Toughs

Toughs

ED FALCO

UNBRIDLED BOOKS

Unbridled Books

Copyright © 2014 by Edward Falco

First paperback edition, 2014
Unbridled Books trade paperback ISBN 978-1-60953-111-9

Library of Congress Cataloging-in-Publication Data

Falco, Edward, author.
Toughs / Edward Falco.
pages cm
ISBN 978-1-60953-111-9 (paperback)
1. Gangsters--Fiction. 2. Criminals--Fiction. 3. New York (N.Y.)--20th
century--Fiction. I. Title.
PS3556.A367T68 2014
813'.54--dc23
2014003503

1 3 5 7 9 10 8 6 4 2

Book Design by SH • CV

First Printing

For Judy

Toughs

Summer

· *1931* ·

TUESDAY ••• JULY 28, 1931

6:28 p.m.

A New York City summer evening and Loretto Jones looked sharp in a dark blue and white pinstriped double breasted suit as he waited on the corner of East 107th Street, between 2nd and 3rd: *Loretto*, the house where the Blessed Virgin was born and where she ascended into heaven, a name pinned on him by the nuns at Mount Loretto Orphanage on Staten Island where he had been abandoned sometime before dawn twenty-one years earlier to the day, July 28, 1910. Sister Mary Catherine Randolph liked to say she'd found him newborn, wrinkled and red as a peach, wrapped in swaddling and left in a cardboard box inside the door to the chapel, where Sister Aloise in long black habit tripped over him and yelped in the predawn light.

Loretto on 107th Street had already sweat through his undershirt, staining the armpits of a white dress shirt he'd bought at Saks for eight bucks the day before, an expensive birthday present to himself. He loosened his tie, unbuttoned the collar, and pulled down the brim of his fedora to keep the sun out of his eyes. He was waiting for Dominic Caporinno to pick him up in his battered 1926 Packard, Dom's pride and his heartache, a once fine automobile with leather interior and dark green carpeting that had been used hard ferrying whiskey out of Canada and now ran or didn't according to its own whims. It was almost 6:30. The temperature midafternoon was 94, making it the hottest day of the year.

Loretto leaned against a lamppost as kids swarmed over the streets escaping the heat of cold-water flats. In this Italian neighborhood of red brick and dull khaki run-down five-story tenements laced with a black stitch work of fire escape railings and ladders, children shouted and called to each other in English while their mothers and fathers, their aunts and uncles and grandparents sitting on stoops, congregating in doorways, leaning out of windows or over fire escapes, spoke among themselves in Italian. Up the block, a few of the older kids had just opened a johnny pump. One boy waved a black monkey wrench in triumph while another straddled the pump from behind and used a soup can to send a spray of glistening water across the street and onto the plate glass window of Ettore's Drogheria. Shirtless boys ran through the spray and a teenage girl pulled away from a younger girl trying to drag her into the bubbling white cascade of water.

Though Loretto had grown up among Italians, could speak the language a little himself and make out the gist of a conversation, his own ethnic heritage was indeterminate. By the time he was thirteen, the Jews, the Italians, the Irish, and the Poles had all claimed him. His skin was neither the olive dark hue typical of Italians nor the fair pale of the Irish. In his dark blue eyes every ethnic population saw its most handsome relatives and ancestors. At five eleven he wasn't too tall or too short for any ethnicity, though the Irish argued he was too tall to be Italian.

Loretto glanced down the avenue, over the throngs of kids running the streets. He was looking for Dom and his beloved Packard but noticed instead a pale green sedan cruising slowly toward him, hugging the center line as if looking for something or someone on the left side of the street. Loretto scanned the sidewalk and spotted Richie Cabo and two of his torpedoes outside his club, a few feet from where Frank Scaletta, a neighborhood kid, had set up a lemonade stand and was selling drinks for a penny to a bunch of little girls crowded around him. Approaching Frankie, a girl of about ten or twelve in an ill-fitting yellow sundress maneuvered a black baby carriage along the crowded sidewalk. Loretto took a step back and positioned himself behind the lamppost. Across the street, Richie Cabo's men went back into the club, apparently having forgotten something. Cabo worked for Dutch Schultz now. He drove around in a bulletproof Pierce Arrow. Once his men were out of sight, he looked up and down the street, and Loretto saw in his eyes the moment when he spotted the sedan rolling toward him. His short, heavy body locked up still as a monument while he watched the faded green sedan roll to a stop in front of his club. A heartbeat later, under a downpour of gunfire, he dove into a doorway and rolled out of sight.

In the confusion of the instant when the shooting started, the shouting kids, the cacophony of voices, came to a halt. The only sounds were the rush of water from the johnny pump and the loud clatter of gunfire as the commotion drew all eyes toward the green sedan and Richie Cabo's club, where the crudely made wooden lemonade stand splintered and collapsed to the sidewalk. A pitcher of water and bright yellow lemons shattered and spilled to the curb. Once the neighborhood grasped what was happening, the screaming and shouting from windows and the street and fire escapes and doorways almost drowned out the shooting. The girl in the yellow dress pushing the baby carriage howled and pulled a bloody infant out of the pram as she herself was shot and knocked sideways. Still, she held the infant and ran for a doorway, calling to her aunt. A boy of seven or eight lay bleeding on the sidewalk, his head on the blue slate curb. An even younger boy, maybe four or five years old, lay on his belly in the street. A woman ran to the older boy and cradled him in her arms. The younger boy in the street lay by himself trailing a wide stain of blood.

When the gunfire stopped and the green sedan started up the avenue again, still rolling slowly, only a few miles per hour, Loretto followed along on the sidewalk, trotting and then sprinting as he got a look at the driver. He recognized Frank Guarracie's pinched face and understood that it had to be Vince in the back seat doing the shooting. He couldn't see Vince's face. The guy had a fedora pulled down almost to his nose, and he was a head taller than anyone else in the car—But if Frank was driving, who else could it be but Vince? The mug alongside Frank in the front seat was probably Patsy DiNapoli. His clothes were rumpled, he wasn't wearing a tie, and his hat sat on his head like a shapeless lump—and that kind of slovenliness was typical of Patsy. He couldn't get a good look at the two mugs in the back seat with Vince, but he'd guess Tuffy and Mike. They'd both been running with Vince since they were kids.

Loretto stopped when Frank turned and saw him. Everyone else in the car was looking the other way, at the two boys on the street and the howling girl who had come out of a storefront holding the blood-soaked baby in her arms once the gunfire stopped and the sedan pulled away. Only Frank, bareheaded, driving slowly as a sightseer, looked the other way, across the street, and saw Loretto peering back at him. In Frank's eyes Loretto read a momentary confusion. A second later, Frank turned away, his narrow face once again an impenetrable mask of nonchalance, as if the gates of hell might swing open and unleash a monster and he would be neither surprised nor bothered.

By the time the sedan turned left on 7th Avenue and disappeared from sight, the wounded kids were surrounded by adults attending to them. The air was thick with the stink of cordite. The commotion of voices was deafening. Loretto found himself, as if he had been transported there magically, kneeling alongside a boy who was screeching in pain, issuing a high-pitched wailing that was a mix of terror and indignation as he tried to grab his leg and was restrained by a stout woman who was probably not related to him, given how calmly she was going about her business. Loretto helped the woman remove the boy's shoes and pants before he took off his own shirt and tried to rip it into strips for bandages. When he couldn't get a tear started, he pulled a stiletto from his pocket, snapped it open, and stabbed the white fabric. At the sight of the knife, the woman paused and then yanked the strips away from him. She took his hand roughly, pressed it to the bloody hole in the boy's leg, and shifted her body so that she was practically sitting on the howling child's chest as she wrapped and tied the bandages. When she was done she spit a few sentences at Loretto in Italian. He made out *attraverso* and *vivra* and took her to be saying that the bullet had gone clean through the child's leg and that he'd live, which Loretto had been able to see for himself.

"Good," Loretto said, meaning he was glad the child would live.

The woman glanced at him with a look of motherly disdain, as if he were a hopeless child, and then waved her hand over her head and shouted, "*Lui è qui!*" at the sight of a scrawny young woman approaching them slowly as if wading through snow. "*Su' madre,*" the stout woman whispered and then lifted the weeping child in her arms and carried him to his mother, who watched speechless, her face white, her arms quivering. Others had joined them at this point, including a crowd of children. They followed the woman carrying the child to his mother and left Loretto alone with the sound of sirens wailing closer and then the first of a dozen green and white squad cars blocking both ends of the avenue and every intersection.

Loretto picked up his jacket and tie from the street. He noticed that the tie was bloodstained, and he crumpled it up and stuck it in the jacket pocket. Then he saw that the jacket was also speckled with blood. He folded the ruined jacket over his arm. Across the street Richie Cabo and his boys were watching him. He met Cabo's eyes and then looked himself over and realized he was covered in blood—his undershirt, his slacks, his hands and arms and shoes. He hadn't realized how badly the child had been bleeding, though he did remember blood squirting out of the hole in the kid's leg when he first pressed his bare hands to the wound.

Cabo and his men stepped out into the street and started for Loretto but were intercepted by a pair of uniforms who separated each of the men, moved them apart, and began asking questions. As cops hustled him back to a storefront, Cabo's eyes lingered on Loretto. Another copper, following Richie Cabo's gaze, approached Loretto warily, his hand resting on the butt of his gun.

"And what would you be doing here?" The officer was burly and tall with a red face and a mop of dark hair pushing out from under a blue saucer cap. The armpits of his blue jacket were stained black with sweat.

"*Non parl' inglese*," Loretto answered and then followed with several sentences of gibberish in rapid-fire Italian.

"Stop the malarkey, Loretto," the cop said. "I remember you from when you were running away from the nuns. I'm asking again: What would you be doing here?"

"I live here," Loretto said. He pointed up the avenue. "Over there a few blocks."

"Would you have a driver's license on you?"

Loretto took his license from his wallet and handed it over.

The cop checked the address, looked up the block, and handed it back to him. "Can you tell me what you saw, then?" He laid a hand on Loretto's shoulder, suddenly friendly.

"Didn't see nothin'. I heard the shootin' and then . . ." Loretto pointed to the blood on the street where he had helped with the wounded child.

The cop looked to the blood and then back to Loretto. "And did you have anything to do with this?"

"Nah," Loretto said. "What would I have to do with a thing like this?"

"Is that so? Well, Richie Cabo seems interested."

"In me? I don't know what about."

The cop put his hands on his hips and stood his ground. Behind him a pair of ambulances were moving slowly along the street.

"Look," Loretto said. He gestured to his bloody clothes. "Can I go? I'd like to get washed up."

"How'd you get so much blood all over you?"

"Helped bandage one of the kids."

The officer glanced at the remaining tatters of Loretto's shirt in the street. "All right," he said. "Go on. Get out of here."

Loretto asked, "Are they going to be all right? The kids?"

The cop seemed mystified by the stupidity of the question. He walked away without answering.

On the sidewalk, still more cops were busy erecting barricades to keep the growing crowd out of the street. Reporters were showing up, press cards sticking out of their hatbands. Loretto's bloody clothes drew stares, and he wanted to get back to his apartment and take a bath. He'd only managed a couple of steps when Dom swooped down on him, linked arms, and pulled him away.

Across the street, in front of the club, Richie Cabo's torpedoes were watching them. The cops had just finished questioning Cabo, and he was moving slowly toward his club while he took in the crowd in the street and on the opposite sidewalk. When he reached his boys, they pointed toward Loretto, and Richie joined them in staring across the avenue.

"*V'fancul'!*" Dominic said. "What the hell happened?" He hurried up the block, away from Cabo.

"Slow down," Loretto said. "Where we going?"

"Getting the hell out of here." Dom pulled him along the sidewalk.

"Wait, wait. *Aspett'!*" Across the street, a commotion caught first Loretto's attention and then Dom's. An old woman, frail and dressed in black, stood in a red doorway with a child limp in her arms. She seemed to be speaking, though neither Dom nor Loretto could make out what she was saying. In another moment she was surrounded, the child was taken from her, and the single word *morto*—dead—made its way through the crowd, traveling outward from the old woman in every direction and seemingly all at once. Frankie Scaletta, the kid whose lemonade stand had been shot up, pushed his way past a pair of coppers and crossed the street hurriedly with his head down.

Loretto caught the kid's arm. "What happened over there, Frankie?"

The kid wiped tears from his face with a furious swipe of his hand. He looked blankly at Loretto before he recognized him and his lips twisted into a sneer. "Your pal Coll killed a bunch of little kids. What do you think happened?"

Dominic slapped the kid across the face, took him by the collar, and pulled him close. "Who do you think you're talking to, you little snot?"

"I ain't said nothin'," Frankie answered, and then he was crying again, the tears glistening on his cheeks.

"Let him go." Loretto found a couple of dollar bills in his wallet and stuffed them in Frankie's pocket. "I didn't have anything to do with this. Neither did Dom."

Frankie took several steps back until he felt he was safely out of reach. "Yeah, well, the Mick's still your friend, isn't he?" He took the bills from his pocket, threw them on the street, and sprinted away.

Dom picked up the bills. "We're attracting attention," he said, and again he linked arms with Loretto and guided him down the street. He was a full head shorter than Loretto and he pulled him along like a tugboat. A block later, crowds were thinning out. "The kid's right, isn't he? This was Irish."

Loretto nodded.

"For Christ's sake," he said, "now he's gone and done it."

Loretto's thoughts were caught up with the stout woman who had grabbed his hand and pushed it over the kid's wound, with the cop who had questioned him, and with the old woman dressed in black with a child in her arms. In his head he heard the word *morto* flying out in a whisper from the old woman and through the crowd.

"Some birthday present," Dom said.

Loretto looked at Dom in a way that made it clear he didn't know what he meant.

Dom added, "Some birthday present Vince gave you."

"Sure," Loretto said once he remembered it was his birthday. They were nearing the faded red brick tenement building where he'd shared a cold-water flat with Dominic for the past year, since they'd both turned twenty. Loretto had moved out of a single cramped room behind the bakery where he'd started working at sixteen. He'd run away from Mount Loretto every chance he'd got since he'd turned twelve, and at sixteen they'd given up on him. Sister Mary Catherine found him a job at the bakery and he'd worked there a couple of years before Dominic's uncle Gaspar took him on. Dominic had moved out of Gaspar's apartment, where he'd lived since he was an infant. His mother had died of pneumonia soon after he was born. A year later his father had been beaten to death. The way the story went, he'd said something fresh to a girl on a trolley and the next day he'd been found on the street outside his home with his head bashed in.

Mrs. Marcello, at the top of their stoop, held her face in her hands and practically screamed. "Loretto!" She hurried down the steps to meet him. "What happened?" She held him at arm's length and looked him over.

Dominic said, "He got blood all over him tryin' to help one of those kids that got shot."

A middle-aged woman widowed since her twenties, Mrs. Marcello had been standing guard in front of her building from the moment she'd heard the shooting. Her late husband had left her the building when he'd died in the 1918 flu epidemic, along with most of the rest of her family.

"I'm taking a bath," Loretto said, and he gently extricated himself from Mrs. Marcello's grasp.

"Dominic," she said, leading both the boys up the steps and into the dim hallway, "go get the kerosene out of the basement. I got a five-gallon jug at the bottom of the stairs."

"Yeah, but that's yours," Dominic said.

She shushed him. "Take it." Her eyes filled with tears at the sight of

Loretto in his bloody clothes. "Go! Go!" She pushed Loretto up the steps with one hand and Dominic down to the basement with the other.

When Loretto opened the door to his apartment, he found it suffocatingly hot, though neat and in order, thanks mostly to Dom, who had taken to picking up after him and doing most of the cleaning. Now he crossed the sparsely furnished living room and made his way to a bowed triptych of windows that looked out over 107th. He opened the windows to let the heat out. At the scene of the shooting, crowds were still gathered behind police barricades, though the last of the ambulances had departed, leaving only police cars and a swarm of cops and reporters. Loretto'd known Vince Coll since he was seven years old and Vince was nine, when Vince and his older brother, Pete, had been sent to Mount Loretto after their mother died. This, shooting children—this was something Loretto couldn't figure.

Dominic entered the apartment carrying a glass jug of kerosene. He lugged it over to the big silver water heater in the kitchen and knelt to fill the tank.

"What are you doing?" Loretto tossed his jacket onto a chair, sat on the window ledge, and went about taking off his shoes.

Dominic filled the tank and screwed the top back on the jug. "What's it look like I'm doing?"

"Are you crazy?" Loretto peeled off his socks. "Don't light that thing! It's a hundred and ten degrees in here and you want to light the water heater so I can take a hot bath? You and Mrs. Marcello, you're both crazy."

Dom sat on the floor and crossed his legs under him. He squinted as if trying to work out a problem. "I don't know what I was thinking. Must be the shooting's got me rattled."

Loretto took off his pants and undershirt and tossed them on the chair with the rest of his clothes. "Do me a favor." He gestured toward the chair. "Throw my clothes in the trash for me." He went into the bathroom, where he sat on the edge of the tub in his underwear and turned on the water.

Dominic gathered Loretto's clothes from the living room chair, tucked them under his arm, and paused a minute at the window to look down at the crowded sidewalks around Richie Cabo's club. The words *Now he's gone and done it* rattled around in his head as he watched a small army of cops and reporters mingling with the crowd, trying to get someone to talk. The cops in their blue uniforms and the reporters with their press cards were not likely to have much luck. This was a Sicilian neighborhood and people here wouldn't be inclined to talk with any stranger, let alone a cop or a reporter. When he looked at his reflection in the window glass and saw that his tie was askew and his hair was mussed, he dropped Loretto's clothes on the chair again and took a minute to straighten himself out. He was short and stocky, with a pudgy face that was so flat it looked unnatural. He ran a pocket comb through his hair, doing the best he could to keep the black curly mop of it in place. When he was finished he picked up Loretto's clothes again and left the apartment, passing the bathroom on the way. Loretto was still sitting on the rim of the tub in his boxers, looking at the blank wall as though a movie were showing there.

On the street, Dom stuffed Loretto's clothes into a battered metal trash can under the stoop. Mrs. Marcello had started chattering at him in Italian as soon as he stepped out the door. She wanted to know how Loretto was doing, had he been hurt, was it their friend Vince Coll that did it, like everybody was saying. Dom answered that Loretto was fine and neither he nor Loretto had any idea who did it. On his way back into the apartment, at the top of the stoop, he asked her what she'd heard about the kids who'd been shot.

Mrs. Marcello answered in English, with a shrug. "It's a miracle no one was killed."

"Yeah?" Dominic said. "I thought that little one was dead?"

Mrs. Marcello pursed her lips and shook her head. "Not yet," she answered. "He's hanging on. So is his brother. It's the Vengelli boys, Michael and Salvatore. And the baby, little Michael Bevilacqua." She shook her head again.

When Dom asked her why she was shaking her head, she shrugged.

"They don't think they're going to live?"

Again Mrs. Marcello shook her head, meaning no, they didn't think the boys would live.

"Who else?" Dom asked.

"Flo D'Amello and Sammy Devino. But they're okay."

Dominic started to ask her how she knew all this and then stopped. No doubt she'd already talked to one of the relatives or friends of the families who'd passed by her stoop, which was how she knew everything she knew about the neighborhood—which was everything. "Five kids shot," Dominic said, talking to himself. And then he added, "Now Irish's gone and done it."

Mrs. Marcello's eyes narrowed. "*Animale*," she hissed. "*Beastia!*"

Dom said, "I didn't see anything myself. It's just everybody else is saying it was Vince."

She held Dominic steady in her gaze. She didn't look convinced.

"I got to go," Dom said. When he was out of Mrs. Marcello's sight and on the stairs, he slapped himself on the forehead for being stupid. Once back in the apartment, he went directly to the bathroom, where he found Loretto up to his neck in sudsy water, working shampoo into his hair. "Nobody's dead yet," he told Loretto, "but the Vengelli boys and the Bevilacqua baby . . . It don't look so good for them." He sat on the edge of the tub, at Loretto's feet, and repeated everything Mrs. Marcello had told him.

"Jesus. They think all three might die? Vince'll be Public Enemy Number One."

"Sure, but that's not our problem right now," Dom said. "Cabo's our problem. He thinks you were Vince's lookout."

"You think Cabo'll come after me?"

"Cabo or Irish."

"Irish?"

"Irish'll put you on the spot if he thinks you can identify him. It don't matter how long we all been runnin' together. Look what he did to Carmine."

"That was different. That was business."

"Yeah? Then what about May? What'd she ever do except see him give it to Carmine?"

Loretto watched a clump of suds slide down his neck and into the bath water. May was Carmine Alberici's girl. Vince had killed Carmine for siding with Dutch, and he'd killed May because she was a witness.

"You know Vince liked May," Dom said. "We all liked May. That didn't stop him from blowing half her head off to keep her from talkin'."

Loretto dropped down under the water and ran his fingers through his hair. He could hear his heart beating, thumping through the water. He remembered sitting on a brownstone stoop with May and Carmine, the two of them chatting and laughing, at ease with the world. When he came up, he said, "So what do you think we should do?"

"I think we shouldn't stay here." Dom got up and leaned against the door frame. The porcelain rim of the tub was chipped, and the mustard-yellow wallpaper peeled slightly where it reached the ceiling. "How come we live in such a dump?"

"Because your uncle don't pay us enough."

"Get dressed." Dom went to a closet in the bedroom and came back with a suit fresh from the cleaners. "I'll drive you over to the Barontis'. You can wait for me there while I go see my uncle. Maybe he can figure something."

"Cabo won't be scared of Gaspar," Loretto said. "Your uncle ain't that big."

"I'm not thinking Gaspar," Dom said. "I'm thinking Maranzano. If Don Maranzano tells Cabo to lay off, he'll lay off. He won't want trouble with the Castellammarese."

"You think Gaspar will talk to Maranzano for us?"

"Yeah, sure. He's my uncle, isn't he?"

"And what about Irish?"

"I don't know about Irish." Dom pulled a towel down off a shelf next to the bathroom door and tossed it to Loretto. "Get dressed," he said. "We'll worry about Irish later."

Loretto watched Dominic walk through the kitchen and into the living room, the late-evening sun casting a reddish tint throughout the apartment. He started to get out of the bathtub and then slumped down again as if he didn't have the energy. He saw the boy on the street with a bloody gash in his leg where the bullet had gone through, and the little one in the arms of the old woman. He couldn't figure it. Vince and Mike, Tuffy and Patsy, even Frank, the only one he hadn't known from the time they were all kids like the others . . . If he hadn't seen them himself, he wouldn't have believed it.

The nuns had tried everything, even for a brief period tying him to the bed at night, but he always ran first chance and the chances came easy till he was spending less time in the orphanage than he was on the street with Vince and Pete and Tuffy and Patsy and dozens more kids like them whose parents had given up or were dead or gone and they were living with old people, aunts and distant relatives, who couldn't keep them in school. There were hordes of kids like him and he preferred their company to the nuns. They stole packages off the backs of delivery trucks, they broke into railroad cars, they burglarized empty apartments. They joined gangs. They went to work for bootleggers. They got mixed up in rough stuff. Sure, they did all these things. But something like this. Shooting kids. This he couldn't figure.

"Hey!" Dom called from the living room. "What are you doing?"

Loretto shook off his thoughts and stood up dripping in the tub. Through the bathroom window he saw a clothesline stretched between buildings, the thin white rope wrapped in a loop around metal pulleys.

Dangling from the rope, pinned with wooden clothespins, were three summery women's dresses, one red, one yellow, the other blue. They were fluttering in a breeze outside his window as if they were alive and watching him as he watched them, mesmerized by their colors, by the way they hovered like bright ghosts against a pale sky.

6:42 p.m.

Frank drove down a concrete ramp, into the mouth of a midtown garage, and cruised past a line of parked cars. Behind him, in the rearview, late-evening sunlight blazed at the garage entrance before ending abruptly at a sharp black line of shadow. In the back seat Tuffy and Mike were laughing over something one of them had said. Frank hadn't been listening. He couldn't figure what might be so funny, and he half wanted to turn around and put a gun in their faces just to shut them up. Mike was a kid. He'd just turned nineteen, making him thirteen years younger than Frank, who was the oldest of the gang. They should have had more sense. The car was hot as hell, they were all baking in the heat, and Tuffy and Mike were laughing like a couple of kids.

"Where the hell are they?" In the back, his fedora pulled down so that his face was hidden behind the brim, Vince was still as a corpse, his hands folded in his lap, a big automatic on the seat beside him.

Frank dropped one hand to the butt of a sawed-off shotgun that lay snug against his leg. He was the only one in the car completely sober: Tuffy and Mike had been drinking gin all day, and Vince had been snorting coke. He brought the car around so that it was facing the garage entrance and parked in a shadowy corner. "We should have planned this all out better." He pulled off his tie, undid the top buttons of his shirt, and blew at the sweat on his chest.

"Ah, shut up, Frank, will ya?" Tuffy threw his hat. It bounced off the back of Frank's head and landed in Vince's lap.

Mike jumped up and leaned into the front seat. "That son of a bitch Cabo is bulletproof," he said. "Him and Diamond."

Vince was silent. This was the second time they'd tried to get Cabo and the second time he'd walked away without a scratch. Vince wasn't talking but Frank knew the kid well enough to know he was steaming.

"We should have planned it better," Frank repeated.

"Ah, don't be a crumb," Mike said, and he fell back next to Tuffy.

Vince pushed his hat back off his face. "This don't look good for us, especially after we screwed up getting Diamond."

"That wasn't nobody's fault," Tuffy said.

Vince rubbed the back of his neck. He handed Tuffy his hat. "Still don't look good for us."

Tuffy found a flask in his jacket pocket and burned down another slug of gin.

Frank considered saying something about the kids they'd just shot up and decided against it. There was nothing to be done about it and less to be said. Vince had taken a shot at Cabo, and then Tuffy and Mike had started shooting. Frank had aimed a shotgun blast at the storefront even with Cabo already out of sight. He still didn't know why he did it. He hadn't noticed the bloody kids until the shooting was done.

In the back seat, Vince ran his fingers through a mat of wavy, sandy-blond hair. It was easy to see why the others had followed him when he'd split with Dutch. They'd all grown up on the streets together, the whole lot of them, including Dutch, and between working for Dutch or Vince, who wouldn't rather be with the kid? Frank was the outsider. He walked out on Dutch and went with Vince because he liked him. He liked his style. That and Dutch was a cheap son of a bitch who didn't like anyone enough not to put a bullet in him if he felt like it.

"That's them," Vince said.

The boys exploded out of the car at the sight of Sally and Lottie pulling into the garage, Lottie at the wheel of a tan Buick Roadmaster and Sally beside her. Frank tossed the keys under the front seat, checked to make sure nothing was being left behind, and then joined the others in the shadows just as Lottie got out from behind the wheel and hurried to Vince. She was wearing high heels and a red dress and a red cloche hat that came all the way down to her neck on the left, hiding that side of her face entirely. Vince took her hand and got into the back seat with her, along with Tuffy. Sally threw her arms around Frank's neck, kissed him on the lips, and got into the front seat between him and Mike.

"Any coppers out there?" Frank turned the car around and drove slowly toward the bright sunlight at the garage entrance.

"We didn't see any," Sally said, "did we, Lottie?"

Lottie had wrapped herself around Vince. She leaned into him, nearly climbing onto his lap, with one arm wrapped around his arm and her free hand caressing the back of his neck. She had known the moment she'd seen him get out of the car that things hadn't gone well. "Come here, baby." She pushed her body into him, pulled his head down to her, and kissed him on the lips.

Sally looked into the back seat. "Where's Patsy?"

"We dropped him off," Frank answered without looking at her.

Sally tried to snuggle closer to Frank, the way Lottie was snuggling with Vince, but he pushed her away. He drove cautiously up the ramp, out into the sunlight, and merged with a line of traffic heading out of the city.

Mike said, "Son of a bitch Cabo is bulletproof. Him and Diamond."

"Ah, give your jaw a rest, will ya?" Tuffy was slumped next to the window with the wide brim of his hat hiding his eyes.

"Where we going now?" Sally asked Frank.

Frank was at first angered by the question, but he softened when he saw the way Sally was looking at him. She was nineteen and though not the beauty Lottie was, still she was a looker, with her finger curls and big brown eyes and a face like an angel in a church painting. "Sit tight, doll," he said. "Things'll be hot for us for a while."

"Yeah?" Lottie said. "How come?" She said this first to Frank but then turned immediately to Vince.

"We missed Cabo," Vince said, "and a couple kids got shot when the lead started flyin'."

"Kids?" Sally said. "You mean like little kids?"

They were coming up on the Williamsburg Bridge. Lottie asked, "How many kids?"

"Three or four," Tuffy said from under his hat. "At least."

"Are they dead?" Lottie knocked the hat off Tuffy's face. "Who the hell started shooting at kids?"

"Don't look at me," Tuffy said. "I wasn't shooting at the little bastards."

Lottie turned back to Vince. "Are they dead?"

When Vince didn't answer, Mike leaned over the back seat. "Couple of 'em might be dead. Looked that way."

"For Christ's sake," Lottie said. "We're in a fine mess if you guys plugged a bunch of little kids."

"Shut up, Lottie." Vince straightened out his jacket and leaned closer to Frank behind the wheel. "How many cars we got in Brooklyn?"

"Three," Frank said. "With Elmira plates."

Vince fell back in his seat and tilted his fedora over his face. "We'll split up for now," he said. "We'll grab a couple more cars, stay away from the Bronx a while, and then meet up tonight again at the new place Florence got for us."

"Will she be there?" Lottie started to reach for Vince's hat when he didn't answer and then thought better of it. She crossed her arms under her breasts and was quiet.

"Gosh," Sally said, "little kids . . ."

7:48 p.m.

Loretto followed Dom up the stairs and through a broiling, dimly lit hallway that smelled of garlic and mold. They were hurrying, taking the steps two at a time on their way to the fifth floor and the Barontis' apartment, where Augie and Freddie Baronti still lived with their mother. The father had left more than a decade earlier, when the Baronti kids—Mike, Augie, Freddie, and Gina—were all children. Whenever anyone mentioned the father, which was rare, they asked after his health, since the story was that he had a heart ailment that required constant hospitalization in a sanatorium out west. The truth, which everyone knew, was that he was locked up in the psych center at Kings Park. He'd been taken away in a straitjacket after stabbing Gina with a kitchen knife, screaming that she was a *puttana* and he meant to cut the *demone* out of her heart. Gina was eleven at the time. The family had been broken up briefly after that, the children shipped off to relatives, before Gaspar, Dom's uncle, helped out with money and then found work for the boys selling newspapers. For years, before Gina got married at sixteen and moved away with her husband, they'd all shared two bedrooms in this same fifth-floor walk-up. Now it was just Augie and Freddie—and Freddie'd been in Elmira for the past two years on a burglary charge. He'd only been back a couple of days.

Loretto stopped on the fourth-floor landing for a breather. From the apartment to his right he could hear meatballs cooking in a frying pan. The smell of meat and tomato sauce wafted out through cracks in the door. "It's like an oven in here."

Dom's tie was undone and sweat stains showed on the front of his shirt. He took off his hat and fanned his face with it. "I keep thinking one of Cabo's torpedoes'll pop out of a shadow and blast us."

"Relax a little." Loretto started up the stairs again. "We don't even know what Cabo's thinking."

"I'll tell you what he's thinking," Dom said as they climbed the last flight together, side by side. "He's thinking you were Vince's lookout. He's thinking when you spotted him coming out of the club, you gave Vince the signal. That's what he's thinking."

"We don't know that."

"I know it," Dom said. "Sure as I'm standing here." He knocked lightly on the Barontis' door and then took a step back when it swung open and Gina stood there looking hot and annoyed. When she saw who it was, she wrapped him up in a big hug and kissed him on the cheek. "Dominic! I haven't seen you in forever!" She held his head in her hands and kissed him again, on the other cheek. "Where have you been?"

"I been right here!" Dom said. "You're the one moved all the way to Canada!"

"Canada," Gina said to Loretto. "I was in Carmel."

"Where's Carmel?" Loretto asked.

"See?" Dom said. "Who ever heard of Carmel?"

Gina rolled her eyes. "It's about an hour from here," she said, and then she laughed with the sudden surprise of recognition. "You're Loretto!" She cocked her hips and offered him a flirtatious grin. "You grew up nice."

"Who, him?" Dom said. "He's a chump."

"Come on in." Gina stood aside. "You must've come to see Freddie."

"Nah, we came to see you, doll," Dom said. "And what do you mean you *was* in Carmel? You're not anymore?"

Gina moved close to Dom and exaggeratedly whispered, "I'm divorced now. We don't talk about it in the family."

"So you moved back?"

"Nah, I got my own place not too far. I'm visiting."

"Boys!" Mrs. Baronti came into the kitchen and flung open her arms. "Dominic!" she said, and she hugged and kissed him before moving on to Loretto. "Federico's up on the roof with Agostino," she said. "It's too hot for them in here with their mother! We already ate dinner!" she yelled as though it were a tragedy that they had eaten without Dom and Loretto.

"You should've told me you were coming! I got some biscotti! You want iced coffee?"

It was hard to believe, as Mrs. Baronti stood alongside Gina, that they were mother and daughter. Gina was slim and cute with short dark hair cut fashionably in a bob, while Mrs. Baronti was built like a small tank: big breasts and belly, hips wrapped in a drab blue housedress, and a pudgy face under a jumble of unruly gray hair. She had a mole on her chin sprouting a pair of dark hairs, and creases and crevices that ran from her neck to her forehead. Gina's skin was blemished only by a small round birthmark above her upper lip, a pencil dot that disappeared when she smiled.

Loretto said, "I'd love a glass of iced coffee, Mrs. Baronti." He fanned himself with his fedora. "It's a scorcher."

"Here, give me that!" Mrs. Baronti advanced aggressively, yanked Loretto's hat out of his hand, and then pulled his jacket off by the back collar. "You, too!" she said to Dom. "You're crazy, both of you, in jackets and ties!

Dom hung his jacket and hat on the back of the front door before Mrs. Baronti could get to him. "We were supposed to go out tonight," he protested. "We were going to the 21 Club. It's Loretto's birthday."

"It's your birthday?" Mrs. Baronti stared at him, jacket and hat in hand, at a loss for words.

"I'm getting too old for birthdays," Loretto said. He read Mrs. Baronti's confusion at a glance. Her first response was that he should be with his family on his birthday, and then she didn't know what to say when she remembered that he didn't have a family. "Say, you think we could go see the boys up on the roof?"

"Why not?" Mrs. Baronti shouted. "Go!" She pointed to a cramped bedroom behind the kitchen. "Gina'll bring the coffee."

Gina, who had been watching from the sink with a glass of water in hand, approached Loretto and stood on her toes to give him a quick kiss on the lips. "Happy birthday, birthday boy."

"Don't be fresh!" Mrs. Baronti said. She took Gina by the arm and pulled her away.

"I can't help being fresh, Ma," Gina said. "Look how handsome he is!"

"What about me?" Dom said to Gina. Before she could answer, he turned to Mrs. Baronti. "Mama," he said, "don't you think I'm handsome?"

"Ah," Mama Baronti said kindly, "*un buon cuore, ma una brutta faccia!*"

Dom held his heart as if he'd been stabbed.

To Loretto, Mama said, "I told him he's got a good heart but an ugly face."

"Nah," Gina said. "Dom's a good-looking boy."

"*Basta*," Dom said to Gina. He hugged Mama, kissed her cheek, and waved for Loretto to join him as he started for the roof.

Dom had played in the Baronti home endless hours as a boy and so was familiar with the apartment. At twenty-one, he was the same age as Freddie, two years older than Mike, and three years younger than Augie. The four boys had played together on the streets as children and sold newspapers together as teens before Freddie went to work for Ciro Terranova, Mike started with the Dutchman's organization, and Augie got a job on the docks.

To get to the roof, they had to go through a room off the kitchen that might have served as a walk-in closet in a fancy uptown apartment but here held two narrow cots on either side of a thin window that looked out to the street. In the foot and a half of space between the cots, a gooseneck lamp and a yellowing newspaper rested on a round night table. The cots were neatly made up with matching blue bedcovers, crisp white sheets, and a single lumpy pillow at the head of each bed, close to the window. On the side of the room opposite the window, a wall ladder led up to a rectangular skylight that was thrown open to a line of filmy white clouds floating high over the city. Dom climbed the ladder, and Loretto followed. On the roof, they found Augie and Freddie sitting on a pair of rickety folding chairs next to an empty wire-mesh pigeon coop and looking out over an avenue of rooftops.

"Freddie!" Dom yelled. "Look at you! *Madon!*"

Freddie was wearing khaki slacks and a sleeveless undershirt that accentuated the bulging muscles of his chest and arms. He was short and solidly built with thick thighs and legs that looked like they could easily kick down doors. He'd been sent up to Elmira for burglary at nineteen. "Yeah," he said to Dom, "I'm the new Charles Atlas." He nodded to Loretto, looked out over the rooftops, and then turned back to them. "I had a lot of time to work out," he said. "Did you ever hear of 'dynamic tension'? I was just telling Augie about it."

Freddie didn't say anything more but instead turned his gaze out toward the ledge.

"Sit down," Augie said. "Take a load off." He nudged his brother. "Don't mind Freddie," he said. "He's come back from Elmira a little batty."

Freddie grinned at that, but his eyes remained on the line of roofs in front of him.

Augie was wiry all over, with knotty muscles and a prominent Adam's apple. He was barefoot in black dress pants, an undershirt, and a straw boater. He looked like he hadn't shaved or been out of the house all day. "You think Mike's mixed up in the baby shooting supposed to be Irish did it? You mugs hear about that?"

"Hear about it!" Dom said. "We was there!"

"Yeah?" Augie grinned as Dom and Loretto sat across from him on the roof ledge.

"You already heard we were there?" Loretto pulled his slacks up as he took a seat.

"Everybody's heard," Freddie said as if talking to the clouds.

Dom started to lean back and then jerked forward when he remembered he was sitting on the roof ledge. "What's the word about us?"

"It's all about Loretto," Augie said. "I heard you saved some kid's life or something."

"Me?"

"Yeah, you. Anybody else named Loretto in the Bronx?"

Dom and Freddie laughed, and Loretto said, "I didn't save no kid's life. I helped bandage one up is all."

Augie pushed a loose strand of hair off his forehead and back up under the boater. "So, like I say, you think Mike was with Vince?"

"Yeah, probably," Loretto said. "I didn't actually see him, but--"

Dom shoved Loretto hard, cutting him off. To Augie he said, "Loretto's got to be careful what he goes shooting his mouth off about."

"What's the big talk?" Loretto said. "I got to be careful what I say to Augie?"

"Word around is Loretto was in on it," Augie said to Dom.

"*V'fancul'!*" Dom shouted. "He works for my uncle! He don't work for Vince!"

"Yeah, we know that," Augie said, "but Richie Cabo don't know it-- and he's sayin' Loretto was in on it."

"I didn't have nothing to do with it," Loretto said. "I was waiting for Dom to pick me up. We were goin' out for my birthday."

"Some birthday," Augie said.

"That's just what I told him!" Dom shoved Loretto again. "I don't think you get the mess you're in," he said. "Cabo's--"

"What about Mike?" Freddie took a step toward Loretto as if he might grab him by the throat. "You sayin' he shot some little kids?"

Loretto remembered Freddie as the most easygoing of the Baronti boys, a good kid who was tough enough but didn't have a touch of meanness in him. "Are you a hard guy now, Freddie?"

"Hey," Augie said, "Freddie didn't mean nothin'. Right, Freddie?"

Freddie took a seat next to Augie. "I ain't trying to be a hard guy, Loretto. I just want to know what's goin' on with Mike."

"See?" Augie said. He tilted his boater back. "Everybody should just relax."

"Besides," Dom said, "who says any of those kids was killed? I heard they're all hangin' on."

"We heard two of 'em was dead."

Dom got up and brushed off the seat of his pants. "I got to go get a newspaper."

"Ah, don't run away," Freddie said. "Nobody's tellin' me nothin' since I been back. I'm goin' nuts! Why don't you just tell me what's what? I'll find out anyway. Is Mike in with Vince or not?"

Augie stroked the stubble at his jaw. To Freddie he said, "I'm tryin' to keep you away from things till you're yourself again. You don't need to know about nothin' till you're feeling better."

Freddie looked to Loretto, ignoring his brother. "Is Mike in with Vince or not? And what the hell happened with Flegenheimer? When I left, everybody was working for Dutch except you guys."

"Dutch don't like to be called Flegenheimer anymore," Loretto said. "I'd be careful about that. You don't know nothin'?"

When Augie shook his head, indicating that Freddie didn't know a thing, Loretto said, "Last year Vince split from Dutch, and Mike went with him."

"Yeah? What made him do that?"

Dom said, "Long story."

Loretto said, "Vince figured Dutch was making twenty million a year and paying him a hundred and fifty a week. He didn't like it."

"I don't blame him," Augie said. He fell back in his chair and tilted the brim of the boater down over his eyes.

"So Vince split with Dutch," Freddie said to Loretto. "Him and Mike?"

"Him and Mike," Dom said, "and Frank Guarracie, Tuffy Onesti--"

"So Vince and Mike and them," Freddie said, thinking about it. "That's a tough gang."

"Don't forget Pete," Augie said lazily, stretched out now in his chair as if taking the sun.

"Pete, Vince's brother?" Freddie asked.

"Who else Pete?" Augie said.

"Was Pete in the car with 'em today?"

"*Madon!*" Dom said and slapped a hand to his forehead.

"Pete's dead," Loretto said. "Dutch put him on the spot."

Freddie looked to Augie, still hiding under his boater, and then back to Loretto. "How'd Vince take it?"

"How do you think, Freddie?" Dominic, who had been standing over them, took a seat on the ledge again. "They been at war ever since. Vince ain't stoppin' till he kills Dutch."

"Who else is dead I don't know about?" Freddie heard a scraping sound and turned to see a big silver platter slide up onto the roof next to the skylight. A moment later, Gina's head popped up.

"Hey," Gina said, "it's cooling off a little." She pulled herself onto the roof. The sun was red and low in the sky, and the windows in the surrounding buildings reflected the crimson light. She carried the platter to Loretto. "Here you go, boys. Coffee and biscotti on the house."

Loretto laughed as he picked up an eight-ounce glass with brown coffee swirling around chunks of ice.

"What do you mean *on the house*?" Augie said. He spooned sugar into his coffee from a porcelain bowl. "Don't I pay for things around here?"

"She was making a joke," Loretto said. "Because we're on the roof."

Augie snatched a biscotti from the tray and bit it in half.

"What are you boys talking about?" Gina sat on the ledge between Dominic and Loretto and placed the empty tray on her lap.

"Nothin'," Augie said. "Don't Mama need help with something in the kitchen?"

"Don't act all tough with me, Augie. I'll tell Mama not to bring you milk and cookies before you go to bed tonight."

"You're funny." Augie took off his boater and dropped it on Gina's head, where it fell comically down to her eyes. "Really, scram, kid," he said. "We're trying to talk."

Gina put the boater on the tray. "Are you talking about Vince? The mayor's on the radio. They're calling him a mad dog and a baby killer."

"Ah, Jesus," Dom said.

"You're not involved with any of this, are you?" she asked Loretto.

"Nah. I had nothing to do with it."

"Did one of the kids die?" Dom asked.

"They're saying two of them aren't expected to live."

"But nobody's dead yet?"

"Not yet."

Freddie said angrily, "How come you're not asking about your brother? Don't you want to know if Mike's in trouble?"

"Leave your glasses on the tray." Gina started for the skylight. Before she climbed down off the roof, she said to Freddie, "I don't have to ask."

"What's she mean by that?"

Augie said, "If there was five guys in the car, you can bet Mike was with them. Hell," he added, "I can tell you right now who was in the car. It was Vince, Frank, Mike, Patsy, and Tuffy. The five of them are like peas in a pod."

Freddie got up and his chair fell over. He looked down at it as if surprised to see it there. He went to the opposite side of the roof and gazed out over the buildings into the fading light.

Loretto and Dom turned to Augie, who gestured in a way that said there was nothing to be done about Freddie. He'd be okay, but they should just leave him be.

"Anyway," Dominic said, "we were thinking Loretto might stay with you till I can see my uncle and get this business with Richie Cabo straightened out."

Augie said, "You think Gaspar can take care of Cabo?"

"Don Maranzano can," Dominic said. "Cabo don't want trouble with the Castellammarese."

"Oh," Augie said. "Sure." He thought about it another moment and added, "You think Gaspar can get Maranzano to stand up for somebody maybe's not even an Italian?"

"Yeah," Dom said. "Besides––" He took Loretto roughly by the chin and turned his profile toward Augie. "Look at that face! Of course he's Italian!"

To Loretto, Augie said, "You'll have to sleep on the floor between me and Freddie. I'd give you the couch, but Gina's stayin' the night and that's where she's sleeping."

"That's fine," Loretto said. "I don't think it'll take long to get this all straightened out."

Dominic pressed his hands together as if in prayer. To Augie he said, "He don't get it. Even if my uncle can keep Cabo in line, that still don't solve the problem with Vince." To Loretto, he said, "You don't know what a mess you're in."

Loretto said to Augie, "He thinks Vince'll bump me off."

"Because you can identify him?"

"Yeah," Dom said. "Loretto saw the whole thing."

"Dom's right," Augie said. "That could be a big problem."

"See?" Dom said. "Now you believe me?"

"I've known Vince most my life," Loretto said. "He likes me."

"He liked Carmine and May, too," Augie said.

"See?" Dom yelled. To Augie he said, "I told him the exact same thing."

Freddie, who had been motionless on the other side of the roof, turned suddenly and joined them. A breeze mussed his hair, and he smelled as if he hadn't bathed in a while. "So now everybody with a gun in this city," he said, "is looking to kill Vince Coll, and Mike's right there with him."

Dom, Loretto, and Augie all watched Freddie with the same confused expression. Between the three of them they couldn't come up with a thing to say.

9:58 p.m.

Patsy DiNapoli walked arm in arm with his girlfriend, Maria Tramonti, and every time he pulled her gently toward the shadows she resisted and pulled him back to the middle of the sidewalk. They were in Brooklyn and the stoops on both sides of the street were busy with families escaping the heat of their apartments, though it was getting late and a wave of clouds had closed over the city, blocking out the moon and stars so that the slate sidewalk was especially dark between lampposts. Everyone, it seemed to Patsy, was watching him, and he was getting more and more frustrated with Maria for telling him to act naturally and walk with his head up and quit trying to hide in the shadows. They'd parked Maria's car in a garage a half-dozen blocks away because it was actually Maria's husband's car and she felt better with it out of sight.

"Come here," Maria said. She kissed Patsy on the cheek and whispered in his ear, "Try not to look so worried."

Patsy laughed in a way that he imagined was lighthearted. He wasn't familiar with this neighborhood, though the tenements here looked like the tenements everywhere: faded red brick facades and black fire escapes with clothes hung out to dry. The people, too, the families, they looked the same all over, with their worn clothes and busted-up faces. It was probably Maria they were all looking at because her dress was new and bright and she filled it nicely, though Patsy couldn't shake the feeling they were looking at him. His ears strained as they passed every stoop and its congregation of people. He listened to hear if they were talking about Vince.

"Is that it over there?" Maria asked. They were under a lamppost and she was looking at a scrap of paper in the palm of her hand.

"Is that the address? I ain't been here before."

Maria nudged Patsy toward the street, around a parked car, and as she did so a woman on a nearby stoop jumped up, pointed in their direction, and yelled, "Get over here! I'll break your neck if you don't break it first!"

Patsy reached for the gun under his jacket and Maria clamped down on his arm. Above them, a boy of eight or nine straddled the top of the lamppost like he was riding a pony.

"Madre mia!" the woman yelled again—but not until a man in an undershirt and suspenders appeared behind her from out of a hallway did the kid swing and leap like an acrobat and shin down the pole to the street.

Maria yanked on Patsy's arm and he followed her across the cobblestones and up a concrete stoop where a family was sitting quietly: a young woman with a baby asleep in her arms and a toddler sleeping with his head in her lap, a brawny mug in a work shirt sitting on the step above them. Patsy nodded to the guy, who nodded back, and then he followed Maria through a pair of open doors and up a flight of stairs. When they reached the right apartment, Patsy knocked twice, paused, knocked three times, paused again, and then knocked once.

Sally opened the door. She squealed and did a little dance at the sight of Maria before throwing her arms around her and dancing her into the apartment.

"Close the feckin' door!" Florence was seated at a round table next to a pair of windows that faced the street. Thick yellow shades were pulled down over both windows. Frank, Vince, and Mike crowded around the table along with Florence's husband, Joe Haley. A few bills and coins were scattered next to three open whiskey bottles, all of them about half full. Except for the table and a dozen folding chairs, the apartment was unfurnished, with dingy, smoke-stained white walls. Florence held cards in one hand and a glass of whiskey in the other. She was tall and skinny with scraggly blond hair, a haggard face, and pasty skin. At age thirty-eight, she looked a dozen years older. To Frank she said, referring to Sally, "You brought around some dumb gashes before, but this one takes the cake."

Frank and everyone else ignored Florence while Sally pulled Maria into the kitchen, where Tuffy was sitting on the stove. He'd been in the middle of telling the girls a dirty joke when Patsy's knock interrupted him.

"Fellas!" Maria said. "Somebody open a window!" Everyone in the apartment was either holding a lit cigarette or had one burning in a nearby ashtray. A gray cloud fed by lines of ascending smoke from each cigarette hovered at the ceiling and drifted toward the back of the apartment, where a hallway led to more rooms.

"Yeah," Sally said. "It's boilin' in here!"

Vince pointed to Tuffy. "Open the kitchen window a little." To Mike, he said, "See if all the windows are open in the back rooms."

Before getting up from the table, Mike threw down the last of his whiskey and stubbed out a cigarette. He was a rough-looking kid with a nasty scar above his right eye, wide and dark as a second eyebrow. He'd gotten it as a boy in a street fight with a bunch of Polacks. Someone had hit him in the face with the pointed end of a spade. Later, his brothers Augie and Freddie found the guy, roped him to a chain-link fence, and broke one of his legs with a baseball bat.

In the kitchen, Lottie, still in her red dress and high heels, took Maria's hand and kissed her on the cheek. "Ain't you a doll?" she said, and stood back to look her over.

Maria posed for Lottie and then turned to look after Patsy as he joined the others at the table. "Give me a cigarette, will ya, beautiful?" she asked Lottie. "My husband don't let me smoke."

Lottie tapped a cigarette out of her pack and placed it between Maria's lips. "Why don't you just walk out on the fat bastard?"

"The girls at Madam Crystal's call him Fatty McMoney," Sally said. She hoisted herself onto the stove and put her arm around Tuffy.

Tuffy said, "Don't be saying nothing bad about Madam Crystal's."

"I ain't!" Sally said. "I'm just saying what they all call Maria's husband!"

Lottie lit Maria's cigarette. "Why do you want to stick with a guy spends every night at a whorehouse?"

Maria exhaled and watched the smoke disrupt the cloud hovering over her. "What do you suppose I'd do?" she said. "Move in with Patsy and his mom?"

Sally and Tuffy laughed, but Lottie was suddenly angry. "Look," she said, lowering her voice. She glanced behind her to Tuffy as if checking to see if she could speak freely with him nearby. "If things go right," she said, "none of us will have to worry about stuff like that."

"Yeah," Tuffy said. He slid down from the stove as Mike came out of the back rooms and rejoined the others at the table, where Flo was complaining about her cards. "Except things didn't go right today at all." He'd been half drunk all day and was only now getting sober. He hadn't had a drink all night.

"This'll blow over," Lottie said, "long as none of those kids dies."

Tuffy wanted to believe her. He was twenty-two, a year younger than Vince, but he looked even younger with his baby face and unmarred skin and not the slightest hint of a beard. "We'll see," he said and pulled a chair behind him from the kitchen to the table, where Mike squeezed over and made room.

Florence tossed a half dollar into the pot, said, "Call" to her kid brother.

"You're calling me?" Vince was smiling in a way that lit up his face and warned Florence she was about to lose the hand.

"Fuck you. Didn't I just say I'm calling?" She slapped her cards down, showing two pair. "What do you got?"

"Straight." Vince laid his cards down on the table, a straight to the king, and pulled the pot to him. Tall and solidly built, with a natural curl to his sandy-blond hair, he had a dimpled chin under full lips, and eyes that seemed to search wherever his gaze fell.

"Ah, but you're a miserable bastard, Vincent Coll." Florence tossed her cards away and poured herself more whiskey.

Vince brushed his hair back, stretched, and looked around the room. "Sally," he said, "be an angel. There's a radio in the back room. Why don't you go entertain yourself?"

"Sure," Sally said. She hopped down from the stove. "Maria, you want to come?"

At the table, Patsy caught Maria's eyes and gestured toward the back room.

"Yeah, why not?" Maria went to Patsy and gave him a hug before exiting the room with Sally.

Vince winked at Lottie as she took Sally's place up on the stove. "We made a mess of things today," he said. He took a whiskey bottle by the neck and filled his tumbler. "Dutch has got the upper hand now."

"I can't believe you idiots missed Cabo again," Florence said. "Again!"

"Say, put a lid on it, Flo!" Lottie leaned over the stove as if she was thinking about leaping at Florence.

"Ah, now the queen bitch puts in her two cents!" Flo pushed her chair back from the table.

"Stop it," Vince said to Florence.

When Florence started to say something more, Joe cut her off. To Vince he said, "Cabo won't show himself out in the open like that again. Not after today."

"That's what I'm saying. We should have planned it better."

Frank looked to each of the boys, to Tuffy and Mike and Patsy. "And you shouldn't have been drinking gin all day, like I said." He'd told them all to quit and they'd all laughed at him and called him an old man.

"Yeah," Mike said. "You were right. I admit it."

"Anyway," Vince said, "we got to go back to the original plan now. We got to get Diamond." He pushed his chair back in frustration, and the table went suddenly dead silent. "It'll be harder now thanks to those feckin' upstate coppers stickin' their noses in our business." He glanced up at the cloud of smoke as if appealing to God against the outrage of that bunch of rural cops that had found his boys in their upstate hideout before they had a chance to get Jack Diamond. "It'll be harder now," he said again and pulled his chair to the table, "but that don't mean it's impossible."

"Irish," Frank said, "between Dutch looking to kill him and us going after him . . . Diamond's not showing his face."

"Hell," Mike said, "it was even in the papers that we were looking to bump him off."

"Why don't you mugs tell me something I don't know?" Vince looked across the room to Lottie, who was sitting quietly on the stove with her legs crossed. "Diamond's organization is ripe for pickin'. All we got to do is kill the son of a bitch."

"Sure," Frank said, "but that's the point. The guy's harder to kill than Lazarus."

"Listen, Vince . . ." Lottie pulled a folding chair to the table and opened it beside Vince while Florence stared bullets at her and the others shuffled to make room. "Legs Diamond," Lottie went on, "he don't seem to want to die—and every time the coppers think they got him, he beats the rap."

Mike added, "He just beat a kidnapping and torture rap."

"Got to hand it to Jack," Vince said, "the way he sticks it to the coppers."

"That's what I'm getting at." Lottie took Vince by the arm and cuddled up to him while she talked to the others. "He's got some kind of charmed

life, this fella. Nobody can get to him. So what if you make him a prop-
osition?" She turned and spoke directly to Vince. "What if you offer to
partner with him?"

"Ah, for cryin' out loud!" Flo yelled. "Vince just tried to kill the guy,
didn't he? And now you think Diamond'll partner with him?"

Lottie went on as if Flo hadn't said a word. "When you think about it,"
she said to Vince, "you and him are natural partners. You both hate Dutch.
He killed your brother, and he shot up Diamond's brother. The Combine's
after both of you. You're both like outlaws' outlaws," she said and then
grinned, pleased with herself for the turn of phrase.

"Legs would never go for it," Patsy said.

Frank said, "Even if we could get a meeting, you can't trust the guy.
That's how Joey Noe got it. Shows up for a meeting with Diamond and
gets a bullet in the head for thanks."

"You can't trust a guy like that," Tuffy said. "There's no telling what
he'll do."

"Nah," Vince said. "Diamond hates Dutch same way I do. Lottie's got
a point."

Mike finished off his drink and poured himself another. "Cheapest son
of a bitch I ever met, Dutch."

"Boys!" Lottie put an arm around Vince's shoulders. "You're not getting the drift. Diamond's still got the feds on him for an income-tax rap,
plus the prohees got a case against him for distributing. Between his legal
fees and I hear he's supportin' two women besides his wife, the guy needs
cash. What do you think'll happen when he gets sent up? You think the
Combine will let you take over upstate? You think they'll let you control all
the routes into the city?"

Vince shrugged off Lottie's arm and nudged her back into her seat.
"That's why I'm saying we got to get to Diamond now. Once we get to
him and they pat the bastard with a spade, we'll be running things upstate."

"Sure, but now we're back to where we were before," Frank said.

"Diamond ain't showin' his face. Nobody knows where he is, and there's no way any of us are getting near him."

Vince lit a cigarette from one still burning in a cut-glass ashtray at his elbow.

"Honey," Lottie said, "I'm saying Diamond's got his back to the wall. You guys got the same enemies, and if you can offer him muscle to fight it out with them, and take over running his operation so he's free to take care of his legal problems and his women, that's a deal the guy's got to take."

"I hear that Kiki dame of his spends money like water," Patsy said.

"Once Legs gets sent up," Lottie went on, "he's looking at losing everything. If he partners with you," she said to Vince, "he knows you're tough enough to run it all without him. You can offer him a way to hold on to a piece of the action, and he can put you in control of his operation before Dutch and them can do anything about it." She turned to the others at the table. "You boys see what I'm saying? Diamond didn't get to where he is by being stupid. I'm telling you, there's a deal to be made."

"Jesus Lord Almighty," Flo said, looking straight ahead at no one, "somebody needs to put this bitch in her place."

Lottie said, "Can it, will you, Florence?"

"All right," Vince said. "Let me think about it." He turned to Frank. "What do you have to say?"

"She might be on to something," Frank said. "If we could get a meeting with Legs."

"All right," Vince said again, and he nodded at Tuffy. "Take Lottie up to Albany tomorrow and scout out a place for us."

"Should I rent a place?"

Flo laughed. "They just tried to kill the guy," she said to her husband.

"You do the driving," Vince said to Tuffy. "Lottie'll pick out the place."

Flo leaned over the table toward Vince. "You must be hitting the pipe," she said, "if you think Legs Diamond'll partner with a guy just tried to kill him. That's all I got to say."

Vince said, "We heard you, Florence. I'm thinking about it. Meanwhile," he said to the rest of the table, "we need to stay out of sight till today's mess blows over."

"Yeah," Mike said. "We're not too popular right now."

Patsy said, "I heard Loretto was there. I heard he saved some kid's life or something."

"What do you mean, Loretto was there?" Vince stubbed out his cigarette.

"That's what I heard."

Frank took a drag on his cigarette, and when he exhaled, he said, "I saw Loretto come up the street behind us after the shooting was over."

"And you didn't say nothin'?"

"Why should I? He didn't see the shooting. He came up the street after it was all over."

"What's that got to do with anything?" Flo said. "Did he see who was in the car or didn't he?"

"Ah, for Christ's sake," Mike said, "half the city of New York seen us in the car."

"But they won't talk to the cops," Flo said. "They're Sicilians in that neighborhood."

"Loretto won't talk to the cops, either," Mike said. "We know him since we're kids. He's your friend, right?" he said to Vince. "You got nothing to worry about."

"Did I say I was worried?" Vince pushed his chair back from the table. "All right," he said. "Enough palaver."

At that, the others all rose from the table as if they'd been released from school.

Patsy started for the back room to get Maria. At the entrance to the hallway, he hesitated and turned to Vince. "I'm thinking," he said, "I might get out of the city for a few days. Maybe go to my aunt's place on Long Island."

"That's a good idea," Vince said. He had slipped his arm through Lottie's and was starting for the door. "Just be sure either Lottie or Sally knows where to find you." He tipped his hat to Maria as she came out of the hallway and threw her arms around Patsy. To Maria, he said, "See you, doll," and he winked at Patsy.

"Come on, Vince, my dogs are killing me." Lottie pulled Vince out the door.

In the alley behind the apartment building, where Lottie had parked the roadster next to a padlocked cellar door, Vince stopped and held his nose while she slipped off her high heels. "Smells like rotten eggs back here."

"Probably that's what it is." Lottie gestured toward the metal garbage pails lining the wall beside her. "That's better," she said once the shoes were off and dangling from her fingertips. "Come here, handsome. You're not letting a lady walk to the car in her stockings, are you?"

Vince was looking up at a bright quarter moon hanging over the alley. Most of the lights in the apartment buildings on either side of them were off, though a scattering were on here and there, throwing a dull yellow light over the red brick of the opposite wall.

Lottie, leaning against the door, wiggled her toes, calling for Vince.

When he heard more footsteps descending the stairs, he kissed Lottie on the neck, picked her up, and carried her to the car, where he deposited her on the roof while he opened the door.

Mike came into the alley looking like he was in a hurry but stopped at the sight of Lottie sitting on the car. "Hey, Vince," he said, "you're not worried about Loretto, are you? You know he's a square guy."

"Sure," Vince said. He pushed Lottie's foot away as if annoyed when she tickled his chest with her toes, but he couldn't hide a smile. "If you see Loretto, though, tell him I want to talk."

"Yeah?" Mike said. "About what happened today?"

"Do I need a reason?" Vince hoisted Lottie off the car, dropped her into the passenger's seat, and closed the door. "Just tell him I want to see him."

Mike was holding his hat in hand, playing with the brim. He put it on and said, "I'll tell him."

Vince patted him on the shoulder as he moved around the car to the driver's side. "Tell Loretto I know where to find him." He added, "Tell him I'll be around." He tipped his hat to Mike and got in the car.

Lottie, stretched out in the front seat with her dress up around her thighs and a playful smile on her face, pushed her toes under Vince's legs as he stepped on the starter. The engine chugged once before it turned over, and Vince drove slowly out of the alley and onto an empty street. He pulled his fedora down low on his forehead.

"Where we going?" Lottie slid one foot out from under his leg and moved it toward his zipper, feeling her way with her toes.

"Got us a room at the Corned Beef Arms."

"Are we Mr. and Mrs. Moran again?" she asked. Before he could answer, she yelped, "What's this!" and her toes pressed down on and wrapped around the bulge in his pants following a straight line up toward his belt.

Vince leaned back as he drove, making it easier for Lottie. Outside, the streets were dark and empty, the lights mostly out in the surrounding buildings. Here and there a car was parked along the sidewalk, and the light from lampposts pooled over the slate curbs and black streets. Beside him, Lottie grinned as her toes probed and pressed, her calves stretching to form a straight dark line toward the shadows under her dress. "You don't quit it," he said, "I won't make it till we get back to a big, comfy bed."

"Yeah?" Lottie pressed down harder. "Then we could just do it this way," she said, and she put her hand between her legs.

Vince pushed his hat back so he could see better. He gazed a long moment at Lottie with her hand under her dress, her fingers disappearing into a dark triangle of shadows. "Baby," he said, turning his eyes back to the road, "you got no shame."

"Somebody seems to like it," Lottie answered, digging deeper with her toes.

Vince slowed the car and scanned the streets for an alley.

"Handsome," Lottie said, "you think Legs'll go for our deal?"

"He might." Vince had spotted an alley and was heading for it.

Lottie pulled her dress up to her waist and undid her garters as Vince parked alongside a coal chute. "I'm sure he'll go for it," she said. Vince cut the engine and threw off his jacket. "And once you're running the upstate operation," she added, "the Combine'll have to work with you."

Vince undid his belt and got to his knees over Lottie.

"We'll be the ones making millions then," Lottie said, "and Dutch and the Combine can go to hell." She helped Vince get out of his pants and pulled him into her.

Behind them, on the street outside the alley, they heard a car approaching. They stopped and held their breath and were still as the brick walls surrounding them. Vince craned his neck to look out the window. When the car appeared and then rolled by, they laughed and kissed gently and went on.

WEDNESDAY ✦✦✦ JULY 29, 1931

12:38 a.m.

Tucked into the slip of space between Augie's and Freddie's beds, Loretto, on his back with his arms folded under his head, listened to the slow metronome of Mama's snoring, soft and distant, coming from behind a closed door on the other side of the apartment. It was late and Augie and Freddie were sleeping soundly on either side of him, their backs turned to each other, both in their boxers, covering sheets kicked down to clumps at their feet. Loretto was also in his boxers, with a folded-over blanket under him and a thin white sheet alongside him on the floor. He ran the heel of his hand along tufts of hair on his chest and wiped away a pool of sweat. It was too hot to sleep and his thoughts anyway were crowded and messy, moving from bleeding kids in the street to memories of Vince from Mount Loretto to concerns about Sister Mary Catherine, who would have heard about the shooting by now and be worried. He found the slow rhythm of Mama's snoring comforting, and he wondered how his life might have been different had he grown up in a home like this, with brothers on either side of him, a sister in the next room, and Mama like an anchor lodged solidly behind the closed door of her bedroom. Sometimes at night in the orphanage, in his single cot among an ever-rotating flux of boys, he'd get to feeling like he was drifting, like his cot was a narrow boat and he might float away out an open window into the night. He imagined it would have been different in the Barontis' home.

Beside him, Augie flung an arm over the edge of the cot before he tucked his folded hands between his knees like a child. Loretto slipped into his pants and undershirt and went to the kitchen for a drink of water. He found a glass in the drain tub, and when he turned the ancient brass sink handle, the pipes groaned and rattled and shook the floorboards at his feet. He quickly shut the faucet, having managed to get only a sliver of water in the glass, and waited with his eyes closed for someone to complain about the noise. When no one did, he drank his sip of water and left the glass in the sink.

"Here," a voice behind him said softly, "I'll show you a trick."

Loretto turned to find Gina approaching him wearing only a flimsy white slip that clung to her breasts and the flat of her stomach. She brushed past him and put the palm of her hand on the faucet. "If you press down hard and turn slowly, like this—" She rose up on her toes and pushed down on the faucet. "No rattling," she said, and she filled Loretto's glass as well as a glass for herself.

"Now I know." Loretto took the offered water glass. He was whispering, as was Gina.

In the kitchen's web of shadows, illuminated dimly by street light from a window over the sink, Loretto and Gina, side by side, sipped from their water glasses. Loretto looked straight ahead. When he had first seen Gina approaching, his eyes had snapped to the lace work of her slip where it dipped around the curves of her breasts. He was pretty sure she had noticed his gaze lingering there.

"Too hot to sleep," Gina said. "Want to go up on the roof?"

Loretto took another sip of water to give himself a moment to think. There was no telling what Augie or Freddie would do if they saw him and Gina climbing up to the roof, Gina with hardly anything on. "What about the boys?" he said when he took the glass from his lips. "We might wake them."

"It's Mama we need to worry about. She's got ears can hear the grass growing." She took Loretto's hand and started toward the back bedroom. "The boys sleep like the dead."

Augie was still on his side with his hands between his knees when Gina entered the bedroom, pulling Loretto along behind her. Freddie was also lying on his side, facing Augie, with his hands steepled and wedged between his cheek and the pillow.

Gina stopped between the two cots. "A couple of tough guys," she said to Loretto. She smiled slightly as if she were both amused and disdainful. At the ladder, she put one hand on a metal rung, started to climb, and then stopped, looked down at her slip, and cocked her head. "You first," she said to Loretto and stood aside.

"Too bad," Loretto whispered, and Gina hit him on the shoulder playfully with the palm of her hand.

A flock of pigeons perched on the roof ledge startled and flew away as Loretto pulled himself up onto the tar paper and then offered Gina a hand. The thick clouds from earlier in the evening had passed over, leaving a black sky threaded with wisps of cloud against a background of faint stars. The familiar smell of bread wafted up from the street and a nearby bakery.

Once on the roof, Gina took Loretto's hand again. "Over here," she said, and she pulled him past the wire and scrap wood of the empty pigeon coop to a shadowy narrow space between two black chimneys. She leaned back against the flat wall of one chimney, leaving room for Loretto to slide in front of her.

"Cozy back here," Loretto said.

"Isn't it?" Gina put her arms around Loretto's neck and pulled his head down as she rose up and kissed him.

Loretto laughed, hesitated, and then held her around the waist and kissed her hard as he pulled her close. She didn't, as he had expected, resist. He thought she was toying with him, and he meant to show her that he should be taken seriously. It was too passionate a kiss, too intense and too fast, and he expected Gina to push him away. Instead, she pressed her body into him and her hands slid down his stomach and undid his belt. He took her by the wrists. "What are you doing?"

"What do you think I'm doing?"

"I didn't come up here for that." Loretto turned as if he could see through the chimney and down the skylight into the apartment. "Your family is right here."

"We're out of sight." Gina took his hand. "It's dark." She glanced toward Loretto's open belt. His excitement was obvious.

Loretto leaned into Gina and kissed her while the fingers of one hand went up and into her hair and the other hand slid down from her shoulder to her breast, slipping it easily out from under the delicate lace.

Gina pulled back a little so that she could undo Loretto's zipper.

Loretto said, "Stop." He was still holding her breast in his hand, his heart jumping at the softness of her skin.

"They won't hear," Gina said. She sounded like she was reassuring a child. "No one will see."

"That's not it," Loretto said. "That wasn't what I was thinking."

Gina looked at Loretto with curiosity. Her eyes dropped to where he was holding her breast. "Well," she said, "what exactly are you thinking, Loretto?"

Loretto let her breast fall back under the lace of her slip. He pulled her shoulder strap up and fixed it in place.

"You're a strange one, aren't you?" When it was clear Loretto wasn't going to say anything, she went to the roof ledge, near the pigeon coop, and took a seat in a folding chair.

Loretto pulled up a chair alongside her. "It would have been too fast," he said. He put his feet up on the ledge.

"Too fast for what?" Gina tucked her legs under her, cuddling up in her seat. She took a deep breath. "Sometimes the smell of baking bread makes me sick," she added, "and sometimes there's nothing better in the whole world."

"Just too fast," Loretto said. "I'd like something more between us be-fore—"

"Before what?" Gina continued making herself comfortable. "What do you mean, *something more*?"

Loretto didn't answer. He wanted to touch her again. He closed his eyes as if that might help him find something to say.

"Do you like me?" Gina asked. Her voice was sleepy and the way she was curled up, it was like she and Loretto were side by side in bed.

"Sure," Loretto answered. "I like your whole family. I like all you Bar-ontis."

"You like me the same way you like my brothers?"

"No. I just meant that I like your whole family."

"But you don't want to make love to me?"

"Sure I do," Loretto said. "You're beautiful."

Gina sighed and pulled herself upright in her seat. "Listen, honey— I just got divorced." She took Loretto's hand, squeezed it, and let it go. "All I want is some fun."

"All right," Loretto said. "Nothing wrong with that. I like having fun, too." He slid his chair closer to Gina and did his best to sound cavalier. "I'll take you on a date," he said, "and then we can go back to my place."

"Oh, you will?"

"Sure." He slid his leg over on the ledge until it was touching Gina's leg. "First, tell me about yourself. What are you doing now that you're divorced?"

"That's too dull," Gina said, and then she threw in, "I've been looking for work mostly."

"Not the best of times to be looking for work."

"No kidding, kiddo."

"What about your husband? You getting something from him?"

"Ex-husband," Gina said. "All I get from him is aggravation."

"How come? Don't you get alimony when you get divorced?"

"Don't marry a lawyer," Gina said. "Especially one whose friends are all lawyers." She seemed to think better of what she'd said and added, "I got some money from the divorce. Enough to hold me for a while. But I'll need to find a job eventually."

"Did he treat you bad?" Loretto turned Gina's face toward him. She'd been looking off at the stars.

"Nah," Gina said. "He didn't do anything."

"Yeah? What happened?"

"I don't want to talk about this." She touched the birthmark over her lip with the tip of a finger and then quickly pulled her hand away as if self-conscious about the gesture. "I should have never married him. He was thirty years older than me," she said, "and he was boring. I thought I liked him enough, but . . . I guess not."

"So why'd you marry him? He was really thirty years older than you?"

"I was sixteen and he was forty-six. Mama was furious."

"How long were you married?"

"Six years."

"So?" Loretto asked again. "Why'd you marry him?"

"Why do you think?" Gina said. "Don't be a baby." She got up and started for the skylight.

"Don't go yet." He patted her chair. "We can talk about something else. I'm not tired enough to sleep."

"You're too serious!" As if against her better judgment, she returned to the ledge and retook her seat. "I needed to get out of the house," she added, explaining why she had married a man so much older. "Too many bad memories here. And it didn't hurt a bit that he had money and his own home nowhere near the Bronx."

Loretto understood that the bad memories involved her father. He wanted to say something but couldn't imagine what.

Gina touched the birthmark over her lip again. "There's a point, though," she said, "where, after that, you can't do it anymore."

"Yeah?" Loretto said.

"Sure," Gina answered. "That's what I've been telling Maria. The dingbat's in love with Patsy DiNapoli. Can you believe that?"

"How do you know Maria?"

"I introduced her to Patsy. Her husband's my ex's client. She's still always calling and asking me to come over."

"How come?"

"Jesus, you're one question after another." Gina got up and stretched. She stood on her toes and reached toward the sky. "She's lonely," she said. "Or at least she was lonely before she went and fell in love with Patsy. Can you believe that?" she asked again. "Have you seen Maria? She's a doll—and she's smart."

"Okay, so," Loretto said, "doesn't sound like she'd go for Patsy."

"You wouldn't think so," Gina said. "Patsy's sweet, but he's not too bright and he's a slob."

"You're too hard on a guy. He's not so bad."

"You all stick up for each other." Gina bent to touch her toes, and her breasts threatened to come loose from her slip. "What are you looking at?" she asked, grinning, when she straightened up. "You think Patsy was in the car with Vince today? I don't put anything past Vince Coll, especially now he's running with that Lottie dame, but Patsy and them— I wouldn't have thought—"

Loretto figured she was really thinking about Mike. "They were going after Richie Cabo," he said. "Vince wants Cabo's end of the beer business in the Bronx."

"But why'd they start shooting with all those kids around?"

"Vince is bent on being a big deal," Loretto said. "He's dead set on muscling in."

"What's that got to do with shooting kids?" Gina flopped back down and retook her seat.

Loretto moved his chair flush against hers. "We don't know for sure that Mike was in the car."

"Yeah, of course we do," Gina said. "I told him Vince was trouble. You guys, you all like him because he looks like a movie star. You think you're all big shots hanging around with him." She slid back in her seat to get a better look at Loretto. "What are you doing with the likes of Vince Coll? I figured you as smarter than that."

"I'm not in Vince's gang."

"You're his friend," Gina pressed. "You and Dominic, both of you. You're always at his club over on Dykman."

"How would you know about that?"

"Never mind how I know. Everybody knows everything about everybody in this neighborhood. You know all about me, don't you?"

Loretto figured she was talking about what had happened with her father, but he wasn't sure. "I've known Vince since he got sent to the orphanage when he was a kid, him and his brother, Pete." The first time Loretto had seen Vince was in the dorms at Mount Loretto, when Vince came through the door in knickers that were a size too small, carrying a battered suitcase. The dorm was set up like a military barrack, with a dozen cots on each side of a long room, forming an aisle down the middle. He hadn't gotten past the first few cots before one of the older boys snatched his suitcase. Vince flew at the kid, though he was nearly twice his size, and got a black eye for his trouble. What Loretto remembered best was that Vince didn't cry. He gave up the suitcase and marched to the opposite end of the dorm while the older kids divvied up his stuff. He sat on the empty cot across from Loretto and winked at him with the eye that wasn't swollen. He didn't even look mad. He looked like maybe what had happened wasn't even as bad as he'd expected, and he might even have been feeling lucky. "He lived in the orphanage with me," Loretto added, "for a few years, till he was eleven or twelve, I think."

"So you spent some years together in an orphanage as kids," Gina said. "That doesn't mean you have to be friends now that you're grown up."

"You don't know Vince." Loretto heard the volume in his voice rise, and there was a firmness in his tone that he welcomed. "Vince's two older brothers, Charlie and Tom, died within a few months of each other while Vince and Peter were living with their Aunt Mary because Florence wouldn't take them in. He had two younger brothers who died when they were little, and a sister, too."

"A sister that died?"

"Died when she was a baby, I think. Pete was the last of his brothers, and now Dutch killed him, too. All that's left of his family is Florence—and she's a piece of work, isn't she? She's got a mouth make a sailor blush, and no great love for Vince, either."

"What's any of this got to do with you being his friend?"

"You don't get it," Loretto said.

Gina said, "I guess not," and laughed, and it sounded a lot like she was laughing at Loretto.

Loretto folded up his chair and leaned it against the pigeon coop.

"Don't be a baby," Gina said. "Sit down."

"For a bright girl," he said, "you don't understand much. Maybe girls care about who's good-looking and who's not, but it don't mean a thing to guys."

"Oh, is that so?"

Loretto pulled the folding chair in front of him and fiddled with it. "Guys care about who's tough."

Gina yawned and covered her mouth.

Loretto moved closer to her, still dragging the chair. "You know who Bo Weinberg is?"

"I've seen him around. He works for Dutch."

"When Vince got out of Elmira, he wanted to get Dutch to hire him, so he goes to Joey Noe's place, finds Dutch and Bo with a couple of dames, and he starts makin' eyes at Dutch's girl. He knows what'll happen, right? Dutch sends Bo over and Vince flattens him, busts him up and leaves him stretched out on the floor. This is Bo Weinberg we're talking about. It's stuff like that impresses guys," Loretto added, "not good looks, which don't mean a thing." He dragged the chair back to the pigeon coop. "You know what Dutch did after that?"

"Sure," Gina said. "He hired Vince to work for him."

"That's right." Loretto closed his eyes and let himself drift a second in the darkness. It was still hot, but there was a night breeze, too, that felt good on his face and in his hair. He put his hand on his chest and felt his heart beating hard. "Look," he said, "I'm getting tired. I'm going back down to sack out."

Gina stood and straightened out her slip, running her hands over her stomach and down her thighs. Loretto watched her at the roof ledge in her white slip with the dark of the sky above her and the dark of rooftops behind her, the white of her slip luminous against her skin. Earlier, when he'd first seen her again after many years, he'd thought she was cute. Now she appeared beautiful to him with the breeze tousling her hair and the way she was looking at him, which seemed to cut and penetrate. Only after she turned away and gazed out at the city did he start again for the skylight.

"What about taking me on that date?" she asked, still looking at the ragged lines of chimneys against the sky. When she faced Loretto, she added, "You wouldn't welsh on your offer, would you?"

"I won't welsh," Loretto said. "You still want to go on a date with me?"

"Sure. What about the new Raymond Novarro movie, *Son of India*? You want to see that?"

"That's okay," Loretto said. "Friday night?"

"You sure Novarro's not too handsome for you?"

"Friday night," Loretto said, and he disappeared through the skylight.

Gina listened as Loretto descended the ladder. She heard him step down from the last rung and knock into something followed by the snap of a sheet as she imagined him stretching out on his blanket and settling on the floor between her brothers. She thought, "Boys," and the single word summed up for her all the foolishness of her brothers and their friends. She'd thought she'd left the world of boys behind when she married a man already in his forties, a dependable man with a career and home, a man who would never be a physical threat to her or to anyone, a good, law-abiding man—and then she had gone and left him and now here she was again, surrounded by boys, and dangerous boys at that.

So why was she thinking about what she'd wear Friday night when she went on a date with Loretto, a boy who probably carried a gun and who worked for bootleggers and was friends with Vince Coll? Aloud she said, "What are you doing, Gina?" and then she sat down in the rickety folding chair without waiting for an answer and allowed herself to remember the feel of Loretto's hands on her body. She glanced back to the dark of the chimneys as if she might see herself there again with her arms around Loretto's neck, pulling him down to her for a kiss in the shadows. In another minute, she'd follow Loretto through the skylight and settle herself again on Mama's shabby couch with its lumpy pillows. For now, though, she'd sit up here on the roof and go over the evening again, moment by moment.

1:38 a.m.

Richie Cabo waited between Dutch Schultz and Bo Weinberg in the back seat of Dutch's Lincoln, with its bulletproof, lead-filled doors and one-inch-thick windows. They had just pulled to the curb in front of the Cotton Club's marquee, under bright neon lights spelling out the club's name and lighting up the street. In the front seat, Dutch's driver looked bored as he got out of the car and exchanged a few words with the driver of the hack parked in front of them. Bo yawned and covered his mouth with his fist. It was late and he was annoyed with Dutch for pulling him away from a card game when he'd been winning. A big guy with short, wavy dark hair and a broad face, Bo had dark, serious eyes that made him appear perpetually sad about the state of things. Richie Cabo didn't like Bo. He didn't like Dutch, either. But he preferred working for them to being dead, which was the way things were heading when he tried to go out on his own.

"I'm gonna put a kimono on this son of a bitch," Dutch muttered. He was talking to himself mostly, but to Richie and Bo, too. He wanted Vince Coll dead, and to put a kimono on Vince, who was the son of a bitch he was muttering about, was his way of saying he wanted to encase his feet in cement and drop him in the river.

"We got to find him first," Richie said. He was short and squat, book-ended by Bo on one side and Dutch on the other. In a wide-brimmed hat with a purple shirt and a white tie under a dark blue suit, he looked clown-ish next to Bo, who was dressed conservatively in a dark Oxford-gray suit, with a crisp white shirt and a silk tie. Dutch, who was looking nervously out the side window, was dressed as usual in cheap, rumpled clothes with his tie loosened at the collar. He was worth millions and he bragged about never in his life paying more than thirty-five dollars for a suit.

On the street, the hack pulled away and the Lincoln took its place. One of Dutch's men checked Lenox once more and then nodded to the driver, who cut the engine, got out of the car, and took up a spot at the back of the Lincoln, next to its gleaming chrome luggage rack.

Bo got out of the car before Dutch. He went to the triptych of entrance doors and pulled one open. When he saw several kids in their twenties, with dames on their arms, exiting the club in a swaying, laughing tangle, he motioned for Dutch to stay in the car.

Richie Cabo said to Dutch, "I want those two punks that set me up dead and in the ground, and I wanna do it now."

Dutch pushed his homburg back and ran his fingers over the strands of unruly dark hair that were always coming loose and falling over his forehead. He turned slowly to look at Cabo as if he were a slightly annoying stranger, and then he looked back to the entrance of the Cotton Club. When Bo waved him on, he got out of the car, straightened out his jacket, and started for the entrance with Cabo following.

Inside the club, Cab Calloway's band was dressed in white tuxedoes with matching white shirts, wing collars, and bow ties, with Cab at the center of the stage scatting and pointing to a band member who looked like he was dancing with as much as playing his big stand-up bass. Dutch and Richie followed Bo to the hat-check window, where Big Frenchy De-Mange was waiting for them. A bulky guy with a broad face and bull neck, Frenchy shook hands with Dutch and Bo and nodded to Richie. He didn't like Cabo—there had been something between them in the past—and he felt no need to hide it. "The Duke is waiting," he said, and he led the men past a heavy red velvet curtain and through a door behind it, where they climbed a flight of stairs to a private room.

Owen Madden was seated at a round polished wood table with a couple of newspapers in front of him. He was dressed impeccably and looked more like a banker than a gangster. "Well, what do you know?" he said, and he pushed the late edition of the *Daily Mirror* to the center of the table. The headline shouted, "Gang Rats Shoot Five Children in Beer War's Worst Outrage," and under the headline was a picture of a heavily bandaged child in a hospital bed with tubes in his arms, looking near death. "Appears our pal Vince Coll has made a mess for all of us."

"The son of a bitch is a lunatic." Dutch pulled up a chair opposite Madden while Cabo and Bo took a seat on either side of him. Big Frenchy retrieved a couple of bottles of Canadian whiskey from a cupboard against the back wall, slid the bottles onto the table along with glasses, and then excused himself, explaining that he had a club to run. Dutch picked up the *Daily News*, read the headline—"Harlem Gang Gunners Mow Down 5 Children"—and tossed the paper away.

Madden said, "I thought you'd have killed the Mick by now, Dutch. I'm disappointed in you."

Dutch pulled a glass to him, filled the bottom with whiskey, and tossed it back to calm himself. "I can't get to the bastard. No one's giving him up. I even walked into the Morrisania station house and offered to buy any cop who killed him a house in Westchester."

"I heard about that," Madden said.

"Everybody's heard about it," Cabo said, and Madden and Schultz looked at him as if surprised to see him at the table.

Bo picked up a whiskey bottle. "Cabo's got a problem," he said, hurrying the meeting along.

"And what's that?" Madden asked.

Dutch said, "He wants to put Loretto Jones and Dominic Caporinno on the spot."

"Who?" Madden turned to Cabo for an explanation.

"They're the Mick's boys!" Cabo shouted. He crossed his arms over his chest and leaned back as if to make himself more imposing. "They fingered me when I left my club!"

"He don't know that for sure," Dutch said as if Richie Cabo gave him a headache.

"So?" Madden said. "What are you coming to me for? What's it got to do with me if you bump off a couple of Coll's boys?"

"That's what I think!" Cabo said from behind his crossed arms. "But Dutch, he says—"

"Dominic Caporinno is Gaspar Caporinno's nephew." Dutch patted his suit pockets, looking for a pack of cigarettes.

"Ah," Madden said. "I thought I recognized that name. So he's Castellammarese."

Dutch said to Cabo, "You can't kill Dominic Caporinno without causing problems for everybody, including me and Owen."

"I got a right to bump off anybody tries to bump me off. Where's it say I don't?"

Bo found a pack of Luckies in his shirt pocket and slid it across the table to Dutch. "You don't want trouble with those guys," he said to Cabo.

"They're right," Madden said. "Forget about Dominic Caporinno."

Cabo leaned over the table. "I'm not forgetting about him," he said calmly. "I'm gonna kill him, and I'm gonna kill this Loretto Jones."

"Who the hell's Loretto Jones?" Madden asked Dutch.

"Him and Dominic, they both work for Gaspar. They're a couple of kids."

Madden turned to Cabo. "I thought you said they were with the Mick."

"They're friends of the Mick. They all grew up together in the neighborhood."

"But they work for Gaspar," Madden said, raising his voice. "And Gaspar works for Maranzano, who's the boss of the Castellammarese family now that Joe Masseria's in the ground. Is there something you don't understand about this, Richie? You want to start a war with the Castellammarese?"

"They fingered me for the Mick," Cabo said, unmoving. "I want them dead."

Dutch pulled a .38 special from a holster under his jacket. He placed the barrel of the gun against Cabo's forehead.

"*Mannag' la miseria!*" Cabo shouted. "They fingered me for the Mick!"

"We heard you," Dutch said calmly, "but I don't think you're hearing us."

Bo gently pushed the gun barrel away from Cabo's head. "You can't rub out Dominic Caporinno," he said to Cabo. To Dutch he said, "What kind of a last name is Jones? He's not Italian?"

Dutch put the .38 down. To Madden he said, "Maybe we can take care of this Loretto kid."

Madden said, "I don't give a damn about either of these two joes." To Cabo he said, "You cannot, however, start a war with the Castellammarese. My friend Arthur here," he added, gesturing toward Dutch, "will blow your head off to make that point, if necessary."

"Okay," Cabo said, though he clearly didn't like it. "So what about the Loretto kid?"

Bo said, "We know where he lives. Him and Caporinno, they share an apartment."

Madden said, "I got a better idea," and turned to Dutch. "You say this Dominic and Loretto, they're friends with Coll?"

"They been runnin' together since they were pipsqueaks," Dutch said. "They're neighborhood kids. I seen 'em around the streets since I was a kid myself."

Madden said to Cabo, "What if I set up a meeting for you and Dutch with Maranzano? I'll tell him you want his blessing to take care of these two mugs. He won't let anybody touch one of his family, this kid Dominic, but he'll agree to the meeting just so he can tell you that to your face and play the big shot."

"And what's that gonna do?" Dutch folded his hands and placed them on the table in a gesture that made him look like he was working hard not to punch someone in the face.

Madden finished off his whiskey. To Dutch he said, "Coll's the object here. You go to this meeting, and let Richie . . ." He opened his hand, searching for a word. "Let Richie express his feelings. He wants to see someone take care of these guys. Maranzano, he's gonna wave his finger in your face and tell you Dominic's his cousin's brother's nephew, or some baloney like that."

"Probably is his cousin's brother's nephew," Bo said.

"You say, okay, you'll restrain yourself, you won't touch Dominic.

You'll do this for the great Don Maranzano," Madden continued, "but the kid, he's got to give up Vince Coll. You see?" Madden waited, pleased with himself.

To Richie Dutch said, "I get them to give up Coll, you get Loretto, and there's no war with the Castellammarese." He pointed to Madden. "That's why this guy's runnin' the whole fuckin' city."

"It's a smart plan," Bo said, and he put a hand on Richie's shoulder.

"All right," Richie said. "As long as I get one of 'em."

"It's settled." Madden leaned over the table to refill everyone's glass. "Coll," he said to Dutch. "I never in my life thought one kid could cause so much trouble."

"I don't know why he hates me like this," Dutch said, holding his re-filled glass up to Madden in a toast. "You'd think I'd killed his brother or something."

All four men laughed at that, and Madden said, "Listen, Dutch, I already got a twenty-five-thousand-dollar bounty on Coll's head since after he kidnapped Frenchy. What do you say you double it, add an-other twenty-five thousand. There's guys'd kill their own firstborn for that money." When Dutch hesitated, Madden snatched up a newspaper and slid it across the table. "This crazy bastard is nothing but trouble. The whole city's gonna be up in arms after this!" He tapped his finger on the headline. "The Mick's sworn to kill you, Dutch, which is your business—but it's making big problems for all of us. You see what I'm saying?"

"I get it," Dutch said. He slipped the .38 into its holster. "I'll tell Ma-ranzano when we meet, and meanwhile I'll spread the word: fifty grand—twenty-five from you, twenty-five from the Dutchman—for whoever kills the Mick."

"Good." Madden finished his drink and slammed the empty glass down on the table, signaling that the meeting was over. "Come on," he said. "I got some beautiful girls that wanna meet you mugs."

4:55 a.m.

Just a block or so away, Big Owney was probably sleeping like a baby in his penthouse apartment. Big Owney, the Duke, with his brewery on 10th Avenue at 26th Street, the Phoenix Cereal Beverage Company, had every copper in the city in his pocket. But Vince rarely slept through the night anymore. In his second-floor room at the Cornish Arms hotel, with Lottie asleep in bed, he stood at the window in striped boxer shorts and a sleeveless undershirt watching a sad-looking gray horse pull a bakery wagon lazily along West 23rd Street. He was twenty-two years old and the last of six brothers. Peter, the most long-lived of the lot, had made it all the way to the doddering old age of twenty-four. Across the avenue from the Cornish Arms, in front of a drugstore, a stack of boxes waited at the curb alongside a milk jug. A beat cop walked by with a hand on the hilt of his billy club. Under the light of the drugstore sign, he stopped and looked across the street. Vince stepped back from the window and when he looked again, the cop was moving on. The name of the drugstore—*London Chemists*—sputtered in neon.

Vince tapped out a quick beat against his thigh, his fingers twitching as much as tapping. A dream about Pete had awakened him. They'd been out together at the Mad Dot and then after that at some hole-in-the-wall speakeasy in Harlem. It was the night after they got Big Dick Amato and Dominic Bologna, two of Dutch's guys, though they'd been gunning for Richie Cabo and missed him. They knew Dutch'd be steaming, and that was what they were out celebrating—he and Pete and Tuffy and Mike. He'd gotten drunk that night, drunk and coked up, and when the memory of it hit him his gut clenched and it was as though there were a sheet of muscle wrapped around his head that pulled tight, making him squint his eyes and turn his head to undo it, to loosen the pull like a tourniquet around his head. Pete had wanted to call it a night and the boys hadn't, and Vince had sided with the boys. It was crazy the way that memory was always right behind his eyes, like he could close his eyes at any moment day or night and see himself seated on a barstool behind a bar that looked like it was made out of plywood painted black and that bartender with a shaved head that seemed too long and wide to be human, that bartender smiling at the four of them with his hands on the bar—and Pete says, "I'm too feckin' old to be spending the night drinkin' with you boys!" and Vince says, "Go on, then! Go home, y' stick-in-the-mud!" and Pete says, "I will, then," and Tuffy slides him his keys and says, "Take my car, Pete. Mike'll drive me home," and Pete tips his cap to Tuffy, gets up from his stool, wraps an arm around Vince's neck and rubs his face in Vince's hair, laughin' while Vince tries to pull away. Everyone's laughing. Everyone's drunk and high. And then Pete's gone and the next time Vince sees him he's dead, slumped over the wheel of Tuffy's car.

That was the dream that woke him. He's driving on St. Nicholas Street on his way home and he sees Tuffy's car on the sidewalk, crashed into a wall, which was what actually happened that night, but in the dream Pete's unhurt. He's behind the wheel trying to start the engine, which only sputters and cuts out, again and again. He's glad, Pete's glad, to see Vince. He slides over and Vince gets behind the wheel. He hits the starter and the engine roars. "See," he says to Pete, "it's easy," and Pete laughs and rests his head against the window. "I'm tired," he says in the dream. Vince backs the car into the street and starts for Pete's place on Marion Avenue. Pete says, "Remember Charlie and Thomas, Vince?" and Vince laughs. Why wouldn't he remember his own brothers? "Remember Aunt May?" Pete says, and he screws up his face the way Aunt May used to all the time when she was furious with the both of them. "Are you getting nostalgic now, Pete?" Vince asks—only when he looks to where Pete was relaxing comfortably a second earlier, there's no one there. He stops the car, and now he's on the docks alone by the river, and then the docks turn into a pier that juts out into endless black water and he's running toward the water and the end of the pier—and that was when he woke up with Lottie beside him sleeping. He found his boxers and his undershirt tangled in the sheets. He slipped into them and pulled the sheets up over Lottie and went to look out at the street.

In the window's reflection, Vince's eyes were dark looking back at him. He raked his fingers through his hair. Women loved the dimple smack in the middle of his chin and when he noticed it himself it brought to mind a moment with his mother when he was little. He could still recall bits and pieces of the place where they'd lived then on Westchester Avenue, he and his brothers and his father, Toaly: the dark hallway up a flight of stairs to the bedroom he shared with Peter, Thomas, and Charlie—Vince and Peter in one bed, Charlie and Thomas in the other. His parents' bedroom on the other side of a thin wall. He couldn't remember much: the stairs, the bedrooms, a hole in the bedroom wall they stuffed with rags to keep the rats out. Their mother crying in the bathroom with the boys around her trying to comfort her, and Charlie, who was already in his teens then and out of school and working—Charlie taking him aside to tell him their father had gone away on business and no one could say when they'd see him again, but it might be a very long time. He remembered a square hole in the kitchen ceiling/bedroom floor, over the coal stove/next to his bed, to help move the heat upstairs. He'd remove the grate over the hole and hang his foot down into the kitchen so his mother could stand on a chair and untie a knot in his shoe. And he remembered a quiet moment, alone with his mother, the boys all out somewhere, Florence married and on her own: it's daylight and he can't really recall what his mother looked like beyond long hair and a skinny body, but he can still almost feel the slight pressure of her forefinger resting in the dimple on his chin as she tells him he's special, that the dimple is a sign he's special—an indentation where God touched his favorites. Those words were etched in memory: *This is where God touched you with his finger and marked you as one of his favorites.* Her finger resting in his dimple, where it fit perfectly. Her name was Anna. His mother's name.

His father he'd never seen again, and that night, with Lottie making a slight whistling noise in her sleep and stirring as if she might be dreaming something bad, Vince wondered if his father had seen him in the headlines. He often wondered about that. He thought he might have, Toaly might have, shown up for Peter's funeral. He'd watched for a man of about the right age, anyone he didn't recognize, at the funeral home and again at Saint Raymond's Cemetery. He'd known exactly what he'd do. He'd walk up to him solemnly, call him Da', and if he acknowledged that he was Toaly Coll, then he'd beat him till he was near dead, spit in his bloody face, and leave him where he lay. He'd say, "That's for Ma, who you left to wear herself out trying to raise us boys alone." But no one unknown showed up for the funeral or the burial at Saint Raymond's, where Vince had bought a grave site big enough for what remained of the family. At the top it said,

In Memory Of

My Beloved Brother

Peter

Died May 30. 1931

Age 24. Years

On the bottom it said,

Rest In Peace

Coll

In between on the headstone there was room for him and Florence.

Vince pulled the shade down over the window, and the shadows in the room deepened. He sat on the bed next to Lottie and put his hand on her bare shoulder. At his touch, she settled down and the whistling and fidgeting stopped. Across the room, her red dress was suspended from a chandelier, and beside the dress, on the blue stuffed chair where he had watched her peel off her clothes for him, her undergarments were neatly laid out, stockings over the back of the chair, the parallel black seams like dark trolley tracks climbing toward the ceiling. At the foot of the chair, a beaded handbag lay crumpled on the floor. Vince retrieved the handbag and returned to the bed, where he folded his legs under him and rummaged through its contents until he located what he was looking for: two pieces of stiff cardboard secured with rubber bands. He removed the rubber bands and found pressed between the cardboard, as he knew he would, a picture of him and Lottie beside Pete and Paulie Cirincione, a friend from the neighborhood. It had been taken at Coney Island, back when he and Pete were working for Dutch, making a hundred and fifty a week and feeling rich.

He went to the window again and lifted the shade enough to let in light from the street so he could see the picture more clearly. A drop of sweat fell from his chin onto the photograph. He shook it off, blotted the stiff paper against his boxers, and then opened the window, hoping for a breeze, before he sat on the floor with the back of his head against the window sash. In the picture, all that was visible of Pete was his head in the notch between Paulie's and Lottie's shoulders. Lottie had her arm around Vince, and Pete had ducked down and pressed his cheek into Lottie's shoulder just as the photographer shouted, "Hold!" Of the four of them, Pete was the only one not smiling. He looked serious, staring at the camera, his dark hair parted in the middle and slicked back. They were all four leaning into a railing, in front of a fake caboose, so it looked like they were on a train, going away somewhere.

Vince laid the picture down on the floor beside him and closed his eyes. From the street, through the open window, he heard metal grating against concrete and figured someone was dragging in a milk jug or a trash can. A moment later, someone walked by whistling "Dancing in the Dark," and Vince figured whoever it was that was whistling must have just seen *The Band Wagon*, and then it gave him goose bumps when he remembered that he had seen that show on Broadway with Lottie and Pete, and Pete had left the theater whistling the same tune. He looked out the window in time to catch the figure of a man as he turned the corner and disappeared. He had no idea of the time, but he figured it was closer to morning than midnight. He went back to the bed and sat at Lottie's feet before lying down beside her, fitting his body into the curve of her body, lifting her arm and placing it over his chest. Air was circulating through the room more now that he had opened the window. He could feel the flow of it coming in through the front window and exiting the open side window behind him. Lottie's red dress, the dark shape of it hanging from the ceiling, swayed and wavered slightly in the breeze.

Vince tried to sleep but an instant later he was thinking about the shooting and the bloody kid on the sidewalk and another couple of kids in the street and the girl who screamed when she was hit and spun around before running off, and then seeing that it was a baby she was holding in her arms. He'd stopped shooting then. He wondered at the sight of all those kids running every which way, and it was as if he hadn't even seen them until he'd noticed the baby in that girl's arms. He'd tilted his hat down over his eyes and slumped back in his seat. All he'd seen was that miserable bastard Richie Cabo standing on the sidewalk like a feckin' target before he'd started shooting. Just Richie Cabo standing there like there was no one else in the world, that was all he'd seen. He figured he must have been blind to have missed him, and then he thought maybe it was the will of God because it was the second time he'd missed him and the stupid fat runt was a car length off and still managed to dive and tumble out of harm's way.

Vince imagined Pete driving along St. Nicholas Street in Tuffy's car when he must have been surprised to see another car draw up alongside him and someone must have leaned out the window close to him and fired four shots through the window glass. Four shots between moving cars and through glass and all four hit Pete—and Vince couldn't hit Cabo, who was standing still as a mannequin in broad daylight. Charlie said, *Dad's gone away on business and we don't know when we'll see him again.* Never was the truth, though Charlie hadn't known it then. Vince thought maybe still he might see his name in the papers. Charlie and Tom. Pete rubbed his face in Vince's hair and then disappeared into the ground never to come back, and Vince put a nice headstone there, with room for him and Florence. He never meant to shoot any kids. He had to be the toughest bastard in the city, that's the only way or else you're doing all the rough stuff and Dutch is getting rich. He had no choice anymore anyway. There were too many bodies. He had to go to the top or to the grave. He had told Lottie that in exactly those words: *the top or the grave*. But he never meant to shoot any kids, and then he said it out loud in a whisper, "I never meant to shoot any kids," and it was like the sound of his own voice woke him from a dream because he opened his eyes and didn't know where he was for a minute until a car drove by on the street and its headlights came through the window and lit up Lottie's red dress that looked like it was hovering in the air, a quick bright shock of red swaying over the bed before it fell back into shadow.

Vince pulled Lottie's arm tighter around him. "Baby," she said and kissed him on the back of the neck and didn't say anything more before she was still and silent again, and he lay there in her arms and tried to sleep.

7:25 a.m.

Gina smacked Augie on the back of the head hard enough to surprise him. Augie was at the kitchen table next to Gina and across from Loretto and Freddie. Everyone was seated behind a full coffee cup and an empty plate, with a knife and fork resting on a triangulated paper napkin. At the center of the table, fat brown pancakes were stacked on a red plate next to a jar of maple syrup. Gina had hit Augie when he'd stuck a fork into a pancake the moment Mama dropped the plates on the table. "Guests first!" she shouted, and she smacked him. Augie yelled, "Hey!" but when Gina proceeded to serve herself, as though she were the guest and not Loretto, everyone laughed, even Freddie. Augie cocked his fist at Gina like he might give her a good punch and she said, "Sure, go on." She tightened the belt around her yellow robe and poured syrup on her pancake. It was hot already at seven in the morning and Freddie and Augie were still in their boxers and undershirts. Loretto too was in his undershirt, though he had put on his pants. Mama turned away from the batter she was pouring into a skillet and gestured toward Loretto's empty plate. "*Mangia!*" she yelled as if she was angry at him for not yet filling his plate.

"Hey, Ma," Gina said in between bites of pancake. She sniffed in Augie's direction. "These boys stink. How do you put up with it?"

"Eat your breakfast!" Mama ordered without looking away from the bubbling pancake batter.

"Freddie," Gina said, "you looking for a job today?" She lifted her coffee cup to her nose before sipping the dark brew, savoring the taste of it. Gina, like all the Barontis, drank her coffee black.

"I'm taking him down to the docks with me," Augie said. "I'm introducing him to some people."

"People who might have work for him?"

"Hey, Gina," Freddie said, "eat your pancakes."

"I'm just asking what you're doing."

"Well, don't." Freddie took the syrup from the center of the table, held it high over his plate, and let it drizzle down in circles. When he looked up and saw that everyone was watching him, he smiled.

Augie said to Loretto, "That's how he always does it. Like he's a pancake artist or something."

"*Mangia!*" Mama yelled again, and she delivered a second stack of pancakes to the table.

Gina stretched and said, "Gee, I'm tired this morning."

Mama wagged her finger at her. "Maybe you should spend less time up on the roof."

"Who's up on the roof?" Augie asked. To Gina he said, "What are you doing up on the roof?"

Mama smacked Augie gently. "Eat," she said. "You'll be late for work."

Augie looked to Loretto. "I'm the punching bag around here." Behind him, Mama left the kitchen and went to her bedroom.

Loretto asked, "Isn't Mama eating breakfast?"

"First she says her rosary," Gina explained.

"Then later when she cleans up," Augie said, making a circle in the air with his fork, "she eats what's leftover."

Gina said, "That's the way she is. She won't have it any other way. Believe me."

Freddie said, "I'm getting dressed," and left the table. He had eaten only a few bites of his pancake.

Gina glanced at Freddie's plate and then to Augie.

Augie speared Freddie's pancake with his fork and dropped it on his plate. To Loretto he said, "Kid's hardly eaten anything since he's back. Mama's getting sick over it." He chopped off a hunk of Freddie's pancake and ate it dutifully.

Gina said, "Maybe we should take him to see Dr. Esposito."

"Sure. Who's gonna tie him up and drag him?"

Loretto checked to see that the door to the back bedroom was closed. "He probably just needs some time to adjust," he said to Gina.

"That's probably it," Gina said, though she didn't sound like she believed it.

Augie said, "He's got too much time to think."

Loretto asked, "Can you get him work on the docks?"

"Haven't you heard?" Augie said. "It's a depression."

Gina said, "Yeah, but you're introducing him around, right?"

Augie started to answer Gina when a knock at the door startled him. "Who the hell's that?"

Gina opened the front door slightly, peeked out, and then pulled it open and returned to the table as Dominic stepped into the room carrying a pair of newspapers under his arm.

"Mornin', Gina." Dominic took off his fedora and hung it from a peg on the back of the kitchen door. "Mornin', fellas." He groaned as he fell into Freddie's seat at the table.

"What are you doing here so early?" Augie asked.

Dominic ignored the question and slid the newspapers onto the table. The *Mirror*'s headline read, "MULROONEY VOWS TO GET MAD DOG COLL!" and the *American*'s screamed, "VENGELLI CHILD DIES!" and in slightly smaller type under it "City Searches for Mad Dog Coll!" Both papers had the same front page picture of Police Chief Mulrooney looking furious.

Loretto and Augie snatched up the papers. Gina got up from the table as if she was angry and left the kitchen without a word.

Dominic said, "I heard the mayor on the radio again this morning. Everybody's calling Vince a mad dog and a baby killer."

Augie said, not looking up from the paper, "They think the other Vengelli boy might die, too."

Loretto tossed his paper onto the table. "Jesus Christ," he said. "They're playin' this off the boards." He thought about it another second, fingered the newspaper as if he might read some more, and then flicked it away.

"They had to be drunk or something," Dominic said. "That's the only thing I can figure."

"Yeah, and that's an excuse?" Augie's face was screwed up in an expression that looked both angry and exasperated.

Loretto said, "Come on, Augie. You know Vince. He ain't a guy would shoot kids."

Augie picked up the *American*, made a show of reading the headline, and then dropped it in front of Loretto. "Yeah," he said. "Looks to me like he is." Dominic started to speak, but Augie cut him off. "Listen," he said, "I been telling you guys since back when I first heard what Vince did to

Joe Rock. Stay away from him." He leaned down lower to the table and almost whispered, "Anybody beats a guy so bad he blinds him. Anybody does what Vince did to Joe Rock—" He stopped and shook his head as if there was nothing more to say.

Dominic said, "He only blinded him in one eye," as if that made things better.

"That was a while ago," Loretto said.

"Sure," Augie said, "and now he's graduated to killing babies." When neither Loretto nor Dominic replied, Augie took another sip of his coffee and then brought his cup to the sink. "Look," he said, "I got to get ready for work." He gestured toward the coffee pot on the stove. "Dominic," he said, "pour yourself some coffee."

"Okay," Dominic said, "think I will." He went to the stove and turned on the water to rinse out Augie's cup.

Augie started out of the kitchen slowly. In the hallway, he stopped and pinched his Adam's apple as if he might pluck it out, and a moment later he returned to crouch beside Loretto, his hand on the back of Loretto's chair. "Listen," he said, "I don't want Freddie makin' his livin' on the wrong side of the law." He glanced up to Dominic. "I'm not getting all holier-than-thou about this, either. You know I've done the same work you're doing and still do at times if I need it. But Freddie . . ." He lowered his voice. "He ain't built for it. I don't think he could do another bit in Elmira." He glanced back to the closed bedroom door. "He ain't right," he said. "I'm worried about him."

"Sure," Loretto said, "but what's that got to do with me and Dominic?"

"Work's scarce everywhere." Augie stood up and touched his back. He made a sound like he was an old man, though he was only a few years older than Loretto. "Dock work," he said, explaining himself. "Kills ya."

"So work's scarce everywhere," Loretto said, repeating Augie's words. He made a gesture like he was still confused.

"'Cept what you mugs are doing," Augie said. "Plenty of that kind of work around." He tapped his finger on the table. "If Freddie comes to you—" he said to Loretto, and then he looked up to Dominic, "or to you or your uncle," he added. "I don't want there to be anything for him." Without waiting for a reply, he pointed to the front door. "Pull it closed when you leave. You gotta give it a little jiggle or it won't lock." Before he disappeared down the hall and joined Freddie behind the closed bedroom door, he added, "Take your time. Finish your coffee."

Dominic raised his eyebrows as if to say, *What's his beef?*

Loretto gestured toward the door and Dominic finished off his coffee in a couple of gulps while Loretto quickly threw on the rest of his clothes.

Out in the hall, Dominic made a joke out of jiggling the door to be sure it was locked.

"Did you see your uncle?" Loretto asked. "Can I go home now?"

"Yeah, sure. That's what I'm here for: to take you home so you can get dressed up all pretty before we go into the city to see Don Maranzano."

"I got to see Don Maranzano?" Loretto stopped and waited while Dominic descended another couple of steps. "What do I have to see the don for?"

"Because I told you," Dominic spoke in a harsh whisper, "Cabo wants to blow our brains out!"

"Both of us?"

"Yeah, both of us. Cabo went to Dutch to okay it."

"Okay what? Killin' us?"

"Yeah—what do you think?—blowin' our brains out."

"How do you know this?"

"Because Dutch knows Gaspar's my uncle and he can't bump me off without trouble from my family, so he got word to Don Maranzano that Cabo wants his blessing, and now they're meeting"—Dominic checked his wrist watch—"in about an hour to have a nice, reasonable discussion about smearin' our brains all over the sidewalk."

"Dutch and Maranzano are meeting?"

"Isn't that what I just said?"

"And we got to be there?"

"*Madon!*" Dominic threw up his hands and continued down the stairs muttering to himself in Italian.

On the street, Loretto caught up with Dominic as he put a foot up on the running board of his Packard.

"Get in the car." Dominic started to get in himself and then stopped and cursed when he noticed a white smear of bird droppings on the glistening blue hood. He found a garbage pail under a nearby stoop and rummaged through it for a brown paper bag, which he used to scrape the spot away.

Loretto watched from the passenger seat as Dominic returned the soiled paper to the garbage pail before getting in the car and straightening himself out behind the wheel.

"You know you're a lunatic," Loretto said, "you and this car."

Dominic adjusted the outside rearview mirror, which was positioned near the car's roof. "Sun's in my eyes," he said. He got out, tilted the visor down over the front window, and then got back in the car and straightened himself out again. He said, "This car's a work of art," before he stepped on the starter and then went rigid with tension when the engine turned over several times without starting. "Give it a minute!" he shouted as if Loretto had hurried him, though he hadn't said a word. He waited a few seconds, shook off his tension, then hit the starter again—and every time the engine turned over without starting his body tensed. By the time he gave up he was red in the face and muttering curses to himself.

"What time's this meeting?" Loretto asked.

"*Sta'zitt'!*" Dominic prepared himself to hit the starter again.

Loretto was already out of the car at the back bumper when the battery went dead. "You ready?" he called.

Dominic waved for him to go ahead and Loretto put his shoulder into the bumper and pushed the car until it started rolling downhill on its own. He ran alongside as Dominic popped it into gear and the engine roared to life.

Back in the passenger seat, Loretto acted as if nothing had happened. "How come you don't look worried about this meeting?"

Dominic tugged at his collar and stroked his cheeks, trying to rub the redness away. He cleared his throat. "Don Maranzano won't let Dutch or anybody else put a finger on me."

"Yeah?" Loretto fiddled with his hat. "You think the don can push around Dutch and Cabo?"

"What are you talking about?" Dominic said. "We're Sicilians—"

"You're all Sicilians."

"If Dutch kills me, Don Maranzano'll burn him to the ground. I'm Castellammarese. And Richie Cabo? That *cafon'*? He wouldn't dare. They'll be findin' pieces of him all over the Bronx."

Loretto pulled the brim of his hat down over his eyes. The sun was brilliant on the street and it glittered off the hood of the Packard. "And what about me?" he asked. "I might not even be Italian."

"Oh, you?" Dominic said. "Too bad about you." He hunched over the wheel and laughed like he'd just said the funniest thing in the world.

At the apartment, Loretto cleaned up and got dressed quickly, and then he and Dom were back in the car and on their way into Manhattan and Maranzano's offices in Grand Central Station. On the Willis Avenue Bridge, Dominic pointed down through the metal truss work to the sun glittering on the gray water of the Harlem River. "I went swimmin' down there once when I was a kid."

Loretto only grunted in reply and then found himself imagining a man dressed in a tux wavering on the bottom of the river, his feet encased in concrete, his body's gases pulling the torso and arms up as if reaching for the surface. He could almost see the man's figure, the black of the tux, its tails rippling in the current, his hair fluttering around his head, the river water swirling around him. He asked Dominic, "How long you think it takes a body to decompose in the water?"

"Decom-what?"

"Fall apart till it's gone."

"You're asking me?" Dominic said. "You're the smart one."

"Maybe a few weeks," Loretto guessed, "before there's nothing but bones."

For a moment, Dominic seemed revolted at the thought. Then he laughed. "Hey, Loretto," he said, "Don Maranzano ain't gonna let Dutch or Cabo or anybody else dump you in the river. You're family," he said. "You're not Castellammarese—we don't leave our *bambinos* in no orphanages—but we forgive you for that."

"Thanks," Loretto said

For the rest of the trip into midtown, Dominic concentrated on driving in traffic while Loretto looked out the window at the soaring buildings and the crowds on the streets. When they passed by the Commodore Hotel and the elaborate columns of Grand Central with its towering statuary, he checked his reflection in the rearview mirror. He pushed his hat back on his forehead and straightened his tie. This gleaming part of the city always made him a little nervous: it was more like another country than another borough, with its fields of glass and metal and concrete, so unlike the dingy tenement walls of Brooklyn and the Bronx, where he and Dominic did their usual business for Gaspar, hauling crates on and off trucks, riding shotgun on shipments, pushing around some dumb mug who didn't want to buy their hooch.

"You about ready, handsome?" Dominic pulled into a parking spot on a side street, took a snub-nosed Colt out of his pocket, and slid it under the driver's seat. "You're not heeled, are you?"

"You told me no guns," Loretto answered, and he got out of the car. On the sidewalk, a tall, thin, middle-aged woman in a blue dress walked by with a black umbrella over her head to shield her from the sun. Loretto had never seen such a thing, and apparently neither had Dominic, who watched her from the other side of the Packard.

"I don't like that," Dom said. When they met on the sidewalk, he twisted around and watched the woman with the black umbrella turn a corner and disappear. "Who carries an umbrella in the sun?"

Loretto looked to the sky and shielded his face with his forearm. "Sun's murder."

Dominic repeated, "I don't like it." As they entered the glass doors to Maranzano's building, he shook himself like a wet dog. "It's just a black umbrella," he said, talking to himself.

"I feel like I'm going to see a judge or something," Loretto whispered. All around him were high ceilings and marble inlays, broad stairways and polished banisters. He shrugged, meaning *What kind of a place is this to have an office?*

"It's not Mulberry Street," Dominic said, also in a whisper. "I hear Rockefeller's got offices around here."

At the top of the stairs, Henry LaSalla, one of Maranzano's men, was waiting outside a closed door. He was a big guy, older, maybe in his fifties, with a bulb of a nose that made him look clownish. Dom and Loretto both knew him, and they exchanged a few words before he opened the door and ushered them into a fancy waiting room with plush carpeting and a bench against one wall, a long table in front of it stacked with copies of *National Geographic* and *Time*. The two torpedoes who had been with Cabo at his club were seated on the bench, and they both jumped up when Henry opened the door.

"Sit down," Henry told them. Behind him, Vic Cinquemanni, another of Maranzano's men, came in. He was buckling his belt as if he'd left the bathroom in a hurry.

"They been frisked?" one of Cabo's guys asked.

"Yeah," Henry said, "I took care of it."

On the far side of the room, a rosewood desk was unattended. It held a black telephone and a silver serving tray with a coffee pot, a milk carton, and a sugar dispenser. To the right of the desk was another door, and behind it men were talking. "The don said I should bring you in soon as you got here," Henry said, and he stood with his back to the door and pushed it open.

Inside, seated around a glass conference table, were Dutch Schultz, Bo Weinberg, Richie Cabo, Don Maranzano, Charlie Luciano, and Gaspar Caporinno. The don was at the head of the table, Dutch was at the opposite end, Cabo and Weinberg were on one side, and Luciano and Caporinno were seated across from them. At the center of the table were two big wooden bowls, one with fresh fruit and the other with a variety of nuts. Each of the men had a white coffee cup and saucer in front of him. Cabo held a nutcracker in one hand and a walnut in the other. He jumped to his feet as Henry pulled the door closed behind Loretto and Dominic. "*V'fancul'* !" he yelled. He turned to Don Maranzano. "What are these two doing here?"

Maranzano calmly gestured for Cabo to sit down. In halting English, he said, "I invite them to join us. We should hear what they say, no?"

Dutch said, "I don't like surprises, Sal."

Don Maranzano smiled at the impertinence of being called Sal. He'd had only a few dealings with Dutch directly, and he was still taking the man's measure. "Arthur," he said, "Gaspar says they're good boys." He waved a hand toward Loretto and Dom, who were still standing behind Gaspar and Charlie with their hats in their hands. "I think we hear their side of the story."

"Yeah, but that's not what I'm talking about." Dutch pushed his chair back and turned to get a better look at Loretto and Dom. "I don't like the way you're pulling a big surprise on us," he said without taking his eyes off the boys. "It ain't copacetic."

Maranzano looked to Charlie Lucky.

"It ain't all right," Charlie translated. To Dutch he said, "It won't hurt nothing to hear them out."

Richie Cabo was still red in the face. He pointed to the boys and said, "You're both dead men! You hear me?"

Maranzano's face paled at Cabo's outburst, and Bo Weinberg put his hand on Cabo's shoulder. He said, "He's angry, Don Maranzano. That's all it is."

In Italian Luciano said, with his eyes on Cabo, "Richie's got a bad temper. Sometimes it gets him in trouble."

Cabo turned his attention to the walnut in his hand. He cracked it and sat down and went about peeling it without a word, but the gesture was a retreat, and it seemed to satisfy Maranzano.

Dutch said, "Okay, boys. Now you're here, what's your story? We're all ears."

Charlie and Gaspar shifted their chairs so they were facing the boys, and Dom looked for a second like he might speak up before he hesitated and turned to Loretto.

"It's nothin'," Loretto said. "Dom and I were going to the 21 because it was my birthday and we were gonna celebrate. I was waitin' for him to pick me up on the corner, and then the shootin' started. That's the whole story. We had nothin' to do with it."

"That's a lot of palaver," Cabo said.

Dutch spoke to Maranzano: "Why should I believe him?"

Gaspar said, "Dominic is my nephew. I raised him like a son in my house since my brother died, God rest his soul. And Loretto is in my employ. I'll vouch for both of them. If they say they had nothing to do with it, they had nothing to do with it. Besides," he added, and his face suddenly got red, "this *infamita*," he waved his finger at Cabo, "this is not something we'd have any part of, none of us."

"I'm telling you," Cabo said to Gaspar, "my boys seen this one," he pointed to Loretto, "runnin' beside the car and talking to the driver, and then this one," he pointed to Dom, "he was with him."

Gaspar hooked his thumbs under his suspenders. He was a man in his fifties with a big belly on an otherwise slim frame. His full head of white hair was slicked back and parted in the middle, and his face was still youthful though weathered. He turned to face Loretto.

"I ran beside the car," Loretto said, "because I wanted to see who was doing the shootin'. I didn't talk to nobody."

Bo said, "Who was doin' the shootin'?"

"*Che cazzo!*" Cabo said, "Everybody knows who was doing the shootin'!"

"All I saw's the driver," Loretto said. He hesitated and then added, "And the guy sittin' next to him."

Dutch said, "Yeah? And who was that?"

Loretto pressed his hat to his chest. "Don Maranzano," he said, "it's no secret who was in that car, but I'm not a guy who talks about what he saw." He looked to Dutch. "Not for nobody."

Maranzano said to Dutch, "We know it was this Vincent Coll. This *animale*."

Dutch watched Loretto. It was obvious he hadn't liked his response.

"Boss," Bo said to Dutch, trying to distract him, "every copper in the city's looking for Coll, and I hear Mulrooney's told 'em all to shoot him on sight and shoot to kill."

Dutch ignored Bo. To Loretto he said, "Hey, kid. You know who I am?"

"Sure," Loretto said. "You're Arthur Flegenheimer."

Dutch turned to Maranzano and Charlie Lucky and then finally to Bo before in a single motion he snatched a nutcracker off the table, snapped it in half so that the metal spring formed a jagged edge, and leaped at Loretto. He held Loretto's shirt in one hand and with the other hand pressed the jagged nutcracker to his throat. Before the men at the table could react, Loretto had his stiletto out of his pocket and at Dutch's jugular.

"Kid," Bo said, "put that away."

Maranzano whispered something into Gaspar's ear, and Gaspar motioned for Loretto to put the knife away.

Loretto took the knife from Dutch's throat, and in the same instant Dutch threw a quick, sharp right. Loretto ducked but the punch still caught him on the side of his head, over the temple, and knocked him back into the wall.

"All right, enough." Luciano pushed Dutch back to keep him from hitting Loretto again.

"Boss," Bo said, and he took Dutch by the arm as the door swung open and Henry entered with a pump-action shotgun in hand. Behind him, Cabo's torpedoes were on the couch looking up at a riot gun in the hands of Cinquemanni.

Luciano said, "Let's all settle down."

Don Maranzano hadn't moved from his seat at the head of the table. He was a slim man in his midforties dressed in a gray three-piece suit with a gold watch chain disappearing into his vest pocket. He pointed to Loretto and said to Dutch, "The boy defend himself, and he don't squeal."

Dutch shook off Bo's arm, straightened out his jacket, and pulled his chair back as if getting ready to take his seat again. Charlie told Henry to wait outside, and Loretto picked up his stiletto.

"You fuckin' dagos," Dutch said, taking his seat again, "you cut a guy's throat and eat off the same blade."

Loretto put the knife back in his pocket, picked up his hat from the floor, and leaned back against the wall. His head hurt where he had taken the punch, and there was a slight ringing in his ear. He acted, though, as if he didn't feel a thing.

Maranzano raised one hand, like a priest giving a benediction. "Nothing is to happen to these boys," he said to Dutch. "They are under my protection." To Richie Cabo he said, "Do you understand?"

Cabo looked away from the don and said nothing.

Bo said, "Don Maranzano, with all due respect, you have to understand that Richie believes these boys fingered him for Coll, and Richie works for Dutch. Dutch has a responsibility to look out for his men."

"*Si*," Maranzano said. He started to reply in Italian and then quickly corrected himself. "Yes," he said, "but these boys, they work for Gaspar, who works for me, and so I am responsible."

"Listen, Bo," Luciano said, "let's cut the bullshit, okay? Caporinno is Castellammarese. You can't touch him. That's the end of the story."

"But this kid's not," Dutch said and pointed to Loretto.

"Maybe you didn't hear," Maranzano said. "I say both boys, they under my protection."

"Dutch," Luciano said, "what's the dirt? You knew," he added, his voice rising, "that the don wouldn't give you what you wanted. What are you doing here?"

"I want Vince Coll." Dutch pointed to Dom and Loretto. "And these two guys are gonna give him to me, or—" he paused and faced Maranzano, "I'm going to fit 'em in concrete shoes and drop 'em in the fuckin' river."

Maranzano said something in Italian to Charlie, and Charlie raised his hand, asking him to wait. To Dominic he said, "Do you know where Vince can be found?"

"I don't know where he is," Dominic said. "Only time I see Vince is at the Mad Dot, his club on Dykman Street. Sometimes I run into him around town. With everybody lookin' to put one in him, he don't give out where he's stayin' to nobody."

Charlie turned to Loretto.

"Same thing," Loretto said. "I don't know nothin'." The ringing in his ear had stopped and he was back to feeling clear-headed.

Cabo stood up and said to Dutch, "We're not getting any satisfaction here." He puffed out his chest and glanced defiantly at Maranzano.

Maranzano snatched Cabo's tie and jerked his head down to the table. With one hand he held tight to the knot of the tie and with the other he pulled savagely, tightening the fabric around Cabo's neck like a noose. In Italian, he said, "I'll cut your balls off and stuff them up your ass, you fat pig." He pointed to the boys and held fast to Cabo, who was choking and sputtering but too off balance to pull away. "If something terrible happens to either one of these young men, even if it looks like the hand of God, I'm still going to hold you responsible. Do you understand?"

Cabo managed to nod, and Maranzano turned him loose.

Bo was looking glumly at Luciano, but Dutch was suddenly smiling. He was watching Cabo, who cut such a comic figure dancing around and clutching at his own throat while struggling unsuccessfully to loosen his tie that in a minute everyone in the room was laughing. When Cabo fell to his knees and looked close to passing out, Bo told Loretto to give him the knife. Loretto did so, and Bo cut the tie off Cabo's neck and then helped him out of the office. As soon as the door closed behind them, Charlie Lucky said to Dutch, "As long as Don Maranzano is head of the Castellammarese family, you can't touch these boys." He pointed to Loretto and said, "Either one of them. However," he added, and he put his arm roughly around Loretto's shoulders, "if one of them should learn the whereabouts of the Mick, they'll come to me right away—and I give you my word, you'll know soon as I do." He looked into Loretto's eyes, his forehead practically touching Loretto's, and the look said, *That's the deal, and you have nothing more to say about it.* He was a solemn-looking guy with thick lips, a right eye that drooped slightly, wavy dark hair, and a scar that ran from his ear to his chin.

Bo came back into the room alone and tossed the knife to Loretto. "That Vengelli kid died this morning. You hear about that?"

Loretto nodded, and Charlie let him loose.

Gaspar stood and said to Dutch, "I'm sure my boys will tell me if they hear anything about Coll."

Dutch got up from his seat, brushed himself off, and left the room without a word.

Alone in the office with Maranzano and the others, Bo said, "Don't pay no attention to that," meaning the contemptuous way in which Dutch had walked out of the meeting. To Don Maranzano he said, "He's a hothead, but he's not stupid. No harm will come to either one of them, not from us, anyway." He offered Don Maranzano his hand, and the don shook it. "Good," he said. "And just so everybody should know, Dutch has put a twenty-five-thousand-dollar bounty on Coll's head. That's in addition to Big Owney's twenty-five thousand. Guy who puts one in the Mick walks off with fifty grand." He tipped his hat to the room and followed his boss out the door.

When they were all gone, when everyone heard the waiting-room door close behind Cabo, who was still wheezing with every breath, Maranzano said, "*Cafon's,*" as if that single word explained everything. He went to Dom and Loretto, stood between them, and put his arms around their shoulders as he guided them to the door. "I like you boys," he said, and he shook them roughly by the neck. "Go on," he added as Gaspar opened the door for them. "You won't get no trouble." He pushed them out the door with a pat on the back.

In the waiting room again, with the door to the inner office closed behind them, Dom turned to Henry and Vic and whispered, "*Madon!*" while gesturing to Loretto.

Vic laughed and Henry said, "You got some balls, kid."

Vic said to Loretto, "I were you, I'd steer clear of Dutch and his gang. Word to the wise."

"Don't worry about it," Henry said. He opened the door and waved for the boys to follow him out into the hall. "Long as Don Maranzano's behind you, even Dutch Schultz ain't crazy enough to do anything." He offered them his hand, and both boys shook with him before descending the steps and walking out into the heat of the city.

On the street, on the way to car, Dom was giddy. He clutched Loretto's arm and said, "When you called Dutch 'Flegenheimer' the way you did, *v'fancul'!* I about shit my pants!"

"Me, too," Loretto said.

Dom shook his arm. "What did you think would happen? *Mannagg'!*"

Loretto didn't know why he had smart-mouthed Dutch, but he liked the way it felt, having done it. "I don't like the son of a bitch."

"You don't like him!" Dom yelled. "Nobody likes Dutch Schultz. That don't mean you can pull a knife on him."

"So what do you think?" Loretto asked. "Should I worry about Dutch or Cabo?" They were at the car, and Dom was stepping into the street, going around to the driver's door.

"Son of a bitch!" Dom stopped in front of the car, where a white mess of bird droppings was splattered over the otherwise brilliant finish. "These fuckin' birds follow me."

"You can clean it up later." Loretto got into the car and waited for Dom to join him.

Dom reluctantly left the hood as if loath to drive the car without cleaning it first. Behind the wheel, he said, "They should kill every fuckin' pigeon in New York. In the whole fuckin' state of New York."

"So what I asked you," Loretto said, "you think I should worry about Dutch or Cabo?"

"No." Dom leaned back, closed his eyes, hit the starter, and then grinned a big self-satisfied grin when the engine turned over the first time. "It's a work of art, this car."

"Why not?" Loretto asked.

"Because no matter how much Dutch wants you dead, he knows if he kills you, the Castellammarese won't rest till he's dead, too." He pulled the car out into the empty side street and started toward the traffic on the avenue. "We're Sicilians," he said to Loretto. "You don't fool around with us."

"And Cabo?"

"Forget about Cabo." Dom straightened out the rearview mirror. "Only one you got to worry about now is Vince."

Loretto looked out the window at the crowds on the street and let his thoughts drift back to the meeting and the men seated around the conference table. Don Maranzano at one end of the table, stylishly dressed but old-fashioned with his gold watch chain strung across his vest. Rumor was he packed two pistols under his jacket whenever he went out on the street, back when he was at war with Joe the Boss. He drove around in a bulletproof Cadillac with a machine gun mounted between the back seats. He had his own brewery in Pennsylvania, a legit real estate business, and was already worth millions before he came over from Sicily. Dutch on the other end of the table in his cheap suit with a sour look on his face: word was he made millions off the Harlem lottery alone, not even counting all the beer and whiskey money. "What do you know about Charlie Luciano?" he asked Dom. "The way he acted, it was almost like he was running things."

"Nah," Dom said. "He's the don's right-hand man now." Dominic looked like he wanted to say something more before he decided against it and went back to concentrating on driving.

"What?" Loretto pressed.

"Nothin'."

"Don't tell me nothin'. What?"

"If I tell you this," Dom said, "you got to give me your word you won't tell another soul. I'm not supposed to know about it myself."

"Yeah, sure," Loretto said. "What?"

"You see that scar on Charlie Lucky's face?"

"I ain't blind. What about it?"

"Yeah, well, Don Maranzano give him that."

Loretto waited for the rest of the story.

"Let's just say there was a misunderstanding between them, and Charlie wound up hanging from a beam getting the shit beat out of him."

"What kind of a misunderstanding?"

"That I don't know," Dom said. "But the don give him that scar on his face, and another one you can't see down his chest."

Loretto started to ask how he knew all this and then caught himself. The only way he could know was through Gaspar, which meant Gaspar had to have been there.

"Salvatore Maranzano," Dom said, "right now he's chief of the Castellammarese, but you watch, in time he's gonna be runnin' everything, the whole country. *Capo di tutti capi*. You watch."

"You admire him," Loretto said. They were at the Willis Avenue Bridge again. It was swinging closed, having just let a barge pass through on the river, and the traffic was backed up.

"Sure, I admire him," Dominic said. "The man has a university education back in Italy. He speaks Greek and Latin! He's got a library in his home, *madon!*, big walls nothin' but books."

"What's a university education got to do with selling hooch to speakeasies and bumping off anybody gives you trouble?"

"You don't get it," Dom said. The traffic started moving again, and he put the car in gear. "It's bigger than that."

"Yeah?" Loretto said. "If you say so."

"Yeah, well, I say so."

Crossing the bridge, Loretto again imagined a body in the river, feet in concrete, wavering in the current. "Maybe the don said something smart in Latin," he said to Dom, "while he was slicing up Charlie Lucky."

"Shut up," Dom said. "You don't know nothing."

Loretto watched the Willis Avenue Bridge recede in the rearview as the traffic started moving. His eyes were on the latticework of the bridge and the rippling water and the lines of cars with headlights like bug eyes, with whitewall tires and running boards and chrome grills and bumpers—but his thoughts were back at the meeting in the conference room.

"What are you smiling at?" Dominic put his hat on the seat between them, pulled a black pocket comb from his pocket, and raked it though a profusion of curly black hair. When Loretto didn't answer, he added, "You're grinning like the cat that swallowed the canary."

Loretto said, "Dutch thought I was a dago."

"Dutch what?"

"When he said that thing about dagos killin' and eatin' with the same blade. He figured me for an Italian."

"How many times I got to tell you!" Dominic gripped the steering wheel and shook it as if he were strangling someone. "You think some WASP family from Westchester drops off their *bambino* at Mount Loretto? *Mammalucc'!*" He slapped the steering wheel.

"Just drive," Loretto said, and he went back to watching the traffic in the rearview.

11:06 p.m.

Gina thought Raymond Novarro was the best-looking man on earth. In the movie she'd just seen with Loretto, Novarro played a Hindu jewel merchant forced to relinquish his love for an American girl, and Gina was chattering about the movie, the girl, and the sadness of it all as she walked hand in hand with Loretto along 107th Street on a perfect summer night. They were on the way to his apartment and the closer they got to his building, the more she seemed to chatter. Loretto was content to let Gina do all the talking. It was one of those rare nights when the stars were so bright they seemed to hover just over the rooftops. Their clasped hands between them swung back and forth with the rhythm of their walking, and he liked the feel of her hand in his, the delicacy of her fingers, the way her palm fit in the center of his closed hand. Along 107th, people were out on their stoops quietly talking with friends and neighbors. From behind an open window, a room full of unseen people burst into laughter. Loretto and Gina glanced toward the window and laughed themselves.

Mrs. Marcello at first smiled at the sight of Loretto coming back to his apartment with a girl, but then she recognized Gina and the smile disappeared.

When she reached the top of the steps, Gina gave Mrs. Marcello a kiss and a hug. In her ear, in Italian, she whispered, "I'm divorced now, and

I'm only staying a little while," and when she pulled away she added, in English, "Mama sends her love. You should come visit. She talks all the time about the wonderful Mrs. Marcello."

"I'll see her soon," Mrs. Marcello said, and she gestured to the sky. "What a beautiful night! The air's so clear!"

"And it's not hot like the last few nights," Loretto said.

"Did you hear both the Bevilacqua boys, they'll be all right? Thank God," she added, "everybody thought Salvatore . . ." She shook her hand, meaning everyone had thought Salvatore would surely die.

"It's a blessing," Gina said.

"The family, they're building a shrine."

Loretto touched the small of Gina's back and nudged her toward the open door.

"*Buonanotte*," Gina said and smiled a little awkwardly.

"Shot three times," Mrs. Marcello said to Loretto as he walked by her.

"Salvatore?" Loretto asked. When she nodded, he said, "Everybody knows I had nothing to do with this shooting, right?"

"*Si*," Mrs. Marcello assured him. She added, "But you know who did."

"Mrs. Marcello," Loretto said, and without realizing it he raised his finger to her, "I know nothing more than everybody else seems to know anyway." When he realized that he was pointing at her, he quickly put his hand in his pocket. "I'd appreciate it," he said, "if you would share that with others."

Mrs. Marcello patted Loretto's cheek. "You're a good boy," she said. "That's what I tell everybody."

"Thank you," Loretto said. "I had nothing to do with it. I swear to you." Before he followed Gina up the stairs, he gave Mrs. Marcello a kiss on the cheek.

Gina was waiting for him at his apartment door. "She's like the neighborhood newspaper," she whispered. "By this time tomorrow, there won't be anyone in the Bronx won't know I came back to your apartment with you." She looked shocked and added, "Unsupervised!"

Loretto unlocked the door and guided Gina into the living room, where she took a seat on the couch. "You'd think I was a girl again," she said, and she crossed her legs. She was wearing a summery blue dress that hiked up over her knees. Loretto's eyes fell to her stockinged legs.

"Aren't you still a girl?" He went to the kitchen, pulled a bottle of Canadian whiskey from a cupboard, and showed it to Gina.

"Just a splash. It is illegal, didn't you hear?"

Loretto went about pouring them both drinks. "Aren't you?" he asked again.

"Just a girl? No. I'm a divorcée, and we all know about divorcées."

"You may be divorced," Loretto said. He started to hand her a whiskey glass and then pulled it back. "Straight okay?"

"I like it straight." Gina took the glass from him. "I may be divorced?" she reminded.

"But you're still only twenty-one. Same as me."

"Twenty-two." She again feigned being shocked. "A divorcée and an older woman!"

Loretto took a seat next to Gina. He put his arm around her neck, drew her close, and kissed her.

"Oh," Gina said, "are we picking up from where we left off on the roof?"

"That sounds good." Loretto's heart was already beating hard. Gina's breasts were somehow even more provocative to him under the thin fabric of her summer dress than they had been that night up on the roof, exposed and in his hand.

"Mrs. Marcello will be listening for every sound that comes out of your apartment, and I told her I'd only be a short while."

"So you don't want to?" Loretto asked. He backed away.

Gina sidled close to him and kissed him again. "Listen," she said, "if we're going to do this, we have to be discreet. The other night, up on the roof, that was a onetime fling with a good-looking boy—and nobody had to know."

"And what's this?"

"That's up to you. Do you want a onetime fling?"

Loretto didn't have to think. "No," he said. He was about to say more when a knock on the door interrupted him. "Who's that?" he asked Gina, as if she might somehow know.

When the knock came again and louder, Gina said, "I don't think he's going away."

Loretto considered getting his pistol from the bedroom, and for a moment struggled with protecting himself versus looking like a gangster in front of Gina. When the knock came a third time, and louder, he settled for standing back and to the side while he opened the door slightly with his toe jammed against the bottom of it. When he heard his name called, he peeked through the crack and saw Mike Baronti's face, with the familiar scar over his eye. He pulled the door open and Mike slipped into the apartment.

Loretto couldn't figure what to say. He was too surprised. He managed only to say Mike's name.

Mike started to speak and then noticed Gina on the couch in the next room. "What's she doing here?" he asked Loretto, as if Gina were somehow out of earshot.

"What business is that of yours?" Gina was off the couch and in the kitchen—and suddenly an entirely different person than she had been a moment earlier. She stood toe to toe with her brother. "Do you realize Mama's worried sick about you? Everybody's saying you were in that car with Vince Coll and you shot up all those kids. Is that true, Mike? Did you?"

Mike seemed not to hear a word she said. To Loretto he said again, "I asked you, what's she doing here?"

Gina shoved her brother and he shoved her back. Loretto got in between them. "Mike," he said, "Gina and I went to a movie, and now we're having a drink before I take her home."

"Yeah? And you're here all alone, just the two of you?"

Gina said, "I swear to God, Mikey, I'm gonna slap you silly. You're asking what I'm doing here with Loretto when everybody's saying what they're saying about you? I'm askin' again: Did you have a part in shooting those kids?" Gina's face had darkened, and the way she was standing, she looked like she was a second away from hauling off and slugging her brother.

Mike put up his hands. "Listen," he said, "let me talk to Loretto out in the hall a minute. Then I promise I'll come back in here and explain everything to you."

"You better," Gina said. She went back into the living room and planted herself firmly on the couch.

In the hallway with Mike, Loretto closed the door behind him. "What's the dirt?"

"Vince wants to talk to you."

"Yeah? What about?"

"Don't worry," Mike said. "He heard you put a knife to Dutch's throat. He wants to give you a kiss."

Loretto looked around the hallway, at the battered door of the apartment across from him and its cut-glass doorknob, at the yellowing linoleum of the landing. "You sure about this, Mike? He wouldn't be worried about me fingering him for Tuesday's shootings, would he?"

Mike scratched the back of his neck. "He might be," he said, "but I'm pretty sure he just wants to talk. I give you my word he ain't said nothin' to me about no rough stuff."

"Where is he?"

"He's parked around the corner, on 108th."

"You know the whole damn city's lookin' for you guys, right? Did anybody see you come up here?"

"Nah. I waited till Mrs. Marcello went in, and I got my hat down to my nose anyway. Where's Dominic?"

"In Pennsylvania with Gaspar." Loretto answered Mike's question, but his thoughts were on Vince waiting for him around the corner. He wished he had more time to make a decision. "They're buying a couple of milk tankers," he explained.

"Shippin' beer in milk tankers," Mike said. "That's smart."

"Sure," Loretto said, and then he and Mike stood there in the hallway staring at each other, neither of them, apparently, with any idea what more to say.

Mike spoke first. "Look, Loretto," he said, "all I think is Vince wants to talk, just to make sure that everything's okay with you and him after . . . after what happened."

"Yeah, but you can't tell me for sure he doesn't plan on taking me for a ride."

"You know Vince," Mike said. "Nobody knows what he'll do. But he didn't say nothing about taking you for a ride. That I swear to you on my mother's life." He waited and then added, "I think you got to go see him. If you don't, then . . ."

"If I don't, then I'll be in trouble."

"Yeah," Mike said. "I figure that's the way it is."

At the bottom of the landing, a mouse took a few careful steps out of the shadows, sniffed at a cigarette butt, and then scurried across the linoleum and disappeared into a hole in the wall. "All right," Loretto said, as much to himself as to Mike, and he started down the steps.

On 108th Street, Vince waited at the wheel of a black roadster with phony plates courtesy of the inmates at Elmira. He was wearing a straw boater and round tortoiseshell glasses. After the Vengelli kid had died and Mulrooney declared open season on him, he'd dyed his hair black, started growing a mustache, and had Lottie buy him the boater and glasses. When he looked at his reflection, he didn't recognize himself.

"What's takin' so long?" Lottie was stretched out in the seat next to Vince with her head against the door and her knees to her chin. Tuffy was in the back seat, sleeping. The plan was to head up to Albany after meeting with Loretto.

Vince didn't bother answering. He felt under his jacket and touched the butt of the pistol holstered over his heart. He figured he needed to have a talk with Loretto. If Loretto had seen him doing the shooting, that could be bad, but he liked Loretto, and he hadn't thought it through any further than this meeting. In the thinking, there wasn't anything about bumping him off to keep him quiet—but then he'd never once thought about killing May Collins till it was already done. It made him jittery to think of that. He'd liked May, too. It was Carmine had to go, and not because he wouldn't come with him when he split from Dutch but because he'd told Dutch—he'd squealed, and he was supposed to be a friend—and it wasn't even the squealing. It was that Carmine showed no respect. He could have just said no, he wouldn't split because he was scared of Dutch, he was happy where he was, anything like that. Instead he'd spit on the ground and said Vince was crazy to rile Dutch and to count him out—and that was saying Vince wasn't tough enough to take on Dutch, and so Vince had to show him and everybody else that he was more than tough enough. He'd learned that lesson with Joe Rock. After he'd blinded Rock that way and sent him running upstate with his tail between his legs, all of a sudden everybody looked at him different. They may have said they were disgusted or it was a sin to do anyone that way—but they were all a lot more careful around him. They watched what they said, and Vince figured out that fear and respect were close cousins. That was the Joe Rock lesson. He knew he couldn't let Carmine talk to him like that, and then Carmine went around telling everybody he had turned down Vince Coll and Dutch would grind Vince and his gang into the dirt—and then he went and told Dutch, and that was that.

But Vince never thought he was going to give May any trouble. She was only a kid from some hick town in Pennsylvania, and he'd told her he just wanted to have a talk with Carmine, man to man, to straighten things out between them because they'd been friends a long time and then they could go their own ways and go on being friends with no one getting hurt—and May lapped it up like the hick from the boondocks she really was, though she dressed like a moll and worked as a dance hostess and liked to talk like she was all wised up, like she'd grown up on the streets with the rest of them. She'd gone along, gotten Carmine to walk her home after work, and Vince was waiting where he'd said he'd be, and she led Carmine right to him. It was late and there was no one on the block. Frank was at the wheel and Vince was in the passenger seat, at the curb, waiting. Vince'd seen them coming, Carmine and May, and they were laughing about something, like whatever Carmine had just said that was so funny might also be a little scandalous. When they came up even with the car window, Vince said, "What do you know, what do you say?" Carmine froze—and Vince put one in him and then got out of the car and put a few more in him for good measure.

May never said a word, and this was the thing Vince kept coming back to in his thoughts: the way he'd looked at May after he'd taken care of Carmine and was standing over him with his automatic still dangling from his hand. Frank was in the car, at the wheel. May was shaking and her mouth was open like there was a word she meant to say but it got frozen somewhere, leaving her eyes wide and her mouth hanging open. Shaking like her whole body was moving, her arms dancing like a Pentecostal at her sides. Vince hadn't meant to do a thing to May, but by the time he turned away from Carmine there was already a buzzing in his blood. He hadn't ever killed anyone up close before. He'd beaten some half to death and tortured a few, like Joe Rock, but he'd never given someone lead poisoning like Carmine up close, and someone who was once a friend, so when he turned around and May saw him do it, he shot her, too. Hadn't planned on it, hadn't even thought of it—just turned around and did it. That was what made him nervous, that he himself didn't know what it was he might do next.

"Here he comes," Lottie said. She straightened herself up and kissed Vince on the cheek. The lights went out in the first-floor apartment closest to the car and the street suddenly got darker. "He ain't gonna talk, honey, even if he did see something. You know Loretto. He's a stand-up guy."

"Sure," Vince said. "And you might have a little crush on him, too. Is that the story?"

"Don't be a big jerk," Lottie said. "You know there's only one man in the world for me." She reached between his legs.

Vince pushed her hand away. Loretto was walking up the street, approaching the car. He was a good-looking kid. In the orphanage, they'd lived in long dorms with rows of beds facing each other against the wall and the nuns would walk down the aisle at night with a yardstick or one of those long sticks for pointing at the blackboard and they'd make all the boys keep their hands on top of the covers. *Fold your hands over your belly and go to sleep*, Sister Aloise used to say. They were tough, those nuns, but Vince figured he'd learned more with them in those three years than he'd learned in all his other years in public schools—not that he was ever really in the public schools much after his mother died, not him or Pete either. Loretto was quiet but no sissy. Sister Mary Catherine took a special interest in him, and he paid hell for that with everyone. Vince had always liked him because he was smart and even if he was quiet he still knew when to speak up for himself, and then once, when Vince wasn't around and a couple of the older boys were giving it to Pete, Loretto took Pete's side and blacked one of their eyes and kicked the other in the balls. After that it was always the three of them—Pete, Vince, and Loretto. Pretty soon the older boys started leaving the three of them alone, and all the boys their own age were hanging around, wanting to be part of their gang. They were only babies themselves, not even teenagers yet.

Vince threw open the door and stepped out onto the street just as Loretto drew even with the car. "Took you long enough," he said. "Where's Mike?"

"Vince?" Loretto had taken a quick step back at the sight of a stranger getting out of a car in front of him. It had taken him a second to realize it was Vince, and he still wasn't entirely sure.

"What's the matter?" Vince said. "You don't recognize your old friend?"

Lottie popped her head out the window. She was wearing a shallow hat with a bright red bow and holding an open gold cigarette case in the palm of her hand. "Don't he look swell?"

Vince bent to the window and kissed Lottie on the lips, a lingering deep kiss. When he was finished, he looked up to Loretto. "Ain't she a beauty?"

"She's a doll."

"Come here and give me a kiss," Lottie said. She took a cigarette and tossed the case onto the seat beside her.

Loretto bent to the car window and gave Lottie a quick peck on the lips. He noticed Tuffy in the back seat. "Is he dead or alive?"

"I don't know," Lottie said. "I ain't checked in a while."

Vince said to Lottie, "We're takin' a walk around the block. There's a gat under the seat if there's any trouble."

"I won't have no trouble." She blew Loretto a kiss. "Don't keep him too long. We got to hit the road."

Vince put his arm around Loretto's shoulders and drew him away from the car. "So where's Mike?" he asked again.

"Gina was with me. He stayed behind to talk to her."

"Gina Baronti? What are you doing with Gina? She's married, right?"

"Not anymore," Loretto said. "We went on a date."

"Yeah?" Vince thought about that for a second before he moved on. "So the word on the street is you put a knife to the Dutchman's throat. Is that what happened?" Before Loretto could answer, he added, "You should have cut the bastard's gizzard for me, Loretto. I'd put twenty-five grand in your pocket just to hear you tell me what it felt like."

"It happened fast," Loretto said. "I wasn't thinking."

"Ain't that the truth," Vince said. They were approaching the corner and a pool of light around a lamppost. With the heel of his hand, Vince pushed the back of the boater up so that the front brim came down low on his forehead, just above the round glasses. "I'm glad you didn't kill him," he added. "Anybody kills him before I do, I'm gonna be mad. I been dreamin' about putting one between the eyes of that cheap son of a bitch ever since Pete got it."

"Can't say I like the guy much myself." The night was still clear and bright with stars, though a few long wisps of cloud had appeared and were floating beneath a sliver of moon. Loretto shoved his hands into his pockets and hunched his shoulders. He was tired all of sudden. "Want to sit a minute?" he asked, and he pointed to a rough concrete stoop smothered by shadows.

Vince pinched the creases of his pants, hiked them slightly, and took a seat. Loretto sat beside him. It was late enough that there was no one left out on the street. Vince said, "So I heard you seen the car and who did the shootin' killed the Vengelli kid. That true?"

"I didn't tell the cops nothin', Vince. How long you known me?"

"That's not the question." Vince leaned back, putting a little more distance between himself and Loretto. "So you saw who was doing the shooting?" he asked again.

"All I saw's Frank doing the driving," Loretto said. "I couldn't identify no one else positively with a Bible under my hand."

"Yeah?" Vince said. "That's good. I'm glad to hear that."

"But I know it was you," Loretto said, and the blood rushed to his face as he spoke. "Who else would be a head taller than anyone in the car, with Frank at the wheel?" He flicked the brim of Vince's hat back off his forehead so he could see his eyes. "What the hell was going through your head, Vince? You shot five kids and killed one of them. What was he, five years old?"

Vince straightened out the boater. "I ought to plug you, you know that? The boys think I should put one in you just to be sure."

"Yeah, well, what's stoppin' you?" He opened his jacket. "I ain't heeled."

"Tough guy," Vince said. "Go on, get up." He stood and snapped his pants at the creases. "Let's keep walking."

Loretto's heart, pounding a second earlier, mysteriously calmed and quieted. Walking alongside Vince now, along a darkened city street, felt like walking with him when they were kids, only Pete was missing. The three of them side by side through the schoolyard together, or down a city street, or running neck and neck like they were racing, which they liked to do, though Vince always pulled away at will and won easily. He understood that it was possible Vince might put a bullet in him—but he wasn't thinking about it. He was thinking about the kids Vince shot.

"You say you won't talk," Vince said, and he sounded like he was arguing with himself, "but once they get you in the sweatbox and start breaking your ribs, you might change your tune. You might sing, and that could be big trouble."

"I already told you," Loretto said, "there's nothing I could swear to. All I saw's a guy in a hat in the back seat. Besides," Loretto stopped and stepped in front of Vince, "it ain't like the whole damn city don't know it was you and the boys doing the shootin' that day. Don't you read the papers?"

"They can't prove it without a witness can identify me."

"They won't need to prove it. Mulrooney put out a shoot-to-kill order on you. 'Put one in him above the waist.' That's what the papers said he told the whole police force. 'If I see him, that's what I'll do.' That's what Mulrooney said."

"Not if I see the fat pig first." Vince pushed Loretto. "Go on, walk," he said. "I ain't got all night."

Loretto walked a way in silence, past empty stoops and garbage pails at the curb, before he asked again, "How'd it happen, Vince? Were you that drunk, the lot of you, that you didn't know what you were doing? That's all I can figure makes any sense."

"Yeah, we were drunk," Vince said, and his voice got quiet and familiar, the Vince at Mount Loretto talking in the dorms at night after lights out, quiet so the nuns wouldn't hear. "Tell you the God's honest truth," he said, "I don't know what happened. We were gunnin' for Cabo. We were gonna hit his club, blast him—and then there he was on the street and he seen us. After that, it was like you just said, everything happened fast." He stopped and took Loretto by the arm. "This is the God's honest truth, too. I don't remember shootin' no kids, and we weren't the only ones doin' the shootin'—so there's no way anybody can say it was me or one of the boys killed that kid. I ain't sayin' it's not possible. I'm sayin' I don't know who shot him and neither does anyone else."

"Who else was shooting?" Loretto asked when Vince let him loose. "I didn't see Cabo get off a shot. Him or anyone."

"Some of Cabo's guys was across the street in one of the apartments facing the club. Cops found guns and ammunition, but they ain't puttin' it in the papers."

"Yeah? Then how do you know about it?"

Vince's body went tight the way it did when he was angry. He shrugged his shoulders as if trying to get something off his back. Calmly, he said, "We got our connections," and then he pulled Loretto so close he was practically whispering in his ear. "I ought to plug you if I was being smart, but I'm not. You know why? Because I figure guys like us stick together." He loosened his grip so that Loretto could walk straight. "But you can't push me too far," he went on, "especially if somebody else is around. You hear what I'm telling you?" As he spoke, Vince watched the street and the stoops and the shadows. He was talking softly again. "In case you didn't notice, there's no real law around here. I plan on makin' millions, me and Lottie. Ask Dutch. He's so scared of me, he don't even hardly leave his place at night anymore. Big Owney is scared of me. Ciro Terranova, the feckin' artichoke king, is scared of me. Legs Diamond, Richie Cabo, the whole feckin' city of New York, they're all scared of me."

They were rounding a corner again, coming up on Loretto's building. Across the avenue, a couple of guys in work shirts and knit caps exited a doorway together, glanced at Vince and Loretto, and then quickly continued down the steps and to the street. Vince was quiet until they disappeared around a corner. "Listen, Loretto," he said, "how much is Gaspar paying you? Hundred a week?"

"Fifty."

Vince spit on the sidewalk. "Fifty," he repeated as if he could hardly believe it. "Come to work for me and I'll give you a fair cut of everything we make, just like I do with all the boys. You'll have more money in your pocket after a week with me than you'll make in a year with Gaspar."

"No, thanks." Loretto told himself not to say anything more and then immediately did. "Every cop in the city is gunnin' for you, Vince. When the Vengelli kid died, the newspapers put up a twenty-five-thousand-dollar reward for whoever brings you in, dead or alive. You know all this, right?"

"Sure," Vince said. "And now I hear Dutch added another twenty-five thousand to the twenty-five grand Big Owney put on my head since I snatched Frenchy."

"That's what I hear, too."

"See?" Vince slapped Loretto on the back. "That's what I was just telling you. They're scared to death of me. You think all the boys on the street don't see that? You think they don't see that I got Dutch shakin' in his boots? When I eventually get to feckin' Flegenheimer—and I swear by everything holy that I will get to him—who's going against me?"

"I don't think you understand," Loretto said.

Again Vince slapped him on the back, only this time not so friendly. "You're the one who don't get it," he said, "working like a slob for fifty a week while Gaspar and Maranzano get filthy rich. The whole feckin' country's like that now. Ain't you been lookin' up at somebody's boot heel since they turned on the lights?"

Loretto said, "I'm not doin' so bad."

"Yeah, you are," Vince answered. "You just don't see it." He was breathing hard and when they reached the last corner before arriving back at his car, he stopped and took off his hat and ran his fingers through his hair. "Listen, don't forget what I said. It's a standing offer." He put his arm around Loretto's shoulders. Ahead of them, Lottie rolled down the driver's window and waved, watching them in the rearview. "We got big plans, me and Lottie."

"If you can manage," Loretto said, "to stay alive."

"We'll manage." They were nearing the car and Vince let Loretto loose. "Just remember," he said, "when you're tired of doing all the work so somebody else can get all the money."

Loretto didn't say anything more. At the car, Lottie was waiting with a smile, her arms crossed in the open window and her chin resting on her hands. You wouldn't have guessed she had a trouble in the world, a beauty with a flirty smile and a twinkle in her eyes looking like someone was about to show her a good time. "Hey, boys," she said, "what's the rumpus?"

Vince got into the car and slid behind the wheel. Loretto crouched to look in the window. To Lottie, he said, "You're getting him out of the city, I hope."

Vince said, "You worry too much, Loretto."

"Sure," Lottie said. "We're takin' us a little vacation."

Loretto knocked twice on the car door and stood to leave but then leaned into the window a last time. "Watch out for yourself," he said to Vince.

"Like I said," Vince answered, "you worry too much." He winked and a moment later Loretto was alone on the street, watching the roadster pull away. At the corner, the car stopped and Lottie climbed half out the window, one hand holding on to her hat and the other waving. She yelled, "Abyssinia, Loretto!"

"I'll be seeing you, too," Loretto answered quietly and then watched as the roadster sped away around a corner with Lottie climbing into its dark interior.

At his apartment, he found Mike waiting for him outside the door. "I can't talk to her," he said, meaning Gina.

"She's worried about you," Loretto said.

Mike looked back at the door, shook his head. "You all square with Vince?"

"I'm still breathin'."

"That's what I figured," Mike said. "You hear the papers are callin' him Mad Dog Coll?"

"Me and the whole country. Yeah, I heard it."

Mike glanced back at the closed apartment door again. "You're treating my sister with respect, right?"

"Hey, Mike," Loretto said, "Gina's all grown up."

Mike shoved Loretto back into the wall and put a finger in his face. "You treat my sister with respect," he said, "or you'll answer to me or one of my brothers. You got it?"

"Sure," Loretto said. "I didn't mean I wasn't treating her with respect."

"Good," Mike said, and he backed off. "How's she getting home?"

"I got Dom's Packard. I'm driving her."

"But first you brought her back to your place."

"Sure," Loretto said. "For a drink."

"Okay," Mike said, "you had your drink. Now take her home." He fit his hat on his head, brim practically to his nose, and started down the stairs.

"What about you?" Loretto called after him. "Where are you going? The others left already."

"I'm meeting Frank," Mike answered and then hurried down the steps.

Loretto waited until he heard the front door open and close, and then he went back into his apartment, where Gina was standing at the window with her back to him. When she turned around, her eyes were puffy, and she had a tissue in her hand. "He says he didn't have nothing to do with the shooting. He wasn't even in the car."

Loretto found his drink on the floor by the couch where he'd left it. He belted it down and went into the kitchen to pour himself another.

"Is that true?" Gina asked. She followed him into the kitchen. "Is it true he wasn't in the car?"

"If he says so." Loretto held the bottle of whiskey out, offering her another drink.

"Did you see him in the car or not?"

"I didn't see him," Loretto said. "Only person I could swear to seeing in that car was Frank Guarracie."

Gina kept her eyes on Loretto's as if hoping to see something there. When she didn't, it was clear in her own eyes, and she walked away, back into the living room. "What am I asking you for?" she said. "You and Mike both, you're a couple of small-time gangsters." She found her purse and started for the door. "I don't know what I was thinking seein' you, Loretto. Mike was in that car, and you know it." She looked like she might slap him, her hand cocked at her side. Instead, she turned abruptly and walked out the door.

Loretto grabbed his hat and followed her. "Where are you going?" Gina held the wooden banister in one hand and her purse in the other as she hurried down the stairs. "Your place is miles from here."

"I can walk it." She threw open the front door and then stopped with Loretto right behind her. "Leave me be," she said. "Go on."

Loretto took the keys to Dom's car out of his pocket and dangled them in front of her. "At least let me drive you."

"No." She went out to the street and started walking.

Loretto caught up to her and tried to press the car keys in her hand. "Then take the car."

"No," she said again. "You've probably got guns stuffed under the seats."

"There are no guns under the seat." As soon as Loretto said this, he realized it wasn't true. Dominic kept a pistol under the driver's seat.

"I want to walk," Gina said. "Clear my head."

"Then I guess I'm walking with you." Loretto put his hands in his pockets and walked alongside Gina, matching her pace. She lived, he figured, at least two miles away, maybe farther. He settled in for a walk. The night, thankfully, was warm and the weather was beautiful, the sky still full of stars, though there were more clouds now, high wispy ones drifting lazily over chimneys and pigeon coops and water towers. They walked together, side by side, for more than a mile before Gina broke the silence. They were on a block of garages and industrial buildings, the streets littered with trash and assorted junk. They stepped over a flattened hunk of metal that looked like it might have once been part of a car and walked around a dusting of metal filings near a tall garage door. "Look," Gina said, and she glanced alongside her to Loretto for the first time since leaving his building, "all I ever wanted with you was a fling. I don't know how I got from there to here. A fling, up on the roof in the middle of the night. That's all I wanted."

"Sure," Loretto said, "but it's not all you want now."

"Who said that?" She stopped and then immediately started again, and at a quicker pace. "I didn't say that. I just got rid of one guy. I don't need another."

"I'm not like him."

"That's true," Gina said. "You're a small-time gangster. You and Mike both, a couple of tough guys, like Freddie was and wound up in Elmira, breakin' everybody's heart. Even my big brother, Augie. He's not clean as a whistle, either. You think I don't know it?"

"You might have missed the news," Loretto said. "There's not a lot of honest work around for guys like Augie."

"And what kind of guy is that?"

They had left the industrial block and were back on a street of tenements and cold-water flats. "Guys that grew up in neighborhoods like this," Loretto said, and then added, "if they were lucky." Meaning if they hadn't grown up in an orphanage or on the streets, like him. And like Vince and Pete.

"Tough guys," Gina said, each word a sneer.

Loretto didn't respond. He had drifted into thinking about all the guys he ran the streets with, how most of them had fathers who were dead, or drunks, or just up and disappeared. Some of them, like him and Vince, didn't have mothers, either. The Barontis, maybe they didn't have a father around anymore, but they had a mother who kept them together, and they had each other. "I make fifty dollars a week," he said. "Even if I could find a legit job, I wouldn't make half of that."

Several blocks later, Gina asked, "You saving any of it, what you make?"

"Sure," Loretto answered. "I am. I have a bank account."

"No kiddin'? I never heard of a gangster putting money *in* a bank."

"I guess I'm unusual that way." He was pleased to see Gina smile for the first time since he'd left Vince and returned to his apartment.

They walked the rest of the way to her place in silence, Gina's eyes focused on nothing, lost in her own thoughts, and Loretto watching everything around him, the streets, the buildings, the cars parked on the streets, the occasional cart, the garbage pails at the curb. In the building across from Gina's, a frilly white dress was suspended from a hanger on a fire escape. It fluttered in the breeze as if dancing alone in the quiet and the dark.

At the entrance to her building, Gina said, "You walked all this way, you might as well come up."

Loretto was too surprised to answer. He waited, watching her as she unlocked the door and held it open.

"If my brothers find out, they'll kill you," she said. She pushed the door open with her back.

Loretto said, "You're hard to figure, you know that?"

"You scared?" she asked.

"Yeah," Loretto said, and then he followed her into the building.

WEDNESDAY ✦✦✦ AUGUST 5, 1931

11:40 p.m.

"This is crazy." Lottie leaned into the bathroom, where Vince was at the mirror, fixing his tie for the second time, pulling a length of blue silk through a loop, grasping the knot between his thumb and forefinger and pulling it smartly to his neck. "It don't add up," she said, and she launched once again into the arguments she'd been making all night, that Jack Diamond couldn't be trusted, that Vince was crazy for agreeing to meet with him alone, at Young's, at night, unarmed. It could be Jack was holding a grudge and planned to kill him and that was all this meeting was about, nothing more, just getting rid of Vince Coll if Vince was crazy enough to show up. "Why's it got to be you alone?" she asked. "Just tell me that. Why's that the deal?"

Vince smiled at himself in the mirror. "'Cause he's scared of me," he said, and he winked at Lottie's reflection over his shoulder.

"You're not being smart about this, Vince." Lottie thought about arguing some more and then gave up. She left Vince alone in the bathroom, crossed the apartment's dingy, barely furnished living room, and returned to the bedroom, where she sat on the edge of their unmade bed. She was close to tears and it embarrassed her. Guys never cried, at least not guys like Vince.

They were in Albany, where they'd rented an apartment not far from Young's on Broadway, Diamond's joint. Frank and the boys were nearby, in Averill Park, with Florence. They'd gotten word to Jack as soon as they'd hit town, and then he'd made them wait days before agreeing to a meeting. Lottie clutched a fistful of sheet, brought it to her nose, and inhaled. The deep red sheets were silky and fine, from Bendel on Fifth Avenue. They turned the bed into a little corner of luxury surrounded by drab, unadorned walls and a pair of uncurtained windows, one hidden behind yellowing venetian blinds, the other behind a faded green shade. Lottie lay back on the mattress, using a clump of sheets for a pillow, and looked up at a slowly revolving ceiling fan that did little more than nudge the muggy air. She was wearing the same black slip she'd had on all day and she ran her hand over her belly and down between her legs. She had the crazy urge to make love to Vince one more time before he left for Young's, though they'd gone at it twice already, once in the morning on waking and then again, long and leisurely, in the afternoon.

For all his toughness, Vince hadn't known anything about lovemaking before she'd met him. All he'd known was whores who went at it fast and wanted their money. She'd taught him to slow down. She'd shown him what to do. He'd seemed mystified at first and then amazed that there could be more to it than a furious rush and finish. Now he liked it. He liked all of it. He opened up for her in bed, became someone only she knew. In the morning she liked to lean over him and hold him in his sleep till he rose up lead-pipe hard in her hand and then she wanted him inside her, wanted him moving slow inside her, and even thinking about it while lying on her back looking up at the ceiling fan she was flushed and wet—and then the sound of the medicine-cabinet mirror clicking shut pulled her out of her dream and she remembered that Vince was on his way to Young's to meet Diamond. She admitted to herself that she was scared.

"What are you doing, Vince?" Lottie shouted at the ceiling, not a question at all, an announcement that she was in the bedroom waiting for him. When he didn't answer, her thoughts drifted to her daughter. Often it happened like that: in the middle of something that had nothing to do with Klara, Lottie'd find herself thinking about her, wondering what she was doing, if she ever thought about her mother. She was a pretty girl, like her mom. Vince knew about her. It wasn't a secret—but Lottie couldn't do the things she had to do with a little girl in her life, and so Klara wasn't around. She was with Jake's people. Jake was Lottie's first husband. She'd married him at sixteen when she got pregnant, and Jake was dead before she was eighteen—which wasn't a shock given he was a thief and a cheat—and then there was nothing to do but leave Klara with his people. She was a big girl already. Twelve years old, that was hard to believe. *Lottie Kreisberger has a twelve-year-old daughter. You'd never guess it by looking.* Vince hadn't guessed, and he still didn't know Lottie's real age. He figured she was a little older but it didn't matter to him.

At first everything Lottie did, everything, it was all for Klara. She wasn't going to raise her daughter in some cold-water flat while she slaved as a housemaid for a banker's wife, like her own mother did till the day she died. Not that life again, she wouldn't have it. So she married Rudy, who made good money in the ice rackets, but then he treated her like a slave and she saw that working as a housewife for a racketeer could be just the same as working for a banker's wife as a housemaid, so she took up with Sam Westin, a guy her own age, with a college degree from Columbia. She'd always known she was smarter than Rudy. Then she saw she was smarter than Sam, too, a guy with a hotshot college degree. She could figure the angles better. She could see the big picture. What she needed was a guy to do the rough stuff, and she thought Sam could be that guy—but then Rudy found out and pulled a gun on Sam, and Sam wound up putting a knife in Rudy's heart and having to hide out from the cops, who caught him anyway and charged him with murder, a rap he beat, and after that they opened Conte's together, a midtown restaurant—and there she was again, working in a restaurant like a chump, but that was where she met Vince, and Vince convinced Sam he should drop out of the picture.

Now she was close. Now with Vince she was close. She was so close she could feel it all around her, the good clothes, the fine homes, and it wasn't too late, she could still get Klara back. She'd raise her in style, with the best of everything, and they'd travel, too, all over the world, Lottie and Klara and Vince. They'd take cruises and there'd be all the money they could ever want, to do whatever they wanted. Who was tougher than Vince? Who was smarter than Lottie? They just needed to get their foot in the door, to get planted solidly, and this thing with Jack Diamond could do it if Jack didn't kill Vince first—and then Lottie's drifting thoughts came full circle and she was back to worrying about Vince going to see Diamond alone and unarmed. "Vince!" she called—and as if in immediate response to her summons, he appeared in the bedroom doorway looking sharp in a three-piece suit, black with a narrow blue stripe. He twirled a gray fedora on his fingertip and then fit it to his head with a smirk that said he knew he looked good. "Ain't you the cat's pajamas," Lottie said. She sat up in bed and rested her chin on interlocked fingers.

"Give me a kiss." Vince offered a hand up. "I've got to hit the road."

Lottie let Vince pull her up from the bed and into his arms. She took his hat off as she kissed him, her free arm wrapped around his neck. When she leaned away, she gave him a look that said she was still worried.

Vince took his hat back and fit it on his head again, the way he liked it, brim down. "Jack won't kill me, doll. Not once he hears me out."

"But that's just it," Lottie said. "How do you know he'll take the time to hear you out? How do you know he's not still all burned up about you going after him?"

"I don't," Vince said, and he pulled Lottie behind him as he made his way out of the bedroom.

"Jeez, Vince." Lottie tugged at his hand. "This is crazy."

"No, it's not." Vince stopped in the middle of the kitchen and for the first time seemed annoyed. "Ain't this your plan, doll? Didn't you figure this for a deal Jack can't pass up?"

"Yeah, sure," Lottie said. "But that's not what's wrong. It's going to see him all alone that's crazy."

"Jack'll hear me out," Vince said, "even if he is still burned up. Why shouldn't he? Do I have guts, showin' up by myself, naked, at his club? You think he won't see that?"

"Sure, he'll see it. Anybody'd see it."

"Besides, he can't help but like me. We're a couple of micks, aren't we? Don't we both hate Dutch? Sure, he'll hear me out, doll." He took her hands and gave her a perfunctory kiss on the lips. "Don't worry," he said, and he started out the door with Lottie right behind him.

In the hallway, as Vince headed for the building's front door and the street, Lottie said, "You shouldn't be battling each other, you and Diamond. You're a pair, you two. You should be working together against Madden and Dutch and the Combine and all them. The two of you together, you can bring them to their knees."

Vince tipped his hat to Lottie and winked, meaning he got it, he knew the spiel, and she shouldn't worry, and then he disappeared into the night and a chorus of insects chirruping like lunatics. Lottie, in her slip, followed him out the door and watched as the car lights came on and he drove off without a look back. She waited there in the dark, surrounded by chirping that rose and subsided in waves, under a sky clotted with roiling clouds.

12:15 a.m.

Their first night in Albany, Vince had taken Lottie to the new RKO Palace, with its soaring neon signs and bright corner marquee grand as anything on Manhattan's Broadway—but the vaudeville acts between shows weren't very funny and they'd left before seeing the second feature. Now, as he drove past the theater, the marquee was dark. Overhead, trolley wires followed the avenue and he cruised over the tracks with one arm dangling out the window, a pistol on the seat beside him. The streets were dead, a long line of shadows and dark windows. He glanced at the gun and checked his wristwatch again. He was supposed to be at Young's at midnight, but he was enjoying the quiet streets and the summer air on his face, and he figured he'd make them wait. Jack and Vince were cut from the same cloth, Irishmen still with family back in the old country, gone from pig poor to in the money and got there the same way, only Jack was getting on and Vince figured he was tired of getting shot up. Vince had on a tailored suit that cost more than his mother had earned in a year scrubbing other people's clothes and washing floors. He straightened his tie and adjusted his hat and figured he looked like a million.

At Young's, he parked in the alley and was out of the car and knocking at the back door without a thought in his head. On either side of the door, a pair of dark stains still wet and stinking. Maybe his heart was beating a little faster than normal, but nothing anybody'd notice. He knocked again and the door opened on two mugs with guns pointing at him and a third guy, huge, well over six foot tall and must have weighed three hundred pounds, a 12-gauge leveled at his waist. The space was brightly lit by a bare electric bulb dangling from a black wire. "Boys," Vince said, "I believe your boss is expecting me."

One of the gunmen motioned for him to come in, and the second pushed him against the wall and frisked him while the first checked the alley and the big guy watched, unmoving, his finger on the shotgun trigger, the barrel resting in his hand. "Gents," Vince said, "I'm alone and I ain't heeled, as agreed upon."

"Okay," the big guy said, "so now we know." His voice was about what Vince expected, low and gruff and slow, like he had to think about every syllable. With the shotgun barrel, he pointed up a flight of stairs behind him. "Let's go," he said. "Jack's waiting." Midway up the stairs, he added, "Jack don't like to be kept waiting."

At the top of the steps, one of the gunmen rushed past him and opened a second door, behind which was a dimly lit room lined with wooden whiskey crates and with barely enough space for the card table and four chairs at its center. Another door led out of the room. From behind it came the muted, tinny sound of a player piano and someone singing, as if there might be another room or two between them and the source of the singing.

Jack Diamond waited at the table with his chair tilted back. He was neatly dressed in a three-piece suit, a gray fedora with a black hatband on the table in front of him, next to a mostly empty bottle of whiskey and a big pistol with a round magazine that looked more suited to a tommy gun. Jack was still the flashy guy newspapers loved to write about, but his eyes were bloodshot and looked tired. He leaned back in his chair and observed Vince as if looking at a horse he might bet on.

Vince said, "Jack! How you been?" He took a seat across from him and placed his hands, palms down, on the table. "Long way from the Hotsy Totsy." Behind him, the door closed and the two gunmen moved to either side of the room, up against the whiskey crates. Vince glanced over his shoulder and found the shotgun pointed at the back of his head. To Jack he said, "Where'd you find this guy? He'll do to intimidate, won't he?"

"Football player," Jack said. "Used to play for the Giants."

"Yeah? At the Polo Grounds?" Vince craned his neck to look behind him again. "What position you play?"

Jack said, "He's not very talkative—but then, I don't pay him to talk."

Vince gave up on waiting for a reply and turned back to Diamond. One by one he took five cash-stuffed envelopes out of his pocket and placed them next to him on the table.

Jack gestured to one of his men and tapped his finger on the table in front of Vince. A whiskey bottle and a glass appeared, and Vince poured himself a drink.

Jack held his own glass up in a silent toast, finished off his drink, and poured himself another. "I had me this dream last night," he said, and though it was evident he'd been drinking hard, he sounded plenty sharp. "I dreamed the dead were all around me like a bunch of ghosts: all the guys I'd plugged or had plugged. Dozens of 'em. Joey Noe was there. A bunch of Dutch's boys. But my brother Eddie was there, too. And my mother. All sorts of people—and while I'm walking along this street I don't recognize, they're looking down at me from windows, from rooftops, from fire escapes, as if they're expecting something of me, or maybe they want something from me. You ever have a dream like that, Vince?" Jack went on before Vince could answer. "Nah," he said. "You're too young. You probably sleep like the angels."

Vince finished off his drink and poured another. "You remind me of your brother," he said, "God rest his soul." He held his drink out across the table. "The two of you with the same funny kind of ears. No offense intended."

Jack said, "It don't hurt me any with the dames."

"Sure," Vince said. "You're famous in that area."

Jack fixed Vince with an unblinking stare. He seemed to be growing angry.

Vince said, "I hate that miserable cheap son of a bitch, Dutch. When he couldn't get to us, he went after our brothers."

"That he did," Jack said, "but he killed yours. He missed Eddie."

"Sure, he missed him," Vince said, "but getting sprayed by bullets didn't help Eddie's health, either, did it? He hurried him to the grave, didn't he? He went after our brothers, didn't he? That's all I'm saying, Jack."

Jack nodded. Some of the anger went out of his eyes.

Vince finished off his drink and poured another. Jack did the same. "I can do the fighting," Vince said. "I'm young, and ain't nobody even put one bullet in me yet. I'm feckin' invincible. I get the chance, I'll send Dutch straight to hell."

"I been hit fourteen times," Jack said. "The bullet ain't been made can kill Jack Diamond."

Vince lifted his glass to Jack in a toast.

Jack asked, "What's in the envelopes?"

"Twenty-five Gs." Vince pushed the envelopes across the table with one hand and finished off his drink with the other.

"And what is it you're hoping to buy with twenty-five grand?"

Vince looked around at the men holding guns on him.

Jack sighed and it sounded as if all the weariness in the world was making its way out of him. "All right, boys," he said, and he picked up his whiskey bottle and glass as he rose from the table. "Vince and I are gonna have ourselves a talk." He put on his hat, left the gun where it lay, and started out of the room.

Vince took his bottle and glass, winked at the football player still holding a shotgun on him, and followed Jack Diamond through the door.

5:20 a.m.

On a tree-lined street of two-family houses, Lottie, invisible in the shadows, watched a storm approach and pass from her apartment doorway, still dressed in her black slip, her back against the door frame, her knees drawn to her chin. First darkness massed in the west, deepening the slate-blue night sky till it turned black and clouds swallowed up the last of the stars; then wind came in gusts that bent treetops and sent a galvanized metal garbage can clattering over the street; finally rain swooped down in wavering sheets and wind blew steadily and hard, accompanied by fissures of lightning and thunder. Vince had left to see Diamond shortly after midnight, and Lottie had spent every minute since either pacing the apartment or sitting in the doorway until now the sky was beginning to show hints of approaching daylight through clouds and steady hard rain. She was exhausted, having passed through in one night emotions ranging from excitement and anticipation to anxiety and dread to despair and terror to, finally, something that felt like nothing at all, like emptiness. She sat listless in the doorway as it gradually grew lighter while rain splashed over grass and concrete, and a few crows cawed now and then in the nearby trees.

Without Vince she'd be back to square one, and that was part of her thinking—but it was in the background. What would she do without him? Where would she go? Without Vince to worry about, would Dutch come after her? She might have to run, and she couldn't imagine where. Since the Vengelli kid got killed, Vince was big news everywhere, all over the country, all over the world. There were newspaper stories every day, and Lottie turned up in most of them. Yesterday the newspapers had them living in Canada, on the run. With Dutch and the Combine looking for her, she'd have to change her name and maybe her appearance.

For most of the night thoughts like these roiled in the back of her mind as she watched trees swaying and listened to the night sounds of crows and wind and rain. She told herself that Vince would be back soon, and she watched the road and the bend where his car would appear, the sound of it first, followed by headlights. A couple of times her eyes misted and tears fell and she wasn't even thinking of anything, at least not that she knew. It was as if as the night wore on she grew so full of fear that it overflowed. Vince's name was on her tongue constantly, the sound of it alone summing up everything. She wanted him back. That simple. That childish. She was filled with wanting him back and it spilled out of her and onto and through everything so that she was looking at the trees and listening to the rain, but it was all the same thing. She wanted Vince.

Her back was beginning to hurt. She thought she might have been sitting in the doorway forever, hidden in the shadows, the night street still but for the rain and wind. She pressed her hand into the small of her back. She still ached a bit between her legs and inside from the afternoon sex, which had gone on and on and was good but now she was raw. Sore down there back and front. She stretched her legs and leaned over—and then froze when she thought she heard a car approaching, the mechanical hum of an engine cutting through the drone of rain. When she was sure of it, she leaped to her feet. At the sight of car lights, she stepped out into the rain, a tentative first step, because it could be anybody's car, a working stiff up early and on his way somewhere. The car moved slowly, only a few miles per hour, rolling along the street in an unsteady line, veering right and then overcorrecting to the left and then veering right again, until it pulled up in front of the house, two tires on the curb and two in the street. Lottie was at the car door, pulling it open before Vince managed to cut the engine.

"Doll," Vince said, and he offered Lottie a flashy smile. His tie was draped over his jacket, his shirt buttons were undone, and he reeked—the whole car reeked—of whiskey. In his lap, between his legs, an empty bottle of bourbon rose up rudely and he grasped it in his right hand.

Lottie tossed the bottle to the curb and helped Vince out of the car. "What happened?" she asked. "What'd he say?"

"Doll," Vince said again, as if it was the only word he could manage. He put his hat on her head to protect her from the rain, though they were both already soaked.

"Jesus," Lottie said. "You're stinko." She tossed his hat into the car and closed the door with her foot as she grasped Vince around the waist and wrapped his arm over her shoulder.

"Say!" Vince said, and he sounded angry. "That son of a bitch can drink!" He paused and then broke into laughter that doubled him over and pushed Lottie to her knees.

"Ah, quit it, will ya?" Lottie righted herself in time to keep them both from falling. She pulled him toward the open front door.

"Doll . . ." Vince kissed Lottie on her temple and whispered in her ear, "You're gorgeous, doll face. You know that?" With his free hand, he fumbled at her breasts.

Lottie pushed his hand away and helped him into the apartment, where she dumped him onto the couch while she went back and closed the door. Rain dripped from their wet clothes and puddled on the floor. When she returned, Vince's arms were spread out across the back of the couch as if to keep himself upright. He looked up at her with a dumb smile and glazed eyes. "That son of a bitch can drink!" he repeated. He seemed unaware of his wet clothes and the rainwater spilling from his hair and off his face.

Lottie decided it'd be easiest to put him to bed on the couch. She went to the bedroom, changed her clothes, came back with a pair of blankets and a couple of towels, and started undressing him, beginning with his shoes and socks. She toweled him dry as she removed each article of clothing. "Vince, honey," she said, "can you tell me what happened? I can see he didn't kill you, so that much is for the good."

"Nah, I told you not to worry. We're a couple of micks, me and Jack. We both come up from nothin'."

Lottie tossed his shoes aside and went about unbuckling his pants and pulling them off. "What about the deal?" she asked. "Did you propose the deal like we said?"

"Sure," Vince said. He looked like he might explain, and then his eyes glazed over and he drifted off. His mouth opened and his lips moved but no sound came out, and a moment later his eyes closed.

Lottie pulled off his jacket and shirt. She knelt beside Vince on the couch and struggled to yank his clothes free. "Baby, just tell me what Jack said. Did he go for the deal or not?" She threw a towel over Vince's chest and he pulled it to his face.

"Sure," Vince said, and he tossed the towel to the floor. "I'm tired." He pushed Lottie away and curled up on the couch.

"Sure, he went for the deal?" Lottie pulled him by the arm, turning him to face her.

"Sure," Vince said. "Hey, listen, Lottie," he added, "it was Cabo's guys shot them kids."

"That's right," Lottie answered. "Why're you even thinking about that?"

"Doll face," he said, and he lit up with a smile.

"So you're saying that Jack went for the deal?" she asked again.

"Didn't I say so?" Vince winked and then closed his eyes. "We're in business," he said. "Me and you and Jack Diamond." He smiled with his eyes closed and then the smile faded and he curled up into himself as he sank down toward sleep.

Lottie sat back on her heels and let it sink in. They were in business with Legs Diamond. She found one blanket, shook it open, and covered Vince. She draped the second blanket over her shoulders and thought about squeezing in beside Vince on the couch, but she was too wound up to sleep. Outside, it was still dark and raining hard but the daylight dark of a rainy day, not night dark anymore. She went out to the doorway again and resumed her position watching the rain with her back against the door frame. She felt as washed out as the rain-splattered streets.

Part of her was excited and another part of her was surprised that Diamond had really gone for the deal and another part of her was suspicious and still another part of her was worried about Vince. She let herself wonder what it might be like if the two of them, just Lottie and Vince, took a car and the money on hand and went someplace far away. Mexico, maybe. Or a cruise to Europe. She had thought of such things before but always the money ran out and she never could see it after that, the two of them in ordinary jobs if they could find even that. And she'd have to give up Klara. There was no possibility of working that out. So the way she saw it she didn't have a choice really, and neither did Vince. They had to bet on the big money. Look at Capone in Chicago living like a king. Look at Big Owney with his brewery smack in the middle of the city and his penthouse apartment.

Big money, that was all they needed and then everything else would come with it. She had to make that bet. She had to. Lottie reminded herself that Vince still didn't have a mark on him, that no one had gotten to him yet, and she thought it could stay like that. It could. Then she said it aloud and it sounded like a prayer: *It could.* When she looked up, it was light enough to see the shapes of the clouds. They were dark, like a long row of faces peering down at her, dark eyes, dark brows, dark faces twisting and torn in the wind. She relaxed and let her head fall to her chest, and only when she realized she was about to fall asleep did she pull herself to her feet, lock up the apartment, and curl up next to Vince on the couch, the two of them under a pair of blankets, pressed tight to each other.

Fall

· *1931* ·

7:00 p.m.

Loretto splashed cold water on his face. He leaned over the sink in the Barontis' narrow bathroom, a fat porcelain tub on black claw feet six inches behind him, a john six inches to his left, a door that opened to the kitchen within arm's reach. After a brutal summer, fall had arrived weeks early, offering generous relief from the heat. Gusts of wind rattled the glass panes of the bathroom window, and the apartment's radiators whistled and groaned as they cranked out heat. Loretto, water dripping from his face, was so stuffed he could hardly move. He'd arrived a little before 5:00 for dinner with Gina and her family, and he'd spent the next two hours eating and talking. First antipasto, then lasagna, then veal and lemon saltimbocca, then apple and lemon meringue pies and coffee, and finally mixed nuts and more coffee. Loretto had cleared his plate with each healthy serving Mrs. Baronti carried from the stove and slapped down in front of him until he had to leave the table and come to the bathroom and splash cold water on his face to clear his senses.

On the other side of the bathroom door, the Barontis were laughing at something. Though Loretto had been seeing Gina regularly—every day, practically—since they'd spent that night together back in July, this was his first dinner with the family as her boyfriend. Gina had worked hard not to make it a big deal: she had invited him on a weekday night rather than a

Sunday, when the family usually had their big meal. She had mentioned it to her mother casually, telling her on Tuesday night that Loretto might stop by for dinner on Thursday. Mrs. Baronti had only nodded as if, sure, it wasn't a big occasion; and then, when Loretto and Gina showed up together, they found the boys wearing suits and Mrs. Baronti in a good dress, and all the makings of a holiday meal cluttering the stove and kitchen sink, the good plates and serving dishes spread over the table. Gina took one step through the door before she looked around and rolled her eyes and said, "Ma!", meaning *Ma, what are you doing?* Mrs. Baronti had ignored her and wrapped up Loretto in a big hug.

Loretto toweled his face dry, shook off a surface layer of sleepiness, and rejoined the Barontis in the kitchen. Augie had just pushed his chair back. He stood and clapped his hands over his belly. "Ma," he said, "you're gonna make us all fat!"

"Eh! Who's forcing you to eat?" Mama snatched a dirty plate from the table.

Freddie pointed a fork at Augie. "Is that how you're grateful?"

"Ah, put a sock in it." Augie went around the table and kissed his mother on the back of her head while she went about rinsing off a dish. To Loretto he said, "Let's go up on the roof." He pulled a couple of cigars from his jacket pocket and held them out as an offering.

"Sure," Loretto said.

Freddie said, "You got one of those for me?"

"What do you think?" Augie tossed Freddie a cigar.

Gina started clearing away the coffee cups. "Go ahead," she said to Loretto. "I'll come up when we're finished down here." She took a step toward him, as if she might send him off with a kiss, and then caught herself. "Go on," she said to her brothers. "Get out of here and let us clean up."

On the roof, Loretto found a chair next to the empty pigeon coops. Freddie and Augie sat across him. The three of them puffed on cigars while a gusty wind blew the smoke away and scattered leaves and dirt over the tar-paper rooftop. Freddie had found work washing dishes and cleaning up in one of Gaspar's restaurants on Mulberry Street in Little Italy. He'd started eating again. Gina and Augie were still worried about him, but they both agreed he was doing better.

"Tell Dominic," Freddie said, "I appreciate what he did, getting Gaspar to give me a job." He loosened his tie and unbuttoned his shirt collar. He'd put on enough muscle in jail that his clothes were tight on him, even with the weight he'd lost since he'd been out.

Augie said, "Where is Dominic? How come he don't come around with you anymore?"

"He's at Gaspar's." Loretto tapped the ash from his cigar. "He's been spending a lot of time there."

"Yeah?" Augie said. "I hear he's moving up. He taking you along with him?"

Loretto ignored the question. Something about the way it was asked came across as a challenge. "Gaspar's got plans for Dominic," he said. "Dom's more like his son than his nephew."

"Dominic's a square guy," Freddie said. "I always liked him."

"Everybody likes Dominic," Augie said, "but maybe it's not too smart, movin' up in Maranzano's family." He took a long drag on his cigar and stared hard at Loretto. "Most guys go that route," he said, "they wind up in jail or the morgue."

Freddie kicked the leg of his brother's chair. "Give Loretto a break!" To Loretto he said, "All that palaver's for my benefit. He wants to make sure I stay out of trouble." To Augie he said, "I told you. I'm playin' it straight. I'm washin' dishes nine to five, ain't I?"

Loretto said to Augie, as if answering a question, "Mostly I load and unload trucks for Gaspar. I sit in the back with a shotgun in case there's trouble. That's it," he said. "It's not like I'm Al Capone."

"Sure," Augie said, "but what kind of future is that?" When Loretto didn't answer, he added, "Look, I do what I gotta do when I need the cush.

I've done a lot worse than what you just said—but now I've got work on the docks, and I'm in the union. When things pick up again, I won't need to be looking for anything on the side. You see what I'm sayin'?"

"I should be a dockworker?"

"Better than washing dishes." Freddie, now that he understood what was being discussed, added, "Believe me, you don't want to get sent up."

Loretto said, "Gina knows all about me."

"Yeah," Augie said, "but Gina's a dame, and smart as she is, dames don't use their heads when it comes to guys."

"Look at that chump she married when she was still a kid," Freddie said, jumping on.

Loretto put up his hands. "Guys," he said, and then he jumped up at the sight of someone emerging out of the shadows on the adjacent roof. Freddie and Augie spun around to see a figure approach the edge of the roof, back up to get a running start, and then leap across the alley and onto their rooftop. "It's Mike," Augie said, and both brothers hurried to meet him with Loretto following.

Mike had almost lost his hat in the leap. He was fixing it in place when his brothers reached him. "Boys," he said, "I thought I'd stop by for a visit."

Augie put his arm around Mike's shoulders and pulled him into the shadowy tight space between a pair of chimneys, the same place where Loretto had first kissed Gina. "They got cops watchin' this place night and day looking for you to turn up here," he said. "They're parked across the street right now."

"They got cops everywhere looking for us," Mike said, "but they ain't on every rooftop."

"Wise guy," Freddie said. He grabbed Mike's chin like he might rip his head off but instead embraced him so tightly that Mike grunted as the air was squeezed out of him.

"Sorry I never came to visit you," Mike said once Freddie let him loose.

"Didn't I tell you not to come? You were sixteen—" Freddie's thoughts seemed to suddenly get crossed, as if he was about to say one thing when something else occurred to him, and as a result he went silent.

"Maybe he should've come to see you," Augie said. "He might have thought twice before taking up with Irish."

"Ah, let up, will ya?" Mike straightened out his jacket, tugging at the lapels. To Loretto he said, "What are you doing here?"

Freddie said, "Gina invited him to join us for a family diner."

"Yeah? Is that right?"

"What are you doing here?" Loretto asked. "According to the newspapers, Vince and his gang are hiding out in Canada."

"Canada," Mike said and laughed. "We're up in Albany."

"Albany?" Augie looked surprised. "What's Diamond say about that?"

"We're in business with him." Mike leaned back against the chimney. He seemed suddenly tired. "Vince bought himself a one-third share of the bootlegging end. It's him and Jack and Joe Rock running things."

Freddie said, "Ain't Rock the one Vince blinded?"

"He's still got one good eye," Mike said.

"Vince is in business with one guy he tried to kill and the other guy he blinded." Augie turned to Loretto as if he needed someone to confirm how crazy that was.

"They're all bosom buddies now," Mike said. "They're building a new airstrip to fly the hooch in from Canada."

"What's Dutch think of that?" Loretto asked. "And the Combine."

"Not much," Mike said. "But they were looking to kill Diamond and Vince anyway, so it don't really matter."

"Mike," Augie said, "are you blinder than Rock? Where do you think this is all headin'?"

"We're bringing in high-quality booze. Dutch and the boys'll have no choice but make nice."

"And what about the cops and the FBI?" Freddie said. "Are they gonna make nice?"

Mike reached into his pocket for a cigarette. "What do you want me to do?" he asked. "Take it on the heels?"

"Hey, Mike," Freddie said. He undid his belt buckle and unbuttoned his pants. "I want to show you something."

"What are you doing?" Augie put a hand on Freddie's shoulder, and Freddie shrugged it off. "What's wrong with you?"

Freddie pulled down his pants and underwear. "See this?" he asked. He lifted his penis, showing Mike a nasty pair of scars on either side of the foreskin. "You know what that is?"

"Jesus," Mike said. "Put your pants on, Freddie."

"Answer me. You know what that is?" Freddie lifted his penis higher and turned it to each side, showing bright red welts against the dark skin.

"Looks like scars," Mike said, his voice full of disgust. "What the hell happened?"

Freddie pulled up his underwear and went about buttoning his pants and clasping his belt. "That's what they do to you in Elmira," he said. "They put a metal ring through your dick."

The boys all watched Freddie in silence. Finally Augie said, "Why would they do that?"

"Supposed to keep you from engagin' in sexual activity," Freddie said, "but it's just the screws makin' your life miserable any way they can. They like it."

"Come to think of it," Mike said, "yeah, I heard they do that to some guys."

"Anybody they don't like," Freddie said. "That and a hundred other things, like beatin' you with a rubber hose so the marks don't show."

"I get the picture," Mike said.

Augie put a hand on Mike's arm. "So what are you doing here?" he asked. "You come to see Mom? Are you alone?"

"I wanted to see all of you," Mike said, "but I been thinking about Mom being worried about me. I thought if she saw me . . ."

Loretto asked, "You come all the way from Albany?"

"It ain't that far," Mike said. "I come down with Vince and Lottie. They dropped me off so I could see Mom."

"What's Vince doing in the city?" Loretto asked. "He's crazy coming here."

"He's got twenty-five grand in his pocket to rub out somebody, and that's only half payment, so it's got to be somebody big."

"Fifty grand?" Loretto said. "Who's payin' him?"

"He ain't sayin'." Mike looked at the cigarette in his hand as if he'd forgotten he was holding it. "He's been tight-lipped. I only found out about the fifty grand from Lottie." He lit his cigarette.

"Fifty grand's a big deal. Got to be Dutch or Big Owney, somebody like that," Augie said.

"Could be Dutch," Loretto said, "and Diamond doing the payin'."

"Nah," Mike said. "Why would Jack pay Vince fifty grand to do something he knows he'd do for free? Happily."

"Besides," Augie said, "if there was some way for Vince to get to Dutch, he'd have done it already."

"So who?" Loretto asked. "Big Owney? Ciro Terranova?"

"We'll find out soon enough," Mike said, and then he nodded toward the skylight, where Gina had just climbed up from the apartment below.

Gina stepped onto the roof with a smile for the boys, a smile that disappeared at the sight of Mike leaning against the chimney and smoking a cigarette.

"Uh-oh," Mike said as Gina approached. "Looks like I'm in trouble."

"How'd you get up here?" Gina crossed her arms over her breasts and shouldered Freddie out of the way so that she could stand face to face with Mike.

"I flew," Mike said, and the words weren't fully out of his mouth before Gina slapped him, knocking the cigarette out from where it was dangling between his lips.

"Hey!" Mike took a quick step toward Gina and was instantly restrained by Augie just as Freddie took Gina by the arm and pulled her back.

"You ain't my mother!" Mike yelled. "You ever slap me again, I'll slap you right back."

"Go ahead," Gina said. She yanked free of Freddie. "Go ahead, slap your sister," she said. "Tough guy!"

"Ah, quit it," Mike said. He fell back against the chimney and reached into his pocket for his cigarettes. "You know I ain't gonna slap you, Gina. You just got me riled is all." He took a cigarette from his pack and shook another loose for Gina.

Gina took the cigarette and let Mike light it for her. When she took the first drag, she was calm, and then a second later she covered her eyes with her hands. Freddie put his arm around her, but she pushed him away.

"Gina," Mike said, "I'm gonna be okay. I swear it."

"No, you're not," she said, her eyes still hidden. "You won't be okay, that's what you don't get." She took a deep breath and finally looked at Mike again. "Listen," she said, "I don't know how you got up here, but you can't stay. The cops are looking for you here, and who knows who else. It's too dangerous."

"I can't stay in my own home?"

"Gina's right," Augie said. "The cops busted in and arrested you with Mom right there . . . It'd be too hard on her, Mike."

"So, what?" Mike said. "I can't even go down and see her?"

Gina said, "If they're watchin' with binoculars and I go down and close all the blinds, I might as well be sending them a telegram: *Come get him. Mike's visiting.*"

"Ah, for Christ's sake," Mike said.

"You can stay with me if you need a place," Loretto said. "Dominic's staying at Gaspar's tonight."

"Thanks," Mike said. He turned back to Gina. "Really?" he asked. "I can't go down and see Mom."

"Mike," Gina said, "the cops could come in shootin', looking to kill you. After what happened with the Vengelli boy, they'd pin a medal on their chests for killing you."

Freddie said, "We can talk up here till it gets dark; then you can go back over the rooftops."

Loretto said, "I'll pick you up around the corner. In the alley by the bakery."

"Thanks," Mike said to Loretto. To Gina he said, "Jeez. I really wanted to see Ma."

Gina covered her face with both hands as if she were a kid again, playing hide-and-seek. She was thinking maybe Mike could talk to Mama through the skylight when, as if she had read her mind, her mother's voice came up from the boys' room. "Eh!" she called onto the roof. "I made some espresso! Who wants?"

Mike looked to Gina, and Gina said, "Go ahead."

Loretto moved closer to Gina while Freddie and Augie stood together side by side, leaning against the flat brick wall of the chimney. The sun had disappeared from the sky, and though it wasn't quite dark yet, night was coming on fast and it was growing both windier and colder. When Mike reached the skylight, Mrs. Baronti shouted his name in a way that was part scream and part lament. He fell to his knees, said, "Ma, wait, don't come up," and he reached down through the opening. The way his right shoulder dipped, it was clear Mrs. Baronti had grabbed him by the hand. It looked like she was trying to pull him down into the apartment.

"Jesus," Gina said and looked away as if she couldn't bear it. Behind her, the boys were also looking away, out over the rooftops.

Loretto watched Mike a moment longer—the way he knelt over the skylight on all fours like a dog, his right arm straining against being pulled in—before joining the others. He put his arm around Gina's waist as the shadows darkened and settled over the surrounding roofs. Behind him, Mike's and Mama Baronti's voices were a murmur, rising and falling, blown around by the wind. He waited, with Gina and her brothers, and tried not to listen.

8:40 p.m.

Gina watched from the chimneys, with Augie alongside her, as Mike leaped to the adjoining roof and slipped away into a maze of shadows. Freddie was in the kitchen with Mama, comforting her as best he could. Loretto had left earlier and would be waiting by now to pick up Mike by the bakery. Gina hugged herself to ward off the cold. She thought she should spend the night, and probably she would, though she didn't know what to say to her mother. She wasn't in any hurry to go back down to the apartment.

When Augie said, "Come on," gently, meaning it was time to go back in, Gina turned on him. "What are we supposed to tell Mom now?" she asked. "Did you hear that crap Mike fed her? He's working as a driver for a trucking company? It's all a mix-up the cops are looking for him? For Christ's sake, Augie."

Augie said, "Mom won't ask us nothing. You don't have to worry about what to tell her."

"How do you know that?"

"Use your head." Now Augie seemed angry. "Mom's not stupid. Did we ever get away with lying to her when we were kids?"

"Okay," Gina said, "but this is different."

"It's not different." Augie turned his back to the wind, lit a cigarette, and handed it to Gina.

Gina said, "Thanks," and watched him light one for himself. "You're saying Mom knows what's going on?"

"I'm saying she don't want to know." Augie looked to the skylight as if checking to see if his mother might be listening. He stroked his Adam's apple. "What can she do?" he said, half talking to himself. "Better not to know."

"And leave us to worry about it."

"Yeah," Augie said. "That's right. She did the best she could raising us. Now it's our turn. Now we worry about each other. And about Mom."

"All right," Gina said, "then what about it? What about Mike?"

"Mike's on his own for now. I got Freddie to worry about. And you."

"You've got to worry about me?"

"You!" Augie said, and it came out sounding like a dog's bark. "What are you thinking, getting yourself involved with a guy like Loretto? You know what he does for a living. What kind of a future can a guy like that give you?"

"Stop it," Gina said. "Loretto's not in the rackets big time. He's not doin' anything worse than what you do yourself now and then." When Augie looked surprised, she added, "What? You think I don't know you got your own dirty hands?"

"My hands get dirty," Augie said evenly, "only when I need to get them dirty to make sure the rent gets paid and the bills get taken care of."

"So why's it different for Loretto?"

"You see him with a family to take care of? You see anybody depending on him?"

"He's got himself to take care of."

"You know what I think?" Augie said. "I think you and Mom are just the same." He tossed his cigarette down, stubbed it out with his toe, and started for the skylight.

Gina watched him disappear into the rectangle of light. Her face stung as if she'd been slapped, and it was only partly from the cold. She went to the edge of the roof and looked down into her neighbors' apartments, though she saw nothing beyond a pattern of light and dark. She saw nothing because she wasn't really looking. "Christ Almighty," she said, and she couldn't tell whether she was cursing or praying.

FRIDAY ✦✦✦ SEPTEMBER 11, 1931

2:35 a.m.

When Loretto opened his eyes, he found himself surrounded by the familiar darkness of his bedroom. Crisp night air pushed into the room through the window over his head, which he'd left open an inch. Across from the window, by the door, the radiator crackled as steam and hot water hissed through its coils. Dominic's bed was empty. Loretto had spent the evening catching up with Mike over a bottle of Canadian Club. Now, as he pulled himself up from sleep, the back of his head throbbed and his stomach rumbled. He'd heard something, a noise loud enough to wake him, though the apartment was quiet as he lay on his back listening to the gurgle of the radiator. He considered that it might have been the heat coming on that woke him but thought it unlikely. Probably it was Mike. Directly across the alley from his bedroom window, in a stranger's apartment, someone left a light on day and night, and the light from that window crossed the alley and dimly illumined Loretto's bedroom. On the floor between his bed and Dominic's, the bottle of CC waited where he'd left it, midway between the beds, bracketed by a pair of empty glasses. Mike and Loretto had gotten into bed while still drinking and talking, and now the blue covers of Dom's bed were turned back, revealing clean white sheets, and the bedroom door was open.

Loretto figured Mike had gotten up to go to the bathroom, so when he heard a cough come from that corner of the apartment, he closed his eyes and tried to settle back to sleep—but the cough was followed by the thunder of the apartment door being battered. First came a loud, dull thump and then a sharp crack as the frame splintered and the door flew open. Loretto couldn't see this, but the sequence of sounds revealed what was happening as clearly as eyesight. He slid to the floor and was reaching for the gun under his bed when the light came on and he found himself looking up at two of Cabo's men, the same two who'd been with Cabo outside the club the evening of the shootings. They stood side by side in the bedroom doorway, pointing a pair of matching cannons at him. The guns were big Colt .45s, something out of a Tom Mix Western, bright and shiny. Loretto showed them his empty hands. He was wearing boxer shorts and a white undershirt. "Gentlemen," he said. He sat up, pulled his knees to his chest, and wrapped his arms around his knees.

One of the torpedoes said in a rumbling, deep voice, "Richie Cabo said to tell you he's sorry he can't be here in person." Both men, shoulder to shoulder, extended their guns, taking aim--and in the same instant Mike Baronti appeared out of the darkness behind them holding what turned out to be the thick porcelain cover to the john's water tank. He wielded it like a baseball bat, catching both men on the back of the head. They went down like dropped stones—one flat on his face, unconscious, the other to his knees, dazed. The two Colt .45s skittered across the hardwood as Loretto slammed the still conscious torpedo to the floor and twisted his arm behind his back.

Mike said, "What the hell is this about?" He picked up the guns and tossed them onto Loretto's bed.

"Jesus," Loretto said. He figured he'd been maybe a couple of seconds from being a corpse. He nodded to Mike and said thanks.

"Forget it." Mike knelt beside the mug Loretto was holding pinned to the floor. A steady stream of blood spilled from the back of the guy's head. "What's your name?"

"Fuck you." He was the one with the deep voice, and the curse came out sounding like a groan.

"His name's Fuckyou," Mike said. "What do you think of that?"

Loretto twisted the guy's arm. "Don Maranzano'll make mincemeat sandwiches out of Cabo when he finds out about this."

"I wouldn't bet on that," the guy said.

"On what?"

"On Maranzano making a mincemeat sandwich out of Richie."

"Why not?" Loretto twisted his arm harder, but if he was feeling the pain, it wasn't showing on his face.

"Ah, shit!" Mike dropped down onto Loretto's bed. "It's Maranzano," he said. He found the CC and a glass and poured himself a drink.

"What's Maranzano?" Loretto let the torpedo's arm loose but held him down by the back of his neck. His hand was smeared with blood, which was pooling now beside the guy's chin.

Mike said, "Vince killed Maranzano."

"What are you talking about?"

Mike held his drink out, gesturing to Loretto. "Maranzano was the only thing keeping you alive after that stunt with Dutch. Now Cabo's goons come after you, Maranzano's got to be dead. No way Cabo would dare otherwise. Vince came here with twenty-five grand in his pocket to kill somebody. I'm telling you, it was Maranzano. Vince killed Maranzano. V'fancul'!" He tilted his head back and downed his drink.

"I don't believe it." Loretto picked up the slab of porcelain and held it over the torpedo's head. "What do you know? Either tell me or I'm gonna bust your fuckin' head in."

When he didn't talk, Loretto pulled the slab back as if getting ready to slam him. When he still didn't talk, Mike said, "Everybody's a fuckin' tough guy." He went to the mug's feet and twisted them like a corkscrew, forcing him onto his back. "Hold that to his neck," he said, and he gestured to the water-tank cover. "Where do you keep that famous stiletto of yours?"

"It's in my pants pocket." Loretto pushed the edge of the porcelain into the torpedo's throat hard enough to keep him still but not hard enough to cut off his air.

Mike found the stiletto, knelt between the torpedo's legs, and sliced his pants open at the crotch.

"Ah, bullshit," the guy said, as though he were talking back to someone who wasn't in the room. To Mike he said, "What do you want to know?"

Mike stuck the tip of the knife into the guy's balls, pinning them to his groin. When he tried to struggle out from under the knife, Loretto pressed down on his neck. Mike said, "I don't know, Fuckyou. What have you got to tell me?"

"You got it wrong," the guy said. He cocked his head over the slab so that he could look past Loretto to Mike. "My name's Jimmy. Take the knife out," he pleaded, his voice an octave higher, which made it sound something close to normal. "Take the knife out, I'll tell you."

Mike took the knife out and wiped it on the guy's pants.

"The Mick didn't kill Maranzano," Jimmy said. "Luciano did." To Loretto he said, "Take that thing off my throat, will ya, kid?"

Loretto took the pressure off but held on to the slab.

"Why would Luciano kill Maranzano?" Mike asked. "They were working together."

"Bad blood," Jimmy said. He looked to his partner, who hadn't budged since he'd gone down. "Is he dead?"

"What's his name?" Mike asked.

"Joey Pizzolatto."

Mike put his ear to Joey's mouth. "Still breathin'," he said, and he gestured for Jimmy to continue.

"Maranzano hired the Mick to kill Luciano. When Luciano found out, he took care of Maranzano first."

"And what happened to Vince?" Loretto asked.

"Nothin'. I heard Luciano's boys were on their way down the stairs after taking care of the don when they ran into Coll on the way up to see Maranzano. They told him to beat it, the cops were on the way."

"Yeah, and?"

"And nothin'. He beat it."

Mike turned to Loretto. "That's an easy twenty-five grand."

Loretto wasn't amused. "So with Maranzano out of the way, Cabo sent you to settle the score with me and Dom—but what about the rest of the Castellammarese? We looking at a war?"

"I told you what I know," Jimmy said. "Cabo sent us here to take care of you."

"To take care of me and Dominic," Loretto corrected. When Jimmy didn't answer, Loretto's face turned white. He didn't breathe for a second while he quickly replayed the moment when Jimmy was pointing a gun at him, about to kill him. Neither Jimmy nor his partner was worried about the empty bed. They weren't worried about anyone else being in the apartment. "Dominic and his uncle Gaspar," he said, the words coming out breathy, his fear showing, which made him angry, "did you take care of them, too?"

"Not us," Jimmy said.

"But somebody?"

"Loretto," Mike said, "if Maranzano got rubbed out, there's gonna be a lot of guys dying tonight."

Loretto snatched his knife from the floor and held it to Jimmy's throat.

"I can't tell you what I don't know," Jimmy said, "'cept your buddy's right. Lot of guys on the spot tonight."

Loretto told Jimmy to stand up, and Jimmy pulled himself to his knees. He looked for a moment like he might throw up or fall over. One side of his face was streaked with blood, and his pants at the inner thigh, below where the crotch was slashed, were soaked black. He clasped his thighs to brace himself and then finally stood upright—and as soon as he did, Loretto clipped him with the slab of porcelain and he fell on top of his partner.

Mike put his hand to Jimmy's throat. "He's gonna have a hell of a headache," he said, "but he's alive."

Loretto found his clothes and started to get dressed. "Let's go."

"Where we going?"

"To Gaspar's. Maybe they haven't gotten to him and Dominic yet."

"You don't have a telephone?"

"I don't," Loretto said. "It's only a few minutes from here."

"I know that," Mike said, "but a phone call's a lot less risky."

"You don't have to come."

Mike said, "I've known Dom since we were both *bambinos*," and he went about getting dressed.

2:45 a.m.

A dozen newspaper pages floated along a slate sidewalk like birds skimming water before wind lifted them higher, some smacking into the brick walls of the surrounding two-family houses, some flying up and disappearing over rooftops. Mike and Loretto were alone on the street. They'd parked a block away and were heading for the narrow alley that separated Gaspar's building from his neighbor's. Loretto touched the gun holstered under his jacket and scanned the streets, where a few cars were parked along the curb. Beside him, Mike had his hands in his pockets and his shoulders hunched against the wind. He didn't appear especially worried, though he too watched the streets. The two of them walked purposefully, fast but not hurried, hats pulled down, heads lowered into the wind. When they reached the alley, Loretto checked the street one more time—and then the two of them disappeared into the dark, narrow corridor. At their approach a black cat yowled and bolted out of the alley.

"Black cat," Mike said. "I hate that."

At the back of the alley, they climbed a cyclone fence, jamming a toe into one of the links and jumping into Gaspar's yard. Loretto took his gun from its holster and pointed to a pair of metal cellar doors over a triangle of concrete rising out of the ground near the back wall. The doors were closed but not padlocked. Mike nudged him and nodded toward the discarded lock where it lay in a patch of grass next to the doors. There were no lights in the house and only silence coming from beyond the walls.

"What's in the basement?" Mike asked.

"Nothing much that I know of."

"Why the padlock?"

"Wine cellar. They got one dug in down there."

"Is it usually locked?"

Loretto nodded.

Mike knelt to one of the doors and pulled it open. Loretto opened the other. Beneath them was only darkness and silence and the acrid smell of earth.

"They got a light down there?"

"Bottom of the steps." Loretto went in first, holding his gun out in front of him as though it were a flashlight. He found the switch and flipped it on, and the basement erupted in light from a bare bulb hanging off a crossbeam.

Yard tools hung from the walls, and a table was covered with terracotta pots and long-dead plants in crumbling dirt. In a corner was a lawn mower with a sharpening tool propped up against one of its wheels. "I don't see nothin'," Mike said.

"Me neither." Loretto crossed the dirt floor to a shadowy corner of the basement and the wine cellar's wooden door, which was circular and looked like a manhole cover. He had seen Dominic climb down there on occasion, fetching a bottle of wine for his uncle. It was tube-shaped, maybe ten feet deep, dug straight down into the earth, a circle barely wide enough to permit one person entry. A long yellow flashlight hung from the wall over the cellar cover. Loretto pulled open the cover and saw nothing but a black hole. He took the big flashlight from the wall, pointed its bright beam into the wine cellar, and saw Gaspar's and Dominic's faces looking up at him.

They'd been stuffed into the hole belly to belly. Their faces were bloody and their heads were bent back so that they were both looking up, as if waiting for someone to find them.

Loretto dropped to his knees. "Ah, Jesus," he said. "Dominic."

Mike joined him, looked down into the wine cellar, and said nothing.

"Who did this?" Loretto turned off the flashlight. "Luciano?"

"Or Terranova, maybe Cabo, maybe a dozen guys . . . It don't really matter."

"What do you mean, it don't matter? That's Dominic stuffed in the ground like garbage."

Mike put his gun away and touched Loretto's shoulder. "Let's go."

"And leave them here?"

"We've got to go," Mike said, and he closed the wine-cellar door.

Loretto looked over his head as if he could see up into the Gaspar's apartment, where he imagined Gaspar's wife sleeping soundly in her bed.

"They wouldn't have hurt anybody else," Mike said.

"Yeah, I understand." Loretto pulled himself to his feet. "But I want to know who did this to Dominic."

"Loretto," Mike said, "think. Gaspar and Dominic were loyal to Maranzano. They would have gone after Luciano and anybody that was with Luciano. There would have been a war. They had to go, Loretto. That's the way it is with these things."

Loretto put his gun back in his holster. Something inside him felt like it was melting or breaking down. He could feel it in his gut, something churning, coming apart. He set his jaw against it and held himself tight.

"Let's go," Mike said again. He took Loretto by the arm.

"Where? Where am I going?"

"With me," Mike said. "You can't stay here. It's too dangerous."

"Where am I going with you?"

"To Albany," Mike said. "Vince'll put you to work. You got no choice now. You can't stay here."

"You're crazy," Loretto said. "Why would I go to Albany?"

"You're not thinking straight." Mike yanked on Loretto's arm, pulling him toward the cellar doors. "Cabo's looking for you. Schultz's looking for you. Luciano might be looking for you."

"Maybe––" Loretto said and stopped. Mike was right. He wasn't thinking straight. He was about to say that maybe Gaspar could help him.

"Maybe what?"

"Nothing."

Mike turned off the light. In the darkness, he said to Loretto, "If you stay here, you could cause trouble for Gina and my family. You understand, Loretto?" He took him by the shoulder and shook him as if trying to rattle him to his senses. "We're going to Albany," he said, and he pulled Loretto up the cellar stairs.

12:15 p.m.

Maria Tramonti poured herself a cup of coffee and rejoined Gina at the kitchen table. They were in Gina's apartment, and both women wore black sweaters over black dresses. At Dominic's burial that morning, the mourners had huddled together around the grave site while a blustery cold wind kicked up leaves and dirt. Summer, it seemed, was long gone. A handsome young priest, new to Saint Raymond's, shivered in his black cassock as he said a few words about Dominic and read a passage from the gospels before sprinkling holy water over the grave. When workers lowered the casket into the ground, Gaspar's wife fainted and was carried to a nearby car. Dominic's cousins and aunts and uncles and a dozen friends of the family wept and moaned and held handkerchiefs to their eyes while Maria and Gina stood shoulder to shoulder, for the warmth and the comfort. Next to them, Augie and Freddie each clasped one of their mother's arms as she held her hands to her face and cried. After, there was food and talk, the women clumped together in circles telling stories and crying; the men talking solemnly, sometimes angrily. Now Gina and Maria were alone in a quiet apartment, sipping black coffee while they talked.

"That poor woman," Maria said. "Her nephew in one viewing room, her husband in the other."

"Dominic was more like a son than a nephew to her," Gina said. "She couldn't have children of her own. Dominic was still a baby when she took him in."

"What happened to his parents?"

"I think the mother died in childbirth. The father got beat to death. I don't know the story."

"Mother of God," Maria said.

Gina went to the stove to refill her coffee. She took a cookie jar down from the cupboard and carried it to the table. "I was in the ladies' room with her." She retrieved two lemon sugar cookies from the jar and put one on her plate and one on Maria's. "She was moaning and pulling her hair out. I never saw anything like it."

"What did you do?"

"Talked to her," Gina said. "Held her hands like I was comforting her." She dipped the lemon sugar cookie into her coffee. "Her sister came in and fixed her up."

Gina's living room was simply furnished with a couch, a coffee table, and matching stuffed chairs. A pair of tall windows that faced the street were hung with floral-patterned chintz curtains pulled back to let in the sun. The apartment was spacious, with a big living room and kitchen and two bedrooms, the second of which went unused.

"Sometimes I worry . . ." Maria said. Her eyes filled with tears.

"Patsy?" Gina asked. "You worry about Patsy?"

Maria took a tissue from her purse and dabbed at her eyes.

"Patsy's a big boy," Gina said. "He can take care of himself."

"Sure," Maria said. "Just like Dominic."

Gina sipped her coffee. Suddenly she was both sleepy and angry. Grumpy, she supposed, after a difficult morning.

"Patsy's so dopey," Maria said. "You know he still can't tell his left from his right? He's got a little scar on his left wrist and he's gotta look whenever anybody tells him something's to his left or to his right." Maria made a face as if she were dismayed with Patsy, though it was clear that she found this endearing.

"Forgive me," Gina said, "but I've got to ask. What are you doing with Patsy DiNapoli? You're smarter than him, you got a college education, you're married to a wealthy man . . . I don't get it."

"I thought you did get it," Maria said. "I thought that was part of the reason we're friends."

"Well, I don't," Gina said. "I don't get it. Sorry."

"I love Patsy," Maria said. "Why are you mad all of a sudden?"

"I'm not mad." Gina threw up her hands, a gesture that said many things, including that she didn't know herself why she was acting the way she was and not to pay any attention to her.

"I get so scared . . ." Maria's voice dropped to a whisper. "I hate the bastard I'm married to, you know that. I was miserable before Patsy came along. Now . . ."

"Now what?" Gina asked. Try as she might, she still sounded angry.

"Now I'm scared something will happen to him," Maria said, and she burst into tears. She used the shreds of the tissue in her hand to dry her eyes. "I'm sorry."

"Don't be sorry." Gina rubbed her back, massaging small circles at her shoulders.

"Here poor Dominic's dead—your friend since forever—and I'm crying 'cause I'm worried about Patsy. I should be ashamed."

Gina hugged Maria and kissed her on the cheek. "You're honest," she said. "I admire that about you." She picked up Maria's empty cup and carried it to the sink.

"I should go," Maria said. She joined Gina at the sink. "I'm sorry about your friend Dominic." She gave Gina a hug and kissed her on the cheek. "If there's something I can do to help his family," she said, "please let me know."

"Don't worry," Gina said, and she was surprised and taken aback by the bitterness that welled up in her. "After they're dead, there's always plenty of help."

Maria took a step back. She looked hurt.

"Gaspar's family, all the women," Gina said, softening her tone, "they'll be there to help. But it's generous of you," she added, "to offer."

"I mean it," Maria said. She embraced Gina one more time before leaving, crossing the kitchen and living room with her shoulders uncharacteristically hunched forward as if carrying something on her back.

Alone, Gina poured herself another cup of coffee, knowing she wouldn't drink it. She carried the cup to the table and sat where Maria had been sitting a moment earlier. She held the coffee cup in the palms of her hands and looked past her curtains out to the red brick building across the avenue. The sun was bright on the window, though it was still unseasonably cold. She was sleepy and considered taking a nap on the living room sofa, but her thoughts held her at the table. Not thoughts, really. She saw Gaspar's widow kneeling at Dominic's casket during the days of viewing, the way she knelt with her head on the lip of the casket and her arms stretched out as if to embrace the whole length of it, as much as she could hold in her arms. She laid her head on the casket and muttered prayers, embracing it with her eyes closed while her sisters stood on either side of her dressed all in black, nodding their heads as if in confirmation of her mourning. Gina had watched from her seat in a line of folding chairs set out in front of the casket. Dominic looked all wrong. He looked like a statue of himself, his face too pink and rosy. His ugly mug fixed up with makeup in a way that would have humiliated him. She wanted to take a wet rag to his face and wipe away all the cosmetics hiding that little bit of impishness that had defined him ever since he was a boy. When she thought of him in the ground that way, his face covered in rouge and paint, she put her hands to her face and cried.

1:55 p.m.

In a knit cap and a khaki work shirt under a jacket frayed at the cuffs, Loretto crossed Gina's street looking like half the other out-of-work young men in the neighborhood. He pushed open the door to her building, hurried up the stairs, and knocked softly on her apartment door. Lottie had dropped him off on the corner and would be back for him in a half hour. Vince was in the city for a meeting, something to do with the kidnapping of George Immerman back in August. From what Loretto could gather, Vince had found himself short of money after buying his way into Diamond's organization and so had kidnapped George Immerman and taken away fifty grand in ransom from his brother, Connie. The story was Patsy and Vince had grabbed George right out of the swanky club Connie ran in Harlem. Now that job was causing problems for some mug who ran one of Vince's speaks, and Vince was here trying to get it straightened out. Loretto wasn't in on the higher-up workings of Vince's bootlegging operation. He was doing the same things he did for Gaspar: loading trucks, providing muscle when needed. When he'd heard Vince and Lottie were coming into the city, he hitched a ride.

Gina opened the door, looked over Loretto in his workman's garb, and stepped back to let him in. Her eyes were red and she had a sleep scar high on her cheek, near her eye. Her hair was mussed on the same side as the scar. Loretto had expected an excited hug. He was surprised by the noncommittal way she simply stood aside to let him in. "You've been sleeping," he said, and he touched the mark on the side of her face.

"Fell asleep at the kitchen table." Gina motioned toward the table and the coffee cup as if she too was surprised to learn that she had fallen asleep there. "Where have you been?" she asked. "You want coffee?" She started for the stove. On the way she added, as if it wasn't a big deal, "You missed your friend Dominic's funeral."

Loretto took a seat on the couch, in a bright rectangle of sunlight coming through the living room window. He folded his hands in his lap and waited.

"Well?" Gina asked, with her back to him. "Do you want coffee?" When he didn't answer, she turned to face him, though she remained rooted at the stove.

"There was nothing I could have done about Dominic."

"Did I say there was? All I asked is if you want coffee."

"Stop it," Loretto said. "I don't have a lot of time."

"Well, I want coffee." Gina poured herself a cup and carried it with her into the living room. She sat on the opposite end of the sofa from Loretto.

"What is it?" Loretto asked. "Why are you angry?" He pulled a pack of Luckies from his shirt pocket and tapped out a cigarette. Before he could put the pack away, Gina snatched it from him, took a cigarette for herself, and tossed the pack onto the coffee table. "Dominic," she said. "Your friend Dominic. Our friend. You missed his funeral."

Loretto found a lighter in his jacket pocket, lit Gina's cigarette first and then his own. His heart was beating fast and when he tried to speak the words stuck in his throat.

"Say something." Gina went to the kitchen, where she took a big cut-glass ashtray from a cabinet and carried it back to the coffee table.

Loretto watched her, the way she looked in her black dress—still young and slim, her hair bouncing a little with each step, but a hint in the black mourning dress of all the old Italian women he'd seen in church every Sunday of his childhood. He willed his heart to beat slower. Whatever was happening with him, the jumpiness and confusion, he didn't think it was obvious on his face. "I couldn't come to the funeral," he said. "It would have been dangerous for everybody."

"And why is that, Loretto? Is somebody looking to kill you, too?"

Gina knew the answer to her question. Everybody knew. Without Don Maranzano around, there was no one to protect him from Dutch or Cabo. Luciano, who might be worried that Loretto would want to avenge Dominic's death—even Luciano might want him dead. "I don't have to tell you," Loretto said. "You know the score."

If Gina felt anything at all for Loretto, it didn't show on her face. The two of them sat side by side on her couch and talked to each other like two strangers in the midst of a business negotiation. "So what are you doing here?" Gina asked. "Could I be in danger, too, because you're here?"

Loretto took Gina's chin in his hand. He looked into her eyes, demanding an answer to a question he hadn't asked. He wanted to know something, though now he didn't know what.

Gina pulled away and got to her feet. "You should go."

"That's it?" Loretto stubbed out his cigarette. "Just like that?"

For the briefest of moments, Gina's hard veneer cracked and her eyes softened—and then the hardness returned. "I said you should go," she repeated, and she went to the door and held it open for him.

Loretto left without glancing again in her direction. On the stairs, on the way down to the street, he felt light-headed. He didn't know what had happened. He zipped his jacket up to his neck and yanked his cap from his pocket and fixed it on his head, pulling the brim down low. He stepped out into the sunlight and the cold. On the sidewalk, on his way to the corner where Lottie would pick him up, he walked along without thinking, his head empty, his eyes on the slabs of deep blue slate at his feet.

10:00 p.m.

Lottie was waiting at the warehouse. She was standing in a pool of light, in front of an open garage door, surrounded by darkness and the rush of a crisp breeze that whipped through the grass at her feet. The way she was dressed, in heels and stockings and a dark skirt and yellow blouse under a jacket that looked like it had been tailored to fit her waistline, she might have been waiting for a date to take her dancing in the city.

"Mister," Lottie said, "can you give a girl a ride?"

Loretto kissed her on the cheek as Tuffy jumped down from the cab of a stake truck and joined them. Loretto and Tuffy had just returned from delivering a shipment of hooch to an Albany roadhouse.

"Hey, beautiful," Tuffy said to Lottie, "what's the rumpus?"

"Vince sent me to fetch you boys," she said. "Big meeting at Florence's place."

"You don't say? What about?"

"What do you think?"

With Vince spending most of his time in Albany, Dutch and Cabo, Terranova and Luciano, and the others—they were all moving on his territories, hijacking his delivery trucks, blowing up his speakeasies and beer drops, and in general making life rough on anybody who worked for him.

It was no secret Vince was going to have to deal with them. "Something new happen?" Tuffy asked.

"Somebody threw a pineapple into the Mad Dot." Lottie's eyes went wide and Tuffy laughed.

"Looks like trouble, then," Loretto said.

"Good guess, Einstein," Tuffy said. "How much damage to the club?"

"Shut it down," Lottie said. "I know that much."

"Anybody killed?"

"Nah. It was closed. Just blew the place up."

"So it's right now," Tuffy asked, "this meeting?"

"I'll drive Loretto," Lottie said. "I need to talk to him about something. You meet us there."

"Jeez!" Tuffy fingered the peach fuzz on his face as if he needed a shave. "They could give a guy a chance to get cleaned up at least."

"Ah, you know you're handsome." Lottie yanked the bill of Tuffy's cap down over his eyes before she took Loretto by the hand and pulled him off into the shadows where her car was parked.

Once in the car, Loretto asked, "Who'll be at this meeting?"

"Everybody." Lottie hit the gas and sped away from the warehouse.

"Slow down. You'll get us killed on these dirt roads."

Lottie shifted up another gear and sailed wide around a curve. The car kicked up a rooster's tail of dust behind them as the headlights cut two clear lines through the dark.

Loretto braced himself.

Lottie laughed and said, "I love going fast."

"I can see." Loretto watched the trees flying past him only inches from the car. "Maybe for my sake," he said, "you could slow it down a bit?"

Lottie glanced into the rearview mirror. When she saw nothing behind her, she downshifted and eased off the gas. "I hate it out here," she said. "Nothin' but bugs and rubes."

"It's not all that bad."

"Yeah? Don't you miss Gina? Aren't you lonely?" Lottie had a way of making everything she said suggestive. He didn't know exactly what she was suggesting, but it made him laugh.

"So what did you want to talk to me about?"

"Vince." Lottie's manner changed the instant she said his name. "Listen," she said, "he respects you, Loretto. You have to talk to him."

"About?"

"About going off half-cocked and shootin' it out with Dutch and the rest."

"Is that what he's planning? Is that what this meeting's all about?"

"Sure," Lottie said. "Didn't I already say that?"

"You didn't say anything about shootin' it out with Dutch."

"Well, that's what's comin'," Lottie said, "unless you can talk some sense into him."

"What about you? He's not listening to you?"

"He's got himself convinced that if he doesn't hit back hard, they'll walk all over him." Lottie pressed the palm of her hand to her forehead as if her head suddenly hurt.

"He might be right about that," Loretto said.

"Well, sure he's right!" Lottie yelled. "But he's got to pick his spots, don't he? You think Dutch is stupid? He wants Vince back in the city, where Mulrooney and the coppers are gunnin' for him. All he's doing is tryin' to get Vince to show his face. He figures between his boys and the Combine and Mulrooney, somebody's gonna get Vince. Dutch isn't stupid," she repeated. "It's Vince who's being stupid now."

"Did you tell Vince all this?"

"Sure, I told him," Lottie said. "He ain't listenin'."

Loretto rolled his window down a little. "I'll talk to him," he said, "but I don't know what good it'll do."

"Tell him this," Lottie said. Her eyes were on the road, though Loretto could see she was looking inward. "Sure, they're walking all over him now—but he needs to wait for the right moment to hit back. He can't let himself get pulled into a fight on their terms. You see what I'm saying?"

"Yeah," Loretto said. "I get it."

"If he goes off half-cocked like this, it'll be bad for all of us."

Loretto stretched and then slumped back against the door and window. Lottie's hand was still pressed to her forehead, her fingers reaching up under her hat's cute bow. She seemed frozen like that, her mind a million miles away while her body sat up straight in the driver's seat and guided the car over the road. In that moment, the features of her face concentrated in thought, she didn't look like the dame everybody said she was, the broad who'd turned up one day running a restaurant in midtown with Sam Westin, then dropped Sam when Vince came around. Everybody figured it was Lottie who pushed Vince to make the break from Dutch. They called her Queen Lottie. Rumor was she had a stash of money from a divorce, and she used it to help Vince start up his operation. She was supposed to be tough and shrewd. Watching her while she drove, Loretto had a hard time making what he'd heard about her jibe with what he saw. She looked like a girl lost in worry.

Loretto said, "Vince can take care of himself," and Lottie snapped back to life. Her hand fell from her hair, she clasped the wheel at ten and two, and she offered Loretto a quick smile.

"You know what I'd like to know?" Loretto was still slumped in his seat as if about to take a nap. "Who it was killed Dominic and Gaspar. Nobody's got a name for me."

"I'm sorry about your friend," Lottie said.

"But you don't know anything?"

"Only what I heard, same as everybody else." The car went quiet for a while before she added, "Does it matter really who pulled the trigger? You and Vince, it's the same enemies, right? Luciano, Dutch, Madden, Cabo—the whole lot of them. They're all a bunch of greedy bastards."

"You've got guts," Loretto said. "You and Vince. You're talking about the toughest guys in the city. They practically got an army behind them."

"Sure," Lottie said, "but they're not the toughest. Vince is. That's the thing, Loretto. It's what I'm always telling Vince. It's the guy's willing to put a bullet in you if you don't do what he says—that's the guy winds up on top. That, and you got to be smart about it. Look at our friend Charlie Luciano. He was tougher than Maranzano: he killed the son of a bitch. Plus he was smart enough to pull it off without having to go to war with the Castellammarese. A guy like that, that's what it takes."

"You're pretty smart yourself," Loretto said. When she didn't respond, he added,

"You think Vince is up to the job?"

"Me and Vince," she said. Her coy smile came back then, and she added a wink for good measure.

Outside, the dirt roads had given way to gravel and then to pavement. Averill Park was a small enough town that you could drive through it and not notice if your thoughts drifted off for a minute. They were coming up on the feed and grain store, where a wagon with two missing front wheels knelt in a puddle of light from the storefront.

"So you'll do it, then?" Lottie asked. "You'll talk to Vince?"

"Sure," Loretto said. "He should hold off and wait for the right moment to hit back. I can tell him that."

"Good," Lottie said. Then she repeated, "He respects you. He'll listen to you."

"If he respects me so much," Loretto said, "how come he's got me loading trucks?"

"Maybe he don't want any competition." Lottie squeezed Loretto's knee.

On the tree-lined street where Florence was staying, Loretto rolled his window down and stuck his head out of the car. The night air was crisp

and cold against his face, and above him the sky was alight with a maze
of stars. Sometimes the stars here were so bright they scared him. Earlier
in the week, on another Albany roadhouse-to-warehouse run, he'd seen
what he understood now was a falling star. At the time, he hadn't known
what to make of it. He'd been in the back of the truck, stretched out on
a line of whiskey crates, watching road and sky rush away when he'd seen
a brilliant blue light streak across the sky. He'd jumped off the whiskey
crates so suddenly that he'd nearly fallen out the back of the truck. Since
then, he was always looking up at the sky, hoping to again see something so
spectacular. By the time he rolled up the window and straightened out his
hair and put his cap back on, he had shaken off much of his fatigue. Lottie
parked on the street, close to a narrow sidewalk and a row of tall hedges.
Unlike everyplace Loretto had lived before, the streets here were utterly
dark at night, not a lamppost to be found anywhere. The only light came
from an unseen window behind the hedges.

Lottie stepped out of the car and said, "I can't see a damn thing!"

Loretto followed her voice, took her by the hand, and led her toward the
dim light coming from the house—and then tripped when his foot caught
on a chunk of narrow sidewalk pushed up by the roots of a tree. Lottie
yanked on his arm and kept him from falling on his face. Once they passed
the hedges and turned at the driveway, they were facing Florence's place,
a nondescript single-story clapboard house painted a dull yellow. Jack Diamond's flashy Chrysler Imperial was parked in the driveway. Shorty—the
ex–football player who worked as Jack's bodyguard—waited outside the
house. Wrapped in a full-length raccoon coat, he looked like a giant animal
guarding the door.

Lottie looked over Shorty in his coat and said, "Jeez, did someone forget to tell me it was winter?"

Shorty coughed into his hand and answered politely, in his one-syllable-
at-a-time manner, "I got thin blood. I get cold easy."

Behind them, Tuffy pulled into the driveway and hurried out of the car. "Am I late to the party?" He had managed to get himself cleaned up and changed into a suit. He straightened the knot on his tie.

Inside, Vince and Jack, with a gallon bottle of gin between them, were seated across from each other at the dining room table, Florence and her husband, Joe, to the right of Vince and Patsy, and Mike to the left of Jack. Frank sat at one end of the table, to the left of Vince, and Tuffy took the empty seat at the other end of the table. The house was run-down, with peeling wallpaper and water stains on the ceiling and walls. Jack and Vince were puffing on cigars, and the dining room smelled of smoke.

Sally peeked out of the kitchen. "You boys want something to eat?" Her question was directed to Loretto. "We're making spaghetti and meatballs."

Loretto had pulled a chair next to Mike. "I could eat," he said.

"Not me," Tuffy said. "I'm watching my figure."

Lottie had moved around behind Vince and was massaging his shoulders. Florence glared at her briefly and then went back to puffing on her cigarette.

Jack filled his tumbler with gin. He glanced up at Lottie as if annoyed by her presence. "So," he said, "as we were saying, Vince. The boys put you out of business in the city, then we don't have the markets we discussed. We got nobody to distribute to, we might as well shove the hooch up our asses." He looked up to Lottie. "You'll excuse my French."

Lottie ignored him.

Florence said, "Don't feckin' worry about her."

Vince said, "We ain't losing our markets." His shirt was open at the collar, and his eyes were bloodshot from drinking. He was hunched over the table. "I said we'll take care of it."

"Sure," Jack said, and he slouched back in his seat. "But when? Give 'em a few more weeks and they'll wipe you out." He tilted the tumbler of gin to his mouth and drank like it was water.

"Ah," Florence said, "those bastards—"

Vince clapped his hand over Florence's wrist. He pointed to the kitchen. "Go help Sally and Maria."

Florence gestured to Lottie. "I don't see this bitch helpin'—"

Vince yanked Florence halfway out of her seat and slapped her arm down on the table.

"Son of a bitch," Florence muttered, the curse aimed at no one in particular. She followed Sally into the kitchen.

Lottie took Florence's seat.

"Look," Vince said to Diamond, "Dutch has got his own problems. I hear Mulrooney snatched his records. They're going after him on taxes."

"He's got lawyers for that," Jack said. He refilled his glass with gin. "And it's not just Dutch that's the problem."

Frank reached over the table for the gin. "We got to hit 'em back," he said to Vince.

Mike said, "We could blow up a couple of their warehouses. Let 'em know they want trouble, we'll give it to 'em."

Vince said, "I'd like to stuff Dutch's head in a fuckin' fishbowl." He toyed with his drink. "Maybe we should toss a couple of pineapples into the Cotton Club. That'll make 'em think."

"Jesus!" Jack said. "Not the Cotton Club. You'll have the whole city on your ass."

Tuffy said, "We already got the whole city on our ass, if you ain't noticed."

Frank said, "That gives me an idea," and he set his glass down on the table. When the room went quiet and everyone turned to him, he said, "You know Joe Mullins? He keeps all the Dutchman's records in his head."

"Yeah," Mike said. "I heard that. He's got one of those what-do-you-call-it memories."

"Photographic," Jack said.

"That's right," Frank said. "He's got a photographic memory. He's got everything from Dutch's inventory to his payoffs all in his head."

"So?" Patsy said. He'd been quiet through most of the evening. Only now, when talk of a particular action was gaining momentum, did he speak up. "What are you sayin'?"

Jack said, "He's saying Joe Mullins would be a tough man for Dutch to lose."

"That's right," Frank said.

Vince asked Frank, "Is he hard to get to?"

"No," Frank said. "Wouldn't be hard at all."

Sally and Maria came into the dining room lugging two big bowls of pasta and sauce. Sally's bowl was filled to overflowing and sauce dripped to the floor and on the table before she finally put it down in front of Jack.

Jack said, "You got dishes and forks and such, doll?"

"Yeah," Sally said. "Comin' right up." She offered Jack a bright smile.

Maria stood behind Patsy and put a hand on his shoulder.

"Doll," Jack said to Maria, "be a sweetheart and go help your girl-friend."

Patsy reached behind him and patted Maria on the thigh. "Don't let it get cold," Maria said. She pointed to the pasta and then joined Sally in the kitchen.

Jack said to Vince, "Man can't run his business without keeping good records, that's all I got to say." He pulled the pasta bowl toward him and sniffed it. "I think I'm hungry."

Loretto pulled the bottle of gin away from Frank. "Hey, Vince," he said. "I'm just speculating— What if Dutch and the syndicate— What if they're trying to get you do something stupid?" He poured himself a drink. "You know what I'm saying? They tossed a bomb into the Mad Dot. Don't you think they know you're going to come right back at them?"

"You're *speculating*?" Jack said before anyone else could speak. "Who's this?" he asked Vince.

"He's a friend," Vince said.

Jack said to Loretto, "I know you?"

Vince said, "He's the mug put a knife to Dutch's throat. You heard about that?"

"You don't say?" Jack lifted his glass in a toast to Loretto. "That was you?"

Loretto said, "I should've cut his throat when I had the chance." As soon as the words came out, he was surprised by them. He didn't know why he'd said it.

"I like this kid," Jack said to Vince. To Loretto he said, "I bet you Dutch was shittin' his pants, the yellowbelly."

"As I recall," Loretto said, "he might have been a little pale."

"Listen, kid. What's your name?"

"Loretto."

"All right, Loretto. In this line of work, it's important to know when to talk and when not to talk. You hear what I'm sayin'?"

Loretto fingered his drink.

Lottie spoke up. "Ah, let him talk," she said to Jack. "It's Vince and his boys puttin' their necks out."

Vince placed his hand on top of Lottie's. "Go find Florence, will you, doll? Tell her it's time to eat."

For a moment, Lottie seemed on the edge of exploding. Then she shoved her chair back and left the room.

Vince said to Jack, "It's settled," and yelled into the kitchen for the dishes. "We're fuckin' starvin' in here!"

Sally and Maria came into the dining room toting stacks of dishes and handfuls of forks and spoons, which they dropped haphazardly around the table. In a minute, everyone was crowded around the food, reaching over each other to pull out chunks of spaghetti and plop them down on their plates. The spaghetti was overcooked and stuck together in clumps. The sauce was watery and the meatballs chewy. None of this seemed to bother anyone as they splattered sauce over the table in a hurry to get at the food. Florence and Lottie came back into the room and Florence took a seat next to Joe. Jack held a meatball on the tines of a fork in one hand and a tumbler of gin in the other. He took a bite of the meatball, washed it down with gin, and launched into a dirty joke about a whore and a priest. When he hit the punch line, Florence laughed the loudest and immediately tried to one-up him with an even dirtier joke, one so full of profanity that even her husband shook his head as if shocked by his wife's language. Lottie was the only one not eating. She tried to catch Loretto's eye, but he looked away toward the front door. He remembered that Shorty was still out there, wrapped in his thick raccoon coat, looking like a marauding beast. Loretto thought it was a wonder no one shot him. When he turned back toward Lottie, she was gone.

12:37 a.m.

Vince and Jack were still drinking, the bottle of gin between them now nearly empty. Frank and Sally, Tuffy, Mike, Florence, and Joe were all huddled around the table, the whole lot of them drunk, drinking and telling jokes, smoking cigarettes and cigars. Loretto watched them through the back window as he leaned against a porch column and smoked one of Patsy's Luckies. Patsy and Maria were seated alongside each other on the porch railing, and Lottie, wrapped up in an old army blanket, was rocking in a swing suspended from the ceiling by lengths of rusty chain, hidden in shadows. With each slight movement back and forth, the chains squeaked. They were all sober and quiet. Beyond the porch, a light drizzle was visible in the glare of a bare bulb screwed into a white ceramic base above the back door. The rain looked like a silvery screen wrapped around the house.

Maria linked her arm through Patsy's and rested her head on his shoulder. She covered her mouth and yawned. "I'm getting tired."

"They'll be making a racket half the night," Patsy said. He put his arm around Maria's shoulders. He was boarding here, in an upstairs bedroom, sharing a room with Tuffy. Mike and Frank had the room across from them.

Out of the shadows, Lottie said, "You boys have all known each other since you were kids." She laughed quietly. "It's funny," she added, "thinking of you all runnin' the streets, climbing fire escapes and lampposts in short pants, like kids do." She laughed again. "I don't know why it strikes me so funny."

"Loretto here," Patsy said, "didn't come around till later. He grew up in an orphanage."

"What was that like?" Maria asked.

"Wasn't so bad." Loretto tapped the ash off his cigarette and watched it fall glowing into the darkness over the porch railing. "I got a pretty good education there."

"Yeah?" Patsy said. "Is that where you learned words like *speculatin'*?"

"Patsy," Loretto said, "you got spaghetti sauce on your cheek."

When Patsy sat up and ran his hands over his face, Loretto laughed at him.

"Ah, leave him alone," Maria said, and she pulled Patsy close again and snuggled up against him.

Lottie said, "Where's your husband think you are tonight, Maria?"

"He'll be travelin' from now till New Year's."

"I wanna put a bullet in his head so she can get the guy's money," Patsy said, "but she don't want no part of it."

"You're not a cold-blooded murderer, Patsy DiNapoli. You talk like you're Al Capone, but I know better."

"Jesus," Lottie said. "He's a real Boy Scout, aren't you, Patsy?"

"What's the big idea, Lottie?" Patsy sounded more tired than annoyed. "What's botherin' you?"

"I already said what's bothering me. Is anybody listening?" she asked. "No. All of a sudden everybody's a genius. I'm telling you, there's gonna be trouble. Dutch and them ain't dumb. The Mad Dot was bait, and Vince is swallowing it hook, line, and sinker. They're just tryin' to get Vince back in the city, where the cops and everybody else is looking for him."

Patsy said, "You're worryin' too much. Vince knows what he's doing."

"Sure, you're all geniuses now." Lottie went back into the house without another word or so much as a glance at the others.

"She's probably got the rag on," Patsy said. He slid down from the porch railing and pulled Maria along with him.

"Don't be a big jerk," Maria said.

"We're calling it a night," Patsy said to Loretto.

"Me, too, in a minute."

Maria pulled herself away from Patsy long enough to give Loretto a kiss on the cheek. Then she and Patsy followed Lottie back into the house.

Alone on the porch, Loretto reached for the brass pull chain dangling from the ceramic fixture over the door and clicked off the light. He made his way to the porch swing and stretched out in the darkness. Lottie had left the army blanket draped over the backrest, and he pulled it over him. The rain continued to fall steadily, though he couldn't see anything other than the small patch of porch floor directly under the back window. He closed his eyes and folded his arms over his chest, his head propped up on the armrest. When he moved, the chains squealed. From inside the house, he heard Vince and Jack talking loudly over the background chatter of the others. It sounded like they were telling stories. Every once in a while there'd be an outbreak of laughter. He tried to tune out the voices and concentrate on the rain. Gina was there in a corner of his thoughts, but Loretto concentrated on listening. He liked lying on the porch swing. He liked the way the night and the quiet made him feel. He closed his eyes and rocked himself, peaceful in the dark.

10:00 a.m.

T he weather had shifted overnight from blustery and cold to bright sunshine and temperatures in the 70s. Joe Haley, bolt upright in the driver's seat, clutched a mug of java in his right hand and the steering wheel in his left. Loretto kept his eyes on a road bracketed by long stretches of green fields and stands of trees with brightly colored leaves—reds and yellows and oranges and every shade in between. It was just the two of them in the car. They were on their way into the city with a list of chores to accomplish. On the one hand, Loretto was feeling surly at being relegated to the role of an errand boy. On the other hand, he was glad not to be privy to any details. He knew enough. He knew Joe Mullins was looking at an early funeral. He knew there were three bombs with short fuses in the back seat of the car under an old blanket. In the trunk, a black valise with a pair of .38 Supers, a .45 automatic, and enough ammunition for a small war was propped up next to a jack and a pump-action shotgun. He knew Vince had plans for a bloody weekend. He knew that, but the only one he knew specifically to be marked for death was Mullins.

"This is some weather, huh?" Joe said. "Indian summer."

And that was the end of the conversation. Joe went back to driving and sipping his coffee, and Loretto went on thinking about Mullins. He knew him a little. They'd met a few times in the course of Loretto's business with Gaspar and Dominic, and he'd never figured him for anything other than a working stiff. Mullins ran a drop for Dutch's empty beer barrels, and Gaspar had done business with him now and then. On the occasions when they'd met, Mullins had been friendly enough, taking the time for a handshake and a slap on the back. He was an older guy, in his forties. One of those men who likes to put his arm around the shoulders of a young guy and give him advice. Once he'd taken Loretto aside, put a finger in his face, and told him to be careful with the girls. "Mug like you," he said, "you don't want to be a father with a family to take care of before you're ready. Do you get my drift?" Loretto had played out his role as the inexperienced kid. "Sure, Joe," he'd said. "I get your drift." Mullins slapped him on the back and sent him on his way. The memory of that little encounter had come back to Loretto fiercely in the past few days. He told himself that Mullins knew the nature of the business. They all did. And he pushed his thoughts elsewhere.

"Listen, Joe," Loretto said, "tell me again what we're doin'?"

Joe put his coffee cup down on the dashboard and fished a slip of paper out of his pocket. "We got to get a room for Patsy and Mike at the Ladonia Hotel on the East Side, a room for you and Tuffy at the Maison on the West Side, a couple of rooms for Vince and Lottie and Frank and Sally at the Cornish Arms." He stuffed the slip of paper back in his pocket.

"He's got us spread out all over town."

"That's the plan. Lottie says it's better that way."

"Queen Lottie," Loretto said. "What about you and Flo?"

"Flo's getting us a room near the Penn Post Garage, over on West 36th." Joe picked up his coffee again. He was an ordinary-looking guy with a leathery face, looked like a million other dockworkers, men who spent their days out in the weather hauling heavy cartons from pallet to pallet.

"So you used to work on the docks," Loretto said.

"Docks, freight yards."

"Ever miss it?"

"Are you kiddin'? I miss it like Flo misses washin' floors."

"Listen, Joe," Loretto said, "can I ask you a favor? You don't need me to make a bunch of room reservations. How about droppin' me off at my girlfriend's place?"

Joe grinned and said, "What do I get out of it?"

"I'll owe you a favor. Never know when a guy might need a favor."

Joe looked at his wristwatch. "All right, but be back at the Maison by one o'clock." He winked at Loretto. "That enough time?"

"Yeah," Loretto said. "That'll do."

11:00 a.m.

The front door to Gina's was propped open with a wash bucket, the black and white squares of the foyer's linoleum floor slick and wet. Loretto managed to reach the steps leaving only one footprint on the newly washed floor. He knocked at Gina's door, waited, and knocked again. When she didn't answer, he rattled the door and called her name, and when she still didn't answer, he took his stiletto from his pocket, wedged it into the door frame, and popped the lock. Once inside, he closed the door behind him and put the stiletto away.

He had no idea what he was doing. It felt urgent to get into the apartment, and so he had broken in—and now he waited and looked around. On the living room couch, directly in front of him, a yellow dress was draped over the armrest, and nylon stockings were balled up in a crevice between two cushions. Spread out on the coffee table, yesterday's newspaper was open to the sports section and a big headline announcing that the World Series was tied at one game apiece, with the Philadelphia A's having taken the last game. A picture of Connie Mack, the A's manager, took up the bottom third of the page. Mack looked like an undertaker in a dark suit, with a narrow face under a straw boater. Loretto picked up the dress and the stockings and carried them into Gina's bedroom. He folded the dress neatly and placed it on her bed. He put the stockings in the bathroom hamper and then returned to the couch, where he stretched out facing the two tall windows that overlooked the street.

He wasn't especially tired but the possibility of a nap was suddenly attractive. He took off his shoes and put them under the coffee table. He draped his jacket over the back of the couch and put his hat on top of the jacket. By the time he loosened his tie and settled his head on a couch cushion, he could already feel sleep sinking into him. It was a strange sense of sleep. It felt more like weariness than tiredness. He thought of Joe Mullins putting his arm around his shoulders and warning him to be careful with the girls, and then he pictured Joe Haley going from hotel to hotel all over town and reserving rooms. He remembered the shotgun in the trunk of the car and pineapples in the back seat, and then he saw Dominic and Gaspar looking up at him from a hole in the ground. His thoughts were doing the crazy things they did before falling asleep, popping around randomly, veering off one way and then another. He saw Sister Mary Catherine kneeling at his feet, untying his shoelaces. He was a child in that memory. He was back in Mount Loretto, seated on his bed, watching the sister untie his shoelaces. She was dressed in her long black habit and white wimple. Before he fell asleep, before he dropped off into silence and darkness, the sister looked up and said something. He didn't know what she said. He couldn't make it out. But she said something to him, of that much he was certain. She looked up and her lips moved and she spoke.

1:30 p.m.

Madon! Are you seeing this?" Tuffy struggled to pull his tweed cap down low on his forehead. He checked the pistol in his shoulder holster, patting it without a thought as he kept his eyes on the scene playing out on the street. They were coming up on the warehouse. An elderly woman and a boy were arguing outside a storefront about whose turn it was to sweep the sidewalk. The woman cursed like a demon and swatted the boy with her broom while the boy stood his ground as best he could and hurled curses right back at her. In the street, a couple of Edison workers climbed out of a manhole and shouted for the two of them to quit making a racket.

"We got a regular circus out here today," Frank said.

"This fuckin' cap," Tuffy said. "It's too small." He yanked it down as best he could over the mop of his hair. "Pull over there." He pointed to a spot on the sidewalk near the loading dock.

"You want to do the driving?" Frank passed the garage and turned the corner.

The car traveled slowly around the block. The next time they approached the garage, the woman and boy were out of sight and the Edison workers were climbing back down the manhole. On the loading dock, a skinny kid in overalls smoked a cigarette, his face turned up to the sun.

"Come on," Tuffy said. "Let's get this over with."

Frank drove past the dock, made a three-point turn, and parked at the curb, where he had a good view of the street and the garage. "I'll keep the car running."

Tuffy pulled his cap down and started for the garage.

Frank opened the passenger-side window as Tuffy climbed the stairs to the loading dock. He heard Tuffy say, "Where's Joe Mullins?" and saw the kid in overalls point back into the shadows. At the same moment, on the street, the boy came hurrying out of the storefront with the old woman right behind him. She shouted and cursed and wielded the broom as if it were a spear, jabbing at the boy with its yellow bristles. Frank put the car in gear. The kid on the loading dock tossed his cigarette away and went back into the garage, and a moment later the pop of a gunshot came from someplace out of sight. On the street, the Edison workers reemerged from their manhole. They were shouting at the old woman as Joe Mullins stumbled into the sunlight and collapsed onto his back. Tuffy came out of the shadows, stood over Mullins, one foot on either side of his chest, and put two bullets in his head. By the time the old woman and the boy looked up from their screaming match at the sound of the gunshots, Tuffy had his back to them and his gun holstered. He jumped down from the loading dock, took one step, and tripped. The old lady and the boy hurried back into the store. Tuffy picked himself up, brushed off his pants, and continued to the car. The Edison workers started for the loading dock. When Frank pulled the car up and threw open the passenger door for Tuffy, they reconsidered and scurried back down the manhole.

"What the hell was that?" Tuffy nodded toward the workers as they disappeared below the street.

Frank drove slowly toward the manhole.

Tuffy saw what he was thinking and said, "Don't worry about them mugs. They ain't stupid. They know what's good for 'em."

Frank drove at a crawl past the manhole cover and then shifted gears and sped away. He glanced at Tuffy. "Where's your cap?"

Tuffy clutched at his hair. "Jesus," he said. "Must have fell off."

Frank laughed quietly, as if everything in the world was a big joke. In the column of sky directly in front of them, enclosed by rows of brick buildings, what looked like a thousand sparrows dipped down into the avenue and soared low over the streets in a dark cloud.

Frank said, "I saw you put two in his head."

Tuffy said, "So much for his photographic memory." A moment later he laughed as if he just got his own joke.

1:35 p.m.

When Mike and Vince drove past Richie Cabo's Majestic Garage on Westchester Avenue, they found a dozen prohees arresting everybody in sight. Three beer trucks were in the loading area, each of them surrounded by agents. Inside the garage, in a shaft of bright sunlight, a pair of agents were looking over a clipboard, two guys in workman's clothes on their bellies in front of them.

"We'll come back later," Mike said.

"Nah," Vince said. "Stop the car."

Vince was in the passenger seat, holding a pineapple in his lap. He had the crudely fashioned black bomb in one hand and a cigarette lighter in the other. He was wearing a crisp dark gray suit and a new fedora. He looked like he might be on his way to a fancy dinner. With his hair dyed dark and his mustache and the Harold Lloyd glasses, he could have been mistaken for a young banker. Except for the bomb.

Mike stopped in the middle of the street and looked back at the warehouse as if he might have missed something. "The place is crawlin' with prohees. What the hell are you thinkin'?"

"Back it up." Vince lit the pineapple's fuse, opened the door, and stepped out onto the running board, the bomb in one hand, the door frame in the other.

Mike yelled, "Jesus H!," and slammed the car into reverse. At the entrance to the garage he jammed on the brakes and the car skidded to a stop.

Vince lost his footing and jumped from the running board to the street, where the prohees were all looking in his direction, some of them already reaching for their guns.

"Hey, boys!" Vince yelled. He threw the bomb, its fuse sizzling, into the back of one of Cabo's trucks and jumped into the car, which peeled away down the street as a pair of prohees leaped from the beer truck to the pavement. By the time the bomb exploded a few seconds later, Vince and Mike were off the avenue and on a side street on their way back to Manhattan. They were both laughing like a pair of fools, throwing glances behind them at the column of smoke already rising over the rooftops.

2:45 p.m.

Detectives Givons and Dwyer climbed the stairs to Commissioner Mulrooney's office with Al Giovanetti behind them. Giovanetti was also a detective, though he was relatively new to the force, having come to New York from Philly only a few years earlier. He was a young guy, still in his twenties, and Givons and Dwyer were both pushing forty. No one knew all the details, but everyone knew the outline: Giovanetti had refused to go along and the brass in Philly had told him he'd best go along or move along. He'd moved along to New York, with his reputation following him, and he'd wound up working with Bill Givons and Jimmy Dwyer, two detectives everyone knew were a couple of straight arrows. Mulrooney had put the three of them in charge of the Coll case and the Vengelli boy's murder.

At the top of the stairs, down a wide corridor of polished wood doors with frosted-glass windows, they found Mulrooney standing at the entrance to his office in a topcoat and derby, shaking hands with Will Jackson, the assistant district attorney of Bronx County. They looked like they were just concluding some business.

"Well, look who it is coming to visit us," Mulrooney said at the sight of the detectives. "Boys," he added, "I hope to hell you've got some good news."

"We might at that," Dwyer answered.

Detective Givons said to Jackson, "You'll be interested in this, too."

Mulrooney slapped his hands together in anticipation. "Come on in, boys." He led the men through a reception room and into his office, where he hung his coat and hat on a hall tree and threw his big body down in a cushioned leather chair behind a redwood desk. He was a man nearing sixty, with a somber face and broad shoulders—a physically imposing man despite his age.

Will Jackson took his coat off, draped it over his arm, and took a seat in a chair next to the desk. The detectives remained standing. Everyone knew this visit had to be related to the Vengelli murder and Vince Coll. With the months ticking by and no progress on the case, newspapers all over the nation were calling for action, and with the papers raising a racket, the politicians were jumpy.

"Well?" Mulrooney grasped the arms of his chair and leaned forward.

Dwyer said, "We think Coll's back in town."

"That's not news," Jackson said. "We get reports of Coll sightings every day."

"This is different." Giovanetti stood beside the door with his arms at his sides. The men all looked at him as if they had forgotten he was in the room.

Dwyer turned back to the commissioner. "Joe Mullins got rubbed out."

"Who?" Mulrooney looked at Jackson as if he might know. Jackson shrugged.

"And isn't that the mystery?" Dwyer said. "Why Joe Mullins? He's a foreman at one of Dutch's beer drops. He makes thirty-five bucks a week. *Made* thirty-five bucks a week."

"There's no question but they were looking for Mullins," Giovanetti said from the doorway. "The killer asked for him by name."

Mulrooney said, "Cut to the chase, boys. What's this got to do with Coll?"

Givons said, "Same time Mullins was getting filled full of holes, somebody tossed a bomb into one of Richie Cabo's beer trucks."

"Here's the point of the matter." Giovanetti sounded frustrated with the progress of the meeting. "There were prohees all over Cabo's garage when a good-looking kid gets out of a car, yells to get their attention, and then throws a bomb in the back of a truck. Who's that sound like? Who's that crazy?" he asked and then promptly answered his own question. "Sounds like Vince Coll."

The district attorney said, "You think Coll's resuming his war with Dutch Schultz?"

"Yes, sir," Dwyer said. "That's what we think."

Givons said, "The capper is somebody threw a pineapple into the Mad Dot just last week."

"Let me guess," Jackson said. "One of Coll's speaks."

Givons said, "You got it," and Mulrooney said, "Was anybody hurt in the truck bombing?"

"Just the poor truck," Dwyer said. "It's seen its last beer run."

"Did we get a description of the kid throwing the bomb?"

"Dark hair, round glasses, early twenties," Giovanetti said, glancing at a notepad.

"That's not Coll."

Dwyer said, "Could be disguised," and Mulrooney nodded.

"We got license-plate numbers and descriptions of the cars in both incidents," Giovanetti said.

"What we'd like," Dwyer raised his voice to take over this part of the conversation from Giovanetti, "is every flatfoot in the city checking every street corner and garage. If we find the cars, we can stake them out and hope that Coll shows his face."

"I'll issue the order," Mulrooney said. "Boys," he added, and he picked up a newspaper from his desk. It was open to the sports pages and a picture of the Cards' third baseman, Pepper Martin, with the caption "The Wild Horse of the Osage." Mulrooney wasn't reading the paper, though. His thoughts were obviously elsewhere. "Boys," he said again, his face even more somber than usual, "if you see this baby killer . . . He's a mad dog, isn't he?"

Jackson stood up. "If we put him on trial, he'll get the chair."

Mulrooney tossed the paper down. "Roosevelt's been all over me," he said to Jackson. "Even Hoover's got his nose in this business." He waved the detectives out the door. "Go on," he said and went to take a seat beside Jackson and continue the conversation.

6:15 p.m.

Loretto woke to find Gina sitting on the couch at his feet watching him. The apartment was dark except for a dim light coming from the bedroom. Outside, beyond the living room windows, the light had faded to a somber shade of gray. Loretto had been dreaming, but the details flitted away as soon as he saw Gina and remembered he was in her apartment and realized he had fallen asleep. "Hey, beautiful," he said, his voice scratchy with sleep. "I conked out."

Gina sighed and pulled her gaze away from the shadows. "You broke in to my apartment."

"I knocked first."

"Good of you." Gina slid away from Loretto and folded her arms over her chest. "What are you doing here?"

"Do you want me to leave?"

"Depends. Tell me what you're doing here and we'll see."

Loretto found his shoes under the coffee table and slipped into them. "I came to see you. Where have you been?"

"Working." She took Loretto's fedora and his jacket from the backrest and held them in her lap. "I'm a ticket taker at the Palace Theater now."

"No kiddin'?" Loretto reached for his hat and jacket, but Gina held tight to them. He asked, "Who's playin' at the Palace?"

"Bob Hope," Gina said. "Why'd you come to see me, Loretto? I thought we were all through."

"We're not through, Gina. You know that." Loretto stretched and rubbed the sleep from his eyes. "How come the lights are all off?"

"You were sleeping peacefully. You were sleeping like a baby."

Loretto put his hand on Gina's knee.

Gina continued to look off into the shadows. "Is Dutch Schultz still out to kill you?" she asked. "Are you part of Vince Coll's gang now? You and Mike?"

Loretto took Gina by the chin and turned her head to him. "What can I do?" he asked. "Tell me what I can do?"

"You can quit being a gangster. You can walk away from it."

"How? What do you think, Gina? I can turn in a resignation some-place?"

"Would you? If you could?"

"Quit? And then what?" Loretto took his fedora from Gina's lap and blocked it while he tried to find the right words. "What would I do? A guy like me. Even if we moved away from here, you and me. What would I do? Pick grapes out in California? Hope nobody ever recognized me and got word back to Dutch or Luciano? Is that a life?"

Gina took the fedora from him and put it in her lap again. "What kind of a life do you have now?"

"I don't know," he said. "Same life as always." He got up and went to the window. He opened it, sat on the ledge, and looked down to the street, where a couple of boys were running full speed and somewhere unseen a woman's voice was shouting a girl's name, calling her home for dinner.

Gina came up behind Loretto and massaged his shoulders. "What are you doing in the city?" she asked. "Isn't it dangerous for you here?"

"I'm with Vince and the boys," he said. "Dutch has been giving us trouble, and Vince is here to hit back."

"Is Mike here, too, then?"

"Everybody's here. Vince has a busy weekend planned."

"But you're here with me," Gina said. The way she said it, it sounded more like a question than a statement.

"I fell asleep," Loretto looked past Gina to the door but didn't move. "I should go."

Gina wrapped her arms around his shoulders and kissed him. "Stay."

She backed up to look him over. She fixed his hair, pushing it off his fore-head. "Stay here with me."

Loretto said, "I can't," but Gina had already taken his hand and he was following her through the living room and into the bedroom, where a small lamp on the night table provided the only light. When she pulled him down onto the bed, he wrapped his arms around her and pressed his face into her neck. "For a while," he said. "I'll stay a while longer."

Gina answered with a kiss as she loosened his tie and unbuttoned his shirt.

Loretto lay on his back and let Gina go about undressing him. Joe Mullins flitted into and out of his thoughts. Dominic had been dead for more than a month, but in some part of Loretto's mind he was still alive, and often, as was the case in that moment, Loretto thought of him as being nearby, somewhere he might go to visit him and talk like they used to, and then always an instant later the recognition came that he was dead. "I think a lot about Dominic," he said, as much to yank himself out of his feelings as to speak. "I can't get him out of my thoughts."

Gina slipped Loretto's tie off from around his neck. She kissed him. "Don't think," she said, and she turned off the light. In the darkness, she knelt and pulled her dress over her head. "Stay with me. Spend the night with me."

Loretto didn't answer. He could make out the shape of Gina as she took off her clothes in the dim light from the bedroom window. When she lay down next to him on the bed he moved to her and his head emptied of thought.

11:30 p.m.

Behind Vince, two pump-action shotguns, two .45 automatics, a pair of tommy guns, and half-dozen pineapples were arranged neatly on the hotel bed's white quilt covering. Vince sat on the edge of the bed, massaging his temples. He was in the Cornish Arms with Lottie at the window and Frank and Sally in the room next door. Through the walls, they could hear Frank and Sally going at it. Lottie grinned at the sound of a headboard knocking out a slow, repetitive rhythm. An hour earlier she and Vince had been making the same music. Now Vince was getting antsy. The front desk had just called. Joe Haley was on his way up. Lottie watched an elderly couple across the avenue as they went into a drugstore. The man was dressed in a shabby jacket and a black derby. He held the door open for the woman and put his hand on her back as if to guide her, as he followed her into the store. Across the avenue, looking down on them from her hotel room, Lottie knew they were man and wife. They had been married since they were kids. They had children and grandchildren. She had no doubt about any of that. She would have bet a million.

"I'm not feeling too good," Vince said. "Get me a drink, will you, doll?"

Lottie went to the armoire and opened it to find a bottle of bourbon on a shelf with a pair of glasses. "What's worrying you? You thinking about Dutch?" She poured them both a drink, carried Vince his glass, and sat beside him.

Vince looked up at the wall. The knocking had stopped. "Maybe he'll get his ass out of bed now." He finished off half the drink in one swallow.

Lottie resumed massaging his shoulders. "Are you nervous?"

"About what?"

"Going after Dutch."

"I've been doing nothing but going after Dutch. Why would I be nervous?"

"I don't know," Lottie said. "You seem nervous."

"You know what I'm thinking?" Vince went to the armoire to pour himself another drink. He was wearing dress shoes and suit pants and an undershirt. "If we can't find Dutch tonight," he said, "I'm thinking we hit his apartment in the Bronx, and if he ain't there, Francis will be—and we take care of Francis. We take care of her good. Give Dutch something that'll really drive him crazy."

"Jesus," Lottie said. "Francis?" Francis was Dutch's wife. She was a dowdy old lady who looked like a church matron.

"Yeah," Vince said. "Francis. Dutch'll go crazy."

"But so will everybody else," Lottie said. "You think the boys will go along?"

"The boys'll do what I say."

"I don't know." Lottie said. "Going after family is something else."

"You mean like my brother Pete?"

Sure, Pete was Vince's brother, but he was also part of his gang. Francis had nothing to do with Dutch's business. Lottie sipped her bourbon and said nothing.

Vince said, "I want Dutch Schultz's blood all over me tonight," and he was interrupted by a knock at the door.

"That's Joe," Lottie said.

"If I can't get Dutch," he said to Lottie, "Francis will have to do." He opened the door, and when Joe slipped in alone, he looked up and down the hallway before closing the door. "Where the hell's Loretto?"

Joe fell back into a chair by the window. "I dropped him off at his woman's place this afternoon," he said. "He was supposed to meet me back at the Ladonia and he never showed."

"Where's Tuffy?"

"He's on his way." Joe looked at his wristwatch. It was 11:45. "You said one o'clock, right?"

Vince banged on the wall to Frank's room. He picked up his drink and took a sip. "What the hell's going on with Loretto?" he asked Lottie. "Why ain't he here?"

"The sap's in love," Lottie said. "He's not thinking straight."

"I don't like it," Vince said, and the way he said it silenced Lottie and made Joe sit up straight. "He's on my payroll, isn't he?"

"Sure, he is," Lottie said. "He should be here."

There was another knock at the door, and Vince let Frank in.

"Loretto ain't here," Vince said. "He's with Gina."

"Yeah," Frank said. He tugged at his ear. "That's not right. What do you want to do about it?"

"I want you to go get him." Vince finished off his drink and thought about pouring himself another. "Go get Patsy and Mike first at the Ladonia; then get Loretto and bring 'em all back here. And tell Loretto I ain't too feckin' happy about him not showing up, either. You got it?"

"Sure, I got it. What about Tuffy?"

Joe said, "He's on his way."

Vince found his shirt in the closet and slipped into it. "Joe," Vince said, "I want you to make the rounds of Dutch's clubs. If you find him, get on the phone and call us here—and then wait till we get there. If you don't, just come back."

Frank said, "So what happens if we can't find him—which is likely because of Mullins. He'll be hiding out like usual."

"If we don't find him, I've got a plan."

"I hope so," Frank said. "We don't want to be stickin' around the city more than a day or two, at most."

"Go get the boys," Vince said. "You, too," he said to Joe. "Let's get movin'."

Once Joe and Frank were gone, Vince poured himself another drink. "I don't like it," he said to Lottie, and he pointed his drink at her. "I don't like this stuff with Loretto."

Lottie said, "He's in love, Vince. That's all it is."

"I don't like it," Vince repeated, and he went to the window, where Lottie had been standing earlier. "He makes me worry," he said as if talking to his own reflection. A moment later, he repeated Loretto's name, and he sounded like he was weighing possibilities.

SATURDAY ✦✦✦ OCTOBER 3, 1931

12:01 a.m.

Frank pulled over at the corner of West 36th. Beside him, Joe put on his hat and snapped the lapels of his jacket. The street was empty, awash in shadows from lampposts and yellowish light spewing from the open mouth of the Penn Post garage. The temperature had dropped and a steady wind swept dust and trash along the sidewalk.

Joe opened his door partway and turned back to Frank. "Say, could I ask you to do me a favor? I left Vince's .38 and a couple of automatics back at the Maison. I was supposed to bring 'em and I forgot."

"Now I'm a fuckin' errand boy?" Frank had already promised Sally he'd stop by her mother's place to drop an envelope in her mailbox with the rent money that was three days late. He'd been paying the old dame's rent ever since he'd first taken up with Sally. Every month it was a different sob story. And now this. "You forgot?"

"They're in a valise under the bed. I put 'em there and then I forgot."

"*V'fancul'*," Frank said. "Yeah, sure. Listen," he added, "don't waste too much time lookin' for Dutch. He's holed up someplace with an army around him now he knows Vince is in town."

"Vince said to look—"

"So look," Frank said. "Just do it fast."

Joe handed Frank the room key and got out of the car. Through the open window he said, "In a valise, under the bed," and then stood back and watched Frank drive off.

Detective Giovanetti, parked in the shadows, figured the mug getting out of the car to be middle-aged, maybe early forties. He was dressed nicely in a suit, looked like a million other guys. When he appeared to be headed for the garage, Giovanetti sat up straight and took a swig from the bottle of Coke he'd been holding between his legs. He'd been watching the garage for a couple of hours, ever since a beat cop located the cream-colored Buick from the Mullins murder parked inside. Dwyer was hiding in the back seat of the Buick and Givons was nearby, behind a concrete column. When the figure entered the light from the garage, Giovanetti got a good look at his face, which was leathery and lined with creases, too rough for an office worker, and so his interest was piqued. He waited until the guy was halfway down the ramp before he followed him and saw that he was heading for the Buick. "Hey, buddy," he called, and to his own surprise he was affecting the manner and tone of a drunk.

Joe looked over the little guy stumbling toward him. He was maybe five six, and at first glance Joe thought the kid was a teenager.

"Buddy," Giovanetti said again. Out of the corner of his eye he saw Givons peek out from behind his column.

"What do you want?" Joe said. "I'm in a hurry."

"D'you see my good friend Jimmy?" Giovanetti asked, slurring his words. "He's a'possed to meet me here."

"I ain't seen your friend."

"What's your name?" Giovanetti asked. "Don't I know you?"

"Joe, and I don't know you." Joe turned his back on the little guy and continued toward the Buick.

Giovanetti moved quietly and quickly toward the Buick. The moment Joe touched the handle to open the car door, he slammed him into the car, turned him around, and showed him the barrel of his gun. "How you doin', Joe?" he said, all the drunkenness gone from his voice.

Givons came out from behind the column flashing his badge and announcing they were cops. Dwyer got out of the car cursing. "What the feck was that drunk act?" he asked Giovanetti, who ignored him.

Givons had already relieved Joe of his pistol. He dangled it in front of him. "Have you heard of the Sullivan laws, Joe?"

"Joe Haley," Giovanetti said to Dwyer. He was looking through Joe's wallet.

Joe said, "I want to see my lawyer." He was leaning face forward into the car with his hands on the roof, the three detectives in a semicircle around him.

"And now wouldn't that make him one Vince Coll's brother-in-law?" Dwyer said, and he turned Joe around to face them.

Givons grabbed Joe by the collar. "Where's Vince?"

"Vince don't tell me nothin'," Joe said. "I ain't seen him in six months."

"So whose car is this?" Giovanetti asked. "You sure it's not Vince Coll's? You sure you don't know where Vince is?"

"This car?" Joe looked at the Buick as if he'd just seen it for the first time. "This is a borrowed car."

"Yeah?" Givons said. "Who did the borrowing?"

"I guess I did."

"You guess you did?" Giovanetti patted down Joe's jacket. "Who do you guess you borrowed it from?"

"Look here," Joe said, "I got a right to see a lawyer."

Giovanetti pulled a bunch of papers from Joe's inside jacket pocket and looked them over.

Dwyer said to Joe, "Of course you've got a right to see a lawyer. You're an American citizen, aren't you?"

"That's right," Joe said.

"Good, then." Dwyer let go a short, quick punch into Joe's solar plexus and watched him drop to the ground struggling to breathe.

"Look at this." Giovanetti showed the papers in his hand to Dwyer and Givons. They were receipts for hotel rooms at the Ladonia, the Maison, and the Cornish Arms.

"Sure," Dwyer said softly. "Vince sends his no-account brother-in-law to rent rooms and pick up cars for him. It makes sense."

At the detectives' feet, Joe pulled himself to his knees, breathing raggedly. Givons and Dwyer each grabbed one of his arms. They dragged him to his feet and out of the garage.

Joe didn't know where he was going, but wherever it was, everybody was in a hurry to get there.

12:45 a.m.

At the Ladonia, Mike was laughing so hard there were tears in his eyes, which he brushed away with the back of his hand. He was sitting on the edge of an unmade bed and Patsy was facing him, straddling a chair and telling stories about the old days, when they ran the streets stealing from vendors or off the back of delivery trucks. "I remember sitting down on the curb and laughing my head off," Mike said. He was dressed and ready to go, his fedora on the bed alongside him. He took an automatic from the holster under his arm, ejected the magazine, looked it over, and popped it back in.

Patsy said, "Alls I remember is that fat copper chasing after me, and I'm running like the Midnight Express. I turn around to look back, and bang! Next thing I know he's standing over me with his hands on his hips and a big smile on his face."

Mike said, laughing, "You hit that lamppost so hard, you bounced off it," and he started laughing again.

Patsy took out his .38 and checked it over. "We better get going," he said.

"Sure," Mike said and again wiped tears from his eyes.

At the Maison, Frank found the valise under the bed, where Joe had said it would be. The room was dark, lit only by a single long fluorescent light buzzing in the bathroom. He tossed the valise onto the bed, opened it to check the contents, and then snapped it closed after looking over each of the guns. He'd just come from Sally's mother's place, where he'd slipped an envelope with rent money into her mailbox. Paying the old lady's rent bothered him more than it should have, and it wasn't about the money. He could afford the money. In the dimly lit room, he sat on the bed and tried to think it through. Why'd it get under his skin like it did, paying the old broad's rent? It wasn't like Sally was holding him up for the money. He'd offered to pay the rent himself when he'd seen Sally crying because her mother was about to get thrown out on the street. Still, paying her rent every month—it was like it was his own bill, come due monthly. And if it was his bill, what was he paying for? Frank told himself to buck up, that he was too sensitive about things. He'd always been too sensitive. He picked up the valise, checked his wristwatch, and started for the door.

At the Cornish Arms, Sally and Lottie were chattering on the bed. They'd kicked off their shoes and were stretched out facing each other side by side, their heads propped on their arms, going on about Maria and Gina and some other girl. They were both wearing silky long dresses and black nylons, as if they were about to leave for a nightclub. On the other side of the room, Tuffy and Vince were standing by the door, talking softly. Vince had just explained his plan to Tuffy, and Tuffy was looking down at the floor, scratching his head.

"Listen," Vince said, and then he stopped and looked over to the girls. He opened the door, went out into the hall, and pulled Tuffy along behind him. "Listen," he said again and closed the door, "I want Dutch to know she didn't go easy."

"Yeah," Tuffy said, "but she's an old lady, Vince. And she don't have nothin' to do with this business."

"So what?" Vince said. "What's that got to do with the price of eggs?"

"The boys ain't gonna like it is all."

Vince tapped Tuffy on the shoulder. "The boys? You mean Madden and Luciano and Dutch and all them? They're already lookin' to put me in the ground. I do this—I put Francis in the ground—they're gonna think twice before coming after me or anyone in my gang. You get my drift?"

"Yeah, but I don't know," Tuffy said, and again he looked down at the ground and scratched his head.

"You don't have to know. I'm either gonna kill Dutch tonight or I'm gonna beat his wife to death so bad he ain't ever getting over it." Vince leaned back and looked away briefly, composing his thoughts. "I'm gonna get Dutch on the phone," he said, "while she's still alive and let him hear her scream. When him and his boys come to get her, we'll be gone, and all they'll find is her beat-to-death body waiting for them."

"Jesus," Tuffy said. "I don't know, Vince."

"What are we gonna do about Loretto?" Vince asked. "Who's he think he is, ditching us to be with his woman? What kind of thing is that to do? He's on our payroll, ain't he?"

"It don't add up," Tuffy said. "You think we can trust him?"

At first Vince looked furious at the suggestion that they might not be able to trust Loretto, and then a moment later his face went dark as he entertained the idea. He started to say that he'd need to have a talk with Loretto but stopped when he heard a noise from the stairwell. Tuffy heard it, too. They both watched the stairs.

At the Ladonia, Bill Givons stationed two men at the elevator, two men in the lobby, and one man at the bottom of the stairwell. He climbed the steps with three more men behind him. When he reached the fifth floor, he sent one man up to the roof. The two coppers he kept with him were both burly

Irishmen in their thirties, men who'd been on the force a good long time and seen a thing or two. At the entrance to the fifth-floor hallway, he took out his pistol and nodded for his men to do the same. "Don't shoot if you don't have to," he told them. "If you have to, shoot 'em dead." He peeked out the door and saw a long, empty hallway with plush maroon carpeting that would muffle their footsteps. Outside two of the doors, food trays waited for the staff to take them away. "All right," he said, and he entered the hall with his gun drawn.

When he reached room 506, Givons glanced behind him and was amazed to see one of the coppers taking a bite out of a chicken leg he'd picked up from one of the food trays. He gave him a death stare, and the copper put the leg down and hurried to his side.

Givons knocked on the door. "Message for Mr. Alfred White." Alfred White was the name the room was registered under.

Patsy opened the door, and Givons hit him hard, knocking him back and down on his ass. Mike Baronti went for his gun, but Givons had his service revolver shoved between his eyes before he could get it out of the holster. "Go ahead," Givons said. "See if you can draw faster than I can pull the trigger."

Mike put his hands in the air. He said, "I want to see my lawyer," and then clammed up.

Patsy's nose was bleeding and one of the coppers handed him a clump of tissues from the bathroom. Patsy pulled himself to his feet. "You broke my nose," he said to Givons.

Givons looked him over. "It ain't broken." He slapped him lightly, twice, on the cheek and then shoved him to the door. "Let's go," he said. "Your friends'll be waiting for you."

. . .

Dwyer had just positioned himself outside the hotel-room door at the Maison, a copper on either side of him, when the door opened from the inside and Frank Guarracie stood in front of him with a valise in his hand. For an instant the two men stared at each other as the coppers drew their guns. Then Dwyer said, "How are you, Frank?" He'd picked up Frank twice before, several years earlier. "We've been lookin' for you."

"Yeah?" Frank said. "Well, here I am."

Dwyer extended his hand for the valise. "And what can I expect to find in this fine valise?" he asked as Frank handed it over.

"I couldn't tell you," Frank said. "I was just picking it up for a friend. I don't have any idea what's inside."

Dwyer opened the valise, looked briefly at the guns, and snapped it closed. He nodded to the coppers, who relieved Frank of his gun, took him by the arms, and followed Dwyer as he headed down the hall to the elevators.

At the Cornish Arms, Giovanetti turned a corner and found himself looking at Vince Coll and Tuffy Onesti standing in the hallway outside a closed hotel-room door. He recognized them both from mug shots. Coll had dyed his hair and grown a mustache, but there was no mistaking him: a tall, handsome kid with a dimple square in the middle of his chin. Neither Coll nor Onesti appeared concerned at Giovanetti's appearance in the hall. They figured him, Giovanetti assumed, for another hotel guest. Behind him, at the far end of the hall and out of sight, four coppers were approaching.

Giovanetti drew his gun. Before he could announce that he was with the police, Coll bolted down the hallway, which dead-ended at a window. Giovanetti took aim as he yelled for Coll to stop. Onesti, white-faced, backed up wordlessly into the doorway. Before Giovanetti could get a shot off, Coll ducked into what appeared to be a restroom.

When the uniformed officers turned the corner with their guns drawn, Onesti said, "Jesus H. Christ," and looked suddenly relieved. "Hey, Irish!" he yelled down the hall. "It's only the coppers! Come on out!"

Coll came out of the restroom with his hands in the air. "Say, officers," he said, "you gave us a scare. We thought you were Dutch Schultz's boys."

Giovanetti kept his revolver trained on Coll. "I'm Detective Giovanetti," he said. When he reached Coll, he patted him down and found only an empty shoulder holster. Behind them, the hotel-room door opened and a beautiful woman stepped out into the hall.

Giovanetti said to Coll, "Let me guess. That's Lottie Kreisberger."

"Yes, sir," Vince said. "That's Lottie."

"Anybody else in there?"

"Sally, friend of Lottie's."

Giovanetti yelled down the hall for the coppers to bring everyone to the station and then pushed Coll back into the restroom at the point of his gun.

"What's the big idea?" Vince glanced around him as if to confirm that he was in a hotel bathroom.

"Take a seat." Giovanetti pointed to an open bathroom stall.

"You want me to sit on the shitter?"

"Why? Does that offend your sense of decorum? Don't you beat guys to death, blow women's brains out, and kill babies for a living?"

"I don't know what you're talking about." Vince looked at the commode one more time and then sat down and crossed his legs. Behind the detective, the restroom door opened and a skinny, tall copper poked his head in. Giovanetti told him to get out and wait for him in the lobby. "What's going on here?" Vince asked. "This ain't no place to conduct an interview."

"*Conduct an interview?*" Giovanetti's tone said he was surprised by Coll's use of language. "I guess you're right," he added. He took a step back from Coll, put his service revolver back in its holster, and removed a .38 snubnose from his jacket pocket.

"What the hell are you doin'?" Vince said. "I'm starting to get annoyed."

"Is that so?" Giovanetti swung out the cylinder, emptied five bullets into his hand, and deposited them in his jacket pocket. He took a step closer to Vince, spun the cylinder, snapped it closed, and pointed the barrel of the gun at his head. "I've got one question," he said. "If I don't like the answer, I'm going to pull the trigger. Then you may or may not have another chance to get it right. I don't expect you to be too good with math, so let me explain: you'll have a maximum, if you're very lucky, of five chances to get it right. You understand?"

Vince laughed. "Sure," he said. "Go ahead."

"Good." Giovanetti moved a little closer and leveled the gun so that the barrel was pointing between Vince's eyes. "Here's the question," he said, and he cocked the hammer. "Who fired the shot that killed the Vengelli boy?"

"Couldn't tell you," Vince said, as casual as ordering dinner at a restaurant. "I wasn't there."

Giovanetti could feel blood draining from his face and he knew Vince saw it, too. Out of anger, he pulled the trigger and when the hammer came down with a loud click, he felt it as a spasm in his heart. He could hardly breathe.

Vince said, "You're no good at this. What's your name? Giovanetti?" He stood up and took his wallet out of his pocket as Giovanetti scrambled back and away from him. "Relax," Vince said. He pulled out a fat wad of cash and started counting.

Giovanetti dropped the snubnose back in his pocket and took out his service revolver. "What are you doing?" he asked. He took a breath and tried to calm himself.

Vince held the money out toward the detective. "It's a little over four Gs. I don't need it," he said. "You take it." He looked off toward the bathroom window.

Giovanetti, in a voice that sounded like a child's, asked, "Why aren't you scared of a bullet in your head, Coll?"

Vince shrugged. "None of my brothers made it past twenty-four. Why should I be any different?" He took another step closer to Giovanetti, extending the wad of cash—and the last thing he remembered before waking in the lobby was the little guy's fist coming at him straight and fast.

8:00 a.m.

Vince watched a patch of blue sky through the barred window of his cell in the Bronx station house. He lay on his back, on a cot with a dirty, inch-thick mattress, his arms crossed under his head. He'd lain there, in much the same position, most of the night, the barred sky through his window changing slowly from black to gray to blue. There'd been a crowd waiting when the paddy wagon pulled up to the station. Mostly they were reporters and photographers and coppers, but there were ordinary chumps out on the street with all the rest, and they shouted curses at him, called him *scum* and *baby killer*. It didn't bother him as much as surprise him. When he'd found out he was Public Enemy Number One, he'd gotten drunk with the boys to celebrate. He was famous. The whole feckin' country knew his name. Did they yell curses at Al Capone? It bothered him and it didn't. Chumps. They'd work two weeks for what the big shots spent on lunch. Enough of that. But he wasn't a baby killer, that he didn't like. It wasn't him shot the kid, and what about Cabo, who was famous for carrying a pocket full of pennies to toss to little kids so they'd gather around him like a bulletproof vest? Why wasn't Cabo a baby killer, the way he surrounded himself with kids? Chumps. They didn't have a witness for the Vengelli thing and they couldn't prove anything. In the paddy wagon with Tuffy and the girls, he'd reminded them of that. They didn't have anything on anybody, and as soon as all the big noise was over they'd be back out on the street.

That feckin' dectective looked so scared when the hammer came down, Vince almost felt sorry for him. He packed a powerhouse right, though. Vince hadn't been knocked out cold like that since his days in Mount Loretto—and it was a nun did it to him then. They were in the kitchen, and he said something rude, something about nuns' panties, and she clocked him with a cast-iron frying pan. He couldn't see out of one eye for a week, and it was a month or more before his face looked normal again. Jesus, those nuns were tough. Vince touched his forehead, where the detective's punch had connected. It was sore, but there was hardly a mark. Must be something they taught them in copper school, how to do damage with nothing showing.

Lottie'd looked like she might faint when Giovanetti came out of the elevator with Vince slung over his shoulder. He was strong for a little guy. He must've carried Vince all the way down the hall and to the elevator. Vince was coming around about the time the elevator doors opened, and he saw Lottie fall backward. He figured she thought he was dead. He struggled to say her name, coming out of a fog, and then quickly he was awake and on his feet. He brushed himself off and called out to her. "Hey, doll," he said. "Must've bumped my head somewhere, but I'm fine now." Then the color came back into her face and she gave him one of her winks. Lottie. It bothered him to see her in the paddy wagon, but she'd be out soon enough. Giovanetti said they had the whole gang in custody, but Vince didn't believe it. Feckin' Loretto. They didn't have him, that was certain. The thought of Loretto bothered him, too. Loretto was too smart to cross him. He knew what'd come of that, but he didn't like it that the kid had disappeared and now he wasn't sure about him. He was sure about Lottie. She was the only thing, and now the only thing that bothered him in a way he didn't want to think about was not seeing her again. But that wouldn't happen. They didn't have anything on him they could make stick.

Vince sat up at the sound of someone approaching his cell. He brushed himself off and straightened his jacket, and then who was it should appear outside his cell but the commissioner himself, Big Shot Mulrooney. And behind him Giovanetti and two more who looked like detectives backed up by a pair of coppers in blue.

"Ah," Mulrooney said at the sight of Coll. "And there he is, the baby killer himself, in person."

Vince smiled amiably and said, "It must be somebody else you're looking for, then. Could you possibly have the wrong cell?"

Mulrooney stood aside and one of the coppers opened the cell door.

Vince said, "Are you sure you're not afraid to step into a cell with the likes of me?"

Mulrooney said, "I've pissed on better men than you, Coll." He was a tall man, which made Giovanetti, standing beside him, look even shorter.

Vince laughed and pointed. "You two should run off to the circus together. Will you look at you, side by side?"

Mulrooney glanced down at Giovanetti and then stepped into the cell and punched Vince in the kidney, a blow that dropped him to his knees. "Enough clowning," he said, and he hauled Vince to his feet and tossed him back onto the cot. "We've got your gang in custody, Vince."

Vince held his head between his knees while he waited for the pain to subside. "What gang?" he managed to say.

Dwyer was standing quietly behind Mulrooney and next to Givons and Giovanetti. "Frank Guarracie," he said. "Tuffy Onesti, Mike Baronti, Patsy DiNapoli."

Givons added, "Plus your sister, Florence, her husband, Joe, your girl, Lottie, and Frank's girl, Sally."

Vince said, "You missed Flo's dog, Scottie. He's gonna go hungry with no one to feed him."

Dwyer said, "That'll teach him to hang around with lowlifes like you and your gang."

Vince touched his back where Mulrooney had hit him. He sat up and said, "You don't have anything. You might as well let us go now before my lawyer gets here and sets you straight."

Mulrooney said, "Now you're thinking wishfully, aren't you, Vince? We've got an outstanding warrant for you from the Sheffield Farm robbery, and you jumped bail last year on a Sullivan rap."

"And then, of course," Giovanetti added, "there's the Vengelli murder."

Vince winked at Giovanetti and said, "We've already had that conversation, Detective."

"And it ended with you unconscious."

Vince said, "I must've passed out."

"Ah, enough of this." Mulrooney crouched down so that he was eye to eye with Vince. "You're a disgrace to your people, Vincent Coll."

"And what people would that be?" Vince said. "The ones on Big Owney's payroll, like yourself, perhaps?"

Mulrooney snatched Vince by the throat. "You make me sick, Coll. All the hard labor over generations to pull ourselves up out of the gutter, and the likes of you dragging us back down." He pulled him close, so that he was within kissing distance, and then tossed him away like trash. "I'll see you burn in the chair—and soon, too."

Vince said calmly, straightening out his jacket, "Not without a witness, I don't believe you will."

To the detectives Mulrooney said, "Bring him along, boys," and then disappeared out the cell door.

Vince stood as Givons took him by one arm and Dwyer by the other. The three of them followed Giovanetti and the coppers down a filthy corridor lined with empty cells and out into another long hallway, this one neat, smelling of vinegar, and lined with offices. "Where are we going?" Vince asked. "I'm getting hungry. You gentlemen plan on breakfasting with me?"

"They'll get you some grub soon enough," Givons said, and he pushed through a door and into a room full of coppers who lined the walls around three rows of folding chairs. Tuffy, Frank, Mike, and Patsy were standing against the wall at the front of the room, facing the chairs.

"Hey, boys!" Tuffy yelled. "They brought Irish to keep us company!" He turned to the coppers and said, "You mugs are swell!"

"Yeah," Mike said. "Very thoughtful of you."

Some of the coppers were laughing. They all appeared to be amused.

"This is like a reunion," Vince said, and he slapped Tuffy on the back.

Dwyer and Givons took up positions at opposite walls, next to a pair of matching lamp poles with the bare bulbs pointed at the front of the room. "Line up," Givons said. "You know the drill."

Tuffy and the gang lined up shoulder to shoulder against the wall, with Vince on one end of the line and Tuffy on the other. Vince said, "Say, where's my lawyer? You can't do this without my lawyer here."

Givons said, "Not if you refused our offer to have a lawyer present."

"Yeah?" Vince said. "Well, I haven't done any such thing!"

"Sure you have," Giovanetti said, and the room exploded in laughter.

Vince looked at the boys and said, "They think they're comedians." He glanced out at the coppers. He added, "They look like a bunch of clowns to me," and then he and the boys had a good laugh.

From the center of the room, amidst the folding chairs, a photographer standing behind a camera and tripod yelled, "Hey, boys, look over here," and a moment later there was a bright flash of light as he took their picture.

"Jesus," Tuffy said, "I'm blinded."

"Ain't that a shame," Givons said, and he and Dwyer turned on their lights, shining them into the boys' eyes. Givons knocked on a door beside him, and Mulrooney entered the room in front of the two Edison workers who had witnessed the shooting at Cabo's garage.

"That's them," one of the workers said as soon as the door opened.

The second worker stepped into the room and agreed with the first. They both pointed out Frank Guarracie as the driver of the car and Tuffy Onesti as the shooter in the Mullins murder, and a minute later they were out the door.

At the front of the room, Tuffy leaned forward to exchange a look with Frank

Vince put a hand on Frank's shoulder. "Don't worry about a thing," he said. "Once our lawyers get here, these coppers will be singing a different tune."

Tuffy grinned as if his problems were done with. Frank's face was expressionless and remained that way as he was led out of the room with the others.

In the hallway, after the prisoners had been taken away, Mulrooney huddled with Giovanetti, Givons, Dwyer, and Will Jackson, the assistant district attorney.

Giovanetti said, "We'll need to give those Edison guys protection."

Mulrooney took a cigar from his jacket pocket. He tapped it against his finger as he looked off down the hallway at a young secretary carrying a sheaf of papers into another office. He seemed to be running calculations in his head. When he turned back to the group, he asked Jackson, "How soon can we bring Guarracie and Onesti to trial?"

"Soon," Jackson said. "Three or four weeks at the most."

"Good," Mulrooney said. "And this son of a bitch, Coll. Don't be telling me we've got nothing on him except these baloney gun charges."

Dwyer said, "There's the Sheffield Farm stickup."

"That's not good enough." Mulrooney shoved the cigar back in his pocket. "I want him for the murder of the Vengelli boy."

Jackson said, "Not without a witness."

Mulrooney said, "Vincent Coll did the shooting and Frank Guarracie was the driver." He looked to the detectives, "That's about the way you figure it, isn't it?"

Dwyer said, "Guarracie's the wheel man. It would have been him doing the driving."

Giovanetti added, "And probably Coll and his boys in the back seat doing the shooting."

"Okay," Mulrooney said. "Indict Coll and Guarracie for the murder of Michael Vengelli." He touched Jackson's shoulder. "Schedule the Coll trial right after Guarracie and Onesti. I want to hang a death sentence on

Coll before the year's out."

Giovanetti said, "And what about a witness?"

Mulrooney took the cigar out of his pocket again and this time went about lighting it.

Jackson said, "I hope you know what you're doing, Mulrooney."

"Me?" Mulrooney winked at Jackson. "I'm going to Philadelphia to see the World Series."

Giovanetti said, "What about the others? The dames and the rest of the gang?"

"Let them go. We got who we want." He took Dwyer and Givons each by the arm and gave them a shake. "Good work, boys," he said, looking at Giovanetti. "The night Coll fries, I'll stand you all to a good stiff drink."

Mulrooney put his arm around Jackson and led him off down the hall, and Givons asked Dwyer who he had in the World Series. "The A's," Dwyer said. "Who do you think?"

Giovanetti said, "I wouldn't be so certain about that," and the three detectives followed the commissioner and the assistant district attorney down the corridor, on their way back to work.

10:00 a.m.

When Augie knocked on her apartment door, Gina was asleep again, as was Loretto, whose chest she was using as a pillow. She recognized Augie's voice calling her name, but it seemed to be coming from a great distance. She'd been up half the night with Loretto and then they'd slept for a few hours before sunlight through the bedroom window woke them and they'd made love again and talked some more and held each other close, sleeping and talking and touching each other as the kids in the upstairs apartment scurried through their rooms and families went about making breakfast and getting started on the day. Sometime during the night, she felt Loretto's fingers exploring her back, gently touching the dark ridges of scar tissue where she'd been stabbed by her father. When she was married, she'd pull her slip up for sex, always keeping something on her back, keeping herself covered or hidden there. If her husband's hands got too close, she'd squirm away or take his hands in hers and move them elsewhere. When she first felt Loretto's fingers on her back, exploring, she tightened up and then willed herself to relax. Loretto didn't say a word. He raised himself up and kissed her on the back of her neck and her shoulders and on her scars, and she let him do it without saying a word, the two of them touching in the dark and quiet of the sleeping building. Later, they talked about their childhoods, Gina about the years with her father, Loretto about the orphanage. They talked quietly, face to face, one or the other's hand now and then reaching out to touch.

She heard Augie knocking and calling her name, but she didn't fully come to consciousness until Loretto shook her by the shoulder, and then she jumped up from bed already aware of what was going on. "Augie!" she yelled. "Hold your horses! I'll be right there." She grabbed a long white robe from the back of the bedroom door, pulled it tight around her, and cinched it closed.

On the edge of the mattress, Loretto was already dressed and scanning the room for evidence of his presence there throughout the night. He tossed his pillow on top of Gina's, snapped the sheets to erase his impression, and then did the same with the covers. He opened the bedroom window quietly and whispered, "Augie will kill me if he finds me here."

Gina nodded in agreement and then put a hand over her mouth to keep from laughing. Loretto's shirt was buttoned unevenly, his jacket dangled from one arm, his hat was on cockeyed, and his shoes were untied. When he climbed out onto the fire escape, she followed him. "Where are you going?"

It was another summery day, the sun bright on the building's red brick. "The roof?"

Gina closed the window behind Loretto and waited until he disappeared up the fire escape before she went out into the living room and opened the door, where she found Augie and Freddie waiting.

"What are you doing sleeping at ten o'clock?" Augie marched past her into the living room.

"It's Saturday morning. Can't I sleep in?"

Freddie kissed Gina on the cheek. "Good morning, sweetheart."

"Good morning," she said and returned the kiss.

Augie tossed a pair of newspapers onto the coffee table. "They got the whole gang," he said, and he took a seat on the couch. "They locked up the lot of them last night."

"They got Mike?" Gina asked. She picked up the *Mirror* and started to read the front-page story as she dropped down on the couch opposite Augie. Freddie sat on the coffee table facing them. Gina gave him a look. When he didn't budge, she sighed and went back to reading the paper. "Jesus," she said, "they're charging Frank and Tuffy with murder."

Freddie said, "And they're charging Vince and Frank with the murder of the Vengelli boy."

"But it doesn't say anything about Mike?"

"Yeah, it does," Augie said. "You got to get to the end of the story. It gives his whole name, Mike Baronti arrested with the rest of the Coll gang."

Gina flipped to the end of the story. "So Mike's in jail?"

Augie didn't answer right away. He watched his sister across the couch, and then his eyes went to the closed bedroom door.

Freddie said, "We already been down to the station house. They're not charging Mike with nothin'. They're letting him out soon as they finish up with all the official stuff."

Augie said, "How come you haven't asked about Loretto?"

"I'm reading the paper, aren't I? I don't see his name."

Freddie said, "Nobody knows where Loretto is. All anybody knows is he wasn't with the gang last night."

Augie went to the bedroom door and flung it open.

"Hey," Gina said, "what are you doing, Augie? Are you my father now?"

"I thought I heard something."

"Sure, you did." Gina watched Augie as he stood by the door, looking like he wasn't sure whether he should be angry or apologetic.

"You haven't seen Loretto, then?"

"I saw him," Gina said. "He came by last night."

"Oh, yeah?" Augie apparently made up his mind and settled on being angry. "I thought you weren't seeing him anymore? I thought it was all over between you two?"

"Well, it isn't," Gina said. "Not after last night."

Augie looked back into the bedroom again.

Freddie asked, "So what happened last night?" He pressed his hands together, doing one of his isometric exercises. The muscles in his chest and forearm bulged. It was hard to believe sometimes that Freddie and Augie were brothers: Augie with his skinny, wiry body and Freddie the opposite, short and thick.

"We had a good talk," Gina said. "We settled a few things."

"Is that so?" Augie said. "So tell us what got settled."

Freddie said, "Ah, lay off, Augie. Can't you see she's in love?"

Gina's face turned bright red with embarrassment, and Augie's did the same, with anger.

"What did I say?" Freddie crossed his legs and grinned. He looked pleased with himself.

Gina got up from the couch and straightened out her robe. "I'll go put up some coffee."

"Good idea," Augie said. They were both speaking softly.

Freddie was still grinning. "You know what Mama always said: there's two things you can't hide, shame and love."

Augie said, "Shut up, will you please, Freddie?" He followed Gina into the kitchen, where he took a seat at the table and watched her as she went about putting up the coffee.

Gina said, "It was Dad used to say that."

"What? About shame and love?"

"Yeah, shame and love. Dad used to say that."

Freddie came in from the kitchen and stood in the doorway. "I knew that," he said. "I don't know why I said Ma."

"So where did Loretto go from here?" Augie asked.

"He said he was staying at a hotel in midtown someplace. I forget the name."

"Gina," Augie said, "what is it with you and men? Can't you pick an ordinary guy? Just once?"

Freddie said, "Loretto's a square guy, Augie. You know that."

"Yeah, sure," Augie said, admitting he, too, liked Loretto. "But he's in a boatload of trouble again, and now if Gina's involved with him, she's in trouble, too. Don't we have enough to worry about with Mike? Now we got to worry about Gina and Loretto, too?"

Gina put the coffee pot on the burner, turned the heat on low, and took a seat at the table next to Augie. "We're all grown up, Augie," she said. "You don't have to worry about everybody."

"I don't?"

"Yeah, you don't," Freddie said. He took a seat on the other side of Augie. "Gina's right," he said. "We can take care of ourselves. Mike, too."

"And who do you think Mama comes to?" Augie asked. "She come to you, Freddie?" He looked at Gina. "She come to you?"

"Mama . . . " Gina said, as if Mama was a part of the problem she had forgotten about.

"She comes to me," Augie said. "You think she's not still cryin' her eyes out over Mike?"

Freddie glanced around the kitchen as if looking for something. His eyes moved from the sink and the line of white wooden cabinets over the kitchen counters to a yellow enamel flour canister next to the stove and to Gina in her white robe. "I hear her at night, too," he said. "Still, Augie—"

Before Freddie could finish what he was saying, someone knocked on the door.

"Who could that be?" Gina said. "On a Saturday morning?"

Augie went to the front door and opened it to find Loretto waiting, hat in hand.

"Augie," Loretto said. "You visiting Gina this morning?"

"No, I'm the landlord here to collect the rent." Augie stood aside to let Loretto in. "What are you doing here?"

"Same thing as you, looks like. I'm here to see Gina."

Loretto took a few steps into the living room and Gina came out of the kitchen to greet him. She put her hands on his shoulders and kissed him on the lips. "I'm glad you could stop by," she said. "Are you hungry? I can make us a late breakfast."

"Sure," Loretto said. He saw Freddie at the kitchen table and they exchanged greetings.

Gina said, "I'll make eggs and pancakes for everybody," and went back into the kitchen.

Augie, who'd been watching Loretto carefully, stepped close and took Loretto's chin in his hand. "You forgot to shave this morning," he said. "You must have been in a hurry."

Loretto ran his fingers along his jaw. "Nah," he said. "I forgot to pack my razor. I got to pick up a new one." He moved to the couch, meaning to put his hat down on the backrest, and saw the newspapers on the coffee table. "Jeez," he said, as he picked up the *Mirror*.

"They got everybody," Augie said. "Except you."

Loretto fell back onto the couch, hungrily reading the news story.

Augie joined him and waited until Loretto finished and tossed the paper back onto the coffee table. "So how come you weren't with them last night, Loretto? I'm thinking Vince and the boys got to be asking themselves the same question."

"I was here," Loretto said, "with Gina." He rubbed his eyes as if suddenly very tired. "I was supposed to be with them, but instead I spent the night here with Gina."

"Till you left to go back to your hotel."

"That's right."

"But you spent the evening here instead of going with the gang." Augie repeated the facts as if he needed another moment to think about them.

Loretto ran his fingers over the stubble on his jaw and then turned to Augie. In the kitchen, he heard Gina and Freddie talking about the best way to make pancakes. Very quietly, he said, "I'm in love with Gina, Augie."

"Yeah?" Augie said, also keeping his voice down. "You know what people in love do, don't you?"

"Sure," Loretto said, "and if Vince can't make it to the wedding, I'll invite Lucky Luciano and Richie Cabo and Dutch Schultz instead. It'd be the shortest marriage in history. I'd be lucky to say 'I do' before someone blew my brains out."

"Yeah, well," Augie said. He thought about the problem a moment before letting it go. He pulled himself up from the couch. "Let's get something to eat."

In the kitchen, Gina rummaged through a drawer and pulled out a wire whisk. "You read the papers?" she asked Loretto as he entered the room with Augie.

"Jesus," Loretto said, "they got everybody." He sat next to Freddie at the table and Augie sat across from them.

Freddie asked, "How come you weren't with them?"

Augie said, "Maybe he decided he didn't want to wind up in jail, Freddie."

"Yeah?" Freddie said, looking at Loretto.

"I don't know. I was supposed to meet up with them, and . . . I don't know. I just didn't go."

"Huh," Freddie said.

Gina turned around with a mixing bowl held tight in the crook of her left arm and the whisk in her right hand. "Good thing you didn't," she said, and she went about mixing the pancake batter. "You'd be in jail now with the rest of them."

"Anybody heard anything about Mike?" Loretto asked.

Gina went back to preparing the pancakes. Freddie said, "They're holding Vince, Frank, and Tuffy—the rest they're letting go."

"That's good," Loretto said, though he didn't seem so sure about that.

Augie said, "They're gonna want to know why you ditched 'em."

"I guess they are," Loretto said. He found a pack of Luckies in his jacket pocket and lit up.

Augie and Freddie joined Loretto, pulling cigarettes out of packs and lighting up. Gina found a couple of ashtrays and slid them onto the table.

Freddie blew a line of smoke up toward the ceiling. "So what are you gonna do?"

Gina went to the kitchen window and yanked it open to let some air in.

Loretto said, "I guess I'll have to talk with Mike and Patsy, see where I stand with Vince."

"Vince won't be happy," Freddie said.

Augie said, "You can't tell Vince you just didn't show because of nothin'. He won't stand for that."

"So? Coll's in jail where he belongs," Gina said.

"That don't mean nothin'." Freddie waved a line of smoke away from his face. "He's just as dangerous in jail as out."

"Is that so?" Gina put plates and napkins in front of the boys and then tossed four forks into the center of the table. "Maybe Mike can straighten it out with Vince."

Augie said to Loretto, "You got to come up with a story. Something happened to you. Maybe you fell down a sewer and broke your leg."

Freddie said, "Want me to break your leg for you, Loretto? I'll do it fast with a baseball bat."

At the stove, Gina had scrambled eggs going in one frying pan, pancakes in another, and coffee perking on the back burner. Each time she finished a batch of pancakes, she placed them on a tin sheet in the oven to keep them warm. "With Vince and half his gang up on murder charges," she said, tending to the pancakes, "maybe Mike will finally see the light."

Augie said, "Stranger things have happened." He asked, "Is that coffee ready yet?"

Gina pointed to a cabinet over the sink. "Cups are over there."

Freddie said, "I'll get it," and went about taking down the cups and pouring everyone coffee. To Loretto he said, "Maybe I can get you a job at the restaurant. It ain't so bad. I don't even mind going in to work anymore. The people there, they're nice. The cooks especially. They're funny, couple of Calabres', right off the boat. They're making peanuts, working sixteen-hour days—and they talk like they couldn't be happier." Freddie thought about this a moment and then repeated, "Right off the boat."

Gina placed two plates of pancakes and a bowl of scrambled eggs on the table and went about dishing out portions for Loretto and her brothers. "I can't see Loretto washing dishes," she said to Freddie.

"But it's good enough for me?"

"Don't get all insulted." Gina gave Freddie a pat on the shoulder.

The men put out their cigarettes and went about digging in to breakfast. Gina pulled up a chair next to Loretto and served herself a couple of pancakes. Next to her, Freddie held the syrup bottle up high and let it drizzle down onto his plate.

Augie said to Loretto, "The Castellammarese got plenty of pull on the docks. Maybe they can work out something for you."

"Maybe," Loretto said, "but they won't want to cross Luciano."

Freddie said, "What's Luciano got against you?"

"Long story," Loretto said.

Freddie held up a bite of pancake on his fork. "I got time."

Gina said, "Leave Loretto be."

"Luciano will know I've been with Vince upstate and I think he may have had the impression that I would let him know Vince's whereabouts soon as I knew them. Which I didn't do."

"He may have had the impression," Augie repeated. "*Mammalucc'*," he said. "Keeping you alive's gonna be a big job."

Gina asked Loretto, "Are you really in that much trouble?"

"Nah," Loretto said. "It'll blow over—but I've got to be careful for a while."

Augie pushed his empty plate away. "You'll stay with us," he said, an order as much as an announcement, "till we find a way to get this straightened out."

"Where?" Gina said. "With Mama?"

"He'll be safe there," Augie said. "No one would dare put a hand on Mama. Luciano would never permit it. They still got some honor."

"I don't like it," Gina said.

"Where's he gonna stay, then?" he asked Gina, and he looked at her pointedly.

Freddie said to Loretto, "We'll be your bodyguards. You can sleep on the couch."

"You won't have to worry, Gina," Augie said. "We'll keep an eye on him twenty-four hours a day. This way, we'll know where he is at all times and you won't have to worry about a thing. See?" He turned to Loretto. "This is best all around till we can figure out something."

"Sure," Loretto said, and he picked up his coffee cup. "I appreciate it, Augie."

"You're welcome," Augie said. He winked at Gina. "Don't worry," he added, "we'll keep him safe."

"I'm sure you'll keep an eye on him," Gina said to Augie. Alongside her, Freddie had cleared his plate and was reaching for seconds. Gina put her arm on his shoulder and gave him an affectionate squeeze. "Eat," she said to the others, and she scooped another pancake for herself.

4:00 p.m.

Lottie waited in a plushy carpeted dining room, a grease-stained brown paper bag clasped in her hands. She wanted not to be impressed by the crystal chandelier dangling over a long polished wood table, by the fine art on the walls or the china cabinet with its arched doors, behind which rows of ornate dishes and stemware were on display. She kept her eyes focused impassively on a winding staircase. She was in Samuel Leibowitz's house. The maid who'd let her in had asked her to wait in the dining room. She'd said Mr. Leibowitz was upstairs, in the library, and would be down in a moment, and so Lottie waited quietly. This was the kind of home where her mother had worked as a maid, where Lottie would come as a child and play in the basement among the soiled sheets and dirty laundry and shelves of cleaning products. The upstairs of that house, the house where her mother worked, was a wonderland of nooks and crannies to be explored, of precious objects to be touched, of bookcases and sculptures and art in elaborate frames. She of course was not allowed upstairs, though she'd sneak up any chance that arose, until the banker's wife put a stop to it and forbade her mother from bringing Lottie to work. Now, all these years later, something in Lottie felt like a child again, a child who had wandered where she was not allowed.

When Leibowitz appeared at the top of the stairs, he was dressed casually in khaki slacks and a blue knit shirt. "Miss Kreisberger," he said, midway down the flight, "though we have no history of clairvoyance in my family, I feel quite certain I know the purpose of this visit."

"Mr. Leibowitz," Lottie said, "I'm here to ask you to represent my boyfriend, Vincent Coll."

"Please," Leibowitz said, "call me Samuel." He approached Lottie and extended his hand. A trim man in his fifties, he was bald to the very top of his head, where the remaining thin strands of hair were carefully combed over and slicked down.

Lottie let go of the brown paper bag long enough to shake hands. "Vince says he'll pay whatever you require."

Leibowitz clasped his hands over his belly and affected a look of amused annoyance. "This is, you realize, Miss Kreisberger, a Saturday evening. I don't work on Saturdays."

"I'm not asking you to work, Mr. Leibowitz." When she tried to hand Leibowitz the paper bag, he waved it off and pointed to the dining room table. "I only want to know if you'll take his case and to leave you this retainer." She placed the paper bag on the table.

"I had heard," Leibowitz said, "that young Mr. Coll was represented by Albert Vitale."

"He doesn't want Vitale." Lottie rejoined Leibowitz at the entrance to the dining room. "He wants you."

"It's Saturday, Miss Kreisberger." Leibowitz went to the front door and opened it slightly. "First thing Monday morning, I'll arrange to have a meeting with Mr. Coll."

"So you'll represent him, then?"

Leibowitz pulled the door open. "You've left your paper bag. . . . I've agreed to meet your boyfriend on Monday. . . ." He shrugged, meaning *Yes, it looks like I'll be representing him.*

Lottie said, "Thank you," shook his hand again, and left the house.

On the street, Joe was waiting for her at the wheel of his old De Soto. Flo was beside him in the passenger seat.

"He'll do it," Lottie said as she got in the car. "He took the money."

"I don't know why Vince's got to have his own feckin' big-shot Jew lawyer," Flo said. "We might need that money the way things are going."

Joe said, "Leibowitz got Capone off, that's why. If he can get Capone off, he can get Vince off."

"Capone didn't shoot no wop five-year-old kid," Flo said.

Lottie laid her head back on the seat, closed her eyes, and almost immediately felt sleep coming on. "I'm exhausted," she said. She heard Flo say, "A night in the feckin' slammer'll do that to you," and then she felt the car moving as Joe pulled out onto the street. She wanted to say something more, something about Vince and his lawyers, but the words wouldn't come—and then she was remembering her mother again and the basement, playing with a rag doll and watching the flight of stairs that led to the upper rooms and everything she wasn't allowed to touch that was up there.

10:00 p.m.

Vince was sleeping restlessly in the Tombs. He didn't think he was sleeping, but he was. When they first brought him in and stuck him on a floor with a dozen cells, he'd complained about the dinner meal: a pair of fat hot dogs that tasted like garlic. The other mugs in their cells heard him complaining and took up with him, and in no time everybody was banging on their cell bars with tin cups and tossing hot dogs till they were bouncing around everywhere, and Vince was in a righteous fury, clasping the cell bars and screaming about the rights of prisoners and the slop they were feeding them that he wouldn't serve to a pig, the others yammering right along with him till the warden came and said he'd get the local restaurants to deliver hamburger steaks if they'd all just quiet down, and a cheer went up, with everybody congratulating Vince soon as the warden was off the floor, congratulating him and every one of them calling him Mad Dog like it was the greatest, most fearful name in the world. Later they moved him to another cell with no one else on the floor, and when he was leaving they all wished him luck, telling him to beat the rap, and again his name was Mad Dog, like they were talking to some kind of hero.

He couldn't fall asleep in this dump, and he didn't think it strange that there was a dog in the cell with him, a big husky like the one from that Alaska book he'd read at Mount Loretto, Buck, the big dog's name in the book. Buck was in the cell with him, right alongside his cot, and every once in a while he'd lean over and pet the big dog's head. He was glad for the company. Did they think he couldn't take some time in the slammer? Hadn't he practically grown up in places like this? *Come here*, he patted the bed and Buck looked at him but wouldn't get up on the cot. Instead, the big dog pawed at an old wooden door that was weathered green like moss. He could see Buck wanted to go out, but Vince was tired and really wanted to sleep, so he didn't get out of bed. He rolled over and buried his head in a pillow. They'd never make this murder rap stick, not if he could get Leibowitz to be his lawyer. He was a big shot now, he needed a big-shot lawyer. He was Mad Dog Coll. Wasn't that what everyone called him? Even the guards, he'd heard two of them talking quietly like they couldn't be heard and one said to the other *That's Mad Dog Coll in there*, like they were talking about a saint or the president. *That's Mad Dog Coll in there.*

Vince rolled over again and cursed himself for not being able to fall asleep, though of course he was sleeping, though restlessly. If he could have stepped out of himself and looked down from the roof of the cell, he'd have seen a young man tossing about in his sleep, turning from one side to the other, throwing his arms about, and all in all looking tortured, like he was struggling in a bad dream and trying to wake himself from the depths of it.

12:30 a.m.

Dutch said, "There's no chance Frank and Tuffy will get off. They got two Edison guys saw Tuffy shoot Mullins in the face, and Frank waitin' in the car." He was sitting in a big stuffed leather chair with his legs up on an ottoman and one of his favorite girls in his lap, a little redhead with a button nose and a sly smile. She was a baby, not yet twenty, but all the men in this little circle knew her intimately. Her name was Vicky, she was one of Polly Adler's girls, and they were at Polly's place on Central Park West. It was storming outside, and through a tall window behind Dutch the trees of Central Park swayed in the wind and rain.

Charlie Lucky sat across from Dutch in another high-backed, deep-buttoned leather armchair. The five men in the tight circle of chairs pulled close to a round marble coffee table were smoking cigars and drinking good liquor. The carpeting under their feet was plush and the walls surrounding them were lined with books. Dutch and Bo had called Luciano and Big Owney and invited them to celebrate Vince Coll's arrest. When Richie Cabo heard about it, he invited himself to the party.

Luciano said, "That Vitale, he's a good lawyer."

Cabo was already half drunk. He had a tumbler of bourbon in one hand and a cigar in the other. "A good lawyer might be able to get them off."

Bo said, "Clarence Darrow couldn't get them mugs off."

Cabo wriggled in his chair, pushing his squat body toward the table, where he flicked the ash off his cigar. "Unless somethin' happens to them witnesses."

Owen Madden, dressed impeccably as always, said, "Nothing will happen to the witnesses." He held a crystal brandy snifter between his thumb and forefinger over his crossed legs. The snifter matched the Waterford decanter on the table. Madden was still a few months shy of his fortieth birthday, but among this group that made him the elder statesman.

Cabo said, "Don't be so sure about that," and fell back in his chair.

Owen paid no attention to Cabo. To Dutch and Bo he said, "My good friend Walter Winchell tells me the trial will be short and sweet and they'll both get the chair." The way he said *my good friend Walter Winchell* made it clear he didn't like the man.

Luciano said to Big Owney, "Is it true what I hear: Winchell's on your payroll?"

Owen offered Luciano a wink and smile as an answer.

Dutch said, "Too bad about Tuffy. I always liked that kid."

Bo said, "Nobody told him to go to work for Vince. He stayed with us like he should've, he wouldn't be in this mess."

Dutch gave Vicky a squeeze and pushed her out of the chair. "Go bring us some more girls," he said. "This party's getting dull."

"That's right," Luciano said. "Bring Polly back with you, too. I like that broad." He raised a glass. "To Vince Coll gettin' the hot seat!"

The men raised their glasses. Bo said, "Good riddance to bad rubbish!"

Vicky gave Dutch a kiss and sauntered away, exaggeratedly shaking her ass.

Cabo said, "I still say, don't be jumpin' the gun. They ain't convicted yet."

The others ignored him until Luciano added, "He's got a point. Without a witness, they can't have much of a case against Coll. Plus, word gettin' around town is he's got Leibowitz defending him."

Owen said to Luciano, "They'll all wind up in the chair. Tuffy and Frank for the murder of Joe Mullins, and Vince for the murder of the Vengelli boy."

Luciano looked around the circle at Bo and Dutch and Owen, all of whom seemed to understand Madden's certainty. "What do you mugs know that I don't?"

Big Owney was silent a long moment, as if deciding whether or not to share what he knew. Finally he said, "They got a witness saw Vince shoot the Vengelli kid. Top secret."

"No kiddin'?" Luciano sounded angry at being the last to know. "Who's the witness?" He tossed down his drink and bent to the table to refill his glass.

Owen said, "That even I don't know."

"And if he don't know," Dutch said, "nobody does."

"Yeah?" Luciano added a touch of defiance to the anger. "Well, I never heard about no witness. It smells fishy to me."

"You don't say?" Dutch took a sip of his drink, spilled a little whiskey on his lapel, and didn't seem to notice. To Madden he said, "Now that's a shame ain't it? Coppers gettin' up to no good."

Madden said, "Breaks my heart when they play fast and loose with the law like that." His tone and manner were so righteously outraged that it took everyone a moment to realize he was joking and break out in laughter.

"You swells haven't started the party without us, now, have you?" Polly came into the room amidst a crowd of girls in lingerie, all of whom went about draping themselves over the men seated in fat leather chairs, massaging their shoulders or sitting in their laps or planting a kiss on their lips. Polly herself took a seat on the ottoman at Dutch's feet and leaned in to him for a friendly peck on the cheek.

Outside, the wind and rain picked up, though everyone at the party was having too good a time to notice the Central Park trees whipping back and forth in the wind as if trying to rip themselves up by the roots, or the way the rain pelted their leaves so that they seemed to be a crowd of hands waving frantically, the whole park like a furious horde beyond the window, whistling and howling in the wind.

Winter

· *1931-1932* ·

TUESDAY ••• DECEMBER 1, 1931

8:00 p.m.

When Gina and Loretto sat down to dinner with Mama and the family on Thanksgiving night, the air had been clear and crisp, and by the time dinner was over an inch of snow covered the streets and fire escapes, with icicles already forming on the tenement ledges and dangling toward the highest windows. Now, six days later, snow had turned to slush, and what was left of it gathered in grimy clumps that formed a small barrier between the streets and the sidewalks. Maria Tramonti was at the window of Gina's apartment with a cup of coffee cradled in her hands. From the kitchen table, where Gina was busy with a spatula scraping a fresh batch of chocolate-chip cookies from a baking sheet, she could see Maria's reflection in the window glass.

Loretto had just started a steady job at fifteen dollars a week clearing trails at Innwood Park, and Gina was telling Maria all about it as she slid the chunky chocolate-rich cookies onto a holiday serving dish, the apartment redolent with the sweet smell of cookie dough and melted chocolate. The trail-clearing jobs, which were employing a thousand men, had been created by the Park Department and the Emergency Unemployment Relief Committee and were supposed to be limited to men with families to support, but a friend of Gaspar's had called in a favor and got Loretto hired. He was working three days a week and driving to and from the job in Dominic's old Packard, which Gaspar's widow had given to him.

Maria listened and occasionally made a sound or threw in a word or two to show she was paying attention, but Gina stopped abruptly when she saw the sadness on Maria's face reflected in the window glass. She pushed the cookies to the center of the table, picked up her own cup of coffee, and joined Maria in looking out to the street. On the table in the living room, a copy of the *New York Evening Post* was open to a story about the Joe Mullins trial. Frank and Tuffy had been convicted of murder and sentenced to death in the electric chair. The trial had lasted four weeks, but it had only taken the jury an hour and half to return a guilty verdict.

Gina put her arm around Maria's shoulders and gave her a quick hug.

Maria said, "That's wonderful for Loretto," and lifted the cup to her lips. She took a sip as if she were drinking from a bowl. "What does he do?"

"Mostly cutting down trees," Gina said. "Grading. Cutting new trails, clearing old ones, that kind of thing." Gina knew what was troubling Maria but couldn't think of anything to say. Patsy was still in the bootlegging business, working with Mike and Lottie and Vince's gang in the city and Jack Diamond upstate—and things had gotten rougher with Vince locked up. A week earlier, Patsy had shown up with a gash on his thigh where he'd been grazed by a bullet. "Loretto's got to be careful," Gina said. "He shows his face in a speakeasy, he's likely to get himself killed."

"But nobody's coming after him," Maria said. "They're leaving him alone, right?"

"For the time being," Gina said, and then suddenly she was as worried as Maria.

After a while, Maria said, "I heard Sally went to live with her grandparents. Someplace in Minnesota."

Gina had heard the same thing from Mike. He'd spent Thanksgiving with the family. "Mike thinks Frank was supporting her and her mother. Without him around to pay the bills . . ."

"She was sweet enough," Maria said and then turned to Gina with wide eyes. "But dumb?"

Gina laughed and said, "Probably best for her, going back to the sticks."

Maria said, "I should be leaving."

"Take some cookies with you." Gina started for the kitchen. "I'll wrap some in wax paper."

"Nah." Maria placed a hand on the flat of her belly. "I got to keep my figure." She went to the closet to retrieve her coat and hat.

In the kitchen, wrapping a half-dozen cookies, Gina said, "You've got a figure would make Fay Wray jealous."

"Patsy's always saying I look like her." Maria slipped into her coat. "I tell him, flattery will get him everywhere."

"That coat is so darling." Gina met Maria at the door, handed her the cookies, then took her by the shoulders and looked over her full-length black wool coat with white fur collar and cuffs.

"Patsy got it for me." Maria extended her arms and turned a full circle.

"You're gorgeous," Gina said. "Patsy's lucky."

"I know!" Maria gave Gina a hug, kissed her on the cheek, and then hesitated before leaving, as if debating what she was about to say. Finally she spit out, "I hope Vince gets convicted. I know he's one of the boys, but, I'm sorry—if he gets convicted, I feel like I can get Patsy out of it."

"I wouldn't be so sure."

"But I am," Maria insisted. "They're all scared of Vince. With Vince out of the picture, we could make a new start, me and Patsy. I'm sure of it, Gina."

"And your husband?"

"I'll divorce him. I've already seen a lawyer. He says between the prostitutes and his never being home, it'll be easy."

Gina took Maria by the hands. "Vince deserves to get the chair for killing the Vengelli boy, and if he gets out, I'm worried about what he might do to Loretto."

"And there's your brother Mike," Maria added. "Maybe without Vince around . . ."

"I don't think so," Gina said. "I think Mike likes being a big shot too much."

"Anyway," Maria started to open the door, "probably we shouldn't repeat this to anyone, even Patsy or Loretto."

Gina agreed. "The boys," she said.

"Sure," Maria added before leaving, "the whole dumb lot of 'em." She gave Gina another hug before pulling the door closed.

Gina went to the window and waited until she saw Maria on the street. She watched her walk to the corner, get into her car, and drive away. This was one of the many times she wished she could afford a phone so she could call Loretto and check up on him. She wondered how he did at work. He wasn't used to hard physical labor, and she guessed he'd be in need of a long, hot bath. She considered pulling the Epsom salt down from the cupboard and bringing it to him—but Mama had Epsom salt, and she'd probably had a hot bath waiting for him as soon as he got in from work. Gina shook her head at the thought of it: Loretto in Mama's house, eating dinner with Freddie and Augie while Mama worked at the stove or put up coffee for them. Truth was, she wished she was there—but they wanted her at the theater in the morning to help with the cleanup, so she found the latest copy of *Vogue* in the kitchen, where she'd left a story about Joan Crawford half read when she'd started baking cookies for Maria's visit. She took the magazine into the living room and flopped down on the couch with it. She'd read till she fell asleep, and she'd see Loretto tomorrow.

10:30 p.m.

On the toilet seat, next to an empty whiskey glass, a picture of Lottie and Vince floated over a *Mirror* story about Vince's upcoming trial. Lottie in the picture was holding a handkerchief to her mouth and Vince had the collar of his coat turned up to hide his face. In the bathtub next to the toilet, Lottie's head alone was visible, the rest of her hidden under foamy dunes of bubbles. She'd been sipping bourbon most of the evening, hoping to bring herself around to a place where she might be able to fall asleep. Since Frank and Tuffy had been sentenced to the chair, she hadn't slept more than a couple of hours at a time. She was staying in Florence's dump of an apartment while Florence was with Joe upstate, where Joe was working with Diamond's boys. Three times a week she'd visit Vince in the Tombs, let him know what was going on outside, and then bring word of what he said back to Mike and Patsy, who were busy making a mess of things while Vince was in jail. By the time she'd settled in her bubble bath with the *Mirror*, all the bourbon had managed to do was give her a headache, and now she lay in the bath with her head on the porcelain rim, looking up at a cracked plaster ceiling.

Earlier in the day she had called Jake's mother to check on Klara, and the witch wouldn't even put her on the phone. She said Klara didn't need to be hearing from Lottie, what with all the publicity. Leave her out of it, she said. Leave her be. What if the newspapers found out about Klara? What if Vince's enemies found out about her? And on and on until Lottie relented and hung up the phone.

Now, in the bath, she tried to put Klara out of her mind. She was always putting Klara out of her mind. It bothered her too much to dwell on. She saw Vince in his miserable cell at the Tombs and her in Florence's squalid apartment and all she wanted was for Vince to get out. Diamond's upstate organization was still ripe for the taking. Dutch Schultz was a pig and no match for Vince once Vince had the foothold he needed. That was how Lottie saw it, saw the whole situation. All they needed was a foothold and they'd climb over everybody to the top, and then things would work out with Klara, the hell with that witch telling Lottie what was best for her own daughter. She closed her eyes. The apartment was quiet and the heat from the bath water was soothing, as was the lemony fragrance of the bubbles—

and then just when she felt a hint of sleep coming on, there was a noise at the door and she sat up quick and alert and reached for the little snubnose on the toilet seat, under the newspaper.

From the front of the apartment, Lottie heard the lock turn followed by the opening and closing of the door. She figured it had to be either Patsy or Mike, since they both had keys, but she waited silently until Mike called out her name, and then she answered and said she was in the bath and would be right out. She put the pistol back on the toilet seat. A second later, Mike opened the bathroom door and walked in on her. He watched her from the doorway, looking cocky in a new tweed suit with his tie loosened, the scar over his eyebrow like a tough-guy badge.

"What do you think you're doing?" Lottie sank down deeper under the bubbles.

Mike glanced at the gun resting on top of the *Mirror*. "What are you gonna do, shoot me?"

"I'm not," Lottie said, "but Vince might if I tell him you're barging in on me in the bath."

"Yeah?" Mike sat on the edge of the bathtub and played with the bubbles. "I wouldn't be so sure about that."

"What's that supposed to mean?"

Mike's only answer was a smirk. He took Lottie's robe from the back of the bathroom door and held it up for her. "Come on, get out," he said. "We need to talk."

"In a pig's eye," Lottie said. "Put the robe back and get out of here. I'll be out in a minute."

When Mike shook his head, Lottie snatched the pistol from the toilet seat and cocked the hammer.

Mike winked at her, a big smile on his face. In leaning out of the tub to grab the pistol, Lottie had exposed herself from the waist up. "Vince has good taste," he said. He took his time putting the robe back on the door. "We'll talk in the kitchen. We got a problem." When he exited the bathroom, he left the door open behind him.

Lottie got out of the tub, slammed the door closed, and put on her silk pajamas. She took the robe down, slipped it on over the pajamas, and dropped the snubnose into a pocket. In the kitchen, she found Mike seated at the table with his chair pushed back and his legs stretched out. She sat across from him. "What's the big idea?" she said. "I thought you were Vince's friend."

"Listen," Mike said, "we got trouble with that big Polack, Jablonski. Some of Madden's boys came around to see him."

"So now he doesn't want to pay us," Lottie said.

"Or buy our hooch." Mike tapped a cigarette out of his pack and lit up. He offered one to Lottie and she took it.

Lottie tapped the cigarette on the table. "You need to convince him otherwise," she said. "Isn't that what you do?"

"Two of Madden's guys were sitting at the bar. They were both heeled." Mike went to the sink and brought back a cut-glass ashtray. He put it on the table between them and lit Lottie's cigarette for her.

"Where's Patsy?"

"He's with Maria at her place."

"So go get him and go back."

"Nah," Mike said. "Me and Patsy's not enough. We need one more guy, at least, to hold a gun on the place while we take care of Big Owney's men."

"Jesus." Lottie blew a line of smoke up to the ceiling. "You can't find some mug looking to make a buck for a couple of hours' work? It's the depression, ain't it?"

"Not this kind of work. We need somebody knows what he's doing and we can trust."

"You know what?" Lottie tapped ashes off her cigarette into the ashtray. "I think it's time Loretto's little vacation came to an end."

"Yeah?" Mike cocked his head, like Lottie might have a point. "Vince won't like it," he said. "He doesn't trust Loretto. He said to leave him be till he got out."

"I'll square it with Vince," Lottie said. "We need him."

"My brothers are watchin' out for him," Mike added, noting another problem with the idea.

"We got to have Jablonski and his speaks," Lottie said, "if there's gonna be anything left for Vince to salvage when he gets out."

Mike pulled his chair closer to the table. "You considered yet what to do if Vince don't get off?"

"No, I haven't given it a thought. I'm telling you, he's getting off."

"That's what Frank and Tuffy thought."

"That's not Vince." Lottie tapped the end of her cigarette against the ashtray so hard that the burning head fell off. "They had witnesses against Frank and Tuffy."

"Word is they got a witness seen Vince shoot the Vengelli kid."

"Who?" Lottie bent to the ashtray and relit her cigarette off the burning head of ash. "Vince says this witness talk is a bunch of palaver. He says there's no one can positively identify him."

"Listen," Mike said, "all I'm saying is, hypothetical: if we've got to go it without Vince, that don't change the way things are with Diamond. He's still weak. The mug's hanging on by his teeth."

"Jesus," Lottie said, "you'd think we'd all learn by now not to underestimate that guy." The way she said it, though, acknowledged Mike's point. Diamond was weak. It was exactly what she'd been saying all along. Diamond's organization: that was the foothold they needed.

"Just think about it," Mike said. "All I'm sayin' is, we need a backup plan. That's all." He picked up his hat from where he'd left it on the kitchen counter, blocked it, and put it on.

"Are you getting Loretto?"

"I got to get him past my brothers first."

"I'm sure you can manage it." Lottie got up and maneuvered around the table to open the kitchen door. "Listen, Mike," she said when he was halfway out of the apartment, "I'm Vince's woman, and Vince is my guy."

"Yeah?" Mike said. "Are you sure?"

"I just told you, didn't I?"

"I think you're your own woman," Mike said, and he winked at her. "I think you'll do whatever the smart thing is—for you."

Lottie said, "What do you think you know about me?"

"Enough," Mike answered, and he pulled the door closed.

11:45 p.m.

Loretto woke to the sound of someone coming up the stairs. He'd been mostly awake anyway, stretched out on the couch under a pile of blankets, watching the ceiling, the muscles in his arms and legs sore from a day spent dragging cut-up tree limbs and piles of brush from trails to waiting trucks. In Mama's bedroom, the steady rhythm of her snoring rose up and punctuated the silence. From Augie and Freddie's room, nothing. Gina was right. They slept like the dead.

It was late for someone to be coming up the stairs, and Loretto listened with his whole body, leaning into the soft footfall. Whoever was on the stairs, he was making an effort to be quiet. When the footsteps stopped at their landing, Loretto retrieved his gun from under the couch cushions and tiptoed into the kitchen. He was in his boxers and undershirt, and he shivered a little in the cold. When he didn't hear any more noises from the landing, he considered the possibility that he'd been mistaken, that what he had thought were footsteps on the stairs were something else, some other set of sounds. He considered it for a second and then overruled it. With the gun in his right hand, he moved to open the door with his left—but before he even touched the doorknob, a key was slipped into the lock and the door opened on Mike Baronti, who looked at the gun first and then at Loretto. He put one finger to his lips, telling Loretto to be quiet, and then whispered, "Get dressed and meet me on the street."

Loretto checked the door to Mama's bedroom, and when he turned back to the landing, Mike was already on his way down the stairs. He went back to the couch, got dressed as quietly as he could manage, and then left the apartment, taking care to be sure the door was closed and locked behind him. He'd taken his gun. It was in the pocket of his overcoat. In the dimly lit space between the bottom of the stairs and the building's front door, Mike was waiting, leaning against the wall with his feet crossed and one hand in his pants pocket. Loretto opened his hands in a gesture that posed the obvious question: *What's this all about?* Mike opened the door for him, and once they were out of the building, he said, "We need you for a job." He pointed across the street, where Patsy was waiting behind the wheel of a new Chevy.

"What kind of a job?" Loretto asked, though he didn't hesitate to follow Mike to the car. "And why do you need me?"

"We're short-handed." He opened the back door for Loretto, as if he were the chauffeur, before he got in himself beside Patsy.

Patsy twisted around and leaned over the seat to slap Loretto on the shoulder. "How you been? You look good."

Mike said, "Come on, drive," and Patsy started the car and drove off.

"Where we going?" Loretto leaned over the backrest into the front seat. "What's the big deal?"

Mike reached under the seat and came up with a .45 automatic. He handed it to Loretto.

Loretto placed it on the floor beside him. "What do I need that for? Where we going?"

"One of Jablonski's speaks." Mike took a blackjack out of his coat pocket and tested the heft of it. "He's forgotten who to pay off. We need to remind him."

"You need me for that?"

Patsy said, "It's a little more complicated."

"And how's that?"

"Big Owney's got a couple of his boys on the premises."

Mike said, "They're meant to persuade us to stay away."

"Yeah? So? What's your plan? You want to go in there and shoot it out?"

Mike twisted around to face Loretto. "You don't have to do nothin' but look tough. Patsy and me will take care of Big Owney's boys."

"What's the angle?"

"Don't know yet," Mike said. "We'll figure it out once we're there."

"So how come the big change?" Loretto asked. "I was under the impression I wasn't on Vince's invite list anymore."

"You're not," Mike said.

"Yeah? So? What am I doing here?"

"Like I said, we're short-handed."

Patsy slowed down for a red light, checked for cars, and then ran it. Outside, the weather was clear and cold, with a crust of grimy snow along the sidewalks, the lingering remains of the last storm.

"Does Vince know you're bringing me in on this?" Loretto asked Mike.

"Nah," Mike said. "I don't think he'd like it."

"So you're calling the shots now?"

"When I need to."

Patsy seemed surprised to hear this piece of news. "Lottie's gonna square it with Vince," he said. "Ain't that right, Mike?"

"That's right." Mike turned to Loretto. "Like I said. We need you."

"I get it," Loretto said, "but where do I stand with Vince? That's what I want to know."

"I already told you." Mike sounded like he was getting annoyed. "Vince ain't saying nothing, but he told us to leave you out of things. If I was you, that'd make me worry."

Patsy said, "If Lottie squares this with Vince, and you do some more jobs with us—maybe that'll calm him down."

"Do you think he believes me that I was sick that night?"

"Yeah, food poisoning," Mike said, like he didn't believe it.

Patsy said, "Here we are, boys," and he pulled over outside a line of shops with windows that looked out onto the street.

Mike said to Loretto, "Forget about Vince for now. Come here." He gestured for Loretto to lean over the backrest as he drew a diagram with his finger on the car seat. "The bar's at the back of the room, like this . . ." He drew a line indicating the curvature of the bar. "Big Owney's boys were sitting on this end when I came by before." He indicated where the men were sitting. "Right behind them, there's a curtain into a back room."

"Sure," Patsy said, "but that don't mean they'll be sitting there now."

"Yeah, I know," Mike said. He looked like he was thinking things over as he opened his door and gestured for Loretto and Patsy to follow. At the back of the car, he popped up the trunk, checked the street to see if anyone was watching, took a pump-action shotgun out from under a blanket, and handed it to Loretto. "You got that .45 I just gave you?"

Loretto patted the back of his coat, where he had the .45 tucked into his pants.

Mike said, "What's it doing back there?"

Loretto said, "I figure better to blow my ass off than my balls."

"Very funny. Look," Mike glanced at the door to the speak, which was in between a stationery store and a grocery shop. "Give me and Patsy time to go around back; then come in the front and blast a hole in the ceiling. While everybody's scurrying around like rats looking for a sewer, me and Patsy'll come in from the back and take care of Big Owney's torpedoes."

Loretto said, "What do you want me to do if they start taking shots at me?"

"Do what you gotta do," Mike said, "but they ain't gonna want to get themselves killed looking after Jablonski."

"You know who they are?" Patsy asked.

"They didn't look too tough to me," Mike said. "Probably a couple of out-of-work Joes that Madden picked up off the street."

"Shouldn't be nothin' to it, then," Patsy said to Loretto.

Loretto hid the shotgun under the flap of his overcoat and waited in the shadows of the stationery store while Patsy and Mike went through an alley to the back of the building. His arms and legs felt light and a little shaky. He took a deep breath and let it out slow. Gina was in the back of his mind. She'd be furious if she knew he was here. He checked the street. A block of stores and shops, only the speak to draw a late-night crowd. Everyone else asleep on a work night. He felt like he could hear the slightest sound: if someone dropped a fork in a second-floor apartment a block away, he'd hear it and see it in his mind's eye.

Chances he'd get shot were slim: he was the one with a shotgun in hand and a .45 tucked under his belt. He checked his wristwatch. He wanted to give them plenty of time to get into the back room. Chances he'd have to shoot someone were also slim. Mike was right. They wouldn't want to get themselves killed. But chances were excellent that if someone recognized him, he'd be getting another visit from Cabo's boys, or Luciano's, or maybe Madden's. Since Vince was in jail, Loretto was out of the picture and the big boys had Vince's trial on their minds, not him, not Loretto—but if word got out that he was in the action again, working for Vince, then the story might be different. Then he might get another visit. He was thinking about this and about Gina and about a dozen other things all at the same time so that the effect was that he wasn't really thinking about anything at all, just a buzz of thoughts rattling around, bouncing off each other. Had there been a single night since Cabo's boys pointed those cannons at his head that he hadn't thought about them, about that moment? He doubted it. His thoughts at that moment were like his thoughts now: not so much thoughts at all as a buzz, a circus of little pieces of thoughts soaring on a trapeze behind his eyes. Gina would be furious, and, still, part of him liked this feeling. Part of him liked it, part of him was scared, part of him knew what he was doing, part of him didn't. And then he moved to the speak door, knocked, and when it opened an inch kicked it open the rest of the way. He punched the air out of a skinny doorman by hitting him hard just under the ribs with the butt of the shotgun, and then found himself striding into a barroom with maybe a half-dozen patrons seated around tables and four or five men at the bar, including the bartender. "Gentlemen," he said, and he pulled the trigger, blasting a crystal chandelier to pieces, the room suddenly full of glass and dust.

The men at the bar and at the tables all dove for the floor. Patsy and Mike came out of the back room, through a bead curtain, and had to get down on the floor to collar Madden's boys. Mike clocked them both with the blackjack, took their guns from them, left them sprawled out on the straw-covered floor. Patsy grabbed the bartender and pulled him into the back room, and Mike used the guns he'd just taken from Madden's boys to blast away at the shelves of liquor behind the bar, liquor and glass flying everywhere. What patrons there were left in the bar crawled or ran out the door and disappeared. One guy scuttled like a crab, his eyes on Loretto, his hand dangling to the ground as if ready at any instant to drop, leap, or run. Thirty seconds after Loretto shot the chandelier dead, he was alone in the barroom, the shotgun aimed at the exit as he backed up through the bead curtain and found Patsy behind the bartender, holding him by the arms. The guy was older, maybe in his forties, wearing a long white apron that tied around his waist and a striped red vest over a white dress shirt with a black bow tie. Mike stood in front of him, holding a bottle of wine. The bartender's lip was bleeding, nothing much, as if maybe he'd been smacked.

Mike said, "This is a good bottle of wine." He showed it to Patsy.

Patsy said, "I never been a big wine expert. Looks like a bottle of wine."

"No," Mike said, "this is an expensive wine." He asked the bartender,

"What do you get for this? Twenty bucks?" When the bartender started to answer, Mike threw the bottle into the wall, shattering it. He picked up what remained by the neck, sniffed it, said, "Nice bouquet," and slashed the bartender's face, gashing his cheek and mouth before tossing the bottle away. The guy screamed, shrill and loud, and Mike shoved a dishrag into his mouth. He held it there roughly until the screaming stopped. When the room was quiet, he removed the dishrag and blotted blood from the bartender's face and then pressed it against the gashed cheek to slow the bleeding. "I don't really care how much it costs," he said. "The point is, it's not our wine. We didn't sell it to you." He leaned toward the bartender, his expression asking the question, *Do you understand?*

The bartender nodded. He was shaking and crying, and his tears drew lines in the blood on his face.

"Good," Mike said. "You tell Mr. Jablonski that I'll be around again." He gestured toward Loretto. "Me and my friend here who doesn't like crystal chandeliers. Tell him we'd like to talk to him, put everything back in order the way it was. Right?"

The bartender nodded, and Mike said, "You're a lucky man, friend. 'Cause if this was Vince Coll here tonight instead of me . . . Trust me," he said, "you're a lucky man."

Patsy said, "Tell Jablonski that when Vince gets out, he's gonna want to talk to him, too." He let the bartender loose and then held him by the shoulders until he felt sure he wouldn't fall when he let him go.

Once they were all back in the car, Patsy said, "The mug'll keep that scar for the rest of his life."

Mike said, "Least he's not blind," reminding Patsy of what Vince did to Joe Rock.

"That's something," Patsy said, and then the car was quiet for the rest of the ride.

When they dropped Loretto off, Mike got out of the car with him. The street was empty and dark, and he and Loretto stood in the center of it.

Mike looked up at the windows of his mother's apartment. "Listen," he said, "I'll leave you out of it, 'cept when we have to."

"Have to what?" Loretto took a cigarette from his jacket pocket and lit up.

"When we need another guy we can trust," Mike said, and he followed Loretto's lead and lit up. Behind them, Patsy slid over into the passenger seat, rolled down the car window, and leaned out to the street as if he wanted to join the conversation.

"Maybe Lottie can straighten things out for you," Mike said, "maybe not."

"And if she can't?"

"You might be able to hide out from Dutch and them, but not from Vince."

"It'd be nice to know beforehand," Loretto said, "if there was trouble coming my way."

Mike looked back to Patsy, who rolled up the window and slid back behind the wheel.

"Yeah," Mike said, and though he said it very softly, the meaning was clear. He'd look out for Loretto. He asked, "How's Freddie?"

"He's doing good," Loretto said. "Real good."

Mike patted Loretto on the arm. "I'll be in touch when we need you." He looked up once more at the windows of the apartment where he'd grown up and then got back in the car and drove off with Patsy.

Alone on the street, Loretto sat on the stoop to finish his cigarette. He ran his fingers through his hair, felt a sharp prick, and his hand came away bloody. Embedded in the soft skin of his forefinger, a half-inch-long sliver of glass drew blood like a tiny straw, sucking it out along its brief length to the end, where drops quickly formed and fell away. He pulled the sliver out, tossed it to the street, and held his hand over the edge of the steps, where the grit and dirt soaked up the blood dripping from his finger. He looked to the sky, found a dark smudge of clouds, and closed his eyes. He thought about the shotgun blast and the chandelier exploding as everyone scurried away from him, as if he were the wrath of God; and then, a moment later, he was back in the basement of Gaspar's house, looking down into the wine cellar. He seemed to see it more clearly now in his mind's eye than he had at the time. He saw the rough dirt wall and the dark circles of the wine bottles where they penetrated the walls, the circles of the bottles in the circle of the wine cellar and Gaspar and Dominic wedged into the center of the circle looking up at him, Gaspar with smears of blood across his face and a thick black clot of blood at the corner of his mouth, as if his bottom lip might have been ripped, Dominic with one eye swollen closed, an ugly mess of yellows and blues, the other eye clear and untouched, open and looking up out of the wine cellar as if watching for something or someone, as if waiting.

Loretto stubbed out his cigarette, checked his hand to see that the bleeding had stopped, and wrapped the cut finger with his handkerchief. He guessed the bartender was in a hospital room somewhere by now, getting his face stitched up. He was tired. He pulled himself to his feet and started back up the stairs. He tried to be as quiet as he could. He hoped to slip back into Mama's house unseen.

1:00 p.m.

O n the first day of the trial, Lottie found that watching the proceedings made her nervous to the point of sickness. Strenburg, one of Vince's lawyers, had arranged a seat for her in the balcony, close to the door, so she could go in and out without making a fuss, though she had to leave her coat and get the guy next to her to guard it or else she wouldn't have a seat when she got back. The courthouse was packed. Coppers every ten feet out in the hall, and it seemed like half the city took off from work to be at the big show. From where Lottie sat, she could see the first few rows of spectators huddled shoulder to shoulder on long benches like church pews that were separated by an aisle where a couple of coppers stood with their hands folded in front of them, watching the proceedings. On the other side of the railing from the spectators, Vince and Frank sat at a table with Strenburg on their left and Leibowitz on their right.

Neary, the prosecuting attorney, had just told the jury he had an eyewitness to the murder of Michael Vengelli and that he would prove beyond a doubt that Vince Coll was the murderer and that nothing less than a conviction for murder in the first degree would serve justice. With Neary's demand for a first-degree murder conviction, Lottie's stomach had cramped and a swell of nausea had threatened to remove her from the courtroom. Now, as Leibowitz rose from the defendant's table to address the jury, she took one of Vince's handkerchiefs from her handbag and tried to pat a sheen of sweat from her face without ruining her makeup. She wanted to be there for Leibowitz's opening remarks to the jury but lasted only long enough to hear him insist that the whole case against Vince was a fabrication invented by unscrupulous individuals more interested in the state's thirty-thousand-dollar reward than in justice. Before the balcony's padded swinging door closed behind her, she heard Leibowitz tell the judge and jury that he would prove beyond a doubt that Vince was hundreds of miles from the scene of the crime on the day the poor Vengelli child was murdered. A minute later she was in the ladies' room, on her knees in front of a porcelain john, vomiting up her lunch. Behind her, a lady copper, the same one who had been keeping an eye on her all day, knocked on the stall door and asked if she was okay. Lottie said, "Give a girl a little privacy, will you, hon?" and then waited for the sound of retreating footsteps and the door closing before she pulled herself up and took a seat on the commode.

Jack had agreed to testify that Vince was with him in Albany at the time of the Vengelli child's murder, but Leibowitz was worried that Jack Diamond would hardly make an unimpeachable witness, given he was currently on trial himself for kidnapping and torture—again. Diamond had come up with the idea of having Shorty go along with him, saying he was with Jack and Vince at the time of the murder. Shorty had no rap sheet at all: he'd been a professional athlete who'd played for the New York Giants. Leibowitz figured between Shorty and Jack, they'd have just what they needed, a believable alibi that would leave the jury in doubt of Vince's guilt. Frank didn't need an alibi: he'd already been convicted and sentenced to the chair for the murder of Joe Mullins; but if Vince got off, so did Frank, not that it mattered much to him.

Lottie straightened herself up as best she could and then went to the sink and washed her face. She knew that Leibowitz planned to make the police look like bad guys who were harassing Vince and maybe even in league with Vince's enemies in the bootlegging business, and while it all sounded fine as Vince explained it to her, her confidence fell apart when she heard Neary addressing the jury and telling them he had an eyewitness. Would the jury believe a couple of bootleggers like Jack and Vince or this mystery witness? The way Lottie saw things, it all came down to the witness, whom the coppers were doing a good job of keeping under wraps. No one knew anything about the guy. Whenever she told Vince that she was worried about the outcome of the trial, he reminded her that Al Capone beat a mug to death in a crowded bar, and Leibowitz had gotten him off.

Lottie put her purse down on the edge of the sink and went about reapplying makeup. Leibowitz had issued an official communiqué from Vince and all the papers had printed it. It was supposed to be in Vince's own words, but Leibowitz had told him what to say and Lottie had helped him write it. She had a copy torn from the *Daily News* in her purse. She stopped what she was doing, found the scrap of newsprint, and reread it for the fiftieth time:

I would like nothing more than to lay my hands on the man who did this—I would tear his throat out. There is nothing more despicable than a man who would harm an innocent child. So far as I am concerned, I am not afraid of the outcome. I can prove I was miles away when this crime was committed. It is a frame-up on the part of my enemies, who have tried many times to assassinate me and have failed. Now they are trying to bring about my death through the law.

When she was finished reading, she folded the paper carefully, placed it back in her purse, and went about applying lipstick. Reading the statement made her feel better. It was almost as if because it was written and printed in a newspaper, it must be true. When she read it, she half believed it herself.

By the time Lottie returned to the courtroom balcony, a cute little girl was on the witness stand. Lottie took her seat and folded her coat in her lap while below her a court attendant rolled a bullet-riddled baby carriage up the courthouse aisle, past the spectators, and toward the bench. The crowd gasped at the sight of the carriage, the way it was torn apart by bullets. Lottie, only seconds after retaking her seat, felt a combination of nausea and jitters coming over her. She tried to settle herself by focusing on Vince and how handsome he was in his new sky-blue suit. He seemed calm and attentive, seated quietly with his hands folded on the table, his eyes on the witness stand. For a moment, Lottie thought she might be able to pull herself together, but then Neary pointed at Vince and asked the girl if she recognized him, and Lottie found herself rising from her seat and pushing through the padded doors. The girl had said "No" almost immediately, but it didn't help. Lottie started down the stairs and toward the street. She needed air. She needed the cold on her skin and to move fast along the street, around the block, to keep walking, to walk off the jitters, to walk until she could take a normal breath. Her stomach was empty, so maybe after the walk she'd try to get a bite to eat. Maybe then she'd be able to return to the courtroom.

8:00 p.m.

At the Barontis', the apartment's windows were black and fringed with frost, and everyone except Mama was in the living room reading newspapers and drinking coffee. Mama was at the kitchen table kneading a lump of dough, the table surface powdered with flour. Every once in a while she'd pick up the dough and hurl it down at the table like she meant to do it harm and a dust of powder would leap up. In the living room, Augie tossed his paper away and picked up his coffee. He had kicked off his shoes and was sitting on one end of the couch with legs outstretched. He held the coffee cup and saucer at his chest. Freddie was at the other end of the couch reading the *Mirror*, and Gina and Loretto were seated side by side in a pair of chairs by the window. Gina was reading the *Post*, and Loretto was reading over her shoulder.

Augie said, "You think those kids can't identify anybody, or you think they're scared?" He was talking to Loretto, but Freddie dropped the *Mirror* to his belly and said, "What are they gonna do? Give Frank the electric chair twice?"

From the kitchen, Mama yelled, "I don't want talk about no electric chair! Go someplace else!"

"Jeez . . ." Freddie went back to reading the paper, and Augie lit up a cigarette.

"Hey, Ma!" Gina yelled. "I forgot to tell you. Mrs. Esposito upstairs, she asked you to come see her for a minute."

"When?"

"Now. I forgot."

"What's'a matter with her?"

"How do I know, Ma? She asked you to come up!"

"*Madon'!*" Mama clapped the flour off her hands, straightened out her housedress, and left the apartment.

Once Mama was out the door, Gina exchanged a look with Augie. She put her hand on Loretto's knee. "Freddie," she said, and then waited a moment until Freddie lowered the paper.

"What is it?" Freddie folded the newspaper and dropped it in his lap.

"It's Pop," Gina said. "Mama heard from the hospital today. He doesn't have long."

"What's wrong with him?" Loretto asked.

"Cancer," Gina said.

Augie patted his chest. "The lungs," he said to Loretto.

Freddie put the paper down on the couch beside him. "That's why Mama's upset. Nobody tells me?"

"We're telling you now," Augie said.

"Mike's coming," Gina said, and then, as if on cue, the kitchen door opened and Mike came in wearing sleek black leather gloves, a handsome black overcoat, and a white cashmere scarf.

"I can only stay a few minutes," Mike said. "I got people waitin' in the car."

"Big shot," Gina said.

"Don't start." Mike sat on the arm of the couch next to Freddie. "You asked me to come, I'm here. What are we doing about Pop?" He put a hand on Freddie's shoulder but directed his question to Augie.

Freddie said, "First I'm hearing about any of this."

Gina said, "You knew he was sick, Freddie."

"Yeah, but I thought he was doing better."

"He was in remission before," Augie said. "Now . . ."

"Now he's dying," Mike said. "Forgive me, but what? I'm supposed to cry?" To Gina he said, "You're shedding tears?"

Gina didn't answer. She took her hand from Loretto's knee and looked out toward the kitchen, as if by looking away she was removing herself from the scene.

Augie said, "The point is, in a few days, a couple of weeks at most, we'll have to arrange the funeral—and Mama wants us all together."

"So what's wrong with that?" Freddie said. "Why shouldn't we all be together for the funeral? We're his family, aren't we?"

"Ask your sister what's wrong with it," Mike said. "What do you say, Gina?"

"If it's what Mama wants . . ." Gina's voice was soft and distant, like she was talking to everybody and no one.

Freddie said, "Hey, Gina," and then his eyes got watery and he looked down at the floor and was quiet, gathering himself. A few seconds passed. He said, "I'm sorry, Gina. I wasn't thinking. Whatever you say. If you don't want to go to his funeral . . . I'll go along with whatever you say."

"Me, too," Augie said.

Gina said, "No. I'll go. Mama wants us all together. I won't disappoint her. We'll all do our part," she said as if finalizing the decision for all of them.

Mike said, "You're a bigger man than me. What he did . . . I'd spit on his grave."

Before Mike finished speaking, Gina got up and left the room. The boys looked at each other and then to Loretto. Mike said, "I got to go."

"Wait a second," Loretto said to Mike. "I want to talk to you, but let me . . ." he gestured toward the back room, where Gina must have retreated.

"I'll meet you outside," Mike said. "Don't be too long."

Loretto found Gina sitting on Freddie's bed, looking out through a circle in the window where she had wiped away the condensation. He sat beside her. "How come you never told me your father was sick?"

"You notice me talking about my father much?"

"No," Loretto said. "I take your point, but—"

"I can't," Gina said, cutting Loretto off. "I can't talk about him. I'm sorry."

In the kitchen, the sink groaned, and then the radio came on with Jack Benny's familiar voice talking about something or other followed by radio laughter. Loretto put his hand on Gina's back. He half expected her to pull away; instead, she leaned in to him and rested her head on his shoulder. "I should go," she said. "They need me at the theater again in the morning."

"Wait before you go. Let me talk to Mike a minute, and then I'll come back and walk you out."

"All right," Gina said. "I'll go get Mama. Mrs. Esposito'll keep her up there till the second coming if I don't get her."

Loretto kissed her again and then retrieved his overcoat from the ladder to the roof, where he had hung it earlier.

Gina shook her arms as if they had fallen asleep. "Don't be too long," she said. "What do you want to talk to Mike about anyway?"

"I want to know what he hears from Vince." Loretto buttoned up his coat and pulled a pair of gloves from the pocket. "Mike'll be talking to Lottie, and Lottie's talking to Vince and his lawyers, so . . ."

"So what?" Gina straightened out Loretto's coat, grasping it by the lapels. She kissed him on the lips. "What's it matter to you what's going on with Vince?"

"Bunch of things," Loretto said. "I still don't know where I stand with him."

"Won't make any difference long as he's locked up, will it?"

"I don't know." Loretto pulled his gloves on. "It's still a mess, my whole situation."

"Sure," Gina said, "but without Vince in the picture, that's at least something."

"I don't know about that." Loretto kissed Gina on the forehead. "I got to go," he said. "Mike said not to keep him waitin'."

"All right," Gina said. "Go on. Don't keep the big deal waitin'."

Outside, on the street, Loretto found Mike alone in the driver's seat of a new Packard Speedster. He got in beside him. "Nice car," he said. "I thought you had people waitin'."

"I lied. What's going on?"

On the street, a couple of teenage boys were hurrying along shoulder to shoulder, huddling close to each other in the cold. "Look," Loretto said, "Gina doesn't know anything about me still doing jobs now and then with you and Patsy. If she finds out, it's gonna be bad for me."

"Yeah? And so?" Mike looked annoyed, like Loretto was wasting his time.

"I guess I want to know what's going on. Things don't look good for Vince. What'll happen if it goes for him like it went for Frank and Tuffy? What'll happen to his business, his speaks and all the rest? Have you thought about that?"

Mike pulled a cigarette from the pack in his pocket and lit up. Loretto did the same.

Mike said, "So what you're really asking is, are you out of it if Vince gets the chair? Ain't that right?"

"I don't want to see Vince get the chair." Loretto rolled down his window a little to let out the smoke. "But, yeah. I can't be in this and with Gina. It won't work. She won't have it."

"Don't be so sure about that."

"I'm sure about it."

"Well, don't be," Mike said, raising his voice.

"Yeah? You taking Vince's place now? You issuing orders?"

"Take it easy," Mike said, and he smiled as if amused by Loretto's anger. "Don't be bustin' a gasket. All I'm sayin' is, Gina's stuck on you. She ain't gonna drop you 'cause she don't like what you're doing for a living."

"I'm saying she will, Mike." Loretto tapped the ash off his cigarette out the window. "She won't have it."

"I know Gina a lot better than you do. She won't like it, but that don't mean she won't put up with it."

"You're wrong about that."

"Well, you got a problem, then, Loretto, 'cause either way, if Vince gets off or he gets the chair, we're still gonna need you."

"See, that's what I'm asking," Loretto said.

"And what would you do anyway?" Mike turned in his seat to face Loretto. "Are you a working stiff now? You breaking your back for fifteen dollars a week?" He pulled a roll of bills from his pocket, peeled off two twenties, and tossed them at Loretto. "Take a couple weeks off. On me."

Loretto gazed at the twenties. For a moment, he was furious. Then he laughed. He stuffed the twenties back in Mike's coat pocket. "I don't know what I'm doing," he said. "Gina's got me crazy."

"Dames." Mike straightened himself out behind the wheel, getting ready to leave. "Listen, Loretto. You're not a working stiff. You don't want to be working like a slave when big money's there for the taking. It's nuts." He started the car.

"What big money are you talking about?"

"I'm talking about Diamond and upstate. If Jack gets sent up, we'll have to move fast if we want to take over his operations. We can't wait to see what happens with Vince."

"Yeah? That sounds like Lottie talking."

"It's me talking." Mike poked a finger at Loretto chest. "If we're doing this, we'll need you. We need the manpower. You're one of us, Loretto. That's the whole story."

"Sure, I'm one of you," Loretto said. He reached for the door handle. "But I'll make up my own mind about what I do or what I don't do."

"Is that what I should tell Vince?"

"Tell him whatever you want." Loretto slid out of the car and walked off toward Dom's Packard without looking back. Behind him, he heard the Speedster pull out into the street and drive off.

It was freezing in the wind but it seemed even colder in Dom's car. Loretto put the key in the ignition, hit the starter—and nothing happened. He rested his head on the steering wheel and wrestled back the desire to find a tire iron and pummel the car till there was nothing left but twisted metal and broken glass. "Dominic," he said aloud, as if Dominic were in the car beside him, smirking.

Loretto wouldn't need the car till the next day, when he had to get to work, but now he knew he'd have to ask Augie and Freddie to help him with a push start in the morning. He tried the ignition once more, and when nothing at all happened, he pulled his coat tight around him and started back to find Gina.

Thursday ••• December 17, 1931

10:15 a.m.

By the second day, Lottie was better able to watch the trial without her nerves getting the better of her. Vince sat at the defendants' table looking like a handsome schoolboy, his hands folded in front of him, his attention focused on the judge or Neary or the detective who was on the witness stand, the short one who'd put a gun to Vince's head and pulled the trigger. Of course that wasn't going to come out, that the little bastard detective, Giovanetti, put a loaded gun to Vince's head. No, because Giovanetti would just deny it and who would believe Mad Dog Coll's word over some straight-arrow son of a bitch detective? Lottie kept her eyes on Vince. She was having a hard time concentrating. Her thoughts kept flying off in different directions. At that moment it was Giovanetti. He was answering questions from Neary and talking about the night he'd arrested Vince at the Cornish Arms, but Lottie was imagining Vince sitting in a bathroom stall with that little bastard holding a loaded gun to his head. Vince had told her the story with a laugh, like it was something funny because he said Giovanetti was more scared by the whole thing than he was, which Lottie could believe. Nothing in the world scared Vince. There were lots of things that made him angry, a million things could throw him into a fury. But scared? No. She'd never seen him scared of anything, not for a second. It was like that part of him was missing, killed off a long time ago. That meant Lottie had to be scared for both of them—and she was, though she did her best not to show it because she'd rather be like Vince, scared of nothing, if she could manage it.

Back when she'd first started seeing Vince on the sly, when she was still with Sam, she was scared of what Sam would do if he found out. In the beginning with Vince it was nothing but a thrill: he was a big-time gang-ster, one of Dutch Schultz's boys, plus he wasn't hard to look at, but then she fell for him the first time they slept together. That was in the Cornish Arms, which was why they kept going back: it was their hotel, it was where they'd made love the first time, and then after, in bed, Lottie got to where she was almost crying, and Vince made her spill it, that she didn't want to be with Sam anymore, that she wanted to be Vince's woman. That was late afternoon and everything in the hotel room was tinged with a reddish light and the red of the hotel windows was reflected in the windows across the avenue so that it was like everything was on fire. She told Vince why she was scared of Sam, because Sam had stabbed Jake in the heart with a bowie knife, killed him like an animal with his hands and a bloody knife.

She hadn't known Vince back then. She hadn't known there was some-thing like a callus where there was supposed to be fear, and all Vince did was look at her, amused by something, and then he told her to wait, not to go anywhere, and he got up and got dressed and left her alone in bed. She thought he'd gone out to get her flowers, to do something nice for her, but forty-five minutes later the phone rang and it was Sam and he was sweet as could be. He said, sure, he understood falling for a tough guy like Vince. He even laughed a little when he said it. *I'll drop out of the picture,* those were his exact words. *You can come by and get your things.* Then he said, *Wait,* and Lottie could hear him talking to someone and when he came back on the line he said, *Listen, I'll move out. You can have the place to yourself.* And after that, Sam was a ghost. One day he was there and then he was gone, left the city, might have left the country for that matter. No one had seen him and not a word from him since—and Vince swore he never laid a finger on him, didn't do a thing but offer him a couple of choices, and Sam chose to disappear.

On the courtroom floor, a wave of murmurs washed over the spectators, and Judge Corrigan banged his gavel to put a stop to it. Behind Lottie, the padded doors opened and Strenburg stepped partway onto the balcony and waved for her to join him. In the hall, he put his arm around her and whispered, "Jack Diamond's been acquitted up in Albany. Verdict's innocent. He's scot-free."

Lottie didn't much like Strenburg, but she clapped her hands to his cheeks and gave him a kiss on the lips.

Strenburg blushed behind a big smile. He was a skinny guy, all rattly bones inside his fancy suit. He pulled himself up straight and winked at Lottie like he was the one to take care of her, nothing to worry about with Strenburg around. "That Diamond's got more lives than a dozen cats," he said, "and isn't that good for us?"

"Sure thing," Lottie said. "Now he can testify with no trouble."

"An innocent man harassed by the coppers," Strenburg said, "just like our boy."

1:45 p.m.

Bo Weinberg tucked a five-dollar bill into the pocket of Lucille's apron and asked her not to seat anyone in the next booth. He was in the Palace Chop House seated next to Dutch and across from Charlie Luciano and Henry LaSalla. "Bring Mr. Schultz a couple of Alka-Seltzer and about this much water in a tall glass." He held his forefinger a half inch from his thumb.

"Smart alec," Dutch said to Bo. He nodded to Lucille, a kid still in her teens. "Yeah, go ahead." When she walked away, he picked up a fat Reuben from his plate, looked at the pink chunks of corned beef like they might be poisoned, and let it drop.

Luciano held a cup of coffee in one hand as if poised to take a sip, a cigarette in his other hand, pinched between two fingers. Beside him, Henry LaSalla might have just rolled out of bed, his eyes were so bleary and his bulbous nose so red and raw and swollen it looked like it had just taken a punch.

"I'll be a son of a bitch," Dutch said. "You'd think Diamond had God Himself in his pocket."

Luciano said, "I heard the judge was putting him away for four years, minimum."

"Well, you heard wrong," Dutch said.

Bo said, "He got to the jury. I know you hate the guy," he said to Dutch, "but you have to admit he's good. Son of a bitch lands on his feet every time."

"I don't have to admit nothin'." Dutch picked up his sandwich and put it down again. "Big Owney's worried," he said to Luciano.

"Yeah, you told me. That's why we're here." Luciano took a drag on his cigarette and tapped the ash off into his saucer. Lucille, the waitress, came back with Dutch's Alka-Seltzer. "Sweetheart," Luciano said to her, "can you bring us an ashtray?" Lucille snatched a couple of ashtrays from the booth behind them. "Sorry, Mr. Luciano."

"That's okay, but be a sweetheart and leave us a little privacy."

"Go on, scram!" Dutch said when Lucille didn't move fast enough.

Lucille scurried away nearly in tears. Bo said to Dutch, "You've got no tact. What do you want to go and yell at the kid for? What'd she do to you?"

"Ain't he sensitive?" Dutch said to Luciano, gesturing to Bo.

"Can we cut out the comedy?" Luciano said. "What's Madden want from me, and why'd you ask me to bring Henry along?"

"Yeah," Henry said. "What am I doing here with you big shots?"

Bo said, "Dutch is thinking, maybe Diamond's feeling lucky, what with getting off when the odds were against him and all."

"So?" Luciano looked to Dutch.

"So," Bo continued, "if he's feeling lucky, maybe he'll let his guard down. We hear he's having a party tonight, celebrating his acquittal."

Luciano said, "I still don't see what that's got to do with me."

"You won't profit with Jack Diamond out of the picture?" Dutch picked up his sandwich and took a bite like the thing was alive and he meant to kill it. "That's what it's got to do with you," he said with his mouth full.

Bo said, "We're thinking me and Henry should take a ride up to Albany tonight, see what we might see, while Jack's still in a party mood."

"Why me?" Henry asked.

"'Cause last Jack heard, you were one of Maranzano's boys. He won't get the picture if he sees you, if he even recognizes you at all."

"But if he sees Bo . . ." Dutch said.

"I don't get it," Henry said to Luciano. "You said this was about the Coll kid."

"It is," Luciano said.

When it appeared no one else was going to do Henry the courtesy of explaining, Bo said, "Madden's worried that Jack'll testify that Coll was with him when the Vengelli kid got it. He'd rather not see that happen."

"Ah," Henry said. "You know your way around Albany?" he asked Bo. "'Cause might as well be Siberia far as I'm concerned."

Bo ignored Henry's question. "How'd you wind up working for Charlie here anyway?" he asked. "Aren't you Castellammarese?"

Then it was Henry's turn to ignore Bo.

Luciano said, answering Bo's question, "We worked it out," and left it at that. He checked his wristwatch. "If that's the way it's gonna be, you boys should get on the road soon as we're finished here."

"We're finished here," Dutch said. He pushed the remains of his sandwich away, dropped the two Alka-Seltzer tablets into a tumbler, and watched them fizz.

"Next time," Luciano said, sliding out of the booth, "let's meet in the city."

Dutch drank down the fizzing water and followed Bo, who was retrieving his overcoat. "Why? I like this place," he said to Luciano. "It's the lap of luxury."

"Yeah, it's the Taj Mahal," Luciano said. He waited for Dutch to join him and they walked out together.

"I get the honor of paying the bill," Bo said to Henry. "You ready to take a ride?"

"Sure." Henry tapped his jacket. "But all I got with me is my peashooter."

"I got what we need in the car," Bo said, and he called for Lucille. "Here you go, honey." He handed her a ten. "Keep the change."

"Is Mr. Schultz mad at me?" Lucille asked.

"Mr. Schultz is mad at everybody," Bo said, and he gestured for Henry to join him as he followed Dutch and Luciano to the door.

1:15 a.m.

B o tilted a half-empty bottle of Seagram's to his lips, downed a searing mouthful, and passed the bottle back to Henry, who did the same. They were parked in the shadows down the block from Packy's, a local speak where Jack and it looked like half of Albany were celebrating his acquittal. Bo recognized some of the figures trooping in and out of the building, including Coll's witchy big sister, Florence, and her husband, Joe—but most he'd never seen before or at least didn't recall. They looked to be a cross-section of Albany's populace, from bums to high society.

"Some party," Henry said. He'd been in and out a few times already. Inside Packy's, Diamond was glad-handing and schmoozing, moving back and forth from the bar to a table where he sat with his wife and his lawyer. He couldn't be gotten to there without risking a massacre.

Bo looked at his wristwatch. "Maybe you should go check again."

"Sure." Henry didn't mind a reprieve from the boredom of sitting in the car and watching the street. He took another pull of the Seagram's, straightened himself out, and exited the car.

Bo watched Henry disappear into Packy's, glanced down at the Seagram's, and screwed the cap on tight. He didn't want to be drunk. Not yet anyway. He was pretty sure he wouldn't be able to get anywhere near

Diamond, but on the off chance he got lucky, he intended to be ready. How many mugs had tried to put Diamond in the ground over the years? Bo himself had put at least two bullets in him: one in the forehead and one in the chest, and Carmine Alberici put three more in him. Five bullets, one in the head, and the son of a bitch recovered and took a cruise to Europe. This was at the Hotel Monticello in 1929. It was early and Jack was in bed with his Kiki dame. The newspapers reported that gangsters burst through the door and sprayed the room with machine-gun fire, but what really happened was that Bo called up from the desk and Jack met them at the door in a fancy white robe, Kiki in bed behind him naked and exposed from the waist up, lying on her back with her eyes closed, her pretty head propped up on a pillow. When Jack saw Bo and Carmine, he said, "Let's go over to my room where we can talk in private." And that was what they did. They left Kiki in bed, went to a room across the hall, and Bo and Carmine filled Jack Diamond full of lead. Bo still remembered what he was thinking when he walked out of the hotel: I just killed Jack Diamond. I put a bullet in his head.

Only it turned out he hadn't killed him. Dutch screamed at Carmine when the news hit that Jack survived: "Ain't there nobody that can shoot this guy so he don't bounce back?" This was the third time Jack had taken multiple bullets and walked away. Bo hadn't killed him in '29, and he doubted he'd get to him tonight, but it was worth a try. It wasn't that he didn't like the son of a bitch. At this point, it was the challenge and the reputation. He'd love to be the guy put an end to Jack Diamond.

When Henry came out onto the street again, he was hurrying. "He ain't there," he told Bo. "He left. Must have gone out a back way."

Bo looked to Packy's and watched a well-dressed couple enter the building. "The party's still hoppin'," he said. "Where'd he go?"

"I asked his bodyguard—"

"Who's his bodyguard?"

"Big guy. Football player. They call him Shorty."

"What'd he say?"

"Nothin'. Asked me why I was askin'."

Bo unscrewed the cap from the Seagram's. "He went out the back with his wife?"

"His wife's still there. You're not lettin' me finish." Henry took a pull from the Seagram's and handed the bottle back to Bo. "I asked the bartender. He tells me Jack went to check on a death threat and he'll be right back."

"A death threat?" Bo took a pull of the Seagram's, gave himself a second to think. "Since when's Jack Diamond run from a death threat?" He tapped his head like he was trying to jog loose an idea. "I don't like this." He retrieved his hat and fit it to his head with the brim down. "Let's go have a talk with this Shorty mug."

"You'll be recognized." Henry went for the Seagram's, but Bo snatched it away.

"I'm not going in." Bo screwed the cap on the Seagram's and stuck it under the seat. "I'll wait in the alley. Bring him out to me."

"What am I gonna tell him?"

"Tell him there's a guy with a message from Big Owney for Jack, but he won't give it to anybody but Jack directly."

"You're the big shot," Henry said. He obviously didn't much like the plan.

Bo glanced to the back seat, where a pair of tommy guns were hidden under a bright red throw. He considered concealing one under his coat and decided against it.

In the alley behind Packy's, a grimy crust of ice and snow lined all but a narrow walking path. A bare lightbulb under a metal half dome over the back door provided more light than was necessary. Bo smashed the bulb with the butt of his pistol and dropped back into the shadows near a couple of galvanized metal trash cans. Henry had gone in the front door. Bo thought about lighting up, decided against it, and then admitted he was a little nervous. That surprised him. He had put down enough men already that it was all business, just the nature of the bootlegger's world and everyone knew it. It was Jack Diamond making him nervous. The mug was as much a celebrity as the president of the United States. You couldn't open a newspaper without seeing a story about him, and the people loved him, probably because he kept getting shot and hauled off to jail and beating the bullets and the rap every time. Or maybe he didn't want to be the guy who killed Jack Diamond. Maybe that's what was bothering him.

When the back door finally opened, a beast of a man walked out into the alley followed by Henry. The big guy had on a raccoon coat.

"You O'Shaughnessy?" Shorty's hands were in his pockets, his shoulders hunched against the cold.

Bo answered by producing a pistol from his coat pocket and placing the barrel under Shorty's chin. "We got a few questions about your boss." He gestured to Henry, who yanked Shorty's hands out of the coat. He searched the pockets before giving Shorty a pat-down and finding a pistol in a hip holster.

Bo pushed him down the alley.

"Where we going?" Shorty went about buttoning his coat as if the cold bothered him more than the guns.

"To have a little talk in my car, where it's nice and quiet." The big mug's face held a look of dull surprise that Bo associated with stupidity. "You're not too bright, are you, Shorty?"

"Bright enough to get by. What do you mugs want with me anyway?"

At the car, Bo opened the passenger door and pushed Shorty across the seat. He got in alongside him while Henry got behind the wheel and started the engine.

"You don't mind if my partner drives while we talk, do you, Shorty?" Bo pressed the barrel of his pistol against Shorty's ribs.

"What do you want to know? I'm no hero," he said. "Jack don't pay me enough to get myself killed on his account. You're Bo Weinberg, aren't you?" he added.

"How'd you know?"

"Seen your picture in the papers with Dutch and what's the other guy's name, the one that's good with numbers."

"Abadabba," Henry said.

"Yeah, him."

"All we want to know," Bo said, "is where to find Jack and who might be with him. Give us the straight dope and we'll let you go. We got no beef with you."

"I don't know where he is, but I can make a pretty good guess."

"And where's that?" Bo asked.

Shorty turned to Henry behind the wheel. "Where are you going?"

"Be damned if I know," Henry answered. "I'm just driving."

"Well, you're heading out of town," Shorty said. "Nothing up this way but farms and woods."

Bo said, "What's that got to do with anything? You worried we're taking you for a ride? Thinkin' we're gonna put one in you out in the sticks?"

"I'm not sayin' it ain't worrying me a little."

"Why would we do that, Shorty?" Bo asked Henry, "Why would we want to harm this big guy?"

"I got nothin' against him," Henry answered.

Shorty said, "I thought it might have something to do with the Vince Coll trial."

"What about it?" Bo was surprised at the mention of the trial.

"I'm supposed to testify that I was with Coll when the Vengelli kid got it last summer. It's an alibi for Coll."

Henry glanced over Shorty to Bo.

"No kiddin'," Bo said. "Well, we don't know nothing about that."

"Good," Shorty said. "So then why don't we turn around and head back into town?"

Bo said, "You haven't told us where we can find Jack yet."

Shorty leaned forward to look out the window. The road was in bad repair, with potholes and long cracks in the pavement. On either side of the car, stands of white pines rose up from a long white beach of trackless snow. The moon was bright enough to cast the skinny shadows of the trees on the snow field. "Nothing out here but woods for miles around," Shorty said. "Woods and old logging trails." When neither Bo nor Henry said anything in reply, Shorty scratched his head. "So why not turn around?" he asked. "Jack's back the other way."

"Yeah?" Bo tapped Shorty's ribs twice with the barrel of his pistol. "Where the other way?"

"If you're gonna kill me out here, why should I tell you?"

Henry said, "Relax, Shorty. We told you, we don't have a beef with you."

"Then take me back to Packy's, buy me a drink, and I'll tell you where to find Jack."

Bo and Henry both laughed.

"What's so funny?" Shorty glanced down at the gun barrel pressed to his ribs and back up to Bo. "Turn the car around," he said, "or I got nothing to say."

Shorty was taller and bulkier than Bo, but Bo was a big man himself, with a powerful chest and muscular arms—and he knew how to fight, been doing it since the day he was born, or at least it felt that way to him. "How do you know we're not here to help out Jack? Maybe we know something about that death threat made him scram from Packy's."

"Nobody heard nothin' about no death threat." Shorty sneered as if disgusted with Bo's story. "That's just a story he used to get away from Alice. Otherwise she'd figure he was runnin' off to see Kiki."

"So is that where he is?" Bo asked. "With Kiki?"

Shorty's face tightened and went red. "I didn't say that."

Bo said, "Yeah, I think you did." The car was coming up on an unmarked gravel road. "Pull over there," Bo said to Henry.

Shorty looked back and forth from Henry to Bo, a hint of panic in his face. He glanced down at the gun barrel again.

"Calm down," Bo said, "or you really are gonna go and get yourself killed."

Henry turned onto the side road, and the car immediately lost traction on a glaze of ice. When he hit the brakes, it skidded a few feet off the road and came to rest against a wide tree trunk. Shorty's breaths were coming short and shallow. He sounded like he was sick with a fever.

"Jesus," Henry said. He cut the engine and a massive silence settled over the car. "We're gonna have to get out and push."

"I ain't getting out of the car," Shorty said. He added, crazily, "It's cold out there."

"Listen," Bo said, and for the first time in the evening he raised his voice, "we're not here to kill you, Shorty, understand? But we sure as hell aren't taking you back to Packy's. Use your head, will you? You're going to tell us where to find Jack, and then we're leaving you out here. By the time you make it back to town, we'll be all done with what we came all the fuck the way out here to do. You got it? You understand now? Calm down. We got no reason to kill you."

As Henry listened to Bo, he smiled slightly as if in admiration.

"You're leavin' me here?" Shorty looked out the car window again, to the moonlit woods surrounding them. "It's miles back to the last house we passed."

"It ain't that cold," Henry said.

"You got good shoes and that coat looks like it'd keep you warm in Alaska," Bo said. "You'll be fine."

Shorty scratched his head and his breathing settled a bit. He coughed into his hand. "All right," he said. "But I hate the fuckin' cold."

"Jack's with Kiki," Bo said. "And where can we find Kiki?"

"Twenty-one Broeck Street. She's got the upstairs apartment. The bedroom window looks out to the street. That's where they'll be. In the bedroom."

"Now we got that over with," Henry said, "help us push the car back onto the road."

"Sure," Shorty said. He was suddenly a new man, comfortable and at ease. "That won't be no trouble at all."

Henry got out first, followed by Bo and Shorty. The three of them stood in the cold and silence. Henry looked up to the stars, which were so much brighter and bigger there than in the city, and Bo took a few steps back into the woods.

"Look at this," Bo said. Two or three feet past where the car had slid into a tree, the land dropped off precipitously into a deep ravine, with a stream at the bottom of it. Bo had heard the soft gurgling of water moving under ice as soon as he'd stepped into the woods. "A few more feet," he said, "and we'd all have been done for."

Shorty and Henry came up alongside him. "Look at that," Shorty said, and he took a step closer to the edge of the ravine.

Henry said, "Let's get the car back on the road."

Bo glanced back to the car and saw that pushing it back to the road wouldn't be a problem, that he and Henry could handle it alone. "Shorty," he said. He lifted his pistol and aimed it at Shorty's chest. "I'm sorry, big guy, but you shouldn't have said nothin' about Vince Coll. We can't have you givin' him an alibi."

Shorty raised his hands in protest but didn't get a chance to speak before Bo shot him four times in the head and chest, the gunshots cracking like hammer blows and knocking him back into the ravine, where he tumbled head over feet down to the stream bed. The big raccoon coat flapped about him as he fell and then settled over him where he landed so that he looked for all the world like a big animal crouched close to the stream, maybe getting a drink of water in the moonlight.

Bo and Henry stood quietly at the edge of the ravine, the silence broken only by the murmuring of water. After a moment, Henry turned a slow circle, taking in the trees and the snow and noticing for the first time a boulder that seemed to push up out of the ground a dozen feet from where he stood. It was tall and massive and black and it looked like it must weigh tons. "Jesus," he said. "It's like the beginning of the world around here."

"If he'd have just kept his mouth shut," Bo said, "he'd still be alive."

"He wasn't none too bright," Henry said.

Bo turned to the car. "Let's get going."

Henry took hold of the door frame and the steering wheel and pulled while Bo crouched at the bumper and pushed. A minute later the car was off the icy gravel road and back on the pavement. Bo took off his gloves, rubbed his hands together, and put the gloves back on.

"You want me to drive?" Henry asked.

Bo said, "Yeah, sure," but instead of getting in the car, he went to the edge of the ravine and looked down again to the stream bed. A moment later, Henry joined him and the two men gazed down the steep hill where the snow cover was pristine, untouched anywhere except those places where Shorty's tumbling body had carved out a dark path to the water. They remained there in the silence a good while before Bo finally looked at his wristwatch and started back for the road with Henry following. Above them, the Milky Way hovered, light screaming down from its bright swirl of stars.

4:05 a.m.

Bo and Henry were drunk by the time Jack finally left Kiki's apartment and was helped into a yellow cab by a little guy in a cracked leather jacket with a knit cap and a bright red wool scarf wrapped around his neck. Jack was so drunk the little guy practically had to carry him to the cab, where he struggled to open the heavy door and deposit Jack in the back seat. Bo finished off the Seagram's and tossed the bottle to the floor. "Will you look at him?" he said to Henry. They were parked on a corner, half a block from Kiki's apartment, but with a good view of the street. "Always the dandy," Henry said. Jack had on a brown velour fedora and a chinchilla coat that was unbuttoned over a classy blue suit.

"That coat costs two grand easy," Bo said.

"Wouldn't know about that," Henry said. "Out of my league."

Henry and Bo had arrived at Kiki's hours earlier. Not a minute after they'd parked the car, Kiki appeared in her bedroom window wearing flimsy, diaphanous pajama bottoms and nothing else. She stretched for the shade and pulled it down just as Jack showed up behind her, reaching for her. Henry had checked his gun, and Bo had told him to put it away. "Let him get laid one last time," he said to Henry. "She's a beauty. It's the decent thing to do."

Henry said, "Then we'll take care of him before he has to fuck his wife again. Ah, you're a saint, Bo."

In truth, Bo was also thinking about '29 and the Monticello Hotel. Kiki had been with Jack then, too, and that hadn't turned out well. At Kiki's apartment on Broeck Street, he made a quick decision to let Jack have his fun and then kill him when he was leaving. He hadn't figured, though, that they'd be at it for hours. By the time Jack finally hit the street, the bottle of Seagram's was empty.

"Jesus," Henry said. "I'm not too confident in my ability to shoot straight at the moment."

Bo slapped his own face, hard, in an effort to sober up. He opened the car windows to let in the cold. "Follow the cabbie," he said to Henry. "See where he takes him."

The cab carried Jack to 67 Dove Street, a two-story red brick edifice with a wooden stoop. Henry followed with the car lights off and twice sideswiped parked cars on the way. "Jesus," he said both times and then broke into laughter, like sideswiping a car was the funniest thing in the world. Bo stuck his head out the window to sober up. By the time Henry pulled the car onto the sidewalk in a drunken attempt at parking, Bo's eyes were watering from the cold and the wind, but his head wasn't swimming quite so badly. Down the block, he watched the cabbie help Jack out of the car and up the wooden steps and then unlock the door for him when Jack couldn't manage it.

"You think Jack spotted us?" Bo asked Henry.

"Jesus," Henry said, "the man can't walk without falling down, let alone spot a car tailing him with the lights off."

"I suppose so." Bo took his gun from its holster and popped in a new magazine. Down the street, the door at the top of the steps opened and the cabbie hurried to his car and sped away, in a rush to get somewhere. "Don't underestimate the man," he added as he tucked his gun away. "We're not the first thought they had Jack Diamond in their sights."

"Maybe we should take the tommy guns." Henry laughed as if the thought of shooting up Jack Diamond with tommy guns was hilarious.

"Cut it out," Bo said, "and sober up!"

"Jesus," Henry said. "We'd better be standing right on top of Jack when we do the job. Between the two of us, we couldn't hit the broad side of a barn with a cannon."

"Shut up," Bo said, and he pulled his coat tight around him. "Come on."

At the top of the wooden steps, Bo tried the door and found it was unlocked. He pushed it open and stepped into a quiet hallway at the foot of a flight of carpeted stairs. Henry came in behind him and closed the door without making a sound. The men, side by side in the musty darkness, were both holding on to something to keep themselves upright and stable: Bo grasped a wooden banister and Henry held the doorknob. The darkness and the nature of their visit hadn't made them sober but had quieted them. Bo unholstered his gun and Henry did the same. Together they climbed the stairs. Each time a step creaked, they stopped and crouched and aimed their guns to the top of the stairway, into the dark, prepared for

Jack to appear out of the shadows—but neither Jack nor anyone else appeared and they reached the top of the stairs and walked past a potted fern and into a dingy little room where Jack lay on his back astride a narrow bed in his underwear.

Bo glanced about the room, amazed at the tawdry surroundings: the cheap dresser and ancient, scratched oval mirror with its backing peeling away around the edges; the thick, smoked-stained shades over the windows; the warped floorboards and dingy walls and cracked plaster ceiling. Jack's pants were on the floor next to his shoes. The rest of his clothes, including the chinchilla coat and velour hat, were piled on top of the dresser or lay on the floor between the dresser and the bed. On a straight back chair next to the bed, a German Luger lay with its barrel pointed at Jack's head. Stretched out on the bed, his head precisely in the center of a pillow, Jack looked stunned as a fish that had just been clubbed, his mouth open and pulling in chunks of air, his hair disheveled, his arms at his sides, palms up and open as if in ecstatic prayer. Henry waited at the foot of the bed, his pistol pointed at Jack, looking to Bo for the go-ahead.

Bo took up a position next to Henry and pointed his pistol at Jack's head. "What's Jack Diamond doing in a dump like this?" he asked Henry.

"Must be where he comes to sleep it off before going home to the wife."

"Think we should wake him?"

"What for? Do you want to say good-bye?"

Bo said, "Nah," aimed, and got off four shots at Jack's head. Alongside him, Henry squeezed off two shots. When the gunfire was over, Henry backed away and toward the door, but Bo went around the bed to get a better look. There were three bullets in Jack's head and three in the wall over the bed. He put his gun back in its holster, took Jack's Luger from the chair, shoved it under his belt, and followed Henry out of the room and to the stairs. Midway down the steps he stopped. "Let's make sure," he said. Though a moment ago he had leaned over Jack's body and counted three bullet holes in his face and skull, he was suddenly unsure that they'd killed him. He had after all shot Jack in the head once before, only to send him off to Europe for a ocean cruise. "I been waiting a long time for this," he said to Henry, and he started back up the stairs. "Oh, hell, that's enough for him," Henry said. He snatched Bo by the arm and pulled him back down the steps toward the front door.

On the sidewalk, on the way to the car, Henry tripped over his own feet and went sliding to the curb. Bo, laughing at Henry, yanked him by the collar, got him standing upright, and then forgot about the curb and fell to the street himself, pulling Henry down with him. By the time they finally got to the car, both men were beside themselves laughing. They drove away like that, amidst their own laughter, partly from the foolishness of their drunken acrobatics and partly from relief at having finished the job that had brought them to Albany in the first place. When they were gone and the street was empty, a light snow started to fall, a scattering of flakes drifting down out of the cold and dark.

5:30 p.m.

At the kitchen table, Gina peeled a potato, chopped it into big chunks, and tossed the chunks into a Pyrex oven dish. She was still in her work clothes, a prim blue skirt and white blouse that fit snugly and were somehow demure and sexy at the same time. Freddie and Loretto sat across from her, both of them smoking and sipping coffee from a pair of matching white cups and saucers, both in blue work shirts and khaki slacks, looking like brothers in their matching attire, Freddie the muscular one, Loretto the handsome one. They were talking about their workdays and laughing at each other's stories. Mama, at the kitchen counter beside the stove slicing up a chicken, occasionally added a comment or asked a question, as did Augie and Mike, who were in the living room, on the couch, smoking with their feet up on the table, drinking coffee and reading the day's papers with their headlines about the early-morning murder of Jack Diamond. Mike was the only one in a suit and tie. Though it was bitter cold outside, the apartment was cozy thanks to an unregulated radiator in the living room that kept pumping out heat, its constant gurgling and clacking a background noise that no one seemed to hear.

Every once in a while, Loretto would sneak a glance at Mama, who mostly stood with her back to him. She wore an apron tied around a plain housedress and occupied herself with preparing the chicken, smothering it in olive oil and seasoning it with spices and herbs. He had spent the night at Gina's and only gotten back around five in the morning. He had settled on the couch in hopes of catching at least a little sleep before work but instead he had lain there quietly, lost in his thoughts, watching the morning approach in tiny increments as the sky outside the living room window grew lighter. Mama was up by 5:30, which was early for her. Loretto pulled a blanket to his chin and pretended to be sleeping, but Mama came into the living room, ran her fingers gently through his hair to wake him, and asked what he wanted for breakfast. When Loretto opened his eyes, he found Mama looking down at him with a mischievous smile. "You gotta be hungry," she said. "You work up a good appetite, I hope?" She patted him on the cheek and held up three fingers. "I make you *three* eggs this morning," she said and laughed. In the kitchen, at the stove, she turned around and added, "And some nice big *sausage!*" And again she laughed before going about putting up the coffee. Loretto hadn't been able to look at her since without feeling a tinge of embarrassment.

In the living room, Augie tossed his newspaper down in disgust. "All this news about Diamond, you'd think the pope got shot."

"Eh!" Mama yelled. "Watch your mouth!"

"They suspect it was Dutch Schultz's boys," Freddie said, twisting around to face Augie. "They're geniuses, these news guys."

"Don't be jumpin' to conclusions," Mike said. He put his paper aside and went about slipping off his shoes. "I'm hearing some talk it might have been the cops up in Albany. They didn't like it that he got off, so they took care of the problem themselves."

"Yeah?" Freddie asked. "Who's sayin' that?"

When Mike didn't answer, Gina said, "I hear from Maria that this is bad for Vince."

Mike said, "What's Maria know about it?"

"Whatever Patsy knows."

"Is that right?" Loretto pulled his chair out from the kitchen table so that he could talk to Mike without contorting himself. "What's Diamond got to do with Vince?"

"According to Patsy," Gina said, "Diamond was going to be the alibi. He was testifying that Vince was with him up in Albany that day."

Loretto, along with everyone else except Mama, turned to Mike for confirmation.

Mike said, "Patsy talks too much."

"Yeah, so, is it true?" Freddie held his coffee up and waited for Mike to answer before taking another sip.

Mike nodded. "I was in the courtroom today when the news hit about Jack. You should have seen the look on Lottie's face when I told her."

Augie said, "*You* told her?"

"We're sitting next to each other up in the balcony, all of a sudden everybody's whisperin' and some of the news guys are bolting for the door."

Augie said, "Yeah, so?"

"So shut up and let me finish!"

"*Basta!*" Mama yelled without turning from the counter.

Augie motioned for Mike to go on.

"So I got up and asked around. When I went back to Lottie and told her, first her face went red, then it went white, then she's holding her belly like she's in pain."

"Jeez," Gina said. "Almost makes me feel sorry for her."

"So is it that bad for Vince?" Freddie asked. "What's he lookin' at now, the chair?"

"It ain't looking good for him now," Mike said, "that's for sure."

At the kitchen counter, Mama slapped a knife down hard enough to get everyone's attention. When she turned around, she said softly, "I don't like this talk. Enough."

Mike said, "Freddie's the one started it."

Freddie said, "Sorry, Mama."

"Listen," Gina said. She carried the Pyrex dish stuffed with potatoes, carrots, and onions to the counter and placed it in front of Mama. "Long as we're all here like this . . ." She paused, waiting till she had everyone's attention. "I talked to Balzarini at the funeral parlor today. They're making all the arrangements for us with the cemetery. Is that okay with everybody? Because if anybody's got any special requests . . ."

"Not me," Augie said. "Let Balzarini handle it. He knows what he's doing."

Mama carried the Pyrex bowl of chicken and vegetables to the oven. "I talk to the people at the cemetery," she said, sheepishly. "We got a family plot. Enough for everybody."

Gina watched her mother as she slid the chicken onto the oven rack and checked the temperature. "All right," she said. "If that's what you want, Ma."

Mama turned from the oven to face Gina. Her eyes were watery. "Thank you, Gina," she said. "You're a good daughter."

Gina said, "Excuse me," but instead of going into the bathroom, which was what everyone expected, she went into the boys' room. A minute later, they all heard her climb the ladder and go up to the roof.

Mama turned to Loretto. "It's freezing out!"

"I'll go talk to her," Loretto said, and he followed Gina to the roof. On his way up, he took his own overcoat from the closet and Gina's from Freddie's bed, where she usually tossed it when visiting. He found her standing by the ledge alongside the empty pigeon coop. Her arms were crossed under her breasts and she was shivering. It was mostly dark out and the lights from the nearby buildings cast a yellow glow over the rooftops and down into the alley. He draped her coat over her shoulders and she turned to him, wrapped her arms around his waist, and pressed her face to his chest. She asked, "How's Mama?"

"I think she's grateful," Loretto said. "How are you?"

Instead of answering, Gina tilted her head to Loretto and they kissed. "I think I'm doing the right thing, going along."

"Sure," Loretto said, "but how do you feel about it?"

"I don't know." Gina looked up to the sky as a light snow started to fall.

Loretto held her tighter, enfolding her in his overcoat. "Do you remember a lot of what happened?" he asked. "You were so young."

Gina was surprised that Loretto would ask such a question. "I was twelve. I remember every little detail. I can close my eyes . . ." She could close her eyes and remember her father pacing the apartment while Mama slept behind the closed door to her bedroom and the boys shared a single bed opposite her, a curtain hung from the ceiling dividing the room. She remembered pulling the covers to her chin and watching the shadowy figure of her father as he passed her doorway muttering to himself in Italian. He was skinny and wiry, an older version of Augie, with the same big Adam's apple. Every once in a while she could make out a word or two of his rambling, whispered monologue—*inferno, demoni, malvagita*—enough to understand that he was off again on one of his rants about the devil and hell and the corruption of the world.

Talk of the devil had started many months earlier, at first more like sermons than rants, warnings of what the devil could do if you allowed him into your life, but gradually becoming more and more frightening until he was pacing the dark apartment at night mumbling about the devil in his head, the devil eating his heart, demons inside him gnawing on his guts, and then a few days earlier getting fired from work for falling asleep on the job, and then sleeping through the days and muttering through the nights while Mama conferred with the priests and nuns—and then he was standing in the doorway with a knife in his hand, a silhouette Gina could never get out of her mind ever again, the shadow image of her father in the doorway with a knife in his hand. *Papa*, she said. She said it loud to wake the boys, to wake Mama. When he took another step toward her with the knife raised over his head, when he said *Puttana*, she called for Augie; when he said, *Ti taglio il demone del tuo cuore*, she screamed for Mama and turned over not to see him, burying her head in her pillow; when he fell on her with the knife, with the terrible sharp gashing pain in her back, she heard Freddie and Augie howling for him to stop; she felt their boys' bodies on the bed wrestling with their father, but the gashing pain happened again and again till it was Mama in the room with them, the heat and bulk of Mama's body pushing everyone aside, and then she could remember being lifted in Mama's arms, being held to Mama's breast, and it was as if she fell asleep there, with her head against her mother's breast. She remembered nothing after that till much later in the hospital; but everything before, her father's muttering, her father in the doorway, the blows of the knife—all that she remembered as if it had happened only a moment ago. All that, she recalled in great detail.

"I remember," she said to Loretto. "It's hard to forget."

Loretto brushed snowflakes from Gina's hair. "It was a long time ago."

"We've got company," Gina said. She pulled back from Loretto as Mike climbed up to the roof.

"Mama's gonna have a heart attack down there." Mike snatched Loretto's coat away from him and quickly slipped into it.

Loretto laughed and Gina said, "Jeez, what's she think? I'm gonna jump?"

"Go on down," Mike said. "Don't make her think you're mad at her."

"I'm not mad at her! Why would she think that?"

Mike gave Gina a look that said the answer to her question was obvious if she'd take a second to think about it.

"Jeez . . ." Gina paused a second and then kissed Mike on the cheek before climbing down through the skylight.

When Loretto tried to follow, Mike stopped him. "Listen," he said, his voice dropping to a whisper, "with Jack out of the picture . . . and Shorty nowhere to be found . . ."

"Shorty? Why would anybody want to kill Shorty?"

"Who the hell knows?" Mike said. "Point is that it don't look good at all for Vince, now he doesn't have an alibi."

"Maybe they can get somebody else—"

"Please. Vince is paying lawyers big money to worry about that stuff. What I'm sayin' here is, with Jack out of the picture, we have to move fast or Dutch and the boys'll take it all before we know what the hell happened."

"So?" Loretto asked. "What are you thinking?"

"I'm not thinking anything," Mike said. "I'm saying we've got to pull ourselves together and show strength if we want to keep the warehouses and supply routes and bring Jack's people in line." He jabbed Loretto in the chest with a finger. "That means we need everybody, includin' you."

"And who's gonna be running things in this new situation?"

"Depends on what happens with Vince," Mike said. "But we can't wait to find out."

"Okay, so I'm asking you again, specifically: What are you thinking about doing?"

"Specifically? Right now we need more men to cover the warehouses, plus to deal with the drivers and ride shotgun on the deliveries and to make sure we keep the speaks we already got."

"What about Jack's organization? What about all his men? Are they workin' for . . . who? You? Us?"

"Bigger problem," Mike said, "is what about Dutch and Luciano and all the rest of the boys? If they think we're weak, it's all over. I'll be out there digging ditches with you and the rest of the chumps." He took hold of Loretto's shirt, feeling the rough fabric with obvious disgust. "What do you think you're doing, Loretto? You're no broom-pusher. Since when?"

Loretto looked up at the few snowflakes falling here and there—more like a random gust of ashes than a snowfall. "I have to figure out what to do about Gina."

"But you're with us," Mike said. "Right? I can depend on you?"

"Yeah," Loretto said. "But I still don't know where I stand with Vince. Last I heard, he wanted no part of me."

"That's only a problem," Mike said, "if Vince gets off and if he's running things again."

"What do you think his chances are?"

"I don't think they're any good," Mike said, "but what do I know? Vince thinks this big-deal lawyer's gonna be just the ticket."

Loretto touched his cheeks. "Hey," he said, "I can't feel my face. Let's go in."

Mike put a hand on Loretto's chest, asking him to wait another minute. "So you're quitting this baloney park job?"

"Give me till after Christmas. That's a week. You can live without me till then."

"What's Christmas got to do with anything?"

"I don't want to ruin it for Gina, if she finds out. Plus Freddie and Augie . . . It's gonna be a mess."

"Don't be all dramatic," Mike said. "I'm still here, ain't I? They know what I do. Plus, Freddie won't be happy workin' in no restaurant. Believe me. He'll want to come in with us. We just got to give him time to get over Elmira."

"I don't know about that," Loretto said. "I think Augie might put us both in the ground we bring Freddie along."

"Let me worry about Augie." Mike patted Loretto on the shoulder. "He ain't so high and mighty."

"Yeah, well, I'm scared of him," Loretto said.

"Don't be." Mike rubbed his hands together and started for the skylight. "Come on, before we both freeze to death up here."

8:00 p.m.

Vince was still in the courthouse, in a dreary, windowless room somewhere down a long corridor where Strenburg and Leibowitz had escorted him, along with a bunch of coppers. He sat at a short metal desk sipping some of the good Scotch that Strenburg had smuggled past the guards. The lawyers had left a few minutes earlier, and now it was just him and Lottie, also smuggled in. Strenburg said he'd give them ten minutes and they should use them to talk. When he said it, he emphasized the word *talk* and winked at Vince. Lottie pulled up a folding chair, sat beside Vince, and put her hand in his lap. She massaged him there in a way that was more comforting than sexual, but he was quickly aroused nonetheless. He had spent the last few minutes reassuring her. It was a tough break, sure, that they'd got to Jack, but that wasn't a death sentence for Vince or anything like it. Leibowitz had his doubts about Neary's so-called eyewitness. If he wasn't on the up-and-up, Leibowitz had said, he'd make mincemeat of him. If he was on the up-and-up, well, that would make it tougher, all right, but they'd deal with that when the time came. But he smelled a rat, he'd told Vince, and he had an excellent sense of smell. "Without a legit witness," Vince reassured Lottie, "they got nothing."

Lottie kissed Vince on the neck, snuggled closer to him, and undid his belt. She had on a black skirt and a simple white blouse, courtroom attire. "You're the handsomest guy in the courtroom," she said. "I swear, all I do is sit up there in the balcony and look at how handsome you are. Do you feel my eyes on you?" she asked. "Do you know I'm watching you every second?"

"When you're not in the bathroom throwing up." Vince tilted his head back and finished off his drink.

"I shouldn't have told you about that," Lottie said, and she peeled open his pants.

"Listen, dollface . . ." Vince kissed Lottie on the temple as her head dropped down into his lap. "Listen," he repeated, "doll . . ." He stroked her hair.

Lottie stopped what she was doing and offered Vince a coy smile while her hands kept busy. "What are you trying to say, handsome?"

"Just," Vince said, and he pushed a strand of hair away from her eyes, "if the law doesn't get me, the boys will. You get that, doll, don't you?"

The smile dropped away from Lottie's face. "Ah, don't talk that way, Vince. Not while I'm doing this."

"Sure," Vince said. He gently nudged her head, and Lottie went back to what she was doing. "Mike's the toughest of the gang," he said as he laid his head back, his thought slowing down. "Loretto's the smartest."

Lottie worked harder, feeling Vince relax and tense at the same time, feeling his body melt into the chair while his thighs tightened and lifted, helping her along.

Vince took a clump of Lottie's hair in his hand and pulled. He heard a small sound issue up from her chest when he tightened his grip, and his body leaned toward it, toward the sound, as, for a moment, all the cares in the world disappeared.

TUESDAY ✦✦✦ DECEMBER 22, 1931

2:15 p.m.

The witness against Vince turned out to be a guy named George Brecht who talked out of the corner of his mouth. He was twenty-seven years old, and nobody had ever heard of him before or seen him around town, but he claimed that he'd been walking along 107th when he'd heard what he thought was a truck backfiring. He had turned around to see a car with five men in it, two in the front, three in the back. For seven years prior to that summer, he claimed he'd worked as a chauffeur and that it was his opinion the car was cruising at no more than four miles per hour while two of the men in the back seat were firing pistols out the car window toward the sidewalk. The man in the front seat had a shotgun, and he fired once. When the DA asked if any of the men in the car were also in the courtroom, Brecht made a big drama out of getting up from the witness stand, walking to the defendants' table, and pointing to Vince as the man in the back seat firing the pistol and Frank as the driver with the shotgun.

Leibowitz questioned Brecht about his finances and established that he'd been in police custody for months, drawing a weekly income from the police department and having all his expenses covered by the city. He even sent home fifteen dollars a week to his family in Chicago, courtesy of the police department. When Leibowitz asked him about the thirty-thousand-dollar reward he would be in line to get if Vince Coll was convicted, Brecht said he'd only learned about it days ago. This would have required him to have read virtually none of the newspaper stories about the shooting, and when Brecht insisted that was the case, Leibowitz made him look like a fool. Then he stopped in the middle of that line of questioning, as if something had just occurred to him. "I have another question I'd like to ask you," he said. "I notice you speak out of the corner of your mouth. Did you ever spend any time in an institution of any sort that might have led you to learn to speak that way?"

There was a flurry of objections to the question, which the judge eventually overruled. Everyone who knew anything about prison life knew what Leibowitz was getting at. Prisoners often spoke out of the corners of their mouths to avoid being overheard by guards.

Brecht said, "No, I ain't never been in prison, if that's what you're suggestin'. Ain't never been in prison, ain't never been charged with a crime. I'm a law-abiding, decent citizen."

"So you've never been on the witness stand before?"

"Never."

"Ever seen the inside of a courtroom before?"

The DA adamantly objected to the question, to the whole line of questioning, and this time the judge sustained the objection.

"One more thing," Leibowitz said, changing course. "You say you'd been looking for work that day, the day the Vengelli child was murdered."

"That's right."

"At a belt factory on 1st Avenue—that's what you testified, am I correct?"

"That's correct."

"You went to this belt factory looking for a job, the watchman told you there were no jobs available, and then when you were walking back from this belt factory, that's when you witnessed the shooting."

"That's correct."

"At this point, Mr. Brecht, I don't think anybody in this courtroom will be too surprised"—Leibowitz stepped away from the witness stand and turned to face the jury—"when I tell you that there is no belt factory on 1st Avenue."

Over the mumbling and scattered tittering in the courtroom, Brecht said, "Well, I got the address wrong, that's all."

Leibowitz turned back to Brecht with the air of a teacher disappointed in his student. "There are no belt factories anywhere in the area, Mr. Brecht."

"Well, like I said!" Brecht again raised his voice. "I got the address wrong is all."

"That leaves us with the question, again, of what you were doing on 107th Street on the day of the incident."

"I was coming back from applying for a job," Brecht said. "Maybe it wasn't a belt factory. Maybe I'm misremembering what kind of a factory it was after all. That could easily be what's going on."

Leibowitz sighed as if more saddened than exasperated by Brecht's answer. "Let me ask you again, Mr. Brecht." He approached the defendants' table and stood behind Vince and Frank, putting a hand on each of their shoulders. "Are you sure these men look like the men you claim to have seen on the day of the shooting?"

"I don't claim it!" Brecht said. He pounded his fist down on the witness stand. "I say it! And they don't *look like* the men that were in the car, they *are* the men that were in the car!"

Leibowitz patted Vince and Frank on the shoulders, paused to collect his thoughts, and then continued with his questions. Lottie, though, couldn't take another minute. She got up and left the balcony and went out to the street, where she lit a cigarette with a shaky hand and smoked it furiously, ripping the smoke down into her lungs and firing it out at the crowded avenue, where hordes of people walked by all caught up in their own lives, without some liar trying to put them in their graves for a thirty-thousand-dollar reward, without Dutch Schultz and Lucky Luciano and all the rest waiting in the wings to take over if the law didn't get the job done. She quickly smoked her cigarette down to the filter and immediately lit another one. When she was finished, she'd go back to her seat in the balcony. Maybe her hands wouldn't be shaking by then. A minute later, with the second cigarette already almost down to the filter, she was surprised when she started to silently cry. She hadn't felt the tears coming. Her eyes were dry one second and wet a moment later. She'd never liked Jack Diamond, and she'd been trying not to think about him, but every once in a while a picture of him all shot up came into her mind and made her sick with the thought of it. The newspapers said they'd put three bullets in his head. Then imagining Jack all shot up turned to imagining Vince with three bullets in his head, and a quiet voice inside her reassured her, told her she'd be all right, she'd figure it out, no matter. The voice seemed almost to be another person, someone both angry and determined. She'd be all right, the voice said. She'd find a way. Her thoughts flashed to Mike Baronti standing in the bathroom doorway, holding her robe out to her. He was the toughest of the lot, Loretto the smartest. She'd be all right, the voice said yet again, and she took a handkerchief from her dress pocket, blotted her eyes, stomped out the remains of the cigarette, and went back into the courthouse.

1:15 p.m.

Lottie was eating her lunch alone in a Horn & Hardart a few blocks from the courthouse. Where she was seated, she could watch people walking along the street under a moving canopy of umbrellas, keeping themselves dry as best they could in a driving rain that was predicted to turn to snow and ice by the evening when the temperature dropped. She was already dreading the subway ride back to Florence's apartment. It wasn't the crowded cars that bothered her as much as the indignity of it, having to ride the subway at all.

By the time she finished her sandwich, the downpour had let up. She watched a little boy on the street dart out from under an umbrella and stomp both feet down in a puddle before the woman holding him by the hand could yank him back to her side and yell something at him that Lottie couldn't make out. She made eye contact with the boy and his face lit up with a mischievous grin. She winked at him, found her umbrella, and left her sandwich half eaten on the table. Outside, on the way back to the courthouse in the rain, she thought about Christmas again and what she could get for Vince. She'd bought a frilly dress and new shoes for Klara, and she liked to think about her daughter handling the package, wondering what was in it, anticipating Christmas morning when she could open it. Those thoughts, though, always led her to Jake's people, especially his mother, and she had to snuff them out or spend the rest of the day angry. Easier and better to think of Vince. She didn't know what to get for him. All the regular gifts, clothes and jewelry and such, were out of the question: the guards wouldn't let him take anything like that back with him to his cell. She'd only get an hour to visit with him on Christmas morning. That was it. An hour.

At the courthouse, she made her way through a side entrance to avoid the press and found Strenburg waiting. He rushed up to her, snagged her by the arm, and pulled her away from the courtroom toward a long line of offices. "Big news," he whispered in her ear.

"No kiddin'?" Lottie said. "They're letting Vince out for Christmas?"

"Better." Strenburg found the room he was looking for, unlocked the door, and held it open for Lottie. "Brecht's a fraud." He switched on the light and closed the door.

"I could have told you that. What happened?" The room was arranged with lines of chairs facing a podium. Two tall windows at the back of the room looked out on a gray, rainy day. Lottie took a seat in front of the podium and crossed her legs.

"Brecht's parole officer from Saint Louie showed up. He saw the kid's picture in the papers and recognized him." He took a seat next to Lottie. His eyes went first to her legs, then to her breasts, and finally to her eyes. "Brecht's been in and out of jail since he was a teenager, and, get this, he's been involuntarily committed to a mental institution. Is that rich?" he asked. "Their only witness, forced confinement in a mental institution."

"What's that all mean?"

"What's it all mean? It means their case just took a header into the crapper! Who's going to believe a nutcase that's been lying to them on the stand under oath?"

"Sure," Lottie said, "but we all knew he was lying anyway. Leibowitz caught him in--"

"You're not getting it," Strenburg cut her off. "Yeah, Sammy caught

Brecht in a bunch of lies, but he never shook his testimony. The guy's been solid as a rock that it was Vince and Frank doing the shooting. But now we've got the guy's arrest record and mental confinements in black and white, undeniable. Plus!" Strenburg added. He stuck a bony finger in air. "Plus, turns out, fours years ago, Brecht was the main witness against a couple of mugs from the Cuckoo Gang. You heard of them?"

"Not me," Lottie said. "The Cuckoo Gang?"

"You would have, believe me, if you lived in Saint Louie."

"So?"

"So Brecht claimed to have witnessed these two mugs commit a murder, and guess what?"

"He was lying?"

"They had to throw the case out when they proved he perjured himself."

Lottie was quiet as what Strenburg was telling her began to sink in. "Are you saying . . ."

"I'm telling you, Neary's case is in the crapper."

"Does that mean Vince will get off? What's it mean exactly?"

Strenburg sat back in his seat and straightened out his vest. He seemed disappointed that Lottie wasn't more excited. "I can't say *exactly* what it means, but this is *very* bad for Neary. Without a witness, he's got no case. And for all intents and purposes, Neary is now without a witness. Even worse, his witness is a nutcase, an ex-con, and a liar. Not only has his case collapsed, but now he looks like a fool at the least, and possibly corrupt if he knew Brecht was lying all along."

"Well, okay, I get all that," Lottie said. "But you said that they threw out that other case because the witness perjured himself. Does that mean the judge will throw out this case?"

"It could very well mean that," Strenburg said, "but it's not guaranteed. He could also declare a mistrial, or he could allow the case to proceed and let the jury decide."

"What do you think he'll do?"

"I don't know, but the important thing is that all of those options, at this point, are good for us."

"But the jury could still decide to convict Vince anyway? Even knowing the witness was lying."

Strenburg sighed as if defeated. He assumed a professional air. "That's possible," he said. "It is *possible* that the jury could find Vince guilty."

"So when will we find out what the judge decides?"

"Corrigan adjourned the case. We're meeting at four o'clock in his chambers. We'll know more after that."

"Jesus . . ." Lottie was sweating through the armpits of her blouse, though the room was chilly. She lifted her arms and waved them, trying to evaporate the sweat. "Why am I more nervous now than I was before?" She looked at Strenburg as if seriously hoping for an answer.

Strenburg, who had always struck Lottie as at least a little foolish, a skinny, chattering kind of second banana, suddenly sounded like someone both compassionate and intelligent. "Because now you have hope," he said, and he squeezed her arm as he pulled himself up from his seat. "Go home," he added as he started for the door. "When you come back in the morning, we'll know more about where we go from here." Before he closed the door he added, peeking back into the room, "But listen, Lottie. This is good news. This is very, very good news." He winked at her, closed the door, and disappeared down the hallway.

Alone in the room, Lottie turned off the light and went to the tall windows at the back, where she sat on a ledge and looked down to a side street and a pair of coppers in their blue uniforms who were standing in a doorway, protected from the rain by an overhang, talking and smoking, one of them with a cigarette dangling from his lips, the other with a cigar between his fingers. She decided she'd write a poem for Vince—either a poem or maybe a love letter with racy stuff in it, something he could take back to his cell and read later, when he was alone and maybe lonely for her. When he got out, she told herself, thinking positively, she'd give him a real gift. From there, her thoughts moved on to Dutch Schultz and Bo Weinberg and the rest of them, and then to Jack Diamond with three bullets in his face. It occurred to her that she and Vince could snatch Klara and move someplace far away, someplace where they could live without someone looking to put three bullets in Vince's face every second—and then she thought of the subway car she'd be riding in a minute on her way to a crappy apartment, and of her mother's hands always red and raw from cleaning products, and of herself as a child looking up those stairs into forbidden rooms, and she told herself again that Vince was tough, that he was tougher than all of them, and she said aloud, the words emerging out of nowhere, *Whatever it takes*. Again, it was as if someone else was inside her, only this time the voice was furious. It unnerved her a little. She focused on where the coppers had been smoking and found that they were gone, disappeared while she was looking but apparently not seeing.

She got up and started for the subway. She decided then that she'd write a racy love letter for Vince, and she left the room and the courthouse with that on her mind.

7:15 p.m.

Mrs. Tintello had a daughter who worked as a nurse at King's Park, and through her word got around the neighborhood that Ercole Baronti was close to death. All day women came around with various foods and fresh-baked bread, trays of lasagna and manicotti, baskets of fruit and bottles of homemade wine, till Mama ran out of room for all the dishes and started giving some to Mrs. Esposito upstairs. To get away from the visitors, Loretto, Augie, and Freddie were hiding out in the bedroom playing pinochle. They'd pushed the beds together and were sprawled across them, lying on their sides with handfuls of cards spread out in front of them like fans. Outside, the snow was coming down fast and hard, blown along the street by gusts of wind that smacked the bedroom window. Augie had rolled up a bright red bath towel and placed it on the window ledge. It didn't do much to keep the room warmer, but at least he didn't feel a brush of cold air over his back every time a gust of wind hit the building.

Loretto and Augie played the game quickly, picking up and throwing down cards, their melds laid out sloppily in front of them, while Freddie studied his cards as if he were reading the Bible and trying to work out the meaning of a parable. Loretto and Augie smoked and talked while they waited for Freddie to move. It was hopeless to rush him. He'd only get frustrated and take even longer.

Loretto tapped the ash off his cigarette into an ashtray resting on the bed between him and Augie. "You've been involved in some rough stuff," he said to Augie. "You ever have dreams?"

With his free hand—the other one clutching a fan of cards—Augie stroked his Adam's apple. "What are you dreamin' about?"

"Me?" Loretto made a face like it was no big deal, just a question to pass the time. "I've been dreaming about Dom and Gaspar, finding them stuffed in the wine cellar like that."

"Ah," Augie said as if he understood. "I wasn't involved in that much rough stuff."

From behind his cards, Freddie said, "You done your share."

"When I was younger," Augie said, "before I figured out it wasn't for me." To Loretto he said, "You keep distractin' Freddie, we'll be here till kingdom come."

"*Sta'zitt'*," Freddie said, and made his play.

"Hallelujah." Augie glanced at his card, put down a meld, and discarded.

Loretto picked up and discarded and then it was Freddie's turn again. Augie lit another cigarette. Loretto stood up to stretch. Someone knocked at the front door and a moment later Mama called, "Loretto! Look who's here!" Augie rolled his eyes and Loretto stared at his shoes, steeling himself to see yet another old lady from the neighborhood who remembered him from when. Once in the kitchen, though, he was surprised to see Sister Mary Catherine. He hadn't seen her in a couple of years, and he was surprised at how much she'd aged in that time. The crow's-feet around her eyes were deep and dark, and her lips were lined with creases. Her blue eyes, though, still had the same sparkle. They lit up her face and undercut the somber black of her long habit and the heavy coat she was bundled in.

"Loretto," she said, "will you just look at you now? You're even handsomer than the last time I saw you!" She was standing next to Mama, whom she had just hugged, one arm still around her shoulders.

"Sister Mary Catherine . . ." Loretto embraced her and then stepped back to look at her. "You're as beautiful as ever."

"Stop," the sister said and blushed, as she always blushed at a compliment. "I can only stay a moment," she said to Mama. "Father Piazza is waiting downstairs in the car." She glanced into the living room, where Augie had put up a small Christmas tree by the window and draped it with multicolored lights. "I wanted to stop and give you these," she said, turning back to Mama. She pulled a long, beautiful string of rosary beads from the pocket of her coat. The polished black beads glittered in the kitchen light as she handed the rosary to Mama. "Perhaps," she said, "when the time comes, you can place them in Ercole's hands."

"Thank you, Sister. *Grazie mille.*" Mama took the rosary. She understood that the beads were meant to be buried with Ercole and that the undertaker would be the one to place them in his hands.

"And surely," Sister Mary Catherine said to Loretto, "you'll walk your old teacher down the steps to the front door."

"Of course," Loretto said. He retrieved his overcoat from the closet and slipped into it while the sister embraced Mama again.

"You can't stay for coffee?" Mama implored.

"The snow," Sister Mary Catherine said. "I can't." She kissed Mama on the cheek as Loretto opened the door and waited.

In the hallway, on the way down the stairs, Sister took Loretto's hand in hers and gave him a squeeze. "I'm proud of you," she said. "When I learned you were working at an honest job, clearing trails at Innwood Park . . . ah, Loretto. That made me so happy." She gave his hand another squeeze.

Loretto had to tamp down the desire to tell her that it was a sucker's job. He wanted to ask her what there was to be so proud of now that he was working like a slave hauling rocks, cutting down trees, spending whole days in the backbreaking labor of dragging away heavy tree limbs and slabs of rock—all for fifteen dollars a week, barely enough to cover food and shelter. Instead he only smiled and said, "It's hard work."

"Ah, I'm sure it is." At the bottom of the stairs, near the building's front door, the sister put her hands on Loretto's shoulders and squared off in front him. "I'm praying for you, Loretto," she said. "Every day my prayers go up to our precious Lord. I pray for your immortal soul." She spoke those words somberly and then added, with a smile, "And now it seems to me that all my prayers and your hard work might, *at last*," she added mock-dramatically, "be getting somewhere!" She pulled Loretto to her and kissed him on the cheek. On her way out the door, she said, "You always know where to find me."

Loretto, seeing that the stoop was slippery and snow-covered, went after her, took her by the arm, and walked alongside her down the steps. At the curb, he helped her into the car, and when the tires spun in the snow as Father Piazza tried to drive off, he put his shoulder to the rear taillight, braced his foot on the curb, and pushed the car out to the street, where the wheels found traction. The father rolled down his window and waved as he drove off with the sister at his side.

By the time he made it back to the kitchen, the boys were at the table with Mama, each with a cup of coffee and a thick slice of apple pie in front of them on a plate.

"Sit," Mama said. "*Mangia'!*"

Loretto held his stomach. "I'm not feeling so good all of a sudden."

"What? You sick?"

"Nah," Loretto said. "I don't know." He gestured toward the bedroom. "I'm lyin' down a minute."

Freddie said, "Don't mess up the game. I'm winnin'."

In the bedroom, Loretto made himself a space next to the wall. He lay on his back on a blanket, his head on a pillow, with a second blanket pulled up over his face. In that self-imposed dark, he lay quietly and listened to Mama and the boys talking about the weather. The boys wondered if the snow kept up whether or not they'd be able to get to work in the morning. He supposed he should be worrying about the same thing, but he didn't want to think about anything, not the snow and his job, not Mike and Vince or Gina and Mama, not Freddie and Augie or Sister Mary Catherine or Dutch or Luciano or Joe Mullins, not any of it. All he wanted was to lie with the blanket over him, his head as empty as he could manage.

10:15 a.m.

Lottie had awakened to a foot of snow on the ground and bundled up for the short walk from Flo's apartment to the subway. At the courthouse, the crowd of press and spectators had been thinned a bit by the bad weather, and she took a seat on the courtroom level. For more than an hour she'd been listening with amazement as Leibowitz asked Brecht question after question, forcing him to admit he'd been lying in every instance with the sole hope of getting a portion of the reward money. The amazing thing was that Brecht happily admitted to every lie and every incarceration, including the involuntary stay in a mental institution, as if it was all an amusing lark and no one should be the least surprised or upset. By the time the questioning was over, Lottie thought the same thing she guessed everyone present thought—that Brecht was at the very least a little crazy.

"Your Honor," Leibowitz said. He stood with his hands on his hips and looked about the courtroom as if to share with everyone present his bewilderment at Brecht's complete lack of remorse. "Your Honor," he repeated, turning to Judge Corrigan, "the defense rests its case." He made of a show of shaking his head in disbelief. He gestured toward the jury box. "I don't think there's any need for a summation at this point, Your Honor." He threw up his hands. "We'll let the jury take it from here."

A rumble of noise and chatter went up among the spectators, and Corrigan banged his gavel once. "I'm sure you'd love that," he said to Leibowitz. "But I'm not sending this to the jury on Christmas Eve." He glanced at Neary, who was seated at the prosecutor's table doing his best not to look like a dog that had just been kicked in the head. Corrigan banged the gavel again. He said, "Trial is adjourned until Monday, the 28th of December," and then practically leaped from his seat and exited the courtroom.

In the commotion that followed as the press scrambled out into the halls, followed by spectators, Lottie made herself small and stood off in a corner until a contingent of armed courthouse guards and coppers gathered around Frank and Vince, getting ready to escort them back to the Tombs.

Before the prosecutor could leave, Frank called across the room to him, "Hey, Neary," he yelled, "a very merry Christmas to you and your family!"

Neary called back, "The same to you and your friend Coll," and despite the traditional good cheer of the actual words, his tone suggested he was telling them both to rot in hell.

Frank and Vince laughed at Neary's response, and then Vince glanced up to the balcony. Lottie called to him and managed to take a step in his direction before the guards grabbed him roughly by the shoulders and hustled him away. He saw her, though, before they got him out a side door. He winked and she threw him a kiss, and then he was gone and she was by herself in a rapidly emptying courtroom.

Strenburg, like an old friend, poked his head through the courtroom doors. "Ah," he said when he spotted her. "You weren't up in the balcony."

"That's because I was down here." She slipped into her coat and wrapped her scarf around her neck. "Say," she added, sorry about snapping at him, "I appreciate your looking out for me. Thanks."

"Vince's instructions," Strenburg answered. "I'm not supposed to let you out of my sight."

"Well, anyway," she said, "Merry Christmas to you."

"And you, too."

When Strenburg started for the doors, Lottie stopped him. "So this is over now, right? No way the jury can convict Vince after this."

"I'd think not," Strenburg said. "But you can never tell what a jury will do."

"You're saying they could still convict him even though the only witness is a liar and a lunatic."

"Listen." Strenburg folded his hands at his waist. "Vince is in a very good position. Things look excellent for him. But it's not over yet. We don't know what Neary might try next. What we got going against us is that Judge Corrigan hates Vince. He considers him a blight on the Irish race. And the jury knows all about Vince's reputation. So," he said, "those are problems. The jury could convict him just because he's Mad Dog Coll, and the judge could stand back and watch it happen. Having said that, though, I tell you it's unlikely. I tell you things now look very good for your boyfriend."

Lottie pulled on her gloves. "So how come I don't feel better?"

Strenburg surprised her with a quick kiss on her cheek. "Merry Christmas," he said. "Try not to worry."

When Strenburg left, Lottie was alone in the courtroom. In the quiet, she put her hands to her eyes and silently cried. The news was good, she told herself—and still the tears wouldn't quit. She took a seat in one of the pewlike benches, buried her face in her arms, and waited for the crying to stop. When she was ready, she'd brave the cold and the subway and make her way back to Flo's empty apartment, where there was a bottle of bourbon and a hot bath waiting.

1:25 a.m.

Christmas Eve the Barontis attended midnight mass and then went home to exchange gifts, as was their tradition. Augie took a seat close to the Christmas tree and handed out brightly wrapped boxes one at time. Each opened his or her present, the others oohed and aahed, and then Augie handed out the next one. After the gift-giving was done, Mama pulled out a tray of manicotti from the refrigerator, and Gina distributed dishes and forks, and at 1:30 in the morning they took their places at the kitchen table—Loretto beside Gina, Augie and Mama at opposite ends, Mike and Freddie side by side opposite Loretto and Gina—for a final meal and a last round of talk before bed or, in Mike's and Gina's cases, before leaving for their own apartments. In the midst of their eating and conversation, there was a knock at the door. When Gina and Augie both got up, Mama raised her hand and they retook their seats without question.

Mama opened the door, saw who it was, and bowed her head. Mrs. Tintello embraced her, whispered in her ear, kissed her on the cheek, and then stepped back into the hall and said, "I'll leave you now to be with your family."

Mama thanked her politely and closed the door. She didn't cry until she looked at Gina. She said, as if imploring Gina to believe, "He was a good man. Not strong—" She stopped and corrected herself. "No," she said, "strong, not strong *enough*." The boys seemed grateful when Gina got up from the table, embraced her mother, and patted her on the back as she cried softly into her shoulder. Augie went to the stove, found the coffee pot, and went about filling everyone's cup as though the hot, dark liquid were the only sacrament appropriate to the moment.

10:00 a.m.

Lottie pressed her cheek to Vince's neck and watched snow falling through a barred window. Strenburg had spent a fortune bribing half the officials in the Tombs to get Vince this hour alone with Lottie on Christmas morning in a bare room with a few surplus office chairs and a half-dozen beaten-up wooden desks. Before he'd closed the door behind them, one of the guards had made a smart remark about the surface of the desks being a little hard and rough but serviceable. He'd said it to Vince with a grin, like a joke between guys, but the grin disappeared with the look Vince gave him in return. Lottie kissed Vince's neck, a little peck, when he stroked her hair, and then she went back to watching the snow flakes flutter down against the background of a gray sky. She was seated on Vince's lap in an office chair, her legs wrapped around his back, Vince still inside her where she could feel him throbbing and shrugging, little by little pulling away. They had just finished and she didn't want to let him go. She watched the snow with her head pressed to his neck, her arms wrapped around his chest, fused to the warmth of his body while he stroked her hair. After a minute he said, "Merry Christmas," which made her smile, though she knew he couldn't see it.

Their hour was almost up and they had spent most of it talking before getting around to making love in an office chair. Vince was full of confidence and wanted to talk business. He had messages for Lottie to deliver to Mike and Patsy. He wanted them to start recruiting more men for the gang. "Hard guys," he told Lottie, "the toughest," and he mentioned names. He wanted the Evangelista brothers and Paul Martone and a bunch of guys from Little Augie's old gang who were working as independents, and an Irish guy Lottie'd never heard of, Jimmy Brennan. Brennan was one of the older boys at Mount Loretto back in the days when Vince was locked up there. Vince had heard from another mug in the Tombs that Brennan's family—wife and six children—had died in a fire in Brooklyn and that he'd been pulling stickups since then and getting a reputation as a man with a mean streak. "You tell Mike and Patsy," he'd said to Lottie, "when I get out I want them to be ready. We're going after all the big shots," he'd said. "Dutch, Big Owney, Luciano, Cabo, all the sons of bitches think they're bulletproof. They're gonna see about that," he'd said, and he'd leaned forward and kissed Lottie so gently she might have been a child. Lottie had mostly listened and let him talk and promised to deliver his messages.

Outside, the snowfall was steady, big flakes floating down past the barred windows, their easy drift interrupted now and then by a gust of wind. "Merry Christmas," she said in reply to Vince and kissed him again, another quick peck of a kiss, before pressing tighter against him, holding him locked up in her arms, keeping him still and quiet and close to her as long as she could.

9:00 a.m.

When the trial resumed, Lottie was back up in the balcony, dressed in a black skirt and sweater over a pale yellow blouse. She could tell that the people seated around her knew she was Vince's woman by the way they leaned away and whispered now and then, but no one was giving her any trouble by asking questions or sharing their opinions, which had happened a few times over the seven days of the trial, forcing her to move to another location or leave for the day. This morning everyone was intent on watching the proceedings as the judge entered and all rose and everyone's attention focused on Neary. Lottie had been unable to eat breakfast that morning. The thought of anything other than a cup of coffee brought on nausea. Now her hunger added to the jitters of the moment and she feared she'd have to leave again and make another trip to the bathroom, with Jennifer, the lady cop who was never far from her sight, once again accompanying her.

Lottie had come to fear Mr. James T. Neary. At first she'd hated him in his crisp three-piece suits with his cocky manner, acting as if he had all the answers and knew all the questions and there was only one way to judge the case that was obvious as the nose on his face and he was going to explain it all to the jury and that would be that, nothing to argue or discuss, and the jury would have no choice but to find Vince guilty. He was so confident, it was hard to believe that even given what had happened to his star witness he wouldn't just pick up and move on and continue explaining it all to the judge and jury, how Vince was the mad dog who'd killed that kid, how it was all perfectly obvious, forget about that nut George Brecht. Lottie had hated him at first, but now she feared him, and her heartbeat slowed to a whisper when he finally stood to address the judge, the courtroom quiet as the grave, everyone's attention fixed on him.

Neary straightened out his tie. He looked like a man about to do something difficult, taking a second to brace himself. "Your Honor," he said, far too loud, the words blasting out of him like a pair of gunshots. "Your Honor," he repeated, lowering his voice. He coughed into his fist. "In view of the fact," he went on, "that George Brecht has lied to the court—as has at this point been proven to our satisfaction—has lied about his former convictions and arrest record," he added, "has lied repeatedly and willfully on the stand, under oath. In view of all this—" Neary paused for the briefest of seconds, as if a word had gotten momentarily lodged in his throat. "In view of all this," he repeated, "I now appear before you, sir, and in the interests of justice I move the discharge of these defendants."

Before he had completed his sentence, newspapermen went scurrying out of the courtroom, hurrying out into the halls to file their reports, the courtroom suddenly loud with open conversation, exchanges of surprise and muttered curses and here and there laughter. At the defendant's table, Liebowitz put his arm around Vince's shoulder and gave him a little shake. Frank Guarracie, whose death sentence still hung over him, reached across Strenburg with a big smile and shook Vince's hand before Corrigan slammed his gavel down and quieted the room.

Corrigan looked like a man inches away from an act of violence: his face was dark red, the veins on his neck pulsed, and his teeth were clamped tight under lips drained of color. When the courtroom was once again quiet he glared at everyone, an animal looking out through the bars of his cage at spectators he'd like nothing more than to rip apart and devour. He turned to the jury, said quickly, "In view of the facts of this case I have no choice but to dismiss the charges," and then slammed his gavel a final time before standing and glaring down from his high perch as if daring anyone not to stand in his honor. When all stood, he swept out of the courtroom, his judge's robes billowing behind him.

"What's this?" Vince turned to Leibowitz as Giovanetti and Dwyer approached him out of the crowd with handcuffs ready.

"We still got you on gun charges," Dwyer said as he grabbed Vince's arm roughly and clamped the handcuffs on.

"And the Sheffield Farm charges," Giovanetti added. "Did you forget?"

Leibowitz laughed and slapped Vince on the shoulder. "It'll take me a few days, at the most, to get all the charges dropped."

Vince, who had thought he'd be free immediately, seemed rattled.

"Listen, Vince," Leibowitz leaned close to him, "a matter of days, I promise, and you'll be out of here and this will be behind you."

Vince looked around the courtroom at the spectators who were watching him with no plans of leaving while the main attraction was still on display. He gave the crowd a nod and a smile and some mug he didn't know shouted, "You showed 'em, Mad Dog!" And then there it was again, that name, Mad Dog, shouted like it meant King of the World. When Dwyer yanked Vince away from the table, he looked up to the balcony, where he saw Lottie leaning over the railing, looking down at him with her hands over her mouth and her face wet with tears. He winked at her, offered her his brightest smile, and followed Dwyer and the others through the side-door exit.

Lottie watched Vince till he was out of sight. Behind her, Strenburg was waiting with hands clasped at his belt and a big grin on his face as if to say *I told you so*. He opened his arms and Lottie happily gave him a hug.

11:00 a.m.

Between the snow and the cold, the ground was unyielding. Ercole's casket, rather than being lowered into the earth where the family might cast roses upon it and say a final good-bye, was carried off into a stone building, where it would wait with others till the weather allowed for interment in the ground. To Mama and the boys, this seemed like a minor issue. The viewing in Balzarini's plushly carpeted funeral parlor had gone well: family members from all over the city had joined neighborhood friends and acquaintances to pay their last respects, to kiss Mama and Gina on the cheek and shake the boys' hands. They'd said their few words and shared their memories of Ercole when he was a young man, healthy and hardworking and funny once you got to know him. Mama cried, but quietly, a tissue in her right hand to blot away the tears. A very few of the visitors believed what they'd been told, that Ercole had been ill with heart problems and away in a sanatorium out west. The rest knew the true story. Augie grew tired of being told how much he looked like Ercole, but other than that there were no complaints. It was only Gina who was distressed by having the casket carried off into a stone building and locked away.

"It's too much like . . ." Gina struggled for the words. She was walking hand in hand with Loretto—Mama and Augie in front of her, Freddie and Mike behind her—along a concrete path out of the cemetery toward a line of waiting cars, the stone building where they had just left Ercole receding behind them. "I don't know," she said, and she squeezed Loretto's hand as if to say she was sorry for not being able to express herself. "When they locked him in that building . . ."

"It was like when they locked him up because of what happened." Loretto tried to finish Gina's thought for her.

"I guess it reminds me of that," she said. "It bothers me."

Loretto put his arm around Gina's shoulders and pulled her close.

When he saw that the snow was sticking to her hair, he brushed it away and then balanced his fedora on the back of her head, where it acted as an umbrella.

Gina pushed the fedora forward and tilted it down so that it dropped over her forehead and covered her eyes. She let Loretto guide her to the car, where they got into the back seat and waited for Mike and Freddie to join them. Once in the car, she took off the fedora and held it in her lap. Outside, the snow was piling up on the lawns and over the graves while a crew of workmen in orange vests scraped wide, flat shovels over the concrete paths in an effort to keep ahead of the accumulation. Freddie and Mike were talking animatedly with Patsy while Maria stood off from their little circle and watched Mama and Augie getting into the lead car. Gina tapped the snow off the brim of Loretto's hat. "What's going on?" She gestured toward Freddie and the boys. Earlier, just before Ercole had been locked away once again, Mike had put his arm around Loretto's shoulders, some piece of news had passed between them, and they had talked about it for a while. She had meant to ask what that was about and forgotten.

"It's Vince," Loretto said. "He got off. Somebody heard it on the radio."

"What do you mean *he got off*? He got off on the murder charge?"

"He got off on everything," Loretto said, a touch of excitement in his voice. "Mike says he'll be out in a couple of days."

"That's it?" Gina tossed Loretto's fedora down on the seat between them. "He doesn't have to serve any time at all for nothing, for no charges, not even for the guns and the shooting?"

Loretto picked up his hat and put it on his knee. "Jeez, Gina. You know how these things work. Vince bought himself the best lawyer in the country." Loretto shrugged as if to say, *Why are you surprised that he got off?*

"For Christ's sake . . ." Gina looked away from Loretto, out the opposite window. "So he'll go right back to what he was doing before, only now he won't have every cop in the country looking for him." With her forearm, she wiped condensation from her window. "What will this mean for us?" She shifted in her seat so that she was facing Loretto. "Do we have to worry about Vince again?"

Outside, the sky darkened suddenly, went from slate gray to a darker shade, and Loretto saw himself reflected in the side window, with Gina watching him. He said, "Everything will be okay, Gina," and he felt suddenly as though he were in a movie. He wasn't looking at Gina. She was twisted around in her seat to face him and he was looking away from her. The figure in the window was a good-looking boy with smooth skin and blue eyes. To Loretto he looked childish, almost innocent, in such contrast with his own image of himself as a tough guy hardened by growing up abandoned and in an orphanage, by stealing and scraping all his life and holding his own—in such contrast with his own picture of himself that it angered him.

Gina said, "Vince knows you've got a job now, right?"

Loretto nodded but still didn't turn to look at Gina—and then Freddie and Mike were getting into the car and the conversation turned back to the funeral and Ercole. Freddie recounted a story he'd been told about Ercole once carrying a neighbor, a man who weighed fifty pounds more than he should have, up six flights of stairs when he'd sprained his ankle walking back from the grocery store—and then carrying the man's groceries up after him. Loretto smiled and pretended to share the others' pleasure in this story, though what he was really wondering was how this could be the same man, this generous strong figure in the story, as the man who'd nearly murdered his twelve-year-old daughter.

"Hey, Loretto," Freddie said. "What are you looking at?"

Loretto was looking at himself in the side window. "Nothing," he said. "I don't know. Just thinking."

Gina asked softly, "What are you thinking about?"

"I don't know," Loretto said again and then added, "It's hard to figure things."

Gina nodded, as did Freddie, assuming Loretto was talking about Ercole and the funeral and the questions of life and death that a funeral might bring to one's thoughts.

"Yeah," Freddie said. "Who knows?" and he fell back into his seat as the car went quiet for the remainder of the short drive home.

2:25 p.m.

A window beside the closed courthouse doors offered Vince a clear view of the newspapermen and spectators crowding the steep steps that led down to the street. He was waiting for Leibowitz to escort him to his car. With Lottie by his side, Strenburg behind him, and a gang of coppers and guards swarming and buzzing around, he entertained himself by watching a couple of mugs with press cards sticking out of their headbands. They were shoving each other and appeared to be on the edge of throwing punches. "Look at those two birdbrains," he said to Lottie. Lottie picked herself up on her toes, peered out the window. "Dopes," she said. She gave Vince's arm a squeeze. "What's taking Leibowitz so long?"

Vince stepped to the side for a better look at the black Lincoln with whitewall tires waiting for them on the street. The car was brand-new and flashy, with a spare tire on the running board, a rearview mirror belted to the tire. "Who's driving again?"

"I don't know him," Lottie said. "Joe Evangelista. He goes by Jo Jo."

"He's Castellammares'. Him and his brother Frank."

"Yeah?" Lottie was more interested in Leibowitz's whereabouts than in hearing about Jo Jo Evangelista.

"Jo Jo and his brother, it didn't sit well with them what happened to Maranzano."

"Don't be thinkin' about that stuff now." Lottie straightened out Vince's jacket and adjusted the tilt of his hat. She had bought him a new pearl-gray fedora with a black band for his release. "First thing we do when we're out of here," she said, "is get rid of the mustache." She kissed him on the lips. "You're even handsomer without it."

"Here's the man of the hour," Vince said.

Lottie turned toward the commotion as Leibowitz made his way through the crowd. "About time," she said. She had begun to worry that something new had come up to delay Vince's release.

Leibowitz put his arm over Vince's shoulders and pulled him away from Lottie. He left Strenburg to hold off the others while he had a few words with Vince in relative private. "We have a problem," he said. "Turns out the Lennox Bonding Company put up your fifty-thousand-dollar bail."

"Never heard of 'em."

"But you have," Leibowitz said. "A little detective work and it's revealed that they're a front for Dutch Schultz and Owen Madden."

Vince laughed. "I didn't know the boys cared."

"Vince," Leibowitz said, "this isn't a laughing matter. Don't forget what happened to your friend Jack Diamond. He didn't last twelve hours on the street after he was acquitted."

"I haven't forgotten Jack," Vince said, and his face reddened slightly. "I haven't forgotten Jack. I haven't forgotten my brother Pete. I haven't forgotten anything."

"All the same," Leibowitz said, "I've arranged for a car to meet you at the side entrance." He took Vince by the wrist and tried to direct him back through the crowd.

"Not on your life." Vince jerked his hand free and grabbed Leibowitz roughly by the arm. "We're going out the front, Counselor." He pushed Leibowitz ahead of him to the courthouse doors.

Once on the steps, the crowd surged toward Vince, shouting a bar-

rage of questions. The bright midafternoon sun reflecting off sheets of
snow and ice was blinding and Vince covered his eyes with a forearm. He
understood that the photographers were shouting for a picture and the
reporters were yelling out questions, but in the fury of all those voices
trying to yell over each other, the only thing he heard clearly were the
words *Mad Dog*, which it seemed everybody was shouting all at once,
trying to get his attention. Strenburg and another lawyer pushed through
the crowd, pulling Vince and Lottie along behind them while Leibowitz
raised his hands and called out to the crowd, telling them he'd answer
their questions. When they reached the car, Strenburg opened the door
and Vince and Lottie piled into the back seat, where Vince looked up to
see Leibowitz at the top of the steps, surrounded by a crowd of reporters
jotting furiously in notepads. Behind them stood the three detectives—
Givons, Dwyer, and Giovanetti—all three with their hands on their hips
and identical angry sneers. They made Vince laugh and he saluted them
as the Lincoln pulled out into traffic. "Boys," he said by way of taking
leave, as if they could hear him.

From the driver's seat, Jo Jo said, "*V'fancul'!* What a mob scene!"
Then, with his eyes on the road, he reached into the back seat for a handshake. "Congratulations, boss."

Vince shook his hand. "Good to see you," he said. "How's Frankie?"

"Eh, you know Frankie. Still betting the ponies."

Vince hardly knew either Frankie or Jo Jo. They were among the older
boys on the streets when he was a kid. Everybody knew to stay away from
them. Jo Jo was crazy and Frankie was crazier. Later they were with Joe the
Boss, and then Maranzano after Joe got his, and then he'd heard they'd
gone independent after Maranzano got it because they didn't like the way
that all happened. They were no fans of Lucky Luciano. "Glad you and
Frankie are on board," he said. "I got big things planned."

"Sure," Jo Jo said. "You're the big shot now. Mad Dog Coll. You're in
all the headlines." He pulled the car into an alley, slid in close to a brick

wall behind rows of garbage pails, and picked up a cannon—a big Colt .45— from under a newspaper on the seat beside him.

"What's going on?" Vince glanced up and down the alley and started to reach under his jacket as if he were heeled.

"We're switching cars," Lottie said, and right on cue a Chevy coupe pulled up next to them.

Jo Jo got out of the Lincoln with his gun dangling at his side, and Mike got out of the Chevy with a tommy gun cradled in his arms.

Jo Jo said, "Okay, boss," and Lottie took Vince by the arm as they switched cars.

Patsy, behind the wheel of the Chevy, drove slowly toward the street, where he waited for a third car, a Packard Speedster, to pull out of a parking space. A moment later the three cars, the Chevy between the Packard and the Lincoln, were rolling in a caravan toward the Manhattan Bridge.

After shaking hands with Mike, slapping Patsy on the back, and exchanging greetings, Vince settled into his seat and put an arm around Lottie. "Who's in the lead car?" he asked Mike.

"Paul Martone and Anthony Domini, from the old days with Little Augie."

"Jeez, those two," Vince said and laughed.

Lottie said, "I hope you can control these guys."

"Remember that thing on the bocce court," Mike said, "with the Evangelistas?"

"What thing?" Lottie asked.

"I remember it," Vince said. "It was some Polack."

"So?" Lottie pressed when Vince didn't offer any further details.

"Frank and Jo Jo are playing bocce with a couple of other *cafon's*," Mike explained. "This Polish guy comes around, doesn't know what bocce is. This and that, he makes some remark about bocce being a dumb dago game—and that was that."

"Shoved a boccino down his throat," Patsy said.

"Looked like one of those snakes that eats a cow," Mike added.

Patsy said, "Here we are," and he pulled into an alley that dead-ended in a courtyard. He took a pistol from his shoulder holster and got out of the car along with Mike. The Packard pulled in behind them, and the Lincoln parked at the head of the alley, blocking anyone else from entering. With Jo Jo at one end of the alley and Paul and Anthony at the other, Mike and Patsy escorted Vince and Lottie through a back door, up a flight of stairs, and into a nicely appointed apartment, where Florence and Joe were waiting along with Loretto and Jimmy Brennan, a thick, bent-over mug with a beer belly who looked like an older, beat-up version of the kid Vince had known all those years ago back in the orphanage.

On a long table in the dining room, Florence had set out sandwiches and cold cuts along with plates of pastries and fruits. The apartment looked like it had been fit for royalty twenty years ago, and it was still impressively plush, with heavy rugs over polished wood floors, plaster ceilings with fancy carvings around the light fixtures, and tall, curtained windows. Florence had gotten dressed up for the occasion. She waited at the head of the table in a frilly blue dress, her hands pressed together as if her prayers had been answered. Vince nodded to her as the rest of the boys filed into the apartment behind him. Florence hadn't shown up for a single day of either trial, but then this was the same woman who wouldn't let Vince and Pete live with her when their mother died.

"Let's toast!" Florence said. "Come on, boys!" She gestured toward a table in the kitchen where a dozen glasses were waiting beside several bottles of whiskey. "Pour yourselves a drink so we can toast to Vince!"

Vince followed Lottie to the kitchen table, shaking hands and exchanging greetings along the way. He poured himself a drink and looked around the room at the assemblage waiting to toast him. Loretto and Jimmy Brennan were face to face by a front window. They looked like they'd been talking for a while, Loretto fresh-faced and sharp in a pale blue double-breasted suit with a pocket square, Jimmy rumpled and sour-looking under a messy clump of barely combed Irish-red hair, wearing a cheap suit, his tie loosened and collar open. He looked like he already had a few drinks under his belt. Jo Jo had gone straight to his brother, Frankie. Jo Jo was slim, looked to be in good shape, and wasn't a bad-looking guy if you discounted the scar that ran from just under his chin all the way down his neck, where it disappeared under his collar. Frankie, his older brother, was bulky, with fat cheeks and droopy eyes that made him look a little drunk even when he was completely sober. Of the two, Frankie was the stronger and Jo Jo the smarter. Paul Martone and Anthony Domini had taken up positions on either side of the front door like a pair of palace guards. Mike and Patsy poured themselves drinks and pulled up seats across from each other at the dining room table, next to Florence's Joe, who looked like he always did, as if he'd just got off work at the docks.

Florence held up her drink. "To Vince," she said—but before she could say anything more Vince cut her off.

"First drink is to Frank and Tuffy."

"Hear, hear," Mike said, and they all threw back their shots.

"And this one's to Vince," Florence went on, "the toughest son of a bitch in the whole feckin' country!"

Before downing their drinks, the Evangelistas, unaccustomed to Florence's foul mouth, exchanged looks as if their sense of propriety was offended.

Vince put his glass down. "Let's get to the business at hand." He pulled up a seat at the head of the table and gestured for the others to join him. Loretto and Jimmy kept their places by the front window while the rest of the boys crowded around and pulled up seats. Lottie perched on the armrest of Vince's chair, her arm around his shoulders, while Florence sat next to Joe, glanced quickly at Lottie, and just as quickly looked away.

"I'll keep this simple for now," Vince said. "First . . ." he lifted his glass and looked to each of the new recruits. "Paul, Anthony, Frankie, Jo Jo, and Jimmy . . . I'm glad you mugs saw fit to come in with us." He threw back his drink and the others followed. "With you mugs on board, there ain't a tougher bunch in the country."

"Or a crazier one," Jimmy Brennan said. When everyone looked at him, he added, grinning, "I mean that with the utmost respect," and drew a cautious laugh.

Mike said, "Once Dutch gets word of this, he's going so deep into hiding, he'll have to look up to see his own ass," and drew another laugh.

Vince knocked on the table. "Here's the down and dirty," he said. "This time next year, we're all gonna be so rich the Vanderbilts will be comin' to us for loans."

Jimmy said, "And just how are we gonna manage that, Vince, if you wouldn't mind fillin' in the peasantry?"

Jimmy's tone walked a fine line between belligerent and amused. "Ah, Jimmy Brennan," Vince said, putting on the Irish, "if you'll shaddup, I'll be telling you."

"Aye," Jimmy said, "I'm quiet as a ghost."

"This is how we're doing it," Vince said. "We're gonna cripple the Combine's ability to produce and distribute beer here, in and around the city, and then we're gonna control all the routes in and out. Once we accomplish that, they'll all be on their knees to us, them that are still alive—and I'll tell you right now, that won't include Dutch Schultz."

"How do you plan to do that?" Anthony Domini asked. He was short and squat, with meaty lips and a ruddy face. He looked like a little fireplug, like it would take a truck to knock him off his feet. "They got a lot of breweries and a lot of men."

"A lot of men," Vince said, "but this is what come to me when I was in the Tombs: not that many breweries." He paused and smiled as if giving everyone a second to think. "One brewery in particular probably serves half the city its beer."

"Big Owney's," Frank Evangelista said. He seemed amused.

"Home of Madden's Number 1," Vince said, and Lottie gave him a squeeze, as if excited for him.

"That place is a fortress," Brennan said.

"No. It ain't," Vince answered.

"You can't park a car on the street there without coppers coming from every direction to give you a ticket!" Brennan took a step toward Vince as if he wanted to make sure he was being heard. "Madden's got every flatfoot within a mile of 25th Street on his payroll. You can't get near the place."

"Sure, we can get near the place," Vince said. He gave Lottie a kiss on the cheek and pointedly didn't look at Brennan. "In fact," he added, nodding to Mike, "we can get inside the place."

"Piece of cake," Mike said. With his thumb, he massaged the scar over his eyebrow and waited till everyone's attention was riveted on him. "We've got the addresses and schedules of everyone who works at Madden's famous Phoenix Cereal Beverage Company. We've bought the ones we need to buy, and when we're ready, we'll walk right in, along with all the rest of the workers."

Frank Evangelista scratched his head. He looked uncertain. "I heard they got machine guns set up at all the windows and on the roof."

"Not every window," Mike said. "Four facing 26th Street and four more up on the roof. Thing is, they're the big belt-fed jobs, and they'll be facing the wrong way. We won't be out on the street or up on the roof. We'll be inside. Behind them."

Paul Martone laughed like he was in on the joke. "They won't have a chance." He was a tall, good-looking guy who was making an effort to keep his eyes on Vince and not to notice Lottie.

Brennan still wasn't buying it. "So we're just walkin' in the front door? Just like that?"

"No, a little more complicated than that," Mike said.

Patsy turned to Brennan. "You'll see when the time comes," he said, making no effort at being pleasant.

"See," Vince said, "Madden's gotten soft. He thinks he's one of those movie stars come to his clubs all the time. We're gonna remind him the nature of his business."

"You don't say." Brennan put an arm around Loretto's shoulders. "I count ten men in this room. You know how many men Owen alone has on his payroll? Let alone the rest of the Combine?"

"Sure," Vince said, "but they can't kill us if they can't find us. My sister, Florence, here . . ." Vince nodded to Florence and she puffed up and looked around the room. "Florence has rented places for us spread around the city. And Joe," he nodded to Joe, who awkwardly saluted the table, "Joe has rented some more places. I'm the only one who knows all these residences. Before you leave, I'll give you an address, and the first thing you're gonna do is take what you need out of wherever you're staying now and move to the new place, where, if you're smart, you'll stay inside and keep your head down. Plus, every week or so we'll move everybody around. I'll know where to find you, but you don't know how to find each other, and nobody knows how to find me." Vince paused, turned to Brennan, and added, "Like I said: they can't kill us if they can't find us."

Brennan lifted his glass to Vince. "You've got moxie!" he yelled. "I'll give you that!"

"I'm telling you, Jimmy Brennan," Vince said, and he turned on his charm, making an effort to convince an old friend, "these mugs have gotten soft, Madden especially. Once they see we mean business, they'll get out of our way. They'll either get out of our way or we'll put 'em in the ground."

"Sure," Jimmy said, and again he lifted his glass to Vince. "You picked the men to do the job, there's no arguing with you there."

"We're starting right away," Mike said, "so you boys might as well enjoy yourselves while you've got the chance."

Paul Martone asked how soon, and Mike told him soon enough.

"Tomorrow," Vince said, "we start hitting their drops and taking out their trucks. The Cotton Club, the Silver Slipper, the Napoleon, the De Fay—these clubs should have a hard time satisfying their customers' thirst if we do our job right."

"*Cazzo!*" Jo Jo said. "We're gonna be making a lot of people very angry."

"That's the point," Vince said. "After three, four weeks of this, then we'll head upstate."

Loretto spoke up for the first time. "Who's running Diamond's gang now? Joe Rock?"

"We are," Mike said. "Only Joe don't know it yet."

Vince said, "Don't worry about Rock. Once we show up in Albany, we'll be running things."

Florence said, "Eat up, boys! Don't be letting all this good food go to waste." And with that, the business of the meeting was over and the men went about helping themselves to sandwiches and booze. Mike and Patsy joined Loretto as Vince and Lottie slipped off into another room, out of sight. A minute later, Lottie came back, found Loretto, and told him Vince wanted to see him.

"Go ahead," Mike said to Loretto, turning his back to the others and lowering his voice. "We got everything straightened out."

"You don't have to worry about nothin'." Lottie slipped in between Mike and Patsy. "We fixed it all up." She gave Loretto a playful kiss on the lips. The three of them—Lottie, Patsy, and Mike—made a small, intimate circle, the old-timers, the remains of Vince's old gang.

"Guess I'll go see what he wants." Loretto straightened his tie and exited the circle. He paused at the entrance to the room where Vince had disappeared, considered knocking, and then pushed open the door and walked in. He found Vince stretched out on a chaise longue next to a bed that looked big enough to sleep six people. Spread out over the surface of the bed was an array of tommy guns, sawed-off shotguns, pistols, and pineapples.

"Vince." Loretto took a seat on the edge of the bed, next to the chaise longue. "Lottie said you wanted to talk to me."

Vince lay with his arms folded over his chest and his eyes on the ceiling. If he was aware of Loretto entering the room and addressing him, he wasn't showing it. His eyes remained fixed on the ceiling for several awkward seconds before he turned to face Loretto and stare at him in silence.

Loretto said, "Did you want to talk to me, Vince? Or am I supposed to be getting some kind of message by the way you're looking at me?"

"How am I looking at you?" Vince asked.

"Like maybe you want to put a bullet in my face."

"And why would you be thinking that, Loretto?" Vince rubbed his forehead as if trying to relieve a headache. The motion took some of the tension out of the room. By rubbing his forehead, he was at least not pulling out a gun.

"Rumor was you weren't especially happy with me."

"You're here, aren't you?" Vince said. "If I weren't happy with you, somebody'd be patting you with a spade about now."

"All right," Loretto said. "So what did you want to talk to me about?"

Vince sighed and closed his eyes as if resting for one more second. Then he pulled himself upright. "I'm glad you're in with us," he said. "I like you. I've always liked you. And I'm gonna make us all rich."

"Great," Loretto said. "I'm in. I quit my job at the park. I'm with you."

"I know that," Vince said. "You been working with Mike and Patsy. I know about you murderin' a chandelier at one of Jablonski's joints. Lottie thinks you're aces. I've been kept informed while I was out of circulation."

"So?"

"So these new guys," Vince said, "between them, they've kept the cemetery business thriving. You understand? They're killers. We're all killers.

Except you, Loretto. You're like a virgin shows up at a cathouse and wants to join the party."

"Yeah, but you invited me to this party, Vince."

"And like I said, I'm glad you're here because we go way back—and I hate to see a guy like you playin' the sucker, breakin' his back for nothin'. I just want to be sure you understand the situation we're in. There's about to be a lot of blood spilled, and we'll be the ones doing the spillin'."

Loretto's arm twitched, a quick spasm that made his fist close as if it were somehow separated from him, a creature moving beside him on the bed. When it twitched again, he stood and shoved his hand in his pocket. "I know what I'm getting into," he said. "I'll do my part."

"Good." Vince gestured toward the door, meaning Loretto could leave. "Ask Lottie to come back in, will you?"

"Sure." Loretto pointed to the bed. "We've got an arsenal here."

Vince said, "One more thing, Loretto. You ever disappear on me again, whatever it was got you sick, you can be sure it'll be fatal."

Loretto thought about saying something more and decided against it. He left the room and closed the door gently behind him.

Vince stretched out again on the chaise longue. He was tired. His thoughts kept going back to Schultz and Madden and the Lennox Bonding Company. He imagined the two of them meeting at Polly Adler's place or the Cotton Club, in a posh room somewhere, sitting over a table with drinks in their hands, talking about killing him, killing Vince Coll, putting up fifty thousand dollars bail like the chump change it was just to get him out on the street and make him an easier target—and what infuriated him, what made his heart start beating like it might tap-dance out of his chest, was the thinking of those bastards, that all they needed was to get him out on the street and they'd kill him, the way they'd killed Pete, the way they'd killed Jack.

He wanted those bastards to fear him. He wanted them to pay fifty thousand dollars to keep him *in* jail because they were afraid he'd get to them if he was out on the street—and it made him crazy that it was the other way around, that they *wanted* him on the street because they thought they could get to him that easily. "One of us is wrong," he said aloud, under his breath, meaning either they were wrong to set him free and it'd cost them their lives and their businesses or he was wrong to think he could take it all away from them. If he could have somehow gotten up from his lounge chair and found himself in that room at Polly Adler's or the Cotton Club, he'd have killed them both and taken his time doing it.

"You want to get out of here?" Lottie asked when she came in and found Vince lying down with his eyes closed. "Are you tired, honey?"

Vince got up, found the new pearl-gray fedora Lottie had bought for him, and put it on. "Yeah, we're getting out of here."

Lottie winked, thinking Vince was ready to catch up on some lost time in the sack. "Where we going?" she said. "I hear the rooms at the Waldorf are the cat's pajamas."

"We're going to City Hall."

Lottie's attitude quickly changed. "Why would we go there?"

"To get a marriage license."

For a second Lottie looked like she might fall over. Then she flew across the room. She leaped into his arms and they fell back together onto the bed.

Vince pushed the guns and the pineapples aside as Lottie leaped up again, locked the door, slipped out of her dress, and climbed over him in her underwear.

Vince looked at his wristwatch. "We got a couple of hours before the offices close."

"That's time enough," Lottie said, and she went about unbuttoning his shirt and helping him out of his clothes to the accompaniment of laughter and shouting voices as the boys got drunker and louder on the other side of the door.

9:00 p.m.

Loretto had moved his two suitcases' worth of possessions out of Mama's before Augie and Freddie were back from work. The weather had turned bitter, and snow piled up on the sidewalks froze into ice barriers between the streets and the tenements. Mike had waited on the street with his car parked behind Dominic's Packard, in case Loretto needed a push, and Mama watched from the living room window as Loretto hauled his stuff out of the warmth of her apartment, down the steps, and out into the cold. "What's the matter?" she asked Loretto before he carried off the last of his suits. "He can't come up to see his mother?" Loretto kissed her on the cheek before leaving. "He'll come up later, probably," he said, and he made his way down to the icy sidewalk, threw the suits in the back of car, and then followed Mike as he led the way to an apartment downtown in the city, on Greenwich Street, a first-floor, two-bedroom flat hidden behind a warehouse.

Mike had settled into the apartment quickly. By the time it was dark, he'd packed his clothes away, made his bed, and stocked the icebox with a week's worth of food. Loretto had also gotten settled quickly, and the two of them were in the kitchen, sitting at the table with a bottle of wine between them, drinking and listening to *The Shadow* on the radio, when someone knocked on the door. The knock was soft and tentative, and the two men looked at each other as if neither had any idea who could possibly be looking for them. Mike took his pistol from the kitchen counter and tucked it into the back of his pants. He stood away from the door, asked who was there, and then opened it with a look of shock on his face when Gina answered and asked to be let in.

"How the hell'd you find us? *Che cazzo!*" He turned to Loretto, who was watching from the kitchen. "How she'd find us?"

"Don't get excited," Gina said to Mike. She stepped into the apartment and closed the door behind her. "One of you dropped this." She took a slip of paper out of her purse with the address written on it. "Mama found it in the boys' room."

Mike made a fist, as if threatening to punch Loretto in the nose.

Loretto, frozen at the entrance to the kitchen, was speechless. Gina said, "I had to see it for myself."

Mike said, "Come on in. I'll make you some pasta. It's not Mama's," he added, "but I'm pretty good."

Gina crumpled up the slip of paper, tossed it to the floor, and left.

"Don't worry about it," Mike said on his way back to the kitchen and *The Shadow*. "That's just Gina. You know how she is."

Loretto snatched his coat and gloves from the living room closet and followed Gina out the door. By the time he reached the street, she was already a block ahead of him, on her way to the subway stop. When he called to her, she ignored him.

"Gina, listen," Loretto said, when he caught up to her. He was still pulling on his gloves. "Jeez, it's cold."

"That's what you came out to tell me? That it's cold?" She walked on, and only after a full block, with Loretto continuing to walk alongside her in silence, did she stop. "Were you even going to tell me?" she asked. "Did you quit your job? Are you with *Mad Dog Coll* now?" She spit out the words *Mad Dog Coll* as if they were both funny and horrifying at the same time.

Loretto rubbed his hands together and then pointed to a Greek diner across from the subway stop. "Let's get a cup of coffee," he said. "We can talk in the diner, where it's warm."

"No. If you're back with Vince, if you and Mike . . ."

"Gina . . ." Loretto shoved his gloved hands deep into his coat pockets. "Try to understand."

"Understand what? I'm listening. Go ahead."

Loretto looped his arm through hers and tried to pull her across the street toward the diner.

Gina resisted. "I'm not having coffee with you," she said. "Tell me right here. What do you want me to understand?"

A plume of condensation rose up from Loretto's lips. "I don't want to dig ditches," he said. "Try to understand that, could you? I don't want to spend the rest of my life like a glorified draft horse, hauling tree limbs, carrying rocks, and getting treated no better than a horse, either. Could you try to understand that, please?"

"Sure, I can understand," Gina said. "So what do you want to do? You're twenty-one years old. There's lots of things you can do."

"I want to make some real dough," Loretto said, suddenly finding confidence. "I'd like a house with some property. Why shouldn't we have that? I want to buy us a reliable car and good clothes. I want to be somebody. I don't want to live six of us crammed into a two-bedroom apartment, like everybody I ever knew growing up. I want to stay in nice hotels when I feel like it. I want to go to the Cotton Club with the rest of the big shots. Does that make me crazy? Is it so crazy to want that?"

"It's not crazy to want it," Gina said. She took a step back as if surprised by Loretto's tone of voice and his manner, which was suddenly different, louder and larger. "But are you willing to kill people for it? That's what's crazy, Loretto."

"And the rich," Loretto said, "you think they don't kill people who get in their way?"

"No. I don't."

Loretto laughed at that, and his look—standing in the street, his hands back in his pockets—his look was a sneer.

Gina said, "What happens if you get killed? Have you thought about that?"

"It's the business," he said. "It's the risk everybody takes. Everybody that signs up knows the deal."

"And that makes it okay?"

Loretto repeated, "It's the risk everybody takes."

"For the fancy clothes and their names in the paper and pockets lined with cash," Gina said. "And what about when a kid gets killed? What about the Vengelli boy? Is that okay? Is that the business, too?"

"That was a mistake."

Gina looked at Loretto as if he were a stranger. "I thought . . ." she said, and suddenly she was pleading. "I thought that night when you stayed with me instead of going with Vince . . . I thought you were done with him."

Loretto said, "It doesn't have to be one way or the other, Gina."

"Yes, it does," Gina answered, and then she shivered, the cold finally getting to her.

"I thought . . ."

"What did you think?"

Loretto didn't know how to answer. His thoughts were tangled. "Don't go, Gina," he said. "Stay and have coffee with me."

"You made your choice," Gina said. She turned and walked off to the subway and then disappeared down a flight of steps, out of the darkness and into the bright light reflecting off the white tiles of the subway walls. Loretto stomped his feet and clapped his hands, fighting off the cold, but he waited a full minute or more after Gina was out of sight before he finally turned around and went back to the apartment, where he went directly to his bedroom and lay down on his bed, still in his coat and gloves.

Mike peeked into Loretto's room and sighed as if frustrated. "Jeez, Loretto," he said. "Look. Gina's a dame, and she loves you. For dames, that's the end of the story. Relax, will ya?" He shut the door as if he didn't want to be bothered by Loretto for another second.

Loretto kicked off his shoes, turned off the lights, and got under the covers, where he lay in the dark, still shivering from the cold.

WEDNESDAY ••• JANUARY 6, 1932

6:00 a.m.

Stretched out in the back seat of a beat-up old Ford, Loretto tried to look like he was catching a little nap before the action started. Under his feet, a grease-stained red blanket covered a black tommy gun. Alongside him, Patsy was talking to Anthony Domini, who was gazing out the window as if bored to tears. Mike was in front, driving, and Paul Martone leaned forward in the passenger seat next to him, humming "Life Is Just a Bowl of Cherries" and tapping his fingers on the dashboard. They were following Vince and Jimmy Brennan and the Evangelista brothers in another old Ford, a two-car caravan making its way through the still-dark streets at an hour in the morning unfamiliar to all of them.

Loretto knew that they were in the city, near Madden's brewery, but he didn't know exactly where they were. He had closed his eyes shortly after getting into the car, mumbled grumpily about the early hour, and hadn't opened his eyes or said a word since. He knew that if he talked, his voice would betray him. He'd been involved in all manner of rough stuff over his years on the street and then with Gaspar and Dominic, but nothing like this. They were riding in cars taken from brewery workers who were spending the night tied up in a machine shop in the Bronx. He was dressed in khaki coveralls, as was everyone else. He knew little of the plan beyond that their cars were full of bombs and tommy guns, with which they hoped to blow up the brewery and kill anyone who tried to stop them. The only thing in their way was Madden's goons, an unknown number of them, all of whom would be well armed. The plan was to go in and get out quick: blow up as much of the equipment as possible and shoot up anything and anyone left standing.

Patsy shook Loretto by the arm, and he sat up as the car descended a long ramp to an underground garage and a couple of men waiting at a sawhorse blockade. When Vince's car approached the blockade, the workers moved the sawhorses aside and waved them through. Loretto glanced back at them as they jogged up the ramp.

"I hope Vince paid those guys enough to get out of New York," Patsy said.

Anthony Domini said, "If they're smart, they'll go all the way to California."

Mike said, "Here we go," and he pulled into a parking spot next to Vince. At the other end of the garage, night-shift workers were filing out through a tall green door and making their way toward an exit or toward parked cars.

"Keep your heads down," Vince said as he joined them. Behind him, Jo Jo Evangelista carried a cardboard box in his arms, clutched to his chest.

"Give these mugs a minute to clear out," Mike said, meaning the workers who were still making their way out of the building. "We bought off the guy at the door."

"How do we get to the brewery?" Anthony Domini asked.

"Same way everybody else does," Mike said. "There's a tunnel goes under the street."

"Big secret," Frankie Evangelista said. Prohibition agents had barred the doors to the brewery, making it appear from the street that the place was shut down. "Like anybody with a nose can't smell beer brewing a mile away."

"All right," Vince said. "Let's be about our business."

The tommy guns the boys were carrying were hardly invisible zipped up under their coveralls, but at least they weren't completely out in the open. Someone not paying attention might miss the bulge extending down from chest to pants leg.

At the door, the guy waiting for them nodded to Vince and then walked away.

"Hey, Vince," Patsy said, "you paying those birds enough for a nice long vacation?"

Vince said, "Don't worry about it," and he held the door open till everyone passed through, with Loretto at the back of the line. On the other side of the door a short, dark hallway led to a second door. Vince looped his arm through Loretto's. "Once we're in the brewery, you're guarding the door for us," he said. "You just stand there. Anybody tries to get out, you shoot 'em. Anybody tries to get in, you shoot 'em. Got it?"

"Sounds simple enough."

"I need somebody at the door with brains and balls enough not to let us get trapped in there."

In front of them, Mike said, "This is where the shootin' starts." He waited at the door for the others to join him. "This opens into a warehouse." He lowered his voice. "Not more than a handful of guys in there usually, and most of 'em will run soon as they see us." He pulled a tommy gun free of his coveralls and zipped up again, as did everyone else.

Vince said, "I'm going through first," and offered everyone one of his light-up-the-room smiles. "Don't any of you mugs shoot me in the back."

"I don't know," Frankie Evangelista said. He waved his chopper around. "My aim ain't so good."

Vince winked at him. To everyone he said, "You ready?"

Mike said, "There's another door across from us. And through that one there's a tunnel under the street that comes out in the brewery. That's where the real fun will start."

Jo Jo held out the cardboard box full of pineapples he was carrying.

"You mugs watch out for me," he said. "I could blow us all to smithereens."

Vince looked everyone over, waiting to see if anyone else had something to say. When everyone was quiet, he saluted them by tapping the barrel of his chopper against his forehead and then threw open the door and jumped into the warehouse, shooting.

The handful of workers scattered with the first burst of gunfire. A few of them hit the ground and crawled behind boxing crates; a few leaped over the crates and dove for cover. Only two mugs went for their guns, both of them dressed in suits that identified them as Madden's boys and not brewery workers. They pulled pistols from shoulder holsters and fired blindly, hitting nothing but the high walls of the warehouse. They both ran for a tall window that appeared to open into an airshaft. Vince went after them, caught them climbing through the window, and emptied two quick burst into them up close before joining the rest of the boys as they pushed through the second door and into the tunnel under the street.

Loretto waited for Vince at the tunnel entrance, his chopper in one hand pointed at the ceiling, his other hand holding the door open. Vince brushed by him without a word and ran to catch up with the others. Loretto lagged behind, keeping an eye on what was going on behind him as well as in front of him. To his surprise, his nervousness, his churning stomach and racing heart, had quieted. He seemed to be moving on automatic, not thinking, not feeling, just moving: all eyes and ears. He saw everything in sharp relief—the makeshift brick walls of the tunnel, the cigarette butts and empty packs and newspaper pages that littered the ground—and his hearing was attuned to the source of every sound, the footsteps of Vince and the boys racing ahead of him like a herd of animals let loose, the way the brick walls muffled every noise, the voices behind him in the warehouse, even the sound of the warehouse door opening and closing, so that hearing was strangely like seeing, as if he could actually see workers charging out of the warehouse by the sound of their footsteps and their voices and the banging of the door.

Before they reached the second set of doors at the other end of the tunnel, someone kicked them open and was met by a burst of machine-gun fire that flung him backward, his own chopper flying out of his hands and skittering across a rough concrete floor. A moment later, they were inside the brewery and Vince was looking up at high red brick walls and a latticework of black catwalks and ladders over a dozen brewing vats with hoses and pipes and gauges everywhere, a row of round metal pipes climbing the walls and disappearing into high vents. Big belt-fed machine guns on tripods were set up on the highest catwalk, each of them pointing out windows to the street and each of them with a folding chair alongside. Of the four, two were unattended. The other two had men working furiously to get them turned around while others lay on their bellies on the catwalk with pistols and choppers, putting down a constant stream of fire at the entrance to the brewery.

Vince and the boys quickly backed into the cover of the tunnel. As soon as they had entered the brewery, Frankie Evangelista had been knocked nearly unconscious by a bullet that grazed his temple, gouging out a slice of skin a quarter-inch deep. He crumpled to the ground before Jo Jo, firing wildly up at the catwalks, dragged him back into the tunnel. From up on the catwalk someone yelled, "Good to see ya, Mad Dog! Come on in! We're waitin' for ya!" Loretto, at the other end of the tunnel guarding the doors, recognized the voice immediately, even though he had only seen him once before and he had only spoken a few words. It was Joey Pizzolatto, the mug who'd pointed a gun at his head and was about to send him to meet his maker before Mike interfered and clocked him with the john's porcelain tank cover.

"Bastards got us pinned here," Anthony Domini said.

Jo Jo peeled back his coveralls, took off his shirt, and wrapped it like a bandana around Frankie's head. "You okay?" he asked his brother as he came around.

Frankie pulled himself to his feet, his face red as the blood seeping through his makeshift bandage.

From the catwalks, more taunting and laughter: "Hey, Mad Dog! What's keeping ya! Come on! We're waitin'!"

Vince peeked around the corner of the door and was greeted by a volley of machine-gun fire that tore one of the doors off its hinges. It fell over like a drawbridge closing. "They got those big machine guns turned around," he said.

"All of 'em?" Paul Martone asked, backing up a little.

Frankie Evangelista laughed and yelled, "Hey! One of you bastards shot me in the fuckin' head!"

While the brewery erupted in laughter, Frankie took a pineapple from out of the cardboard box and lit the fuse. It took a second for the others to catch on, but when they did, everyone pulled a pineapple out of the box with one hand and a cigarette lighter out of their pockets with the other.

"Hey, boys!" Frankie yelled. "You hear that?"

The brewery went silent then, the only sound the crackling sizzle of fuses protruding from a half-dozen pineapples. The homemade bombs looked like huge black versions of the cherry bombs everyone set off on the Fourth of July.

Somebody high up on the catwalk yelled, "Son of a bitch," and Loretto heard a quick succession of footfalls on metal as everyone up there scampered for the ladders, realizing the bombs were coming—but no one could have made it down from the catwalks before Frankie tossed the first pineapple directly under the steam engine, and the others followed suit, tossing pineapples out into the maze of machinery and temperature gauges, vats and pipes and hoses. The first explosion ricocheted off the walls and was followed by a screaming hiss of steam and the screams of men falling from the catwalks, scalded by the steam and thrown through the air by the blast. The next explosions collapsed the inner brick walls and left only the outer facade of the building standing.

A rolling cloud of dust, steam, and hops rushed into the tunnel, pushing Vince and the boys in front of it, all of them moving with a fleetness of foot that was surprising even to themselves, not stopping till they were out of the warehouse, which quickly filled with steam and dust, and then out in the underground garage, where they stopped for a moment and looked themselves over. They were all soaking wet and covered with grime that reeked the yeasty smell of malt. Their hands and faces, any part of them that hadn't been covered, were pink from the steam. Jo Jo, who had been shirtless, looked like a lobster from the chest up. They stood around in a mob looking each other over.

Jo Jo, gazing down at his chest, said, "Last time I was this pink it was at the beach. I got drunk and fell asleep in the sun."

"Jesus," Anthony Domini said, "no more Madden's Number 1! Now we're in trouble!"

"Come on," Vince said, and they made their way to the cars. Loretto alone among them was quiet. He walked quickly with his eyes focused on the ground, his face somber, as if he had just remembered something troubling. Patsy noticed and asked if he was okay. "Yeah," Loretto said. "It's that malt smell. It's making me sick." Once he was in the car, he put his head down between his knees.

Patsy said, "Open the windows. The stink's gonna make us all sick."

The boys laughed and opened the windows, and Patsy slapped Loretto on the back, and then the car was climbing the ramp and squealing out on the street, where the sun was just coming up, casting a red glow up and down the avenues.

10:00 p.m.

Duke Ellington with his top hat cocked jauntily atop his head leaned over the table, listening attentively as Big Owney told a story about Cab Calloway, Harold Arlen, and a couple of the Cotton Club dancers. Ellington was decked out in a tux with a white bow tie, his mustache trimmed so thin it might have been drawn on, while Madden was dressed elegantly as usual in a tailored suit with a blue silk tie. Walter Winchell, in comparison, looked like a vagrant in a cheap suit with his tie loosened and a flask in hand. The sprawling room around their table buzzed with conversation and laughter as Ellington's band warmed up after a break, waiting for him to join them. When Madden finished his story, the three men laughed and Ellington slid his seat away from the table, ready to go back to work. Winchell looked toward the entrance to the club and then to an exit by the stage. Four or more of Madden's boys lingered at every exit or entrance. "What gives with all the extra security?" Winchell asked Madden. "It couldn't be that young Master Coll is giving you a case of dyspepsia, could it?"

Madden's smile dropped away. "Are you saying a punk like Coll might cause me problems, Walter? I'd think a man in your position would know better."

"You know me," Walter said, "always looking for a scoop."

Ellington got up from the table, tipped his hat to his companions, thanked them for their gracious company, and did a little rhythmic dance, dipping and bouncing on his way up to the stage, which brought on a round of applause from the room.

Madden got up and leaned over the table to Winchell. "You want a scoop?" he said. "Here's your scoop: Mad Dog Coll's not long for this world."

Winchell raised his flask to Madden. "A few more details would make for a better story."

"When the time comes," Madden said, and he slapped Winchell on the shoulder, friendly but maybe a little rougher than necessary. He pointed to the back of the room, where Big Frenchy was standing beside a closed door with his hands in his pockets. "Got to go," he said. "My partner's waiting for me."

"They're upstairs," Big Frenchy said as Madden joined him and they went together through the door and up a flight of stairs. When they reached Madden's private rooms, Frenchy opened the door for him. Inside, seated at a long table, were Lucky Luciano, Dutch Schultz, and Bo Weinberg. There were several bottles of whiskey on the table, and the men were drinking and talking. No one looked particularly happy.

As soon as Madden came through the door, Dutch slapped his glass down. "That son of a bitch torched two of my beer drops and jacked three shipments—and it's not even five full days since we bailed him out!"

Frenchy took a seat next to Dutch. "That's why we're here," he said calmly.

"You're talking about your shipments and your beer drops?" Madden asked. He sat at the head of the table. "It'll take me months and a small fortune to get my brewery going again."

Luciano said, "He hit two of our breweries in Pennsylvania. They're also gonna be out of action for a while."

Dutch's collar was unbuttoned, his tie loosened, and there was a stain on the lapel of his jacket. "Where's he hiding, this little bastard? You mean to say between all of us, we can't find him and put him out of his misery?"

Madden poured himself a drink and tapped his glass on the table. "Obviously," he said, "we can't let this go on. The kid's crazy. He's causing serious problems."

"That's what you called us here to tell us?" Dutch said. "You thought maybe we hadn't noticed?"

"Between us," Madden went on, "we've lost more than a dozen men already. He's hitting our breweries, our speaks, our drops, and he's blowing up our trucks, not even bothering to steal them."

Dutch finished his drink and slapped the empty glass down, making his frustration with Madden obvious.

"What's that tell you?" Luciano asked Madden, ignoring Dutch. He sipped his drink with one hand and straightened his tie with the other.

"It tells me his point is to disrupt our business."

"When are you gonna quit telling us what we already know?" Dutch poured himself another shot. "What's Coll thinking? We're gonna go to him on our knees and beg him to play nice?"

Madden tapped the table again. "I don't know what the little lunatic is thinking."

Frenchy opened his arms, addressing the whole table. "Is he really crazy enough to think he can take on the whole Combine?"

Madden took a cigar from his pocket and pointed it at Dutch. "Soon as he shows his face, we'll kill him. Meanwhile, we've got a problem. At the rate he's going, if we don't get him soon, he'll wreck our businesses—"

"He's already wrecking our businesses," Dutch said. "We got speaks, we can't fill their orders."

Madden said, "In Chicago, Capone's asking what's going on. He's lost shipments from us and from Atlantic City. The Atlantic City shipment, they didn't even take the whiskey. They blew it all up along with the trucks."

"That's my point," Luciano said. "He ain't actin' reasonably. What's he up to? What's his plan?"

Bo said, "Might be right now he's sending us a message. He beat the rap and he's back—and we'd better cut him in or else."

"I'll cut him in," Dutch said. "I'll cut his throat from ear to ear."

"Gentlemen," Madden said. He waited until he had everyone's attention. To Luciano he said, "I don't care what his plan is. I have no intention of dealing with him. There's only one thing you do with someone like him, and we all know what that is."

"But we can't find him, or any of the boys he's got workin' for him," Bo said. "We're lookin' everywhere."

"They all got to go," Dutch said, slapping the table. "The Evangelistas, Domini, Martone, the Loretto kid, Mike Baronti, Patsy DiNapoli—all of them! And I wouldn't be against puttin' one in that Lottie bitch, either."

Madden played with his whiskey glass. "Let's concentrate on Coll for now. We'll worry about the rest of them later."

"Like I said." Bo took a pack of cigarettes from his pocket and tapped it on the table. "We're looking."

"But we're not making progress quick enough," Madden said, "so this is my plan. I'm calling another meeting here in New York for next Friday night. I'm inviting the Chicago boys, Capone and Nitti and them. If we get Coll before that, I'll call it off, obviously. If not, then we'll put our heads together and figure out what to do next. Coll can't take on the whole damn world. Between all of us, we'll get him."

"This is bullshit." Dutch got up and motioned for Bo to join him. "Call your meeting," he said to Madden on his way to the door. "If I find Coll first, I'll bring you his heart on a platter. You can feed it to your dogs." He walked out without bothering to close the door behind him. Bo gave Madden a look as if to say, *That's just Dutch*, and then followed him out to the stairs.

"He has an especially mercurial temperament, that one," Frenchy said of Dutch. He took a pear from a bowl on the table and bit into it. Down-stairs in the club, the band was playing "The Devil and the Deep Blue Sea," and the bouncy rhythm floated up the stairs and into the room.

Luciano asked Madden, "Can you at least get us a good table at this joint?"

"That I can do," Madden said, and he held the door open for him.

"Just keep that Winchell creep away from me," Luciano added.

"He's useful," Madden said, and he left the room with Luciano and Frenchy following behind.

1:10 a.m.

Somewhere someone was laughing and the sound of it snaked through the darkness and became something different, a voice speaking though Loretto couldn't make out the words. In his spare room, with snow falling beyond a curtained window, he tossed and turned on a bare mattress, fully dressed, a pillow clasped to his breast, a bottle of Canadian Club and an empty glass on a table beside the bed. He'd been going nonstop since hitting Madden's brewery: hijacking shipments, torching beer drops, bombing speaks, hitting Dutch's banks.

In Harlem, they'd taken more than fifty grand out of one bank. Vince and Mike knew the setup from the days when they'd worked for Dutch. They'd pulled two mugs into a back room while Loretto held a chopper on a half-dozen runners, all with their faces to the ground, eyes closed. They might have all been holding up signs saying, *I don't see nothing, I don't want to see nothing.* Loretto was blind to what was going on behind him in the back room, but he could hear. For several minutes, the place was quiet as a stone, the only sounds traffic from the street and Vince and Mike, Vince asking one guy to open the safe and getting some cock-and-bull story about how the combination had just been changed and even he didn't know it, and Vince saying, *I'll tell you one more time,* and then the guy starting up on his excuses and getting only a few words out of his mouth before a gunshot brought his story to its end. Then Vince saying to another mug *Open the safe* and coming out of the back room a few minutes later with two bags of cash in his hands. Fifty grand, which Vince split up with the gang, Loretto's share, over six thousand, in a cardboard box under his bed along with several thousand more from the other banks and speaks and drops they'd hit, and all this in a few days, more money than he could earn in years of work clearing trails, more money than he could save in decades—in a few days.

Loretto struggled to hear what the laugher was saying, something dark that made him nervous though he couldn't make out the words. He was half drunk and half asleep, half listening and half dreaming. It was cold in his room and he clutched the pillow tighter. He pulled himself up from sleep and poured another drink. Mike was in the kitchen, on the other side of his closed bedroom door, with Paul Martone and Patsy. They were drinking and telling stories and laughing. He pushed the curtain back and peered out his window, where a light snow was falling, the small flakes lit up in the glare of a streetlight, falling onto yesterday's snow already going sooty with the city's grime. He finished off his drink, found a crumpled blanket on the floor, and covered himself with it. He closed his eyes and drifted off. He hadn't slept three hours in a row in days. The rest of the boys were doing lines of coke, and he'd done a few but they made his heart race like it was raging out of his chest and he'd gone back to drinking, between jobs, before trying to sleep, soon after he woke, always a glass in his hand and a bottle nearby. He hadn't spent much time thinking about Gina only because he hadn't spent much time thinking. He was either on the move or trying to sleep. When he was on the move, all his thoughts were in the moment. When he was trying to sleep, Gina would come to mind but then he'd fall off into dreams where one minute he might be back at Mount Loretto with Vince and Peter and the next minute at the dinner table with the Barontis and a minute after that in a tunnel on his way into a brewery, blood and malt like a river at his feet.

"Hey, ugly," Vince said. "You in shape for work?"

Loretto opened his eyes to Vince sitting on the edge of his mattress. Mike and Patsy were in the doorway, grinning.

"What is it?" Loretto knew where he was and what was going on, but his thoughts were sluggish. There seemed to be a lag between what he thought and what he said.

Paul Martone pushed past Mike and Patsy with a mug of coffee, which he handed to Vince.

"Sit up." Vince handed Loretto the coffee mug. "We're getting visitors."

Paul found a chair and pulled it into the room. He was wearing a blue silk cravat around his waist, passed through the belt loops and tied in a knot at his side. He'd been told so often that he looked like Fred Astaire that apparently he felt he could dress like him, too. "What's the word?" he asked Vince.

Vince patted Loretto on the back as he sat up and sipped his coffee. "We found Jablonski," he said. "He was hiding way out on Long Island, East Hampton or something."

Patsy came into the room and took a seat on the windowsill. "He's coming here? Who's bringin' him?"

"The Evangelistas." To Loretto he said, "You know that red bandana Frankie's been wearing to cover the head wound? Now Jo Jo's wearing one, too. He says it's *stylish*."

"Stylish my patootie," Paul said.

"They look like a couple of pirates." Vince was laughing, in a good mood.

"Why are they bringing him here?" Loretto asked.

"'Cause you're moving." Vince slapped the bed. "Let's go." He jumped up. "Help 'em get their stuff in the car," he said to the others. "It's parked out front."

Loretto followed Vince into the kitchen, where he found a bottle of orange juice in the icebox, looked it over, and then lifted it to his mouth and drained it. He wiped his lips with the back of his hand. "Where we going?" he asked Vince.

Vince took a seat at the table, laid out two lines of coke, and snorted both through a straw, which he put back in his pocket when he was done. "New place," he said. "I told you we'd be switchin' places regular."

"Yeah, you did." Loretto went to the sink and splashed water on his face. In the living room, he saw Mike carrying a couple of suitcases out the door. One of them was Loretto's. "I'd better help," he said, meaning help the boys empty out the apartment.

"Sit down a second." Vince kicked the chair across from him out from under the table. "The boys'll take care of it."

Loretto sat across from Vince. There was a bottle of bourbon on the table. When he reached for it, Vince pushed it aside. "You're drinking too much."

"And you're doing too much coke."

"Coke don't slow me down," Vince said. "It makes me sharper. You want some?"

"Nah. Makes my heart bang like it's about to explode."

Vince smiled, amused. "You're doing good," he said to Loretto. "I was worried about you, but you're holding up your end."

Beyond the window, snow was falling light but steady. "I got close to fifteen grand stuffed under my bed," Loretto said. "Lot of money. I could buy a house for me and Gina with that."

"That ain't nothin'." Vince took Loretto by the wrist, his eyes bright and bloodshot. "That ain't nothin'," he said again, raising his voice, and he squeezed Loretto's wrist hard enough to hurt. Then just as suddenly he let go. "We're showing these sons of bitches, Dutch and the Combine."

"How much longer?" Loretto asked.

"How much longer we keepin' this up? Another couple of weeks. Then we head upstate."

In the living room, the Evangelista brothers pushed Victor Jablonski through the door, followed by another guy. At first Loretto didn't recognize the second man; then he saw the scar across his cheek.

Jablonski lumbered into the living room behind a gut big as a pregnant woman. He was an older guy, probably in his sixties. Other than the gut, he was an average-sized man. It looked like everything he ate or drank, it went straight to the belly. "I'm caught in the middle!" Jablonski yelled before anyone could say a thing. "I stay with you, Big Owney kills me. I go with Big Owney, and you're gonna kill me. What am I supposed to do, Vince? You tell me! I'm a businessman, that's all! I own a bunch of speaks. All I want is to do my business. That's all I'm askin'!"

"Victor . . ." Vince was still seated at the kitchen table. The Evangelistas stood one on each side of Jablonski while Mike and Patsy held the bartender by the arms with a light touch. "Victor," Vince repeated, and he mussed his hair and shook his head as if trying to clear away the cobwebs, "you may find this difficult to believe, but I'm sympathetic. I understand. You're right. You're caught in the middle."

Jablonski huffed and put his hands on his hips. "So tell me, Vince! What should I do?"

"Too late for that," Vince said, and finally he got up from the table. He went to the kitchen cabinets and rummaged through the drawers and cupboards as if looking for something. "You made your choice," he said, not looking up from his search. "You decided you were more scared of Big Owney than you were scared of me."

"Vince," Jablonski said, pleading, "I'm scared of both of you. I'm a family man," he added. "I got a wife and kids. I gotta make a living!"

"Ah. Here we go." Vince took a ball-peen hammer from a kitchen drawer. "How in hell," he said, "could you be more scared of that old man's been pretending like he's high society . . . How could you be more scared of Big Owney than me?"

"I'm scared of both of you," Jablonski repeated, his voice gone softer, weaker, at the sight of the ball-peen hammer.

"But you were more scared of Madden," Vince said. He flipped the hammer in the air, catching it by the handle.

"Why do you do this?" Jablonski got down on his knees and put his hands together in prayer. "I'll only buy from you from now on! I swear to you, Vince."

Vince approached Jablonski but looked beyond him to the bartender. "You been with Victor a long time, I'm told."

Jablonski said, "Since the beginning," answering for the bartender. "Bogda," he added, telling Vince the bartender's name. "He works for me, that's all. You don't have to hurt him!"

Vince said, "I'm not gonna hurt him." He hadn't yet looked at Jablonski. He'd been staring at Bogda. He hesitated for a moment, and the room went quiet. Finally he looked down at Jablonski, who was still on his knees, his hands steepled in front of him. "Victor," he said, "you made the wrong choice," and he hit him once at the top of the forehead, viciously, with the round end of the hammer. It penetrated his skull like a bullet, leaving a round hole from which blood at first seeped and then poured. Victor fell over on his face. "Bogda," Vince said, trying out the sound of the bartender's name.

"Bobby," the bartender said. "Everybody calls me Bobby except Victor."

"Bobby," Vince said. He leaned over Victor, hit him several more times, violent blows to the back of the head, and then tossed the hammer aside. "Bobby," he repeated, "who scares you more, me or Owen Madden?"

"You," Bobby said without hesitating. "You scare me more."

"Good," Vince said. "Let's get out of here." He slipped into his coat and put an arm around Bobby's shoulders. He led him out the door with the rest of the gang following. "You're running things now," he said to Bobby. "What was Victor's is now yours. You own a gun?"

Bobby shook his head, and Vince turned to Frankie Evangelista behind him. "Get this man a gun, Frankie, would you, please?"

"Sure, boss." Frankie pulled a pistol out of his coat pocket and handed it to Bobby.

"My boys, we'll protect you from the Combine," Vince said. "But we can't be there all the time. Meanwhile," he tapped the gun that Bobby was holding in his hand. "Meanwhile, if anyone tries to force you to buy their hooch, now you've got your own gun, right?"

"Right," Bobby answered, though he sounded like he would have said *right* if Vince had asked him if he owned his own spaceship.

"Don't be afraid to use it," Vince went on. "Like I said, we'll deal with the Combine, but we're stretched a little thin right now, so for a while you might have to take care of yourself."

"That's okay," Bobby said. "I won't buy from anybody but you. I swear."

"Good." They were all outside then, standing in the snow next to three cars parked on the street.

Vince turned to the Evangelistas and smiled at the matching red bandanas they wore under their fedoras. "Take our man wherever he wants to go, gentlemen, would you, please?" He took a roll of cash from his pocket, peeled off four fifties, and handed them to Bobby. "You work for us now," he said. "We'll take care of you better than the Combine ever did."

Bobby put the money in his pocket. Softly he said, "Thanks, Vince."

Vince didn't answer. He looked around till he spotted Loretto. "Ride with me," he said and got into the back seat of the lead car.

Loretto glanced up to the sky, at a line of dark clouds sliding over the rooftops like a low ceiling. Between the tops of the buildings and the black clouds a small space of moonlit sky looked bright in comparison, making the slab of dark clouds sitting over the city look like a black lid about to close. Loretto brushed snowflakes from his hair and then wiped the wet palm of his hand across his eyes.

Vince had left the door open, and his voice came out of the darkness of the car. "Where are you, Loretto?"

"Right here," Loretto answered, and he got in and pulled the door closed.

10:45 a.m.

Lottie woke with Vince wrapped around her: his face pushed up against the back of her neck; one arm around her waist, the other under her head; his knees folded into her thighs. He'd come in sometime in the middle of night and she'd awakened to him already making love to her, opened her eyes to his brightest smile, a boy pleased at having sprung a big surprise. She'd petted his hair, his face, wrapped her legs around his back, and when it was over she wanted to talk but he fell asleep within minutes, his head still propped up on his hand as if he'd been trying to listen before sleep overwhelmed him. Now she wriggled out of his grasp, sat up in bed, and looked out through a line of uncurtained windows onto a dreary day, the sky gray as ashes over an empty field. They were someplace way up in Yonkers, in an old farmhouse. She climbed out of bed, found her heavy white robe in the closet, and went to the window, where she pulled a pack of Chesterfields from the pocket of her robe, lit up, and inhaled deeply as she gazed at a long expanse of untrammeled snow that dipped and rose, following the contours of a plowed field, the long lines of furrows flowing into shadows. Farther off, there was a farmhouse with a silo and a green tractor outside a barn.

Behind her, Vince groaned and made a sharp, high-pitched sound, as if something had hurt him, and a moment later he jerked onto his back, waved his arms, and then turned onto his stomach and dropped off into stillness and silence. Lottie sat beside him and stroked his back. Most nights he was like this, flailing in his sleep, groaning and making noises. Once he'd bolted out of bed and made it halfway to the front door before he realized he was dreaming. More than once he'd soaked the sheets with sweat. On the floor beside the bed, she found an ashtray and stubbed out her cigarette. She noticed the corner of an old leather suitcase, pulled it out from under the bed, opened it, and found it stuffed with cash and guns. She took two hundred in twenties and put them in the pocket of her robe. One of the pistols looked like a small cannon with a long, fat barrel and a wooden grip. She picked it up, felt the weight of it in her hands, and placed it back where she'd found it, atop a pile of bills. She started to close the suitcase and then noticed, peeking out from the clutter of crumpled fives and tens, the corner of their marriage license. She put it back in the suitcase with the guns and cash and shoved the suitcase under the bed again. They were thinking that they'd get married upstate, where they'd be safer, and they might even be able to have a party, at least with their closest friends. She closed her eyes and imagined the real thing, a real wedding with a classy white gown and a long, flowing train. She knew that would have to wait till the fighting was over—but still she enjoyed the imagining.

When Vince groaned again and turned onto his back, throwing a forearm over his eyes, she got back under the covers with him, found a copy of *The New Movie* on a bedside chair, and propped up a pillow under her back so she could read. The magazine was several months old, from last August. It was light green, with a picture of Helen Twelvetrees on the cover. Next to the actress's face, in bold type: *COULD YOU Be a MOVIE STAR? Turn to Page 33 and Find Out.* Lottie turned to page 33 and settled into reading, *The New Movie* in one hand, the other hand stroking Vincent's hair, comforting him as he wrestled with his dreams.

8:00 p.m.

Capone was in a foul mood. Whenever someone else spoke, he glared at him like he might pull a pistol out of his pocket and shoot him dead. He was one of a dozen men seated around a long table in a conference room at the Forest Hotel, where Madden had booked suites for his visitors and stocked them with booze and women. With Capone from the Chicago Outfit were Frank Nitti and Paul Ricca. Luciano was also there, with Meyer Lansky and Bugsy Siegel. Dutch and Bo were seated directly across from Luciano with Richie Cabo, Ciro Terranova, Vannie Higgins, and a half-dozen more big shots from the city and upstate, New Jersey and Buffalo. Owen Madden sat at the head of the table, across from Big Frenchy at the other end. Madden had spent the last half hour pressuring the men around the table to stop whatever they were doing and put all their efforts into finding Coll and his gang and eliminating them. "Listen," he said, frustrated in particular at Capone's carping and complaining, "the Mick's costing all of us money. He's a lunatic. He'll kill your mother if he thinks it'll get him what he wants. He's a baby killer!" Madden yelled and slapped the table. "Ask Dutch about his wife! Ask him about Francis!"

Capone turned to Dutch as if curious. For the first time since the evening started, he looked interested.

Dutch might have been constipated the way he squirmed in his seat and clutched his belly. His suit was more rumpled than usual and his face was strained, as if he'd been under a lot of pressure for a long time.

"Well?" Capone said. "What about Francis?" He had met Francis before, on an earlier visit to New York with his family. They'd gone out to dinner together, Capone and his wife and Dutch and Francis.

"I got it on good authority," Dutch said, "the son of a bitch—on the night he got rounded up with the rest of his gang—he was on his way to kill my wife." Dutch paused and his face went so dark he looked like he might slump over in his chair with a heart attack. "Francis!" he exploded. "My wife! He was gonna beat her so bad I couldn't recognize her, and he was gonna call me while he was doing it so I could hear her scream!"

"You see what I'm saying?" Madden was talking to Capone. "He's a lunatic. He'll make us all look like rabid dogs. We need to do something about him, and we need to do it before he costs us more money and more trouble."

Capone nodded to Dutch and then turned to Madden. "All right," he said. "We'll send you twenty men, and they'll stay till the job is done. I'll make sure they're nobody Coll'll recognize."

After Capone, one by one the big shots around the table promised men and money. Madden's plan was to put together a small army of men that Coll didn't know and wouldn't recognize. He'd break the city up into zones, with men on the streets at all times, all of them with orders to fill Coll full of lead as soon as they laid eyes on him. In addition to the men on the street, he wanted men roving the city, four to a car, in case they came across Coll and his boys. He wanted them all armed with choppers.

"Good," Madden said, and he sat back in his chair, signaling the meeting was about to be over. "With your men and the boys I'm bringing in from Kansas, Coll won't last another week."

Capone lit a cigar and pointed it at Madden. "You put my men up," he said. "Whatever they need."

"That's taken care of," Frenchy answered for Madden. To the whole table, he said, "We'll treat your boys good."

Madden stood and straightened out his jacket. "Gentlemen," he said, "Frenchy's got something special planned for you all over at the Cotton Club."

Luciano declined, as did Lansky, but Siegel and all the others were more than happy to take up Madden on his hospitality. They filed out of the room, talking and laughing, leaving only Madden, Luciano, and Lansky behind with Dutch and Bo. "Jesus," Madden said when they were alone, "who shoved something up Capone's ass tonight?"

Luciano said, "He's got that tax beef hanging over him. I hear he's going away for a long time, and soon."

"Ah," Madden said. "I should have figured. Gentlemen," he added and gestured toward the door, meaning it was time for them all to get on with their own business.

"Nah, wait," Luciano said. He motioned to Lansky, who slipped out of the room.

"What the hell's this about?" Dutch said.

Madden took his seat, folded his arms over his chest, and waited.

Dutch and Bo followed Madden's lead and took seats at the table. Luciano lit a cigarette, offered the pack to the others, and then went about pouring himself a drink from one of a dozen liquor bottles scattered over the table.

"Good idea," Dutch said, and he poured drinks for himself and Bo.

After five minutes had passed with Dutch and Bo talking between themselves about business, Madden pulled a cigar from his jacket pocket. To Luciano he said, "This better be good."

Luciano winked at Madden, and a minute later the door to the conference room opened and Lansky walked in with Jimmy Brennan.

"Who the hell's this?" Dutch said.

Bo said, "I know you. You're the one's family passed away in a fire. Am I right?"

"That's right," Luciano answered for Brennan. "Now he's working for Coll."

Brennan took a seat opposite Madden and poured himself a drink. He knocked it back, poured himself another, and then ran his fingers through the unruly mess of hair tumbling down onto his forehead. "I want a hundred thousand dollars," he said. "The fifty you already offered and fifty more for the risks I'm taking with this crazy son of a bitch."

Madden said, "A hundred thousand?"

Dutch said, "Fuck you. Seventy-five."

Jimmy downed his drink and placed the glass gently on the table. "Done," he said and looked to Madden.

"You'll kill him yourself?" Madden asked.

"Or tell you where you can find him and get the job done."

"Fifty for that," Dutch said. "Seventy-five if you kill him yourself."

Jimmy shrugged. "Sure," he said. "That's fair."

Madden asked Luciano, "Where'd you find this guy?" When Luciano didn't answer, Madden turned back to Jimmy. "How do you know Coll?" he asked. "What's a guy like you doing with the likes of the Evangelistas and Domini and them?"

"I was in the orphanage with Vince," Jimmy said. "I gave him a bunch of shellackin's. I guess he remembered me."

Madden was quiet a while, watching Brennan. Finally he said, "A mick to kill the Mick," and he got up from his seat. "You report to me," he said, "not Mr. Luciano." He took a pen from his coat pocket along with a slip of paper. "Here," he said. He wrote his name and phone number on the paper, carried it to Brennan, and slipped it into his jacket pocket. "That's my office number at the Cotton Club. That's where I can usually be reached. Call when it's done or when you've got information for me. Are we clear?" He pointed to his own chest. "You call *me*."

Madden turned to Luciano and pointed a finger at him. "I see I'm gonna have to watch out for you," he said. "You're a man knows how to get a job done."

"Ah," Bo said to everyone, "too bad. Looks like Mad Dog Coll's days are numbered."

"Yeah," Dutch said, standing up. "My heart's breaking." He rose and left without offering anyone a word or a handshake.

Madden said, "Business," meaning Dutch was the kind of guy you had to work with in this business. He shook hands with Luciano, Lansky, and Bo. "You can go," he said to Jimmy. "You know how to reach me." He crossed his arms and waited for Jimmy to leave. When he was alone with the others, he said, "I hate a Judas," and then he added, again, "Business."

"That's how it is," Luciano said, and the four of them left the conference room together, Madden between Luciano and Bo, his arms around their shoulders. Lansky took a last look around the room, at the conference table with a half-dozen bottles of liquor spread across its dark wood surface. He found an unopened bottle of Russian vodka, slipped it into his jacket pocket, and followed the others out the door.

7:17 p.m.

Maria Tramonti sat across the kitchen table from Gina. She was drinking coffee with Gina and talking nonstop about Patsy and Loretto and the position she and Gina were both in now that the boys were back working for Vince Coll.

"Let's sit in the living room," Gina said, and she carried their cups to the coffee table, where she put them down next to a copy of the Saturday Evening Post before she went to the window to pull the shade. It was dark out. On the street, a couple of boys were in the midst of a snowball fight, running along the sidewalks parallel to each other, scooping up snow and hurling shots across the street.

Maria sat on the edge of the couch, picked up the magazine, and looked it over. When Gina sat next to her, Maria slumped down as if defeated. "I don't know what to do about Patsy," she said. "I hardly ever see him anymore, and when I do we have to sneak around."

"I haven't seen Loretto since the day he moved out of Mama's."

"If I didn't love him so much . . ." Maria sipped her coffee. She didn't know how to finish her thought. If she didn't love him so much, she'd leave him? No. She couldn't imagine that, though the thought must have been in the back of her mind, or why would she have said what she did?

"I don't know what will happen with me and Loretto," Gina said. "I guess I'm hoping he'll come to his senses before he gets himself killed. Augie's furious at him."

"Why's Augie mad? 'Cause he's not treating you right?"

"I guess so. He don't like it that Mama's all worried about Loretto. What's he doing? Where's he living? Why he no stay here with us? I swear, I think she likes him better than me."

Maria laughed at that. "She's a darling, your mother."

"She's got enough to worry about with Mike. She don't need Loretto on top of it."

"Look," Maria said, "there's something else I wanted to tell you." She picked up her cup from the table and held it close to her chest.

Gina sat up straight, newly attentive.

"I'm leaving Bill." Maria put the cup down again without taking a sip.

"About time," Gina said. She squeezed Maria's knee. "You should have left him years ago."

"Sure," Maria said, "but until Patsy came along . . ."

"Are you moving out? Where will you stay? Have you told Bill yet?"

"My lawyer thinks I'll wind up with plenty of cush once the divorce is settled."

"I'd be careful about that," Gina said. "Didn't work out like that for me."

"But your guy wasn't spending half his time in whorehouses and the other half on the road."

"Still," Gina said, "I'm just saying be careful."

"My lawyer's pretty sure about it. And what I'm thinking is this: maybe, if I wind up with as much moolah as my lawyer says, maybe Patsy can start a business of his own. Who knows, maybe Patsy and Loretto can do something together. You see what I'm thinking?"

"You're dreamin' more than thinkin', honey."

"Really?" Maria's eyes were suddenly full of tears.

Gina slid close to her and gave her a hug. "I don't know. Maybe it's possible. What kind of business were you imagining?"

Maria found a tissue in her purse and blotted her eyes. "I don't know what kind of business. Whatever Patsy wants. Listen," she said, "I'm serious about this, Gina. Bill comes from money. I could wind up in the dough. Maybe if Patsy and Loretto can find something to do together, I can bankroll them. You see what I'm saying?"

"Is that why you're leaving Bill?"

"Yes," Maria said, suddenly firm, almost angry. "That's a big part of it. I'm scared to death for Patsy. I got to get him away from Vince and them. Maybe this could be the way."

"Have you talked to Patsy about it?"

"About leaving Bill? We talk about it all the time."

"No, about setting him up in business."

"You know guys," Maria said. "I'll have to make it look like he came up with the idea."

Then it was Gina's turn to laugh. "Well, when's the big day? When are you telling him?"

"Bill? Tomorrow. That's why I wanted to see you tonight. I wanted to tell you first."

"Where will you stay?"

"The Clarion Arms. It's in midtown."

"A hotel? Why don't you stay with me? It wouldn't cost you anything, and I could use the company."

"No kidding?" Maria jumped at Gina and gave her a hug. "I'd pay half the rent," she said. "I insist. And it'd only be till after the divorce is settled."

"We should have a party," Gina said. "Girls only. To celebrate."

"Are you sure about this?"

"About the party or you movin' in with me?"

"Me movin' in!" Maria followed Gina into the kitchen and watched as she stood on her toes to take a calendar down from the wall. "Are you really sure?" she asked again.

"I'm excited about it! It's been lonely, especially with Loretto never here anymore." She put the calendar down on the kitchen table and pointed to January 31. "Let's have it Sunday after next. We'll invite all our girlfriends."

Maria gave Gina another hug. Then all of a sudden she was blubbering.

Gina patted her hair. "It'll be okay," she said. "It'll all work out."

"I know," Maria said. "I'm serious about Patsy and Loretto," she added, sobbing.

"I know you are." Gina patted Maria's back and let her cry. "Go ahead," she said. "Cry. You need it."

Maria nodded and did as she was instructed. She leaned into her girlfriend's shoulder and cried.

MONDAY ••• JANUARY 25, 1932

2:15 p.m.

Madden had just tossed one of the Chicago boys out of his office, taking him by the collar and the seat of his pants and heaving him out the door. For more than a week he'd been paying these mugs and putting them up, buying their meals and their women and their booze—and Coll was still on the street. He fell back into the leather cushions of his rolling chair, put his feet up on his desk, kicked a ledger book across the room, and glared at the heavy black telephone next to his feet. It occurred to him, staring at the phone, how the years had changed him. His urge now was to pick up the phone and order someone to get off his arse and finally take care of this little bastard. When he was a young man, he would have used the handset to bash Coll's head in. He saw himself then as a boy standing in the middle of 201st Street with a pistol in his hand and a lead pipe tucked into his belt, standing over the dead body of Joey Macario, blood pouring out of Joey and onto the cobblestones. He'd just shot him through the heart and he'd have shot him again if it would have done any good. Instead, he turned to the empty street and the closed tenement windows and yelled, "Owen Madden! Tenth Avenue!" He'd killed more men in those days, when he was running the Gophers and warring with the Hudson Dusters—he'd killed more men than he cared to remember, with his bare hands, with a lead pipe, with knife and gun. Now he picked up a telephone.

"Duke." Frenchy opened the office door and peeked in. "Your brother-in-law's here."

"Connor?"

"You got another brother-in-law?"

"Don't get wise with me," Madden said, but with a grin. "What's Connor want?"

"It's your sister," Frenchy said. He was wearing a yellow ascot and he tucked a loose corner into his shirt. "He's says she's sick, but it's not serious."

Madden leaned back in his chair. "I saw her yesterday."

"You want me to send him away?"

"No. Tell him I'll be right there." Madden brushed himself off and straightened out his suit. At the bottom of the stairs, he found his brother-in-law waiting for him. He was a tall, thin man with an elaborate handlebar mustache.

"Owen," Connor said, "I'm worried about Mary."

"What's wrong with her?"

"Ah, I think it might be the flu," he said, "but you know Mary. I can't get her to see a doctor."

"She was fine yesterday." Madden brushed off the step and took a seat.

"Came on all of a sudden," Connor said. "That's why I think it's the flu."

"You want me to tell her to see a doctor?"

Connor said, "You know she'll do whatever you tell her. Come and pay her a quick visit and send her on her way to see a physician."

Under Connor's smile and his casual attitude, he seemed nervous, as if the smile and attitude were an act. Madden wondered how sick his sister might really be.

"Come back to the house with me," Connor said. "It'll only take a few minutes, and if you tell her to see a doctor, you know she'll do what you say. My car's parked right outside."

"Give me a second." Madden trotted up the stairs and retrieved his coat and gloves from the office hall tree. In his desk drawer, he found a snub-nose .44 and slid it into his coat pocket before he rejoined Connor. The hallway was dimly lit. A splash of light from the street came in through a narrow window that ran the length of the exit door. Two of Frenchy's boys were stationed at the door, and Madden had them check the street before he stepped out into the cold.

"Snowing again," Connor said. "You'd think we lived in Siberia, wouldn't you now, with how it's snowed this winter?" He led the way to the car, waited for Owen to get in beside him, and drove off over streets already covered with a layer of new snow. "Owen," he said, "you know I love you like my own brother," and he turned onto a side street and pulled over in front of an empty storefront with a blacked out glass doorway bracketed by two boarded-up display windows. As soon as the car stopped at the curb, Mike Baronti pulled the curb-side door open and put a pistol in Madden's ribs. He patted him quickly, found the .44, and dropped it into his coat pocket. "How are you, Mr. Madden?" he asked politely. "Vince Coll would like to have a word with you." He gestured toward the storefront with the boarded-up windows.

On the other side of the car, Patsy DiNapoli opened Connor's door and put a pistol to his chest. Connor ignored the gun and grasped Madden by the coat sleeve. His face was red and panicked. "They swore they wouldn't hurt you, Owen," he pleaded, "but they said they'd kill me and Mary unless I did this. I swear to you, Owen, I had no choice." By the time he finished speaking, there were tears in his eyes.

Madden pulled his sleeve free from Connor's grasp. To Mike he said, "Vince doesn't need to see him," meaning Connor. "Let him stay in the car till this is over."

Mike looked to Patsy, who shrugged. "Okay, sure. My friend'll keep him company." He stepped back, giving Madden room to get out of the car as Patsy slid in behind the wheel, changing places with Connor.

Inside the boarded-up store, Vince sat at a round table in his black overcoat and white scarf, his fedora on the table in front of him. When Madden entered with Mike, Vince gestured to the chair opposite him. "Sorry we couldn't meet someplace more suitable," he said, "but I'm afraid it's dangerous for me to go out in public these days."

"So I've heard." Madden took his seat at the table. He crossed his arms over his chest and waited. The store was empty except for a few dust-covered cardboard boxes scattered across a grimy floor. What light there was came in around the edges of the boards covering the windows. The two men sat on opposite sides of the table, staring at each other. Behind Madden, Mike leaned against a bare wall, his arms crossed at his waist, a pistol in hand.

"What's the matter, Big Owney?" Vince said finally. "You look a little pale."

"No, I don't," Madden said. "If anyone looks pale, it's you." Without giving Vince a chance to reply, he said, "Is my sister okay?"

"Why would I hurt your sister?"

"I don't know. Why would you?"

"I wouldn't," Vince said. "I'd prefer to leave family out it, myself. But ever since Dutch killed my brother . . ."

"What do you want, Coll? I can't see what good it'll do you to kill me."

"I'm not planning to kill you, Mr. Madden."

"Then what am I doing here?"

"You're too important to kill," Vince continued. "And you're from good Irish stock. I'd prefer to keep you around for the company."

"Then I'll ask you again," Madden said, "what am I doing here?"

"But your brother-in-law, that Connor fellow," Vince went on, "I'd take him for a one-way ride. I only met him briefly, but I never liked a man with one of those mustaches."

"What do you want, Coll?"

Vince pushed his fedora aside. "I want you to understand that I'm not going anywhere, Duke. That's what your friends call you, isn't it? Duke?"

"My friends call me Owen."

"Owen, then. I want you to understand that I'll kill your brother-in-law, I'll kill your sister, I'll kill Frenchy. I'll blow up your clubs, steal your whiskey, and kill your people and their damn pets till you got no choice but to do business with me. That's what you're doing here. So I can look you in the eye and give you that message."

"I didn't need to see you to get the message," Madden said. "You've been making yourself eminently clear."

"Good," Vince said. "I don't want all that much. I want to be a partner in your breweries and in the beer business, and I want Dutch Schultz delivered to me—and then of course I want all of Dutch's businesses. That's all I need. Then everything goes back to being nice and peaceful again. That and a cash payment to make up for all the money you and the Combine have cost me. A hundred thousand should do it."

"Those are your terms?" Madden asked. "You want in on the breweries and the beer and you want Dutch and a hundred grand. And then all this is over with, and we go back to making money without having to worry every time we step out on the street."

"That's it," Vince said. He put his hands in his pockets. It was cold enough in the abandoned store that the men could see their own breath.

"I'll tell you a secret," Madden said. "Nobody likes Dutch Schultz."

"That's not a secret," Vince said. Behind Madden, Mike laughed.

"This is not something I can do on my own, though. I've got partners."

"So?"

"So give me two weeks." Madden pulled his chair closer to Vince. "I'll see what kind of a deal I can arrange. Dutch was wrong, going after your brother when he couldn't get to you. The man's a miserable son of a bitch, and everybody knows it."

"That's my point," Vince said. "Better to work with me. We're the last of the Irishmen." He looked up to Mike and winked at him.

"Give me two weeks," Madden repeated. "I've got to work it out with my partners and get the cash together. Meanwhile," he said, "lay off my people and my businesses. You're costing me a lot of money."

"I'll lay off *your* people and *your* businesses," Vince said, meaning he wouldn't lay off Dutch and the others. "I'll give you two weeks," he said, "and if you double-cross me, I'm gonna be mad. And then I'll come after you, Mr. Madden." He sat back in his seat. "You don't want that."

"You're a tough guy," Madden said, and for the first time since he'd entered the empty store, he smiled. "You remind me of myself when I was your age."

"Yeah?" Vince said. "Somebody kill your brother?"

"No. But if I had a brother somebody killed, I'd do exactly what you're doing." He extended his hand to Vince.

Vince looked warily at Madden and then stood and shook hands with him. "Two weeks," he said.

"Two weeks," Madden answered and then turned to Mike, who escorted him out of the store and back to the car, where he switched places with Patsy and got behind the wheel.

As Madden drove off, he watched Vince come out of the store with Mike and Patsy on either side of him. Connor was rambling, but Madden didn't hear a word. He was watching Coll standing brazenly on a street corner like he owned the whole city while a small army of men was out hunting for him.

To his brother-in-law, when he finally stopped talking, Owen said, "Something like this ever happens again, Connor, no matter what they tell you, you've got to figure they plan on killing me. Understand?"

"Owen—"

"Then you'll have to choose. If it's between me and Mary, you did the right thing. You had no choice. My friends, of course," he added, "they won't understand. So the next thing you'd need to do is get out of the country. Fast."

"Owen—"

"Shut up, Connor." They were already back at his office, and he pulled the car to the curb and cut the engine. "It's not something you need to worry about. I'm just explaining how it is."

"And why don't I need to worry about it?" Connor asked. "Didn't I just get taken for a ride?"

"If you'd been taken for a ride," Madden said, "we wouldn't be sitting here talking." The snow was falling heavily now, covering the streets and sidewalks and rooftops. "You don't need to worry about it because only an animal like Coll would pull this kind of stunt. You read the papers. He's a mad dog. And you know what you've got to do with a mad dog, don't you?"

"That guy, Patsy, he told me you'd be going into business with Coll."

"I'd rather rip my balls off with my own hands," Madden said. He stepped out of the car into the snow. The wind was picking up and the clouds looked ominous. He leaned down into the car. "Go take care of Mary," he said. "Call me and let me know everything's okay." He closed the door, checked the street, and scurried to the protection of his office doorway. Across the avenue, on a fire-escape landing, someone had hung a line of stuffed animals—bears and rabbits and monkeys—from a clothesline. Their fur was matted, as if they'd gotten soaked somehow and someone had hung them out in the weather to dry. Now they were covered with snow and they looked to Owen like they'd all been executed by hanging and left out to dangle in the wind. He watched them spin and sway. Above him, clouds rolled over the rooftops. He shook off the snow and stomped his feet and went back inside.

10:17 p.m.

At the new place in Brooklyn, Loretto stretched out in a squarish stuffed chair with high armrests and propped his feet up on a window with a view of the East River. Mike was in the kitchen watching the stove like an expectant father, waiting for a loaf of bread he had made from scratch to finish baking. He stood over the oven with a drink in hand, a bag of tea on the table behind him next to a sawed-off shotgun, a bottle of Scotch, and a copy of the *New Yorker* they'd inherited with the apartment. Vince had given everyone a day off after Anthony Domini'd taken a bullet in the leg jackin' one of Luciano's shipments of Canadian hooch. Vince had sent him off to a family he knew in West Virginia, all the way up in the hills somewhere, and they were taking care of him till he got back on his feet. The gang had been lucky for weeks, with no more than a few scratches and bruises to account for all the mayhem they'd created while stealing from the Combine, with the exception of Madden, whom they were leaving alone while they waited for him to work out a deal.

"Look at this!" In the kitchen, Mike pulled his loaf of bread from the oven and carried it on a plate over to Loretto for inspection.

Loretto leaned over the bread and filled his lungs with the delicious smell of it. "You're a man of many talents."

Mike laughed and said, "And you're high as a kite." He took the bread back into the kitchen and set it down on a counter to cool. Half to himself and half to Loretto he said, "My mother taught me how to bake bread." He took his seat at the kitchen table and went back to flipping through the *New Yorker*, stopping to read the cartoons while he sipped his Scotch.

Loretto had cut back on his drinking and replaced it with smoking tea. He was high at that moment, but it was different from being drunk. He was relaxed and sleepy, though he found himself speeding off along crazy trains of thoughts and memories rather than falling asleep. He thought of Gina and that first night when she'd wanted him to make love to her and he'd refused. He closed his eyes and he could almost feel her leaning in to him, her arms around his neck, pulling him to her for a kiss. He hadn't seen Gina now in weeks. He'd stopped at the docks once, right after Augie's shift let out. He'd worn his coat collar turned up over his ears and his hat pulled down, and he'd found Augie in one of his usual watering holes, drinking by himself in a booth, a newspaper spread out on the table in front of him. Loretto joined him in the booth, sliding onto the bench across from him. Augie looked up, saw who it was, and went back to reading his paper. Loretto said, "Aren't you glad to see me?" and Augie glanced up at him in a way that seemed to Loretto to be pained. Loretto told him he was making enough money with Vince to buy a house somewhere and settle down with Gina once the fighting was over, and Augie listened without comment. When Loretto was done talking, he asked Augie to relay his message to Gina, that he was making enough money to buy a house and settle down with her when the time was right. Augie looked up from his newspaper and spoke as if he hadn't heard a word. "We put ourselves out for you," he said to Loretto. "We took you into our home. We stood up for you." Then he slid out of the booth and left the bar.

"Hey, Mike," Loretto called into the kitchen. "Roll me another joint, would ya? You're good at it."

"You don't need another joint," Mike said. "You're high enough."

"No I'm not," Loretto answered, but when he stood up the room spun around and he was briefly nauseated.

The apartment was sparsely furnished: a few chairs spread around, a table in the kitchen, mattresses on the floor in the bedrooms. Bare walls. Loretto looked out the window at the gray water of the East River and the expanse of the Williamsburg Bridge, where the lights of subway cars flickered as a train rattled into the city. The snowy weather of the past several weeks had given way to a deep freeze, and the corners of the windows were coated with ice and frost.

Mike turned a page of the *New Yorker*. "If it wasn't so cold," he said, "and if I wasn't likely to get my head blown off, I'd be on my way to Madam Crystal's about now."

"You wouldn't make it through the front door," Loretto said, and then both he and Mike went for their guns at the sound of footsteps coming up the stairs. Mike took the shotgun from the table and positioned himself in a corner of the kitchen, protected by a wall but with a shot at the front door. Loretto knelt behind his chair, a big .45 in one hand and a smaller .38 in his pocket. In the hallway, someone knocked three times, paused, knocked twice, paused, and then knocked three times again.

"Who is it?" Mike said.

"It's your uncle," Patsy answered, and Mike went to the door, let Patsy in, and quickly locked the door behind him.

"What are you doing here?" Loretto put his .45 back in its holster.

"I'm staying with you guys now. I think I got spotted at my place." Patsy had his coat collar turned up, a long scarf wrapped around his neck, and a pair of newspapers under his arm. "Who's making bread?" he asked as he took off his gloves.

"I am," Mike said. "You want some?"

"Sure. I'll have a slice." Patsy tossed the newspapers onto the kitchen table. "Get a load of this," he said.

Mike and Loretto snatched up the papers and Patsy went to the counter and cut himself a slice of bread. "It's still warm," he said, and he took a small bite. "It's delicious."

On the front page of both papers were pictures of a shot-up bar with two men dead on the floor, one of them an Italian New York City police detective. There'd been a gunfight in a Manhattan bar between "hoodlums from rival gangs." The detective had come in off the street when he'd heard the shooting and gotten himself killed. The other dead guy was identified only as "a gangster from Chicago." Two men had been in the bar drinking, both papers reported, when four men came in from the street and opened fire on them. The men at the bar drinking were identified as Giuseppe and Francis Evangelista. Both men had long records of arrest for everything from arson to murder. "It was a shootout," one of the witnesses said. "Two mugs jumped behind the bar and shot it out with those guys come in off the street." The Evangelista brothers escaped through a back door. Neither of them appeared to be injured, though several bystanders caught in the crossfire had been wounded and taken to area hospitals.

Mike threw the paper down. "Jesus Christ," he said. "Those *cafon's* went out for a drink? Are they crazy?"

"I guess they got tired of being cooped up," Patsy said. He took another bite of bread. "This is delicious, Mike."

"Yeah?" Mike went to the counter and cut himself a piece.

"A New York City police detective," Loretto said, holding the newspaper like a baton. "Now in addition to Dutch and the Combine, we'll have every cop in the state looking for us."

"He was an Italian detective," Mike said with his mouth full. "They probably won't care as much."

"Baloney," Patsy said. "We're in for it now. You guys been outside?" he added. "It's below zero out there."

Loretto sat at the table and poured himself a drink. "Those guys are tough," he said, meaning the Evangelistas, "but they're crazy. They go to a bar for a drink like a couple of citizens? While Dutch and everybody else is looking for us? *Che cazzo?*"

Mike and Patsy laughed. Loretto didn't often curse in Italian. When he did, they found it amusing. "Have some bread," Mike said. He carried the loaf to the table, made a space for it next to the shotgun, and then brought out some butter and jam from the icebox. "It's perfect just with a little butter," he said to Loretto.

Loretto cut himself a thick slice and then watched as Patsy and Mike did the same. The three men sat at the table in silence, spreading butter on the warm bread. Loretto found that he was famished and could hardly spread the butter quick enough.

Mike lifted his drink to Patsy and Loretto. "*Salut'*," he said, "*buon' amici*," and then he bit into his chunk of bread as Patsy and Loretto did the same.

11:30 p.m.

Gina showed Freddie her new phone and wrote down the number for him on a slip of paper. "EV4-4504," she said as she wrote. Maria had the phone installed as soon as she moved in.

"It's nice," Freddie said. He picked up the heavy black handset, held it to his ear, listened a second to the dial tone, and then replaced it in its cradle. "I've never lived anyplace had its own phone."

Gina kissed Freddie on the cheek. They were in her kitchen, where a half-dozen of her friends were gathered around the table with its spread of pastries and party foods. She was a little tipsy from mixing wine and liquor, and it made her more animated than usual. More friends were in the living room talking and drinking while Carmen Lombardo's voice came over the radio singing "Goodnight Sweetheart." Augie stood alongside the radio talking to one of Maria's girlfriends from work. The party had started out as a girls-only gathering, celebrating Maria moving in with Gina, but then a few girls called their boyfriends and one of Maria's friend's brothers showed up with a few of his friends. When Augie and Freddie knocked on the door, arriving unannounced for a Sunday-evening visit, Augie with a grease-stained pastry box under his arm, she invited them to join the party.

"Hey, Gina," Freddie said. He was looking into the living room where a girl with short platinum-blond hair leaned against the wall, a wineglass in her hand. She was one of a threesome of young women, two of whom were talking and gesturing while she stood by quietly. "Who's that?"

"Who's who?"

"The platinum blond over there. The one with the black dress and the…"

"Plunging neckline?"

"Yeah. That one," Freddie said and grinned.

"Come on. I'll introduce you. She's sweet."

Gina took Freddie by the arm, but before she could pull him away from his spot by the phone, where his feet seemed suddenly stuck, Maria interrupted her.

"Hey," Maria said, "the place is crawlin' with guys! I thought we said girls only!"

Gina gave Maria a quick hug. "We can't help it. They can't stay away from us! I've got to go introduce Freddie to Celeste." She yanked Freddie away from the phone and pulled him into the living room.

Maria put her hands on her hips. There were a couple of dozen people crammed into the apartment, talking, drinking, listening to music coming over the radio. The buzz and chatter of talk was so loud she could hardly hear herself think. She glanced around the room at the dozen or so men chatting with each other or with the girls, then found a slip of paper in her purse, placed it on the counter beside the phone, and dialed Patsy's new number.

11:45 p.m.

I t's probably Maria." Patsy crossed the room, picked up the phone, lis-tened, exchanged a few words, and hung up. "Sorry," he said, speaking into the kitchen, where Vince and Mike were seated around the table with Loretto, Paul Martone, and Jimmy Brennan.

Vince had shown up a half hour earlier with Paul and Jimmy in tow. They had news about the Evangelistas. The brothers were on their way to Argentina. They'd left a message with Florence, since they hadn't known how to find Vince. They'd said to tell the boys they were sorry, but it was too hot for them now that they'd killed a cop. They had family in Argentina who would take them in and set them up in business—and that was where they were heading. Florence had called Vince with the news, half hysterical, convinced they'd all wind up in jail now that a New York City detective had been killed. Vince had told Florence and Joe to pack up and go on vacation for a while. He'd stopped by their place, given them money, and sent them off to Niagara Falls. "They weren't doing much for us anyway," Vince had told the boys, and they'd all lifted a drink to that. Then he'd laid out a few lines of coke on the table. "We're losing manpower, though," he'd told them, "with the Evangelistas gone, Domini laid up, and now Florence and Joe." He'd snorted a line of coke and Mike had joined him. "We're gonna have to look around again," he'd said, meaning they were going to have to recruit new members for the gang.

"I know you said not to give anyone our numbers . . ." Patsy was talking to Vince. "I figure it's Maria, though," he said. "I can trust her."

Vince said, "If the cops get the number, they can figure out where we are." He shook his head, trying to clear his senses. "Did you tell her not to write it down?"

"Sure." Patsy joined the boys in the kitchen and poured himself a drink. "I told her to memorize it and not to call unless it was important."

"So what's so important?" Loretto asked. He had just finished off the last of Mike's bread. He wiped away strawberry jam from the corner of his mouth.

Patsy grinned but didn't answer.

"What's the deal?" Vince slid his chair back, suddenly curious.

Jimmy Brennan reached for the shotgun. He said, "Want me to beat it out of him, boss?" and drew a laugh.

"It ain't nothin'. She's at a party over at your sister's place," Patsy said to Mike.

"Gina's having a party?"

"Yeah," Patsy said. "They're celebratin' because Maria finally dumped her old man for me, and she's moved in with Gina till things settle down and we can get our own place."

Paul Martone straightened out his bow tie. He was the only one of the gang not drinking, smoking tea, doing coke, or indulging in all three. "What a dish like that is doing with a dope like you, I'll never understand."

"Tell you the truth, I can't figure it out, either," Patsy said, and everyone laughed.

"Who's at this party?" Vince asked. "Any other good-looking dames?"

"It was supposed to be girls only," Patsy said, "but then a bunch of mugs started showing up. That's why she called me. She wanted me to come to the party."

"What'd you tell her?" Vince found the bottle of bourbon and refilled his glass.

"What do you think? I told her nothin' doing. I'm with the boys."

"What mugs are at this party?" Loretto asked, and the way he asked it made it clear he didn't like the idea of other guys showing up at Gina's place, party or not.

Vince turned to Loretto. "Maybe we should go see for ourselves."

"Now you're talkin'!" Paul was out of his chair and heading toward his coat, which was hanging from a hall tree in the living room.

"Don't be crazy," Loretto said. "We can't show up at a party with Dutch and the cops all looking for us."

"Ah, let's live a little," Paul said to Vince. "This is getting tired being cooped up like this."

Vince thought about it for a couple of seconds and then got up from his seat. To Loretto he said, "Nobody's gonna spot us. And Paul's right. We all need a little fun."

"But what if someone does?"

"Nobody will," Vince said, his mind made up. "And if they do, we'll kill 'em."

Paul and the rest of the gang laughed.

Loretto said to Mike, "What do you think about this?"

Mike looked a little worried at first, but then he shook it off. "It'll be fine," he said. "Nobody's gonna spot a couple of cars driving to the Bronx."

Patsy chimed in. "Come on," he said to Loretto, "let's go see our girls."

"Count me out," Jimmy Brennan said. "I ain't one for parties."

"You're too old for the dames that'll be there anyway, Jimmy," Paul said.

"I won't argue with you there. I'm not much for anything but a whore now and then anyway."

"You'll get over that," Vince said. "Give yourself time." He was in the living room with the rest of the boys, bundling up in their coats and scarves, fixing their hats the way they liked them. He meant that Jimmy would eventually get over the loss of his wife and family.

"How do you know she wants the rest of us there?" Loretto said to Patsy. "She only invited you, right?"

Patsy said, "You know Gina wants to see you, Loretto."

"And she's my sister," Mike said.

Vince said, "And who's gonna keep me out?"

The gang all laughed with Vince and then followed him through the door.

Loretto was the last one out. Before he pulled the door closed behind him, he looked back to Jimmy. "Will you be all right?"

"Sure," Jimmy said. He held up a bottle of whiskey. "I got all the company I need."

"We'll see you later, then." Loretto followed the rest of the gang out the door, down to the street, and out into the frigid cold.

12:00 a.m.

Dorothy Dunbar smiled and winked at Owen while Max Baer, sitting alongside her at Owen's private table, focused his attention on a line of young dancers prancing to the stage. The club was noisy and busy for a Sunday night, and patrons kept walking by the table trying to get a better look at the hulking boxer and his movie-star wife. Owen was starting to ask Max about his last fight when Frenchy came up behind him and whispered in his ear.

"Excuse me," Owen said to Dorothy. To Max he said, "Business." He slid out of his seat, and Frenchy took his place at the table.

In the hallway at the foot of the stairs leading to his office, Owen found Jimmy Brennan waiting, his homburg pulled down so far over his face it might as well have been a mask. Owen snatched the hat from Jimmy's head. "This better be good."

"It's better than good," Jimmy said, and the two men climbed the stairs together and disappeared into Owen's office.

12:20 a.m.

Augie huddled in a corner of the kitchen with Gina and Loretto. Vince had shown up at the party a few minutes earlier with his gang in tow. Maria had opened the door and squealed at the sight of Patsy. She'd thrown her arms around his neck and kicked up her heels. While she dangled from Patsy's neck, the boys made their way into the living room and by the time Augie, who'd been in the kitchen with Gina, realized what was happening, it was too late: Vince and his gang were there at the party, pouring themselves drinks, laughing and telling stories to the girls, who surrounded them as if they were movie stars. Vince had a quartet of women around him, hanging on his every word. Patsy was on one side of the couch with Maria in his lap, next to Freddie on the other side with Celeste. Paul and Mike were by the radio, lighting cigarettes for a couple of dames Gina only knew as friends of one of her friends from work.

Mike edged away from Paul and the girls. He took a couple of backward steps toward the kitchen, where he had spotted Augie taking Loretto in one hand and Gina in the other and pulling them along behind him.

In the kitchen, Augie said, "Get them out of here." He held Loretto firmly by the arm.

Before Loretto could respond, Mike pushed his way into their circle. "Jesus Christ, Augie." He snatched Loretto's arm away from Augie. "Relax, will you? And lower your voice. The last thing I need is for you to get into a beef with Vince."

"You want me to lower my voice?" Augie said, loud, almost shouting.

Gina said, "Augie, a brawl won't solve anything."

Behind them, Vince entered the kitchen. He spotted Augie, Mike, and Gina with Loretto, the four of them huddled up as if in a private conference. "Augie," he said when Augie turned in his direction.

Mike looked to Gina as if about to ask her to intercede before Augie said something stupid—but he hadn't managed to get out a word before he was interrupted by the loud, cracking sound of the front door being kicked open, followed instantly by gunfire, several guns firing in rapid succession, not the rat-a-tat-tat of choppers but close to it.

Vince and Mike rushed to the living room, guns already out of their holsters.

Loretto spun around and threw Augie into Gina, knocking them both off their feet. He overturned the kitchen table and pushed it in front of them as a barricade, the food and drinks crashing to the floor. In the next instant, he had his gun out, and when he turned around he saw that Mike had been hit and was sprawled across the kitchen floor, blood spilling out of him and mixing with the spilled liquor and beer, the broken glass and scattered food.

Vince knelt over Mike, a gun in each hand, firing into the living room.

Loretto joined Vince shoulder to shoulder and got off a couple of shots at a pair of masked figures who quickly backed out of his line of vision. They were young guys wearing long overcoats and fedoras, bandanas tied over their faces like stagecoach robbers in a movie Western. There were more gunmen somewhere behind them. The living room had emptied of everyone but the dead and wounded. Both windows were open and a freezing wind blew through the apartment, which was suddenly cold as an icebox. Through one window, Loretto caught the bright flash of a white dress descending the fire escape ladder. Through the second window, he saw Paul Martone's body on the fire escape, facedown and unmoving. On the far side of the couch, Maria was draped over Patsy as if she had flung herself on top of him, trying to shield him from the bullets. She'd been shot in the back several times: her blouse, a red smear, looked like a soaked-through bandage. Patsy was slumped under her, half his face turned to a bloody pulp. Alongside them, reversing their positions, Freddie was draped over a girl with platinum-blond hair. Freddie, like Maria, had been shot in the back, but he'd also taken a bullet to the top of his head, and blood dripped down out of his hair and onto the unmoving figure beneath him.

From someplace out of his line of sight, a voice yelled, "Mad Dog! Time to put you down!"

Vince responded by leaping to his feet and firing blindly as he jumped backward to a sitting position on a counter and opened the kitchen window. "Hold on," he yelled back. "I'll be with you in a second. Just got to make sure I've got a full clip." He motioned for Loretto to go out the window.

Loretto stood, fired twice in the direction of the voice, and started toward Augie and Gina where they were hunched down behind the overturned table, Gina looking paralyzed with fear, Augie holding her in his arms. Before he reached them, Vince, who was already sliding backward toward the open window, grabbed him by his coat and tried to pull him along with him.

"Go!" Gina yelled when she saw that Loretto was resisting. "Get out of here!"

When Loretto ignored her, she struggled free of Augie's grasp and pushed him toward the window. She yelled, "Get out before they kill you," and the words were hardly out of her mouth before a bullet hit her in the face, spinning her around. As she fell to the floor, Vince fired back at the figure who had just shot her.

Loretto tried to kneel to Gina, but Vince yanked him up and toward the window. He held Loretto by the neck in the crook of his arm, and with his free hand he aimed and squeezed off shots at figures that appeared and disappeared in the shadows of the living room.

In Vince's grasp, Loretto could hardly breathe, but he continued to struggle until Augie, who was holding a towel to Gina's face, pushed him away.

"Go!" Augie yelled. "Get out! It's you they're after!" He picked up Mike's gun and fired a shot through the kitchen wall.

Loretto struggled to breathe. When the apartment started to waver and spin, his legs went weak and Vince lifted him bodily and pulled him out through the window. There were more gunshots then, and he saw that it was Augie, kneeling over Gina, next to Mike, shooting with one hand and holding the bloody towel to her face with the other.

From the living room, someone yelled, "They're going out the window!" and then there was the noise of footsteps rushing down the stairs toward the street as Vince grabbed Loretto under his arms and pulled him onto the fire escape. He dragged him down the steps and pushed him to a ladder that ratcheted them down to a dark alley. As soon as they hit the ground, Vince took off running, pulling Loretto behind him.

For Loretto, as they raced through alleys, leaping fences, charging around corners, speeding through the maze of the city's narrow passages and cramped yards in the dark of night, an old instinct kicked in. How many times had he done this growing up on the streets—torn through alleys and yards at night, being chased or giving chase? It was familiar to him, this rush of speed, and he let himself concentrate on it. He told himself that Augie was with Gina. He put the picture of her falling, her face a sudden swell of blood, out of mind. Mike on the kitchen floor, Patsy and Freddie on the couch, Paul on the fire escape—all of these images he put out of mind. Running beside Vince, he quit thinking. He ran to keep up with Vince, to leap and sprint, to keep moving. It was something he was good at, and he did it with Vince beside him, the two of them tearing through the dark.

12:30 a.m.

They came out on 2nd Avenue, across from a tenement building with a rat-hole speakeasy in the basement. They both knew the place. The street was deserted and they leaned close to each other against a brick wall, in the shadow of a sandstone stoop with a pair of matching gargoyles on either side of the steps, the monstrous figures glaring out at the street. The apartment windows up and down the block were uniformly dark. Loretto didn't know what time it was, but he figured it was late, a Sunday night, and these tenements were home to working stiffs, guys with families, guys who had to get up in the morning and drag themselves to their jobs. Still, that there wasn't a single light on spooked him. The street was quiet as the end of the world.

He crouched down deeper in the shadows and Vince did the same. Their breath issued from them in long white streams. Neither had said a word since they had come out of the alley, jumped a wooden fence, and hid themselves in the comforting shadows of a stoop. Their hard breathing eased some while they rested, and then the sound of a car approaching, rolling slowly along 2nd Avenue, still out of sight on the other side of the stoop, set them both on edge, crouched, ready to run. There were four garbage pails in a cramped space under the stoop. Vince pulled two of them out quickly, lifting them so they wouldn't scrape along the sidewalk. By the time the car passed, creeping along the avenue, two men in front, two in back, peering out the windows, Vince and Loretto were hidden behind the garbage pails, under the stoop and out of sight. Five minutes later, a second car passed, again cruising slowly as four men scanned the sidewalks.

"They'll give up in a while," Vince said. He took his gun from his holster, reexamined the empty clip, and slipped it back as if it had disappointed him.

Loretto's holster was empty. He'd dropped his gun when Vince pulled him through the kitchen window. "It's freezing," he said.

"That it is." Vince fell back against the wall, pulled his knees to his chin, and wrapped his arms around his legs.

Loretto sat next to Vince, close to him for the warmth. "I don't think we'll make it till morning," he said. "We'll probably freeze to death."

Vince nodded in the direction of the speakeasy. "Somebody'll come out of there drunk soon enough. We'll follow him back to his car."

"What if he's not driving?"

"Then we'll follow him back to wherever he's going and hope he's got a phone so we can call Lottie."

Loretto pulled his legs closer to his chin, huddled into himself. Something about Vince's plan made him angry. It was as if he were upset because the plan might work and they wouldn't have to freeze to death or get filled full of lead by Dutch's boys. He asked, "How bad do you think Gina's hurt?" When he turned to look at Vince, they were so close they were practically touching.

"She got hit in the face." Vince covered his own face with his hands as if the memory of Gina getting shot pained him. "I saw her get hit. She took a bullet in the jaw. It won't kill her." He lowered his hands. "She may not be as pretty as she was before."

Loretto only nodded. The extreme cold seemed to make everything dull and slow, even his memories, even his feelings. "Patsy's dead. It looked like half his face was gone. His woman, too. Maria."

"And Mike's brother, Freddie. He got it in the back of the head." Vince watched the bottom of the stoop as if recalling the shootings, trying to see them again. "I don't know about Paul," he said. "He got hit trying to get out the window."

"Mike?"

"He was still breathing when we left. He took a bullet in the right side of the chest."

"You think it was Dutch's guys?"

"Probably," Vince said. "Probably Dutch hired some out-of-town boys to do the job for him. That's like Dutch."

Loretto shivered, his body convulsing as if he had the shakes. He pulled his knees tighter to his chest and Vince put his arm around his shoulders. It surprised Loretto, Vince putting his arm around his shoulders and pulling him closer. It wasn't like Vince to touch anyone, even when they were kids, back in the dorm, when they might sit side by side on one of their cots, reading a comic book. There was always some distance between them. He couldn't ever remember actually touching Vince, except once, when they were kids, after a fight, when Vince had helped him up. One of the bigger kids had pinned Loretto to the ground. He was sitting on him and throwing punches at his face, relentless. Then Vince was there, with

Pete. Vince knocked the kid off him, and Pete pummeled him, sent him running. Loretto remembered Vince leaning over him, extending his hand, helping him up, and then he put his arm around him and they walked off, the three of them, Vince on one side of him with his arm around his shoulders, Pete on the other side.

Loretto said, "How'd we get here?" and took a deep breath to tamp down the roiling feeling building in his stomach.

"What do you mean?" Vince answered. "We got here through the alleys. Sometimes it's like," he went on, dismissing Loretto's question, "it's like there's only one thing that matters to me anymore now, and it's that I get to kill Dutch." He was quiet then, as if he wanted to say more and was trying to come up with the words—but a door opened across 2nd and he jumped to peer out from under the stoop.

He was a little guy, the mug coming out of the speak and onto the street, clutching a frayed peacoat by the lapels, wrapping it around him tighter. He was wearing one of those crazy Russian hats that look you've got a live animal on your head, a big black woolly thing pulled down to just above his eyes.

Vince said, "Get a load of this guy." He pushed a garbage pail aside and scurried out from under the stoop with Loretto following. "If a car comes by, we go for the alleys again." He stepped out of the shadows and onto the sidewalk.

Loretto kept pace alongside Vince as they followed the little guy, who was walking briskly on the opposite side of the street, his hands shoved in his pockets and his shoulders hunched forward, making him appear even shorter. Loretto figured he couldn't have been more than five four.

"We're in luck," Vince said as the figure with the funny hat stepped into the street and crossed to the driver's side of a black Ford coup. "Hey, fella!" he called.

By the time the guy turned around to look, Vince had him by the neck with one hand, and with his free hand he relieved him of his keys. "We need to borrow your car," he said with a big smile. "Sorry for the inconvenience."

"Well, you can't borrow my car!" The big voice that came out of that small frame was startling. "Give me those keys!" he boomed, and he lunged at Vince.

Vince hit the guy once with a right that knocked him down—but he was up again immediately. He threw his head into Vince's gut and wrapped his arms around his waist as if he might upend Vince and throw him to the ground.

Vince snatched the guy's hat off, took him by the hair, and yanked him off his feet. He threw him back against the car and hit him several vicious blows to the gut, which doubled the guy over and left him flat on his face on the street, where he tried to crawl under the car for protection. Vince dragged him by the feet, pulled him out from under the car, lifted him by the waist, and carried him to the sidewalk, where he picked him up high over his head and plunged him down in sitting position onto a spear picket fence. The scream that issued from the guy then was loud enough to be heard for blocks. Vince hurried to the car and drove off with Loretto beside him and the guy still yowling and screaming as he struggled to extricate himself from the picket fence.

Vince turned quickly onto a side street and piloted the car through a maze of narrow cobblestone roads. Loretto figured he was trying to avoid the main thoroughfares, where they were more likely to run into Dutch's boys. After a while, he saw that they were heading out of the Bronx, up toward Westchester. "Where are we going?"

"To Lottie," Vince said. "I got another car there."

"You're not taking me back to my place?"

"Too dangerous."

"Dangerous? Why?"

"Give me a minute," Vince said. "I'm still thinking." He leaned close to the steering wheel, his eyes on the road.

Loretto tried to figure why it might be too dangerous to go back to his apartment in Brooklyn. He closed his eyes and sank down into his seat. "Jesus Christ," he said. "Jimmy Brennan."

"Yeah," Vince said. "That's what it looks like—but we don't know for sure."

"My money." Loretto pictured the cardboard box in his closet, all his money neatly stacked and banded in piles. "Christ, it was Jimmy," he said. It seemed obvious to him now: Jimmy staying behind, the gunmen showing up so soon after they'd arrived at the party.

"Probably," Vince said.

My money, Loretto thought. For a second, he let himself hope that he might be wrong, that Jimmy might not have turned on them, that his money might still be there in the closet waiting—but he quickly let that notion go. No. Jimmy had turned on them, and his money was gone. He felt oddly distanced from the realization—as if it didn't matter. He leaned his head against the window. He would have liked to fall asleep, but he knew he wouldn't. He'd stay where he was, in a dark space, moving, with everything hovering around him, just outside the range of thought.

1:00 a.m.

Lottie woke to the sound of a car pulling up the drive. She sat up in bed as headlights flashed through the bedroom, throwing a bright light on the plaster ceiling before racing down the walls and then leaving the room locked in darkness again as the engine cut out and quiet returned. She reached for the light on the night table and then thought better of it. Instead, she felt around under the bed until she found the sawed-off shotgun Vince had left for her there. She pulled it under the covers and turned on her back with the shotgun pointed at the bedroom door. There was no lock on the farmhouse door, and now she regretted not propping a chair under the knob. Outside, she heard the car doors open and close. She listened, her body tensed toward the quiet, hoping to hear a familiar voice.

The room was cold and she was sleeping in her robe under a quilt and a pair of red flannel blankets, the coverings mounded over her. Before going to bed, she'd smoked some tea with a glass of wine to help her sleep—but as she waited in the dark, listening, she didn't feel anything other than sober. Her heart wasn't racing, though her arms and legs were tingly, the way they got when she was afraid. She held the shotgun with both hands, her finger on the trigger, and when the lights went on beyond her closed door and someone climbed the stairs toward the bedroom, she snuggled down into the pillows with her eyes squinted closed and tried to look like she was sleeping. Then the door opened and the light went on and it was Vince standing in the doorway.

"Jesus H. Christ," she said, the words tumbling out of her. "You scared the hell out of me! You said you were spending the night in the city." Only after she'd spoken did it register that his shirt and jacket were blood-stained. "What happened?" She tossed the heavy covers aside and stepped onto the cold hardwood floor.

Vince glanced at the barrel of the shotgun sticking out from under the covers. "Get dressed and packed," he said. "We're leaving tonight for Niagara Falls."

Lottie pulled Vince's jacket open, examining the bloodstains on his shirt.

"Not my blood," he said. "Loretto's downstairs getting cleaned up." He gently pushed her aside and made his way to the bathroom as he stripped out of his clothes. "Bring Loretto one of my suits. His is a mess."

Lottie followed him into the bathroom and watched as he sat on the john and pulled off the rest of his clothes. "Are you going to tell me what happened?"

"We got ambushed." He leaned over the sink and took a washcloth to his face and chest. "Mike wanted to go see his sister, Gina. She was having some kind of a party. We didn't want him to go alone, so we all went with him. Everybody but Jimmy Brennan." He opened a cabinet door under the sink, found a clean towel, and dried himself off. "A couple of minutes after we get there, a carload of Dutch's boys bust through the door." He shrugged as if he didn't want to tell the rest of the story. He went back into the bedroom and started getting dressed.

Lottie watched Vince as he pulled on underwear and an undershirt and then moved to the closet to pick out a suit. "Who got hit?" she asked. "Whose blood is that?"

Vince didn't answer right away. He put on his pants and slipped into his shirt before he turned to face her. "Patsy's gone," he said, buttoning up his shirt. "Mike and Paul got hit. We left them there."

Lottie looked as if she had a sudden headache. She sat on the edge of the mattress, next to the shotgun.

"Mike's brother Freddie got it, too," Vince said, and he pulled a jacket from the closet. "And Maria, Patsy's woman. They're all dead. I don't know about Mike and Paul."

"Jesus," Lottie said. "Anybody else?"

"Gina got hit in the face. And, I don't know, there was a broad under Freddie. She might have got hit, too. I never saw her before."

"God Almighty," Lottie said. She took a moment to think and then asked, "Is it all over now? Are we on the run?"

"You ever known me to run?" Vince snatched a suit from the closet and tossed it at Lottie. "Take this to Loretto like I asked you. Go on."

"Where are you going?"

"We got some business to take care of."

"What kind of business?"

"Jimmy Brennan business. He ratted us out to Dutch." He stared at Lottie where she stood with the suit draped over her arm. "I got to ask you a third time?"

"If he squealed on you," Lottie said, "don't you think he'll be expecting you? You can't go after him now. You'll get yourself killed."

Vince rubbed his chin like he was trying to hurt himself. Then he snatched Lottie by the back of her robe, yanked her across the room, threw her out of the bedroom, and slammed the door behind her.

In the hallway, Lottie clutched the suit to her breast. When she saw Loretto at the bottom of the stairs, she hurried down to him. He had a bath towel wrapped around his waist and a second one slung over his shoulder. His hair was wet and still dripping. "Jesus, get dressed before you freeze to death." She handed him the suit.

Loretto looked up to the closed bedroom door. "Everything all right?"

"Sorry about Gina," Lottie said. She pushed Loretto back toward the bathroom.

"She'll be okay," Loretto said as if he was sure of it. "She got hit in the jaw." He stepped into the bathroom, and Lottie followed him in.

"Go on, get dressed." Lottie took a seat on the edge of the tub, her feet in the tub, looking away from Loretto. "Vince says you're going after Brennan. Don't you think that's pretty crazy?"

"Not really." Loretto stepped into Vince's pants. They were big on him, but then he wasn't going anyplace where style mattered. He tucked the shirt in and cinched the belt tight.

Lottie said, "I thought you were the smart one? Jimmy'll be looking for you to come after him."

"Not if he thinks we're dead."

"Yeah, but what if he doesn't?" Lottie said. "What if he knows you and Vince got out?"

Before Loretto could answer, Vince appeared in the doorway. He was wearing a winter coat, gloves, and a hat, and he had a second coat slung over his arm and a second hat in hand. "You can turn around," he said to Lottie. "He's all dressed."

"Jesus, Vince," she said when she saw him. "We should just go, right now, the three of us. We can meet Florence and Joe and figure out what to do next from there."

Vince handed Loretto the coat and hat and then took a Super .38 from under his belt and slipped it into Loretto's holster. To Lottie he said, "Do what I just told you to do. Get dressed. Get packed. As soon as I get back, I want you ready to go out the door."

"Vince, honey—" Lottie sounded as if she was going to try one last time to convince him not to go after Jimmy, but Vince snatched her by the neck, lifted her close to him, and slapped her across the face.

"Soon as I get back," he said, and he tossed her down into the bathtub, where she landed awkwardly on her back.

For a second, Lottie thought she might cry, but then something different rose up inside her, something huge and angry, and she wrapped her arms around herself to keep it contained. It was as if the slap had detonated an explosion—and then an instant later another part of herself had clicked into gear, a part that was mechanical and calculating. She counted the dead and wounded: Patsy, Mike, and Paul. She counted the missing: Domini and the Evangelista brothers. She added Jimmy Brennan to the calculations as a traitor, probably gone over to Dutch and the Combine. That left only Vince and Loretto, and now Vince was flying out of control. These calculation happened in an instant, but she didn't look up until she heard Vince leave the bathroom. She caught Loretto glancing back at her just before he followed Vince out the door to the cars. He had a mystified look on his face, as if he had no idea what was going on. He'd opened his mouth, and she'd thought he was going to say something, but he only turned and followed Vince, and then Lottie was alone in the big farmhouse

again. When she heard two cars start up and pull away, she switched off
the bathroom light and closed the door and sat down on the john in the
darkness and tried to think.

1:45 a.m.

A couple of miles out from Westchester, Loretto ditched the stolen Ford
and drove the rest of the way into Brooklyn with Vince in his Buick.
Brennan owned a couple of houses side by side on Ainslie Street in a quiet
Italian neighborhood. Before the fire, he'd had a steady job as a welder, and
he'd pulled in money on the side as a shylock. His wife had worked at home
as a seamstress. Loretto knew all this from conversations with Brennan, who
was proud of owning two houses. His family had come from County Donegal, same as Vince's family, and the only thing they'd ever owned was debt
and misery. With a few drinks in him, Brennan talked freely about his life,
about growing up one of six brothers and three sisters, about working in
factories from the time he was a child, too young even to know how to read,
about the fights he'd had with his old man, who was good-hearted but with
a weakness for drink and women, about his mother who was a scold and a
shrew and beat all the boys while pampering the girls, about the years he'd
lived in Mount Loretto because his family couldn't afford to feed him and
couldn't find anyplace to put him to work, about how he'd been in and out
of trouble with the law. He talked about everything but the fire that killed his
wife and children. About that he'd never uttered a word.

"That's it," Vince said, and he pulled over on a quiet street of two-family houses, under a tree with branches that reached out toward the rooftops.
Down the block, a lamppost cast its yellow light over a slate sidewalk and a
cobblestone street. "That's the one that burned," he said, gesturing across
the street toward a house with a basement apartment under a wooden stoop
and a second apartment on the upper level. "You can still see the scorch
marks by the windows."

Loretto crouched down to get a better look at the building. "I don't see any lights."

Vince buttoned up his coat. "Feckin' coldest night of the year. You ready?"

Loretto nodded, but Vince kept his eyes on him. "If you're still thinking about what happened at Gina's, don't," he said. "Don't think. Just keep moving." He waited another moment, watching Loretto, before he got out of the car and started across the street.

Loretto followed Vince to a narrow alley between two buildings, where they jumped a wooden fence and followed a dirt path to a small backyard littered with old paint cans and an assortment of car parts, including a red car hood and a chrome fender draped over a wire fence like a pair of wings. While Loretto watched, Vince found a rusted blade of metal amidst the junk and used it to deftly unlock and open a tall window. A second later, the two of them were creeping through a dark kitchen. Vince knew his way around, and Loretto realized he had to have been here before, probably on business. Beyond the door, a dim light illumined a flight of stairs that led to another door, this one open and beyond which Brennan was stretched out on an old-fashioned bed, a four-poster that looked like it might have been carried over with his family from the old country. He was fully dressed, on his back, his head propped up on a pillow, with a pistol by his knee. Alongside him on a night table, an almost empty bottle of gin lay on its side next to a table lamp, a greasy tumbler, a pack of Camels, and an ashtray stuffed with cigarette butts.

Vince took the pistol from the bed and handed it to Loretto, who tucked it into his belt. He turned on the lamp. "He's sleeping the sleep of the dead," he said to Loretto.

"He's drunk." Loretto set the bottle of gin upright.

Vince told Loretto to search the place. "Maybe you'll be lucky and find your money."

Loretto started by looking under the bed and moved from there to the closets and dresser drawers and then on to the other rooms. He found nothing, and when he returned to Vince, he saw that he'd used belts to tie Jimmy's feet and hands to the bedposts, and that Jimmy was awake and alert.

"Jimmy was just telling me he don't know nothing about your money," Vince said to Loretto. "Right, Jimmy?"

Jimmy said, "Give me a drink at least, will you, Loretto?"

"Not much left." Loretto picked up the bottle of gin and tilted it to Jimmy's lips.

Jimmy swallowed and said thank you. "I don't know nothing about nothing," he said to Loretto. "Once you mugs left, I picked up some gin and came here. I don't know nothing about no ambush."

Vince sat on the mattress at Brennan's feet. "Jimmy," Vince said, "do we look stupid to you? Do we?"

"I'm telling you the truth. What can I do to prove it?"

"Why would you come back to your own house, Jimmy? Why would you come here—where anybody knows to look for you—instead of our place in the Bronx? Why would you do something stupid as that?"

"Ah, I wanted to sleep in my own bed, that's all it is, Vince. It don't mean nothing."

"Or you felt safe here because you knew no one was looking for you. That could be it, Jimmy. Couldn't it?"

"I'm telling you, Vince! I just wanted to sleep in my own bed." Jimmy turned to Loretto and nodded toward a closet on the other side of the room. "There's a bottle of whiskey on the shelf in there," he said. "Be a good lad and bring me another drink."

Loretto looked to Vince, and when Vince nodded, he retrieved the whiskey bottle and held it to Jimmy's lips.

Vince scratched his head. "I know you squealed on us," he said to Jimmy. "Why are you making it hard on me?"

"I didn't do it, Vince." Jimmy tried to sit up a bit, but his feet and arms were fastened securely and all he could manage was to lift his head. "I'm telling you, Vince, you're making a mistake."

To Loretto Vince said, "What do you think? You think it's possible he's telling the truth?"

"Anything's possible," Loretto said, though he had little doubt about Jimmy's guilt.

"Give me his wallet." Vince gestured toward Jimmy's pants, slung over the back of a chair by the window. "Let's see how much money he's got."

Jimmy's face brightened, and he tried again to sit up. "All I've got's a couple of twenties in there," he said. "And all you'll find in the Bronx is my share of the jobs we've pulled. That should tell you something. If I was the Judas, then where's my pile of gold?"

Loretto tossed Vince Jimmy's wallet, and Vince pulled two lonely twenties out of the billfold.

"What did I tell you?" Jimmy said, struggling against his restraints.

Vince continued looking through the wallet, which was stuffed with receipts and business cards and scraps of paper. He tossed each item onto the bed after examining it casually until he came to something that caught his attention. As he held it up to the light and examined it carefully, his face grew darker. "Why would you have Owen Madden's name and phone number in your wallet, Jimmy?" He handed the scrap of paper to Loretto. Madden's name was scrawled but clearly legible, and under it was a phone number.

Brennan's head fell back onto the pillow. "Must be from a long time ago," he said, but he didn't sound like he expected anyone to believe him.

"What business would you have had with Madden a long time ago?" Vince asked. When Jimmy didn't answer, Vince added, "That's what I thought." To Loretto he said, "Let me see your knife."

Jimmy lifted his head. "Ah, just put a bullet in me, Vince," he said. "I only done what anyone else would have done. Can't you see you're good as dead already? Why shouldn't I have made a little cush in the process?"

Loretto said, "Patsy's dead, too. And Freddie, Mike's brother."

"That's the business they were in," Jimmy answered with his eyes closed, as if he was ready to take a nap. He sounded tired.

"And Maria Tramonti," Loretto said, "she's dead, too."

"She should have been more careful about the company she kept." Jimmy settled back into the pillow, making himself comfortable.

Loretto said, "Why don't you tell me where my money is, Jimmy?"

"I never went back there," Jimmy said. "I don't know nothin' about your money." He seemed to think about it a second and then added, "You might want to talk to Big Owney's boys. I gave him the address."

Vince gestured for Loretto to hand him the stiletto. Loretto waited another moment and then gave it over. When the blade snapped open, Jimmy's head shot up from the pillow. "Ah, Vince," he said. "Don't send me out screaming. Put a bullet in my head and be done with it. For the sake of the old country, Vince, if nothing else. For County Donegal."

Vince made a circle with the knife, taking in Loretto and Jimmy and himself. "You know why I picked you, Jimmy Brennan? Because you were one of us, and I thought I could trust you for that."

"Trust me for what? Because we were all in the orphanage together?"

"That's right," Vince said. He stood, took a handkerchief from his pocket, and stuck it in Jimmy's mouth. He said, "That's exactly what I'm doing, you son of a bitch. I'm sending you out screaming."

Jimmy spit the handkerchief out. "Go ahead," he shouted. "I'll be waitin' for you on the other side—and I won't be waitin' long."

Vince punched him in the face, splitting his lip. He stuffed the handkerchief back into his mouth and held it there with one hand while with the other he cut his shirt away, exposing his belly before plunging the stiletto into him. He locked his eyes on Jimmy's as he pulled the knife up slowly,

Jimmy's eyes wide and fiery as he strained to free himself and screamed into Vince's hand.

"Here," Vince said once he had sawed through Jimmy's belly from navel to breastbone. With his bare hand he reached into the bloody gash and pulled out a handful of blood and gore, which he wiped on Jimmy's face.

Brennan's eyes darted from side to side before settling on a spot on the ceiling and glazing over, going blank as his body collapsed into the mattress and spilled out a stinking stream of urine and blood.

Vince closed the stiletto and shoved it back into Loretto's pocket. He said, "Let's go," but in the same instant spun around, picked up the gin bottle, broke it over Jimmy's head, and went on stabbing him in the face until he wasn't recognizably human. When he was done, he stood, out of breath from the effort, and wiped his hands on the sheets. He found the scrap of paper with Madden's name and number, read the number aloud as if memorizing it, and then jammed it in Jimmy's mouth.

In the car, on the ride back to Westchester, Vince held the wheel in both hands, steadying himself with it as much as steering. Alongside him, Loretto smoked a cigarette and watched the road and the cloud-blotted sky at the horizon, a line of black clouds settled like ink at the bottom of a gray field. The memory of the comet he'd seen upstate came back to him, the white-blue slash of it across the sky, and he was thrown back to his nights in Albany, sitting quietly on the back porch watching the night sky. He let himself settle comfortably there, hundreds of miles from this car driving out of Brooklyn, leaving Jimmy Brennan's mutilated body behind.

For a brief while, Vince talked quietly to Loretto. He explained that he planned on taking Lottie upstate, to Niagara Falls, for the rest of the week, and that he'd be back on Friday. He wanted Loretto to stay at the farmhouse, where he'd be safe. When he came back, Madden's deadline would soon be up, and he'd learn whether or not he had a deal.

"It was Madden just tried to have us all killed," Loretto said.

"And he failed," Vince answered. "Now he knows he's still got to deal with me, one way or another."

After that, they both fell silent. They drove through deserted streets in the dead of night, under a black sky, the weather too cold to snow but the feel of snow and winter everywhere.

9:05 p.m.

In the chair beside Gina's hospital bed, Augie ran his fingers through his hair, lowered his head into his hands, and massaged his scalp with his fingertips and his temples with the heels of his hands, over and over again, with the solemnity of a ritual. Every now and again he'd take a break and rub his eyes and touch his eyebrows lightly, but then he'd fall back into the ritual. He'd spent the morning finalizing the funeral arrangements with Mama. Freddie would be laid out at Balzarini's Funeral Parlor Wednesday morning with one day of viewing and the burial on Thursday. The bullet that had hit him in the back of the head had exited under his right eye and taken a portion of his face with it. When Balzarini had explained that it would have to be a closed casket, that even with all his experience he could never make Freddie's face look natural, Mama had wailed and pleaded with him so desperately that even Balzarini, a man on friendly terms with grief, couldn't keep himself from shedding tears. Augie's thoughts were full of details—of bills and expenses, of arrangements and agreements, of food orders and mass cards, of priests and cemeteries. When now and then there was room for the thought of Freddie being carried out of Gina's apartment in a body bag, or the image of his shattered face, Augie's body slowed to a stop as if drained momentarily of life, as if empty.

Gina scribbled, *Augie quit it will you?* on a yellow pad and then threw the pad onto his lap.

"What am I doing?"

Gina gestured for Augie to return the pad so that she could write her response.

"Doctor said you should talk."

"It hurts," Gina said. The bullet had hit her low on the jaw and taken off a piece of her chin. She touched one finger gently to the bandages that started under her lower lip. "Let him talk," she said and winced.

"Quit what?" Augie placed the yellow pad back on the bed next to Gina. "I wasn't doing anything."

Gina picked up the pad and then dropped it and sighed. "Rubbing your head," she managed. "It's driving me crazy."

When Augie saw that Gina's eyes were tearing from the difficulty of speaking, he kissed her on the forehead and straightened out her hair.

Gina took Augie's hand in hers and squeezed it. They were both crying, though neither acknowledged it. "You sure Mike's okay?" she asked and wiped away tears. "You're not keeping anything from me?"

"You know what they say: God looks out for fools and drunks." Augie dropped back into his chair and roughly brushed a forearm over his eyes. "The bullet went through clean and he's gonna be fine."

"What about the other guy?"

"Martone? Not so lucky. He got hit four times. He's losing a couple of internal organs, and his knee's smashed so he won't be doing any more dancing for a while."

Gina's eyes welled with tears. Augie knew it wasn't Martone she was crying for.

"I heard Maria's husband is arranging a quick funeral."

"You know where?"

"Not here. Papers said Midwest someplace, in a family plot."

"And Patsy?"

"His family's burying him at Saint Raymond's, same day as Freddie."

"The DiNapolis . . ." Gina said. She was sorry for the family. The mother was a religious woman, in her sixties. Patsy was her baby.

"The girl Freddie was with at the party," Augie said, wanting to change the subject, "looks like she packed up and went back to wherever she came from. Celeste," he added when Gina only looked away, "the one that played dead."

Gina nodded. She was gazing at the wall as though there were something going on there beyond a couple of charts hung from hooks. She whispered, "I'm tired," and offered Augie a wan smile.

Augie figured Gina was thinking about Freddie. She looked the way he felt when he thought about Freddie. Empty. Quiet and empty.

"Go take care of Mama," Gina said. She closed her eyes and settled into her pillow as if about to drop off to sleep. "Tell her I'll be there for the burial. Tell her I promise."

"I will." Augie kissed Gina on the cheek, pulled her blankets to her neck, and then stood at the foot of the bed and watched her. Her face was a little pale, but other than that, she looked okay. The feistiness was gone out of her, but that would come back in time. It was her nature. He thought, *She's the only one I have left*, as though she were the last of his siblings. He realized that he was thinking of Mike as already dead. Mike, the last of his brothers. He bowed his head and concentrated, trying to imagine what he might do to save Mike from the Combine and the cops and everybody else set on killing him. When these thoughts felt like they might tear him apart from the inside, he cast them out. He looked around at the various pieces of hospital equipment scattered about the room and tried to settle down. He didn't move until Gina opened her eyes again. She whispered, "Mama shouldn't be alone," and gestured toward the open door.

"I'll come by to see you first thing tomorrow morning," Augie said.

Gina responded with the hint of a smile. "Go on," she said, and she watched until Augie finally pulled himself away from her bed and left the room.

Mike was on the floor below Gina, and when Augie reached his room, he found him dressed and sitting on the edge of his bed with his hands on his knees.

"Good," Mike said at the sight of Augie. "Help me out of here. I'm still a little weak."

"*V'fancul'!*" Augie cocked his arm as if to give Mike a smack. "Get undressed," he said. "You're not going anywhere."

"Augie," Mike said, his voice weary. He wiped sweat from his forehead. "Are you heeled?"

"Since when you known me to carry a gun?"

"Then neither one of us is safe here. You understand? If you don't want me to end up like Freddie, then help me get out of this place."

Augie again raised his hand to Mike, and this time he did slap him. "Don't mention Freddie," he said. "Don't even say his name."

Mike glared at Augie, his face a snarl. "Yeah," he said a moment later, the snarl melting away—and in that single syllable there was an admission of responsibility for Freddie's death, an acceptance of his guilt. "Yeah," he repeated, and he dropped his head into his hands to hide his face.

Augie sat on the bed alongside him. When he put his arm around his shoulders, Mike laid his head against his brother's chest. "Don't look at me," he said.

"I'm not." Augie ran his hand over Mike's head as if Mike were suddenly a little kid again and he was comforting him.

Mike pulled away and sat up straight. He rubbed his eyes with the heels of his hands. "You know I can't come to the funeral."

Augie noticed Mike's hat on a shelf under the window. He went and got it for him and dropped it in his lap. "I'll make Mama understand," he said. "But you've got to come see her soon as you can."

"When it's safe."

Augie put an arm around Mike's waist and helped him up. "When will that be, Mike?" he asked. "When's the Combine gonna stop looking for you? Dutch Schultz and Lucky Luciano and Big Owney—when are they likely to forget that you've robbed their money and killed their men? Anytime soon, you think?"

"Vince has got a plan," Mike answered. "If it works, we'll be okay."

"A plan? What kind of plan?"

"You don't want to know too much." Mike fixed his hat on his head and pushed Augie away. "We're waiting to hear from Big Owney. If it works out, we'll be okay."

To himself Augie whispered, "Jesus Christ." To Mike he said, "Owen Madden is not making a deal with Vince. Get that out of your head. The deal is that you and Loretto and Vince are all dead men. That's the deal."

"Maybe," Mike said, as if he hadn't heard a word Augie said. "Come on. Let's get out of here."

"Where? Where are we going?"

"Hotel somewhere. Seedier the better." Mike winced and stopped. "If you could try to get word to Loretto about where I'm staying, that'd be good. But only Loretto, Augie. Nobody else."

"Loretto," Augie said. "Are you even sure he's still alive?"

"I'm not sure of nothin', but like I said, if there's a way to get word to him, that'd help."

Augie was tempted to smack Mike yet again. If he thought it would have done any good, he would have. Instead, he put his arm through his brother's arm and helped him out the door.

9:00 a.m.

The below-zero cold spell of the previous days had given way to temperatures in the low teens, still cold enough, though, for Saint Raymond's to discourage long graveside ceremonies. Mama, Gina, and Augie waited in the back of a limousine while the cemetery staff carried Freddie's casket to the plot of earth where he would be buried once the ground thawed. When the site was ready, Augusto Balzarini came to the limo door and opened it for the family. Once Mama exited the limo, followed by Gina and Augie, three more cars emptied of family and friends and neighbors who joined her as they walked in a solemn procession to the grave site. There the priest said a brief prayer with the family gathered around, and then stood aside as the cemetery workers once again lifted the casket and carried it off to the same stone building where Ercole Baronti had been carried a little more than a month earlier.

Gina held Mama around the waist on one side while Augie held her around the shoulders on the other side. Mama had cried silently at times, loudly at others, throughout the previous day of viewing and through the following night. If she had slept at all, it couldn't have been more than a few minutes. In the funeral parlor, she had wailed every time she looked up to find the casket closed, as if she couldn't bear being denied a final chance to see the body of her son. Now, graveside, she appeared to be so worn out and exhausted from her mourning that both Augie and Gina were taken by surprise when she flung them aside like a pair of scrawny children and screamed after the casket, "Go! Go! Be with your papa!" In an instant, Mrs. Esposito and Mrs. Marcello had taken Augie and Gina's place at Mama's side, each of them whispering in her ear and patting her hair, kissing her on the cheeks and holding her. With everyone in the gathering, priest and funeral director included, holding tissues or handkerchiefs to their eyes, the women took Mama by the arms and led her back to the waiting limousine.

Augie had closed his eyes and looked up to the sky as if he might find some strength there. When he opened them again, he saw that Gina was watching one of the cemetery workers, a young guy in denim overalls under a bulky winter coat with a knit cap pulled low over his forehead. The worker was walking toward Gina, who was also walking toward him, and when they met, they embraced before Gina quickly pulled away and looked around worriedly—and Augie realized that the cemetery worker had to be Loretto. He didn't recognize him, though, until he was standing between him and Gina in a small circle. "You're crazy to be here," he said to Loretto, and he pulled Gina away from him. At first Augie was furious with Loretto—but when he saw his face, it was so stricken that he relented and touched his shoulder in a gesture that made Loretto struggle to swallow his tears.

"I had to be here," Loretto said. "I'm sorry."

Gina asked Augie to give her and Loretto a minute, and Augie agreed, but first he pulled Loretto aside to have a private word with him. "Don't be long," he said. "It's too risky."

"Just give us a second."

"Sure," Augie said. At the curb, the last of the guests were climbing into their cars. "I need you to do something for me," he added. "When you see Vince, tell him I want to work for him. Tell him I want the chance to put a bullet in whoever it was that killed Freddie. You understand?"

"Augie—"

"Shut up." Augie moved in closer to Loretto. "Tell him I need the money, too. For the funeral and the loss of Freddie's income. We've got to eat. Tell him. He'll understand."

"I'll tell him," Loretto said, though he was pretty sure he wouldn't.

"And I've got a message for you from Mike. He's staying at the Breslin. He says you know the place. He's registered under the name of Wilson."

Loretto said thanks, and Augie told him again not to be long. Then he went to join Mama in the limo.

When Loretto was with Gina again, he found he had nothing to say beyond *I'm sorry* and then repeating himself. He searched her face, hoping to see forgiveness—but all he saw was grief.

"Augie tells me to forget about you," Gina said. "He tells you and Mike, both. You're good as dead."

"Maybe," Loretto said. "I hope not."

"You hope not," Gina repeated, and on her lips the words were a rebuke.

"How are you?" Loretto asked. Gina was wearing a scarf, and he pushed it aside to reveal the white bandages that covered her chin. "Is it too bad?"

"It's not too bad," Gina said. She glanced back at the cars. "It hurts to talk."

"But you'll be okay?"

"Sure, I'll be okay. A little deformed, maybe, once the bandages come off. But nothing I can't live with it."

"It won't matter to me," Loretto said. "It won't matter a thing to me."

Gina only nodded and said, "I've got to go." She turned once again to the waiting cars. She opened her mouth as if she wanted to say something more—and then she gave up and walked away.

Loretto watched her get into the limousine. The cars pulled away and drove off, leaving him alone in a field of headstones and frozen ground and empty paths. He went to the stone building that held Freddie's casket and stood beside it in the shadows. Up close, he could see that the stones were covered in a thin layer of ice. He took a glove off and held his hand to a stone and felt his body's heat sucked out of him. His only thoughts were the two words *I'm sorry*, which repeated themselves again and again in a mindless litany. When he put his glove back on, he thought he was ready to leave. Instead, he found himself observing a barren tree, its branches spread over a line of grave sites. It was quiet and peaceful in the empty cemetery, surrounded by the dead, and he stayed as long as he could, quiet, leaning against the stone wall, looking out at a single tree and a line of graves. He stayed until the cold urged him on, and then he walked back slowly among the gravestones to his waiting car.

10:00 p.m.

H ere they are," Mike said. Vince and Lottie had just pulled up, the headlights of their big Buick first lighting up the trees and the gravel path and the bright red face of the nearby barn before cutting off with the engine, the car disappearing again into the night. Loretto, in the kitchen, slipped into his jacket as if preparing for the arrival of guests. He had picked up Mike at the Breslin after Freddie's funeral and taken him back to the farmhouse, where they'd both been waiting for Vince's return. Lottie had called from a gas station two hours earlier and said they'd be at the farm in an hour.

Mike found a flashlight in the foyer and went out to meet them at the car while Loretto watched from the window. At Mike's approach, Vince put his suitcase down, and the boys shook hands and patted each other on the back while Lottie walked on as if she had nothing to do with either of them.

Loretto met Lottie at the door and tried to take her suitcase.

"Thanks," Lottie said. "I've got it." She continued on to the stairway to the bedrooms, climbed a couple of steps, sighed, and turned back to Loretto. "It ain't you," she said to Loretto. "Me and Vince been fightin' all week, that's all." She gave Loretto a wink and then trudged up the stairs and disappeared into the master bedroom.

When Vince and Mike came through the door, they were already talking business. Vince had plans to recruit a dozen guys from a gang he knew that operated out of New Jersey. "They're strictly small time," he was saying to Mike, "mug named Tony Nannini runs the show—but they're all tough enough, and once I tell 'em how much cush they'd be making, they'll be all for it." At the sight of Loretto, he dropped his suitcase to shake hands. Upstairs, Lottie was banging around in the bedroom. It sounded like she was tearing the place up more than unpacking. "Don't mind her," he said. "She didn't want us to come back."

"Speaking of that," Mike said, "where's Florence and Joe?"

"Look at this guy," Vince said to Loretto, talking about Mike. His eyes lit up with a mixture of amusement and joy. "I was worrying he might be dead, and here he is, like nothing happened."

"Ain't exactly like nothing happened," Mike said. "Every time I take a deep breath, it's like someone's sticking a knife in my back."

"Yeah, but here you are," Vince said. "Let's get a drink." He started for the kitchen. "I'm still freezin'. The heater in the Buick is on the fritz."

"It's this cold," Mike said. "Probably something's frozen somewhere."

In the kitchen, Vince found a bottle of bourbon under the sink and three glasses in the cupboard. He went about pouring everyone a drink. Loretto and Mike pulled up seats at the table while Vince tossed his coat over a chair and then joined them. He lifted his glass. "To the boys," he said, and the three of them clinked glasses and drank. "Florence and Joe ain't comin' back," he said. He finished off his bourbon and poured himself some more. "They're headin' up to Canada. They're gonna lay low there till things cool off."

Mike said, "No offense, Vince. I know she's your sister, but she wasn't doing us much good."

"Yeah," Vince said, "but she and Joe were good for taking care of the little stuff."

Loretto said, "We are in a bind," meaning he could understand why

Florence and Joe took off for Canada. "It's just the three of us left now—and Lottie."

"Don't worry about that," Vince said. "There's a dozen guys in this New Jersey gang, and I'm gonna get them all to come in with us. We'll be stronger than we were before."

"I don't know," Loretto said. He was fidgeting with his drink. "You think we can trust a bunch of new guys? Small-time hoods from New Jersey?"

Vince's good humor faded. "You sound like Lottie," he said. "She wanted to run to Canada with Florence. She figured that was the right move."

Loretto sensed the atmosphere in the room shifting with Vince's mood. "All I'm sayin' is—"

"Pete always really liked you," Vince said, cutting Loretto off. "He thought you were a smart guy. Once he told me he thought you were almost as smart as me." Vince grinned, and Loretto knew better than to say anything more.

Vince topped off Mike's and Loretto's drinks. "To Patsy DiNapoli," he said, and they all three emptied their drinks.

Vince refilled their glasses. "To Frank and Tuffy," he said, and again they drank up and slapped their glasses down.

Then he refilled only his and Mike's drinks. "To our brothers," he said.

When Vince and Mike slapped their glasses down once again, Loretto refilled his own drink and followed suit. "To Freddie and Pete," he said, and he downed his drink.

Vince nodded to Loretto, acknowledging his gesture. He leaned close to him, his eyes bright with whiskey. "We had Madden on the ropes before he got to us at Gina's party," he said. "And what did he do? He took out two of our guys." He turned to Mike. "So what do we do? We come back with a dozen more guys." To Loretto he said, "You see? This ain't the time to back away. They're not beatin' me. I'll beat them and bleed them, take their money and kill their men, till they got no choice but to cut us in. Understand?"

"Sure," Loretto said.

"Nothin's changed," Vince went on. "Madden's got till Monday. If he don't cut us in, we're going after the big man himself. In the Cotton Club. He thinks he's safe there? He's not safe anywhere. He's not tough as us, not anymore, he ain't. Maybe once but not anymore."

Mike said, "Listen, Vince. Another thing. My brother, Augie. He wants to join up with us, at least until we find out who got Freddie. He wants to kill the son of a bitch."

Loretto sipped his drink and was quiet. He'd regretted telling Mike what Augie had said to him at the funeral as soon as the words were out of his mouth and he'd seen Mike's reaction, like he was proud of Augie. Now there was nothing to do but shut up.

"I didn't think Augie liked me," Vince said.

"Augie don't like anybody, but he's tough as they come—and we know we can trust him."

"We'll see," Vince said. "Sunday night we'll take the ferry over to New Jersey and meet Nannini's gang. Tell Augie to come along—and tell him to make sure he's heeled. We can talk on the ferry." Vince's hair was sandy blond again, the last traces of black dye finally faded away along with the mustache, which he'd cut off soon after his trial ended. He looked like Vince again, like Irish, down to the mixture of mirth and murder in his eyes and the distinctive dimple smack in the middle of his chin. "I'm beat from the drive," he said. "Lottie'll make us breakfast in the morning." He lifted his glass to the boys and started for the stairs.

Once Loretto heard the bedroom door close, he turned to Mike, drink in hand. "You think we've got a chance?" he asked. "Really?"

Upstairs in the bedroom, Vince and Lottie's voices could be heard faintly. Mike shrugged as if to say he didn't know. He took his drink and started up to his room.

Loretto poured himself more bourbon, turned off the lights, and sat in the living room chair by the window. He drank his bourbon and concentrated on the dark until he was able to see the branches of a nearby tree wavering in the breeze. Later, when his eyes adjusted, he could see the clouds, dark and tumbling. He watched the sky as if it might have a message for him, and every time a thought of Freddie or Patsy or Dominic or Gaspar came to mind, he sipped some more bourbon, till finally he fell asleep drunk in the living room chair, facing the darkness beyond the window, the glass falling from his hand and rolling along the rough wood planks of the farmhouse floor.

8:13 p.m.

Augie got up from his place at the table and shook hands with Owen Madden first, then around the table to Lucky Luciano, Big Frenchy, and Bo Weinberg. Dutch didn't stand for a handshake, and Augie acted as if he didn't notice. He tipped his hat to the table, and Frenchy led him down a narrow staircase and out to the street, where a crowd was waiting to get into the club. He hailed a cab and as he drove away he looked back at the Cotton Club's glaring lights. He thought that it was the first and last time he'd ever enter the premises.

He gave the cabbie the address for a twenty-four-hour diner he knew downtown, in the meat-packing district. He figured it to be a quiet spot, even on a Saturday night. When the cabbie let him out and drove off with his fare and a tip, he found himself on a deserted street, looking into the long window of the diner, where a young couple—a dame in a red dress and a swank-looking mug in a dark suit with a steel-gray fedora—were talking with the counter attendant, a blond kid in a white uniform. Other than Mike, they were the only people in sight. The polished wood counter-top formed a curvy triangle, and Mike sat across from the couple, facing them, with his back to the window. He was hunched over what looked like a half-eaten sandwich on a white plate, his hat pulled low on his forehead.

Augie knew there were a couple of quiet booths at the back of the room, and when he entered the diner, he didn't take a seat on the stool next to Mike. Instead, he put his hand on his brother's shoulder. "We need to talk in private," he said. He gestured toward one of the booths. To the counter boy he said, "Bring us two cups of coffee." Then he took a seat in the booth and waited for Mike to join him.

11:25 p.m.

When Madden saw Winchell crossing the crowded dance floor and heading in his direction, he lowered his head and muttered to himself that he'd like to lay a lead pipe across the creep's skull, but when he looked up, he was smiling. He'd been having a pleasant night, enjoying a quiet drink with one of the dancers, a new girl, and he was about to take her upstairs to his private rooms. They were seated next to each other at his table, listening to the band playing "Night and Day," a brand-new Cole Porter number. She was light-skinned enough to pass for white, a beauty with big round eyes and soft lips. Though she'd given her age as eighteen, he didn't figure her for more than sixteen, if that. He was looking forward to getting her upstairs.

"Big Owney!" Winchell leaned over the table and winked at the dancer. He wore his fedora pushed back high on his head, and he tipped it to the girl before turning back to Madden. "Looks like you got better things to be up to than talking to me!" he half shouted. "Say, give me something for my column and I'll skedaddle."

"I got nothing for you tonight, Walter," Madden said. "You'll have to find your gossip someplace else."

"Sure," Winchell said, "but a little bird told me a bunch of you tough guys got together a few weeks ago at the Forest Hotel. A big powwow, I hear, with mugs flying in from all over the country. What about that? I already got the story. I was figuring you might add to it, that's all."

"Don't know nothing about it."

"Sure," Winchell said. He straightened up and tugged on his ear. "Then just tell me this, Duke. How much trouble is young Master Coll making for you and the Combine that requires convening a meeting of the sort that took place at the Forest Hotel? One kid and his scrawny gang's got the whole mob in an uproar? That's quite a story, don't you think?"

Madden got up from his seat, went around the table, and put an arm over Winchell's shoulders. He led him away from the table. "Get out of here," he whispered in his ear, "before I lose my temper."

"Ah, take it easy," Winchell said.

"I am taking it easy. Try not to forget that you're on my payroll, Walter. As for Coll, here's a tip for you: tell the paper to get his obituary ready."

"Didn't you tell me roughly the same thing last time I broached the subject?"

"This time you can bet on it." Madden patted Winchell on the back, pushed him away, and returned to his table, where he offered the young woman his hand. She smiled and followed him out of the room.

12:25 a.m.

Loretto followed Vince with his hands in his coat pockets, his collar turned up against the wind, and his fedora low on his forehead. They might have been matching figures drawn by the same artist, the four of them—Vince, Loretto, Augie, and Mike—all in long winter coats with turned-up collars and hats pulled low. They were on West 23rd, on their way back to the Cornish Arms, where Lottie and Vince were staying in the same room they'd stayed in many times before, the one that faced the street on the second floor. The trip to New Jersey had been a bust. They'd arrived at the meeting place, a warehouse on the docks, to find nothing but seagulls and rats. Vince had shot up the warehouse door for the hell of it. Then they'd taken the Hoboken Ferry back to 23rd, and now they were strolling along the avenue, a quartet of tough guys with hands in their pockets and backs to the wind.

When they reached the hotel, Vince checked the lighted windows on the second floor as if he might see Lottie there, watching for him. "It's after midnight," he said. "That makes it Monday." Loretto and the others waited for him to explain. "Monday's Madden's deadline." They were outside a drugstore across from the hotel. The entrance was a narrow door between two plate-glass windows full of medical supplies. A banner on one of the windows announced that breakfast and lunch were served at all hours. Vince glanced up at the neon sign above the door—*London Chemists*—and then back to Mike. "What the hell," he said. "Let's get it over with."

"What?" Mike asked.

"I'm calling Madden. Tomorrow we're in business with him or we're at war with him."

"You're the boss," Mike said without so much as a second's pause, "but I've got to take a leak." He gestured toward the Cornish Arms. "I'll be in the lobby."

Vince said, "What's wrong with the drugstore?"

"What's wrong with the hotel?" Mike slapped Vince on the arm. "Augie and Loretto'll keep you company in there. I'm about to bust a gut," he added, and he trotted across the street to the hotel.

Vince looked to Augie and Loretto. "All right," he said as if Mike was acting like a goof, but what the hell. "Let's have a talk with Big Owney."

Inside the drugstore, a couple of older men sat at the soda fountain. A clerk behind the counter was taking an order from one of them while the other sipped a drink and read the newspaper. At the drug counter, a woman talked to the pharmacist. Vince looked over the place, seemed satisfied, and started for a pair of telephone booths.

Augie joined him. "I'm gonna call my girl," he said. "Tell her to wait up for me."

Vince pointed at Loretto. He said, "Keep an eye on the door," and then pushed open the booth, stepped inside, and closed the glass door behind him. He dropped a coin in the slot atop the phone and dialed a number.

Alongside Vince, Augie stepped out of his booth, having quickly completed his call. He joined Loretto where he'd taken a seat at the far end of the counter. When the clerk came for their order, Augie raised his hand and told him they'd only be a minute while they waited for their friend, and he gestured to Vince in the phone booth.

"Since when do you have a girlfriend?" Loretto asked Augie. "And Mike's got a weak bladder all of a sudden? Something don't smell right, Augie. You have anything you want to tell me?"

"Sure, I have something I want to tell you." Augie talked softly, his elbows on the counter, leaning close to Loretto. "Your friend Vince Coll, Irish over there," he glanced behind him to the phone booth, where Vince appeared to be waiting for someone to come on the line, "he's living in a dream world."

"What are you talking about?"

"Open your eyes, Loretto." Suddenly Augie's voice was harsh and angry. "Vince has been beat," he said. "Except for you and Mike, his boys are dead or gone or in jail waiting to get the chair. He's got nothing, and he's in there—" Again he glanced behind him to the phone booth. "He's in there talking to the most powerful gangster probably in the whole damn country, and that includes Capone in Chicago. Owen Madden's got an army working for him. He's got connections that go up to the mayor and beyond. Vince has got nothin' left, and he never had much to begin with— and he's in that phone booth thinking he's got a shot at Madden bending over for him. He's living in a dream, Loretto. Understand? It won't happen. Owen Madden is not going to cut him in on his business. Owen Madden was never going to cut him in on his business. Owen Madden is going to kill him. That's done and over with, and it's been done and over with ever since he took on Madden in the first place."

Loretto spun around on his stool. Vince was talking on the phone now. He'd say a few words, nod his head, listen, and then talk some more. He didn't seem at all unhappy or angry. "Looks to me like he's having a conversation about something," he said to Augie.

"I'm sure he is," Augie said. "I'm sure somebody on the other end of that line is telling him everything he wants to hear. He's probably explaining what Vince's cut will be and what's expected of him. They're probably setting up a party for him at the Cotton Club."

At first Loretto didn't grasp what Augie was getting at. "Who did you call?" he asked. When Augie didn't answer, Loretto grabbed his arm. He was about to ask a second time when Bo Weinberg came through the door with a chopper dangling from his right hand. Outside, a black Cole waited at the curb, its engine running, and Henry LaSalla stood at the store entrance, his clown's nose bright red in the cold, the barrel of a chopper protruding from under his coat.

Loretto went for the pistol under his jacket, but Augie caught his hand before it got any higher than the counter. Bo noticed and froze where he stood, the chopper still dangling beside him. His eyes were on Loretto while his body was angled toward the phone booth. Maybe a second passed like that, maybe two, with Bo watching Loretto, his body angled toward Vince, Augie grasping Loretto's wrist.

Augie said, "What are you going to do, Loretto? Shoot Bo Weinberg? Then will you shoot me? Because if you don't, Vince will."

Bo shifted his body toward the phone booth. Loretto got up from his stool and stepped back from Augie. He pulled his pistol from under his coat and pointed it at Bo.

Bo partly raised the barrel of the chopper. The way he was standing, when he lifted it again, he could aim at either Vince or Loretto.

Augie held his hand up to Bo, asking for another second. At the same moment, Vince looked out from the phone booth and saw Bo holding a chopper, watching Loretto with one eye and him with the other. Augie said, "For Christ's sake, Loretto, are you standing with Vince against everybody? Against us?" he added, meaning him and Gina and the whole Baronti family. "This is enough," he said. "It's over."

Vince was smiling, watching Loretto holding a gun on Bo. He had that cocky look that was typical Vince, like things were playing out one more time, against all odds, to his advantage.

Loretto put his gun back in its holster. It took only a second and felt like an eternity. Vince's smile faded and then disappeared. He turned to face Bo, and Bo unleashed the chopper, which spit lead into the phone booth, shattering the glass and pummeling Vince's body, knocking him about in the tight confines of the booth until he slumped down in a lifeless heap, his bloody face pressed into the glass, his sandy blond hair dyed black with streaks of blood.

Bo turned to Augie and jerked his thumb toward the door. Augie grabbed Loretto by the arm and pulled him onto the street, past LaSalla and toward the waiting Cole. At the door to the car, Loretto resisted getting in the back seat as Henry got behind the wheel and Bo climbed into the passenger seat. Lottie was at the hotel window, looking down at the car, at Loretto, her face a solemn mask. There was no surprise in her look, no fear or hysteria in her eyes—only a glaze of sadness, of sorrow. Mike appeared alongside her at the window. He put his arm over her shoulders, and she rested her head on his chest. From the passenger seat, Bo said to Augie, "Get the kid in the car," just as a beat cop appeared on the corner. The cop first noticed a commotion as people fled the drugstore and then Augie and Loretto at the door to the Cole. He yelled, "Stop!" and raised his baton. A big guy with a mop of unruly hair, his Irish accent was evident in the single syllable. Augie shoved Loretto into the back seat, and Henry stepped on the gas. The Cole's V-8 roared as it sped out onto 23rd and turned quickly on 8th. When they looked back, they saw that the cop had commandeered a yellow cab and was following them, standing on the sideboard, his pistol in the air.

"You got to love these micks," Bo said. "Look at that mug. He's got balls big as potatoes." He hadn't gotten the final word out of his mouth when a bullet broke the rear window and tore a hole in the seat back just over Henry's shoulder.

Henry swore and hung a quick right. The Cole straightened out and lurched forward, quickly leaving the yellow cab far behind. Twenty minutes later, after maneuvering through a maze of side streets and quiet avenues, Henry pulled up outside a warehouse at the Chelsea piers.

"This is your stop," Bo said. He got out and opened the back door for Augie.

Loretto slid out of the car and found himself looking at an expanse of black water. A seagull swooped low, skimmed the river, and lighted on a nearby pier. It was quiet, the only sounds water slapping against the docks and a bell clanging softly with the rhythm of the water.

Bo buttoned his coat and turned up his collar. He looked out over the water and then back to Loretto. "This squares you with Dutch," he said. "Charley Lucky, too, and Big Owney and all the rest of the boys. You and Mike both." He paused, thought a second. "Richie Cabo . . . I'd still stay away from him if I were you. But he's part of the deal, too."

Loretto turned to Augie. "What deal?"

Bo seemed not to hear the question. "He was a fearless son of a bitch," he said, talking about Vince. "I'll give him that. One of the few guys who ever put a beating on me. *Once*," he added, and turned and spit toward the river. "Now it's all over," he said. "Everybody'll be happier, and Dutch can come out of his hole." He shook hands with Augie and nodded to Loretto before he got back in the car with Henry and drove off.

When the car was out of sight, Loretto asked Augie again, "What deal?"

"Do you need it spelled out for you?" Augie put his hand on Loretto's back and directed him to a walkway between the pier and the warehouse. "My car's over here."

"Go ahead," Loretto said. "Spell it out for me."

ED FALCO

"You're in the clear. You and Mike both," Augie said. "No one's looking to put one in you anymore. No one. Both of you. You're both free and clear. You can do whatever you want now." Augie paused and they walked together a moment in silence. "And I'm taking enough money out of the deal to move Mama and Gina out of the city with me, to Long Island. I already got a house picked out for me and Mama, with an apartment for Gina if she wants it."

"Gina knows all this?"

"No. Not yet."

At the car, Loretto said, "And all it cost us was Vince."

"Didn't cost us anything," Augie said. "Vince wound up exactly where he was going to wind up, only maybe a few days earlier, that's all." Above them, the moon came out from behind a long shroud of thin clouds. Augie opened the car door. "You did the right thing, " he said. "Get in. It's cold out here."

"I'll walk." Loretto found a pair of gloves in his coat pocket and slipped them on.

"You sure? It's a long way."

"I'm sure," Loretto said, and he started back for the piers.

"Where are you going? Do you still have your apartment?" Augie called after him.

Loretto didn't answer. He continued toward the water and the piers. When he heard Augie drive off, he stopped at the dock's edge and sat with his back to a pylon. He watched a pair of gulls hurry along the dock side by side, their wings flapping now and then. He saw Vince again looking at him from the phone booth with a smile on his face, and then he watched the smile disappear. He saw Lottie looking down from the hotel window with Mike behind her. He heard the rattle of Bo's chopper and glass shattering and he saw Vince crumple and fall. He didn't have his apartment anymore, and so he had no idea where to go. He took off his heavy coat and his gloves and dropped them both in the river. Then he took off his jacket and his hat and his holster and gun. He threw them all in the river. He watched them sink and disappear into the murky water before finally, with the cold already cutting through him, he turned away from the piers and started back toward the lights of the city.

Spring

· *1977* ·

Sunday ••• April 10, 1977

2:15 p.m.

Loretto wore a sweater against the chill in the April air and a straw hat to keep the sun off his head. He was stretched out on in a lounge chair with a copy of the *New York Times* in his lap, a picture of Walter Winchell staring up at him from the front page. Winchell had died some five years earlier, and the story appeared to be about gossip columnists—though Loretto hadn't read past the first few sentences.

"Loretto!" Gina opened the screen door onto the backyard and stuck her head out. "*Madon!* Come in the house! The kids are already at the table. We're eating in a few minutes."

Loretto raised a finger, meaning he'd be there in a moment. He put the newspaper aside and crossed the patio to watch one of his koi swim in a pond he'd built with his sons—slate, with a waterfall and a wide ledge where the grandchildren loved to sit and drop food in the water and watch goldfish swarm and peck flakes off the surface. He and Gina had raised their family in this house, a two-story colonial in Northport, Long Island. The yard had a patio and the pond and gardens—and up a small hill, a long in-ground pool. He sat down on the pond's slate ledge and rippled the water with his fingertips, drawing the goldfish to him.

Winchell's picture in the paper brought the memories back, all the things Loretto could never forget, not through all the years, through the children, the grandchildren, the great-grandchildren; through the depression, the war, the boom; through all of it the memories, the images, the dreams remained.

The night Bo Weinberg killed Vince Coll, Loretto had walked in his shirtsleeves through the cold till he came to an all-night diner, where he drank coffee and sat in a booth till he stopped shivering and he could feel his feet and fingertips again. Later, he ordered food, and when the sun came up, he called Gina. She and Augie came to pick him up, and he moved back in with Augie and Mama until they left for Long Island that spring, for Northport, where Augie bought a house within walking distance of the house Loretto bought a couple of years later. Augie started a construction business that struggled through the depression, did well during the war, and exploded in the boom that followed the war. Now he was a wealthy man, with a second house on the ocean in Palm Beach, where he and his family spent the summers. He'd married late, in his thirties, but not too late to have five children with his wife, Karen, who was some ten years younger.

Loretto and Gina married the summer of '32. They lived in Mama's apartment another year till Gina got pregnant and Augie lent them the money to buy their house. Later, Loretto put the skills he'd learned on his first job as a boy together with Gina's talents, and—with another loan from Augie—they'd opened a bakery, which did well enough for the loan to be repaid within a few years and for Loretto and Gina to live a comfortable life and raise six children, the youngest, twins, born in '41, right before the war started. They were all grown now, and Loretto had lost track of the grandchildren. Between his family and Augie's, they were a clan—with only Mike missing.

Once Vince was gone, Mike had taken up with Lottie, and the two of them had gotten themselves in more trouble with the law. Lottie wound up doing a couple of years in prison, after which she disappeared. Loretto liked to think that she had gone off somewhere to live an ordinary life and raise the daughter he hadn't known about till years later, when Mike told him—but the chances were better that she was at the bottom of a river, even her bones long ago washed away. She'd made a lot of enemies in her years with Vince. Still, she disappeared utterly once she was out, and it was possible she was still alive. It gave Loretto some small pleasure to think so.

Mike had eventually gone to work for Luciano, and for the last thirty-five years he'd been in and out of jail. Augie washed his hands of him, and his name was never mentioned at family gatherings. In time, the kids came to know that they had another uncle—Mike turned up in the newspapers more often than anyone would have liked—but they learned not to mention him. He was the family's dark secret, the uncle in the mob. About Loretto's and Augie's past, they knew nothing. Only Loretto stayed in touch with Mike. Once a month he drove up to visit him in Ossining, where he was currently serving the tail end of a sentence for racketeering.

When Loretto saw Mike, they talked about the '30s as if they were yesterday. Dutch killed Bo in '35, put him in a cement kimono, as he used to call it, and dropped him in the East River because he thought he was conspiring with Luciano. Luciano had Dutch killed a month later because Dutch was threatening to assassinate Thomas Dewey, even after the Combine had ruled against it. Madden left town in '35 when he realized no Irishman could stay on top in New York, not with Luciano running things. He retired to someplace in Arkansas, where he lived to be an old man, into his seventies. In '39, Big Frenchy died. Mike never got the whole story on that, but he'd heard it was natural causes. Luciano got deported after the war, though Mike said he was still running things until he died of a heart attack in Naples. Richie Cabo, he'd heard, died of cancer in his sixties. Every visit, they'd talk about the old days, Mike doing most of the talking, Loretto listening and adding something now and then. Most of all, they talked about Vince. In their conversations, they brought him back to life: what he looked like, how he acted, the things he'd said—all that energy, all that power, his good looks and charm, his fierceness and his rages. The only thing they didn't talk about was the night he was killed. That they left alone.

"Loretto!" Gina opened the screen door, gave Loretto a look, and closed it again when one of the grandchildren crashed into her legs. With the children and the years, she had gained more and more weight, till now, put her in a black dress and she'd look exactly like her mother, like Mama Baronti, long gone and still missed by everyone who'd known her. When the children asked about the scar on her chin, which had grown less noticeable as her face grew heavier, she told them she had tripped and fallen down a concrete stoop in the city.

Loretto took off his hat and ran his fingers through what was left of his hair. He retrieved the *Times* from the lounge, glanced again at the article on gossip columnists, and recalled the piece Winchell had published predicting Vince's murder only hours before it had actually happened. He'd called him "Master Coll," and he'd written about the meeting at the Forest Hotel. He'd gotten in hot water for that and had to go before a grand jury. They wanted to know where he got his information, and then the Combine didn't like it either, and for a while it appeared Winchell wouldn't be long for this world—but he'd weaseled out of it somehow. Loretto shook his head at that, at a weasel like Walter Winchell living a long and prosperous life and Vince dead at twenty-three. Then the thought of Winchell's article predicting Vince's murder led, as so many things so often did, back to the image of Vince crumpled up in that phone booth, his bloody face against the glass, his hair streaked with blood; and that memory led to the memory of Jimmy Brennan screaming into Vince's hand as Loretto's knife sliced open his belly; and when Loretto blinked those images away, others surfaced to replace them: Gaspar and Dominic, the two of them looking up at him out of a hole in the ground; Tuffy and Frank hooded and burning in the electric chair; Freddie spilled over the couch with a bullet in the back of his head; Patsy with half his face blown away, sprawled on top of Maria, her back blood-soaked around a maze of bullet wounds; the whole bloody swirl of pictures and memories rising up and overpowering him, knocking him back into a stunned silence.

Overhead, the clouds were fat and white. They tumbled in slow motion across a blue sky. He watched them and the thought came to him, as it had many times before, that the clouds and the sky were watching him rather than the other way around, as if something he didn't know and couldn't understand was watching, watching everyone, watching and waiting. It was a feeling more than a thought, and it brought him back to the night he'd seen that comet streak across the sky when he was in Albany—which was another image that never faded, the brightness of that blue streak, the way it lit up the night sky.

"Loretto! *Mannagg'!*" Gina yelled to him through the screen door, and this time he nodded and joined her.

Inside, the whole brood was waiting, all his sons and daughters and most of their children. The adults and the older children sat at two tables pulled together across the length of the dining room. The younger children had their own space in the kitchen. Loretto took his seat at the head of the dining room table, and the house went quiet, everyone waiting for him to start the meal. Trays of lasagna, plates of meats, and bowls of sauce waited. Every Sunday, Gina and the women made the meal while, in a new twist, the men helped put out the dishes and care for the children.

Loretto looked over his family. On bad days, he'd sometimes see the face of the Vengelli boy in one of his grandchildren or the face of Vince or Freddie in one of his sons. But this was not a bad day. This day, he saw his family gathered in his home. He started the Sunday meal as he always did, as was their tradition. With all the children and grandchildren waiting to dig in to their food, he lifted his wineglass. "Eat," he said. "Eat and be grateful."

Author's Afterword

Toughs is a novel built around the following series of historical events.

July 28, 1931. The gun battle on 107th Street in New York, where several children were shot. One of the children, a five-year-old, died from his wounds. Twenty-three-year-old Vince Coll was the assumed shooter. The city's newspapers tagged him "Mad Dog Coll."

September 10, 1931. The murder of Salvatore Maranzano.

October 3, 1931. The arrest of Vince Coll and his gang in New York City.

December 16–December 28, 1931. The trial of Vince Coll on murder charges stemming from the July 28 shootout.

December 18, 1931. The murder of Jack "Legs" Diamond.

January 15, 1932. A meeting of gangsters from all over the country to deal with Vincent Coll. The meeting was convened by Owen Madden and held at the Forest Hotel in New York.

JANUARY 31, 1932. The murder and wounding of several Coll associates in a Bronx apartment.

FEBRUARY 8, 1932. The murder of Vince Coll.

Though based on these events and the characters involved in them, *Toughs* is a work of fiction. The particulars of the events, including the people involved, are entirely imagined. I have used history as a touchstone for the novel. Gangsters don't leave accurate records of their lives, and, regardless, attempting to present an accurate picture of *anyone's* life is the work of a journalist or a biographer. As a novelist, I've satisfied myself with presenting these historical figures as the people I imagined them to be in the context of the story I created. I've changed the names of many of the secondary and minor players in the Vince Coll story and kept the names of the most famous figures.

The difficult-to-find *Mad Dog Coll: An Irish Gangster*, by Breandán Delap, is to my knowledge the only biography of Vince Coll, and I relied on it heavily in the writing of *Toughs*. I would like to express my appreciation to the author. I also researched newspapers and magazines from the era, and of course I scoured the always useful though wildly unreliable Internet.

As always, I'd like to thank my family and my writing community: friends, fellow writers, students, teachers, and readers.